The Golden Age of
Chinese Drama:

Yüan *Tsa-chü*

Modern copy of Wall Painting dated 1324, still existing in Ming-Ying Wang Temple near Chao-ch'eng, Shansi.

The Golden Age of Chinese Drama:
Yüan *Tsa-chü*

CHUNG-WEN SHIH

PRINCETON UNIVERSITY PRESS

Copyright © 1976 by Princeton University Press
Published by Princeton University Press
Princeton and Guildford, Surrey
ALL RIGHTS RESERVED

Library of Congress Cataloging in Publication Data
will be found on the last printed page of this book

Publication of this book has been aided by a grant from
the UNIVERSITY RESEARCH FUND, THE GEORGE WASHINGTON
UNIVERSITY, and THE ANDREW W. MELLON FOUNDATION

Printed in the UNITED STATES OF AMERICA by
Princeton University Press, Princeton, New Jersey

Foreword

YÜAN drama is at once the first full florescence, the Golden Age and the grand classical forebear of all Chinese theatre. In performance, the most we could hope to see of it today would be a reconstruction of its lost music and largely unknown stage conventions. Yet, thanks to Ming period enthusiasts like Tsang Mao-hsün, remarkably complete versions survive of about a hundred and seventy plays, a corpus four times the size of the entire classical Greek drama. In these texts we can find many of the glamorous beings still portrayed in the traditional drama today: the favored Imperial consort Yang Kuei-fei, loyal or treacherous generals of early dynasties, the wise and upright Magistrate Pao, and the Monkey King battling demons that menace the quest for the holy scriptures.

Historically, critics have defined two poles of the Chinese theatre, or of the hundreds of forms of theatre that have flourished at one time or another in local districts or in several provinces. Very approximately, "Southern" has meant softer, more elegantly poetic and refined, symbolized by the plaintive flute. The *K'un-ch'ü* plays of the present-day stage preserve this kind of "Southern" distinction for us. The "Northern" pole has represented a more raucous, energetic art, with lively string music and much percussion. In geographical terms Yüan drama is certainly "Northern." It was the theatre of the Mongol capital, the great city we now call Peking. But it is a truly protean art. There is no more a typical Yüan play than there is a typical Elizabethan. Working within sharply defined formal conventions, the dramatists of thirteenth- and fourteenth-century China made the world their stage, and show us an old vagabond drinking poisoned

soup, or a stouthearted prostitute hoodwinking a boor to
save a sister from his clutches, as readily as an Emperor bemoaning his lost love.

It is this protean character that explains the fascination
of Yüan drama for scholars. The finest poetry of the age
found its way onto the Yüan stage, a literary banquet from
which Peking opera merely sweeps up the crumbs. As material for the history of the Chinese spoken language, the
texts of the plays have unique value. The social historian,
too, finds rich sources in the work of these dramatists and
their storyteller associates, who gave us the earliest portraits
of people from the humblest walks of life. To the student of
drama, the era of the Yüan provides one of those rare moments in human history when poet, trained actor, and ap-
preciative audience achieved happy conjunction. To thirteenth-century Peking we should have to compare the
Athens of Pericles, Elizabethan London, or the Versailles of
the Roi Soleil.

The translation of Yüan plays into Western languages has
a history of more than two centuries. Unfortunately, the attitude of the pioneers towards their originals was cavalier at
best. As Professor Shih suggests below, Voltaire might have
been more impressed by the passion of *Chao shih ku-erh*
had not its translator, the good Father Prémare, omitted
virtually all of the forty-three songs that are the soul of the
play. (The only actual Yüan dynasty printings that survive
omit almost everything *but* the songs.) Perhaps the apparent
and so often misleading modernity of the language has been
to blame. Even the best dictionaries are inadequate for the
pre-modern colloquial language. For whatever reason, it is
only in the last few years that we have begun to see successful translations of Yüan plays, made by careful scholars
whose sensitivity to English as well as to Chinese can match
the severe demands the texts impose.

Professor Shih's study, the first full-length book in English
on the great age of the Chinese drama, is most timely. In the
pages that follow, she shares with us her understanding of

the Yüan theatre and her appreciation of its rich legacy. Her description is comprehensive, her interpretation enlightening, and her scholarship up-to-date. Quoting poetic and prose passages from a select number of plays, she renders faithfully these two prime values of Yüan drama. As only the skilled guide can, she makes a rich exotic landscape swiftly and warmly familiar.

CYRIL BIRCH

University of California, Berkeley

Preface

CHINESE theatre first began to flourish during the Yüan period (1260-1368), and the 171 extant plays (*tsa-chü*) are the earliest surviving and most brilliant body of Chinese dramatic literature.[1] As poetry, Yüan drama has long been considered by scholars a supreme form of lyric beauty; in addition, the drama of this period has bequeathed to the later Chinese stage many of its techniques, conventions, and themes. Thus the Yüan plays command scholarly interest not only because of their intrinsic literary merit but also because of their relation to the vernacular tradition and their substantial influence on the development of Chinese drama.

Although Yüan dramatic literature has finally begun to receive the attention it deserves, there has been as yet very little material available in English or any other Western language offering the kind of information necessary for an appreciation of the achievements of the Yüan dramatists. At present, there is no single book in any Western language on the subject, except for several unpublished doctoral dissertations that deal with more specific problems of the genre, and a few translations of the plays. Hence there is a pressing need for a comprehensive study of Yüan drama. It is the

---

[1] Yüan drama is also known as *pei-ch'ü* (Northern drama). It is believed to have reached the height of its development in the early part of the Yüan period and is thus often referred to as thirteenth-century Chinese drama.

All 171 extant plays are collected in the following two works: *Yüan ch'ü hsüan* (hereafter referred to as *YCH*), edited by Tsang Mao-hsün, 1616 (reprint, Peking: Chung-hua Book Co., 1958), and *Yüan ch'ü hsüan wai-pien* (hereafter referred to as *WP*), edited by Sui Shu-sen (Peking: Chung-hua Book Co., 1959; reprint, 1961). References in this book are to these two collections.

aim of this study to help to fill that need by making available information about the essential aspects of the genre and by offering more detailed interpretations in those areas which constitute the central artistic values of the form.

In order to place the work of the dramatists in its historical setting, this book begins with a description of the popular genres that contributed to the flowering of Yüan drama. Following this, conventional features of dramatic construction, methods of characterization, and recurring themes are given detailed consideration. The dramatists' use of poetic language, a central focus of interest in this study, is then discussed. Finally, such important technical matters as the nature of music used in the plays and some physical aspects of staging are explored.

Predominant among the influences that combined to mold the complex art that is Yüan drama was the long heritage of oral narrative, which contributed many formal conventions to the drama. In the examination of this subject, an effort is made to identify the structural elements and to consider their history and aesthetic qualities.

A delightful feature of Yüan drama is its great variety of characters, made interesting by their individual as well as their universal traits. The influence of earlier traditions is also apparent in the predominant use of type characters. Skilled playwrights, through the richness of their poetry and their flashes of insight into human thought and feeling, succeeded in endowing their characters with life and vitality.

The themes of the extant plays cover a wide range of subjects. Many of them suggest a preoccupation with ethics, presented from Confucian, Taoist, or Buddhist viewpoints; there is also a concern for social justice in plays about wise judges and justice-minded outlaws. The treatment of love is particularly remarkable for its candor. Many themes that were prominent on the Yüan stage have proved their endurance by appearing again not only in later plays but also in other literary forms, suggesting that they are representative of persistent ideas among the Chinese.

Poetry is the essential material from which the fabric of Yüan dramatic literature is woven. The sense of human significance and of beauty in the plays, perhaps for the modern reader as well as for the Yüan audience, is effected primarily through poetry. On the modern stage elaborate scenery and staging are often used to draw the audience into the fantasy world of the play, but on the Yüan stage verse must have been the chief medium through which the audience passed from the crowded pit into the splendors of the Han palace or the atmosphere of a moonlit garden in spring. The newly emerged poetic form, the *ch'ü*, became in the hands of skilled playwrights a pliable medium for dramatic effects.

Although the power of Yüan drama resides primarily in its verse, the use of vernacular prose for dialogue and description enriches the plays' texture by lending fullness and life and by varying tone and mood. Passages in prose have the effect of freeing the plays from some of the strictures imposed by highly organized verse sequences. While lyrics are conventionally sung by only one of the characters, prose is spoken by all, and frequently becomes the vehicle for expressing the more earthy and often coarser feelings and thoughts of everyday life. Prose is the chief instrument for the creation of realistic effects in the dramatic form, and the skill of the playwrights can be seen in the vitality with which they represent the spoken language of their time.

Music also played a major role in Yüan drama. It complemented the lyrics, carried the action forward, and contributed to the structure of the plays. The exact nature of the music can be ascertained to a certain degree through a study of the modes and song-sequences, contemporary references, and comments by Ming dynasty musicians, who in all likelihood still had some firsthand knowledge of the performances.

Finally, the Yüan drama was a living medium, which had to attain its success through actual performances on stage before a diverse audience. The physical stage presentation, the expectations of the audience, and the background of the dramatists all played an essential part in determining the nature of the Yüan drama; consideration of these factors is helpful to our understanding of the genre.

The artistic emphasis of Yüan drama as a whole is very different from that of Western plays. Attention in Yüan drama is primarily focused upon stylistic excellence in the poetry and music, while plot structure seems to have been a secondary consideration. The moral codes and social conventions that formed the background for the Yüan audience's reaction to characters and events are often different from those of Western readers, so that the stories may at times seem unsatisfying. In instances of this kind, an attempt has been made to describe the formal and social presuppositions underlying Yüan drama, in the hope that this may help Western readers to respond to the genre on its own terms.

Since there is a general lack of useful critical terminology in both traditional and contemporary Chinese scholarship on the drama, Western terms familiar to the English-speaking public have been used when appropriate as an aid to understanding. Despite the use of such terms and occasional references to Western dramatic literature, the present work is not intended as a comparative study, and I have not attempted to make any judgments concerning the different characteristics of Chinese and Western drama.

There is some controversy as to the best texts to use for a study of the genre. It would have been preferable to rely on a contemporary edition, but the only extant Yüan edition, *A Yüan Printed Edition of Thirty Plays* (*Yüan k'an tsa-chü san-shih chung*), consists of about one-sixth of the existing plays, and the text contains very little prose and is often unclear. As David Hawkes noted, "Our scholarly gratification at the discovery of an early text must not blind us to the possibility that it may be a very *bad* text."[2] The adoption of

[2] David Hawkes, "Reflections on Some Yuan Tsa-chü," *Asia Major*, xvi (1971), 81.

later collections, when the plays were published as one work, presents a disadvantage as well; they may have been edited to be made more readable. The many editions from the Ming dynasty nevertheless remain the best sources available. Again, as Hawkes points out, "It is to the Ming editors, and above all to Tsang Mou-hsün, that we owe practically all we know about Yuan drama as such. In a description based exclusively on the Yuan editions there could be very little about *drama* at all."[3] In the present study, both the Yüan edition and various Ming editions are consulted.

In addition to the problem of texts, there are a number of other points over which scholarly opinion is still much divided. To examine in detail the various viewpoints regarding each of these questions would have been unsuitable in a book of this nature, for it would have made for unmanageable length and perhaps obscured the general picture. The views that seem most reasonable in the light of recent scholarship have been adopted; references to other viewpoints are presented in the footnotes when necessary.

In the course of the discussion, several of the major plays are analyzed in detail, with a number of plot summaries of other plays included for the benefit of readers who may be unfamiliar with the extant works. It is hoped that this book may be of use to anyone interested in the subject; however, it is primarily intended for students in the field of Chinese language and literature. Some of the more technical points are included in the footnotes instead of the text. Romanization for each Chinese title is given on its first appearance in the text. Cross references between Chinese titles and their English translation are given in the index. Tune titles, however, are not translated (see p. 21, n. 2); Chinese characters for them are given in the glossary.

I wish to acknowledge my indebtedness to the American Association of University Women, the American Philosophi-

---

[3] *Ibid.*

cal Society, and the American Council of Learned Societies for a joint travel grant that enabled me to visit the Research Institute in Humanistic Studies at Kyoto University, Japan, a center for the study of Yüan drama. Discussions there with Professor Yoshikawa Kōjirō helped me to formulate the basic approach. The assistance I received from my colleagues and students has been valuable. I wish to thank Professors Jane Evans, Y. K. Kao, C. T. Hsia, and James J. Y. Liu for reading the manuscript and for their criticism and suggestions, and to Professor Iris Pian for reading the chapter on music. I am especially indebted to Professor Fritz Mote not only for reading the manuscript but also for his generous support in many ways. I should also like to express my appreciation to R. Miriam Brokaw at Princeton University Press for her expert advice and assistance, and to Josephine Silcox for typing the manuscript. The Research Committee and the Institute for Sino-Soviet Studies at The George Washington University have provided financial support, for which I am grateful. The mistakes and omissions are my own; I shall welcome corrections from readers.

C. W. S.

Contents

Contents

Illustrations

The Golden Age of
Chinese Drama:

Yüan *Tsa-chü*

I

Historical Background and
Social Milieu

The Theatrical Tradition

THE Chinese have traditionally found pleasure in theatrical entertainment. For centuries before the development of Yüan drama, song, dance, and pageantry had been a part of Chinese life. Song and dance rituals stemming from the practice of shamanism have been singled out by Wang Kuo-wei as the possible origin of Chinese drama.[1] The male and female shamans, referred to as *hsi* and *wu* respectively, date back to before the Chou dynasty (1122?-221 B.C.), and are mentioned in the Chinese classics. In accordance with the ancient Chinese belief that the gods could move righteous persons to speak oracles, these male and female shamans, clad in ceremonial costumes, danced and gesticulated to the accompaniment of music in order to evoke the revelation of divine will. This form of worship was most likely as pleasing to man as it supposedly was to the gods.

Court jesters and entertainers skilled in impersonating well-known figures represent another early form of acting. These jesters and entertainers were known by various names: *yu, ch'ang, ch'ang-yu, p'ai-yu, ling,* and *chu-ju*. Reminiscent of fools or court jesters in medieval Europe, their roles were not limited to formal performances, but also included making satirical observations, telling jokes and stories, and impersonating historical and contemporary figures. A few of them capitalized on their wit and insight to become official advisors to their masters.

[1] Wang Kuo-wei, *Sung Yüan hsi-ch'ü shih* (1915), pp. 1-4.

Both the shamanistic rituals and the activities of the court jesters may be seen as a rudimentary form of acting, but these exhibitions cannot be considered as true drama, because in the performance of such songs, dances, and episodes, whether in a jesting or serious vein, there is no telling of a sustained story or unfolding of a plot. Only with the emergence of the following theatrical acts, did Chinese theatre begin to assume recognizable form.

"Hundred Entertainments" (*Pai-hsi*). Performances embodying an essentially dramatic principle—the telling of a story by acting—existed at least as early as the first century. In a descriptive composition on the capital city of Ch'ang-an, Chang Heng (78-139) mentions various activities during a public festival. He describes one scene in which "Nü-e sits and sings, her voice clear and lingering, while Hung-ya [an immortal], clad in beautiful feathers, stands and waves his hands. Before the song is finished, clouds gather and snow falls." In another scene, "old man Huang of Tung-hai, carrying a red metal knife . . . fights against a white tiger and is defeated."[2] While in the first, impersonation using costumes and physical gestures is presented, in the second, a story is dramatized. Although the "hundred entertainments" may have been mainly feats of physical strength and skill, this scene between the old man and the tiger is strictly acting, since it is decided beforehand that the tiger will win and the man will lose.

"The Big Face" (*Ta mien*) *and "The Stomping-Swaying Wife"* (*T'a-yao niang*).[3] During the sixth century, dramatic performances integrating stories with singing and dancing are known to have existed in the state of Northern Ch'i. Two dramatic skits, "The Big Face" and "The Stomping-Swaying

[2] Chang Heng, "Hsi ching fu" in *Liu ch'en chu Wen-hsüan*, ed. by Hsiao T'ung (*SPTK so-pen*), *chüan* 1, p. 58.

[3] The former is sometimes also called *Tai-mien* (mask), and the latter *Su Chung-lang* (Secretary-of-the-Board Su).

Wife," were probably based on actual events. Concerning the first, *The Old History of T'ang* (*Chiu T'ang shu*) relates that Prince Lan Ling of Northern Ch'i was a brave warrior with a delicate face. On the battlefield he often wore a mask to frighten his enemies. The people of Northern Ch'i composed a dance celebrating his valiant deeds and named the act "Song of Prince Lan Ling Entering Battle" ("Lan Ling wang ju chen ch'ü").[4]

"The Stomping-Swaying Wife" evidently evolved from a domestic situation, as recorded in a T'ang document, *An Account of the Music Academy* (*Chiao-fang chi*):

"A certain man named Su of Northern Ch'i had a red nose. Although he held no official post, he called himself by the official title of *chung-lang*. Whenever he was intoxicated he beat up his wife, and the wife, in turn, would complain to the neighbors of her plight. Their contemporaries made fun of them in a dramatic sketch as follows: A man wearing a woman's outfit walks slowly onto the scene, singing as 'she' walks. At each refrain, others join in:

> *Where do you come from, swaying as you walk?*
> *What grieves you, swaying lady?*

Because she sings as she walks, she is known as the 'stomping-singing' wife. Because she complains, the word 'grieve' is used. When her husband appears, the two engage in a heated argument in order to amuse the spectators."[5]

Two comparable versions are also found in *The Old History of T'ang* and in *Miscellaneous Notes on Songs* (*Yüeh-fu tsa-lu*).[6]

---

[4] "Treatise on Music" (*Yin-yüeh*) in *Chiu T'ang shu, chüan* 29, p. 9a.

[5] Ts'ui Ling-ch'in, *Chiao-fang chi* in *Chung-kuo ku-tien hsi-ch'ü lun-chu chi-ch'eng* (hereafter referred to as *CKKT*), Vol. I, p. 18.

[6] *Chiu T'ang shu, chüan* 9, p. 9a; in the second source, it is added that in T'ang times, the actor playing the part of the husband "wore a red outfit and a hat, and his face had a drunken red hue" (Tuan An-chieh, *Yüeh-fu tsa-lu*, p. 45).

"The Military Counselor" (*Ts'an-chün*). In the T'ang period (618-906) a new type of theatrical act known as "The Military Counselor" appeared, and its introduction of dialogue is regarded as a significant step towards the development of drama. The act originated in the story of a corrupt official who was degraded to the level of an actor, traditionally of extremely low social status in Chinese society:

"Chou Yen, military counselor to Shih Le [reigned 330-344, of the Later Chao dynasty], served as magistrate of Kuan-t'ao. He was put in jail for embezzling thousands of bolts of silk, but his sentence was later commuted on the grounds of one of the 'Eight Excuses.' Thereafter at banquets an actor was made to wear a headpiece and an unlined yellow silk robe. 'What official are you that you should come among us?' one actor would ask him. Thereupon he would reply, 'I was the magistrate of Kuan-t'ao'; and shaking his robe he would add: 'Because I took this, I come to be among you.' This made people laugh."[7]

A prestigious well-to-do official whose fortunes are reversed when his dishonesty is exposed must have provided an excellent situation for a jester to display his wit and to provoke laughter. "The Military Counselor," originally a skit based on a certain event, soon became a kind of dramatic act with a stock comic main character.[8]

"Variety Plays" (*Tsa-chü*) *and Yüan-pen.* In the Sung period (960-1279) the expansion of trade and economic growth brought new prosperity to the middle classes. Contemporary accounts provide a picture of a bustling urban scene in Pien-liang (the present-day K'ai-feng), the Northern capital, and Lin-an (the present-day Hangchow), the South-

---

[7] *Chao shu,* cited in *T'ai-p'ing yü-lan, chüan* 569. A somewhat similar version of this story appears in Tuan An-chieh, *Yüeh-fu tsa-lu,* p. 49.

[8] Jen Pan-t'ang's *T'ang hsi-nung* (1958) provides good source material on "The Military Counselor" and other types of theatricals in the T'ang Period, but his conclusions, often based on insufficient evidence, are not convincing.

ern capital. Popular entertainment flourished in the amusement centers, the so-called "tile-districts."[9] Meng Yüan-lao, writing about the Northern Sung capital, states: "Since Ch'ung-Kuan [the Ch'ung-ning and Ta-kuan Reigns, 1102-1107 and 1107-1111], performances in the 'tile-districts' in the capital consist of . . . 'variety plays' (*tsa-chü*) . . . storytelling (*hsiao-shuo*) . . . 'popular entertainment acts' (*san-yüeh*) . . . and shadow plays. . . . Every day, rain or shine, the places are crowded with spectators."[10] "There are the Sang Family Tile-district on the south side of the street, the Middle Tile-district near the northern side, and next to it the Inner Tile-district, wherein are located some fifty theatres (*kou-lan*). Among these, the Lotus Tent and Peony Tent in the Middle Tile-district, and the Raksha Tent and Elephant Tent in the Inner Tile-district are the largest, accommodating several thousand spectators."[11] Popular entertainments in the Southern capital seem to have been even more prosperous, with seventeen theatrical districts inside and outside the city.[12]

The "variety plays," an important feature of the amusement centers, consisted of four parts: a prologue that was usually low comedy; two middle acts that portrayed the main action in one or two scenes, usually accompanied by singing and dancing; and an epilogue. There were four or five characters, each known by a conventional role or title, and a musician: *mo-ni*, the leading male role and probably the producer as well; *yin-hsi*, probably the director: *fu-ching*, a comic performer; *fu-mo*, the secondary male role; *chuang-ku*, the role of an official; *pa-se*, the musician.[13]

That these Sung "variety plays" had scripts is suggested

---

[9] The term "tile-district" (*wa-she* or *wa-ssu*), applied to "amusement centers," appears in Kuan-p'u-nai-te-weng (pseudonym), *Tu ch'eng chi sheng* (1235; reprint, 1962), p. 95. The pseudonym means "The old man who can put up with watering the garden."

[10] Meng Yüan-lao, *Tung ching meng hua lu* (1147; reprint, 1962), pp. 29-30.

[11] *Ibid.*, p. 14.

[12] Wu Tzu-mu, *Meng liang lu* (c. 1275; reprint, 1962), p. 298.

[13] Kuan-p'u-nai-te-weng, p. 96.

by a reference in *The Wonders of the Capital* (*Tu ch'eng chi sheng*): "Formerly Meng Chüeh-ch'iu, a delegate from the Music Academy (*chiao-fang*) in the capital city of Pien, was able to compose scripts for 'variety plays.' "[14] The exact nature of a "script," however, is not clear. Of the 280 "variety plays" listed in *Memoirs from Wu-lin* (*Wu-lin chiu shih*), some 150 seem to be titles of songs.[15] The close association of the Sung "variety play" and the Yüan drama is seen in the similarity in name (*tsa-chü*), the four-act division, and the use of a role system.

Yüan-pen, believed to be an ancestor of the Yüan drama, was in Chin times merely a different name of the "variety play," according to the contemporary author T'ao Tsung-i.[16] It seems that beginning with the Yüan period, the "variety play," centering on comic episodes, retained the name of *yüan-pen* while the name *tsa-chü* was adopted for the emerging new drama based on plot.[17]

Southern Drama (*Nan-hsi or hsi-wen*). In addition to these rudimentary theatrical arts, a fairly well-developed

[14] *Ibid.*

[15] Chou Mi, *Wu-lin chiu shih* (completed in 1280-90; reprint, 1962), pp. 508-12.

[16] T'ao Tsung-i (fl. 1360), *Ch'o keng lu* (*SPTK so-pen*), *chüan* 25, p. 5b.

[17] Feng Yüan-chün, *Ku chü shuo-hui* (1956), p. 222. On *yüan-pen*, see Wang Kuo-wei, pp. 68-73 and 133-37; Chou I-pai, "Hou-ma Tung shih mu chung wu-ke chuan yung te yen-chiu" ("A Study on the Five Clay Figurines in the Tung Tomb at Hou-ma [Shansi]"), *Chung-kuo hsi-ch'ü lun chi*, pp. 384-90. These figurines unearthed at the Tung tomb of the Chin dynasty (1115-1234) have been identified as actors; they were originally placed in a small stage-shaped niche in a wall of the tomb. Three of them were exhibited in Europe and America in 1972-1975; photographs of these appear in the catalogues (*The Exhibition of Archaeological Finds of The People's Republic of China*, 1974, picture edition, p. 101, and text edition, p. 56). Exhibited with these are three larger and more lively pottery figurines, one whistling, one stepping sidewise with clappers in hand, and one dancing; unearthed at Chiao-tso, Honan, they are believed to be actors and dancers of the Yüan period (see photograph and description on the catalogue pages cited above).

drama also seems to have existed in southern China around
this time. Rediscovered in 1920 among *An Imperial Collection of the Yung-lo Reign* (*Yung-lo ta-tien*) are three handwritten play scripts: *Sun, the Little Butcher* (*Hsiao Sun t'u*)
by a "writing society" in Hangchow; *An Official's Son Goes
Astray* (*Huan-men tzu-ti ts'o li-shen*) by a playwright in
Hangchow; and *Chang Hsieh, the First-place Graduate*
(*Chang Hsieh chuang-yüan*).[18] They are believed to be from
the Sung or Yüan period and the forerunners of Southern
ch'uan-ch'i drama, which was to thrive in the Ming period
(1368-1644).[19] These surviving plays vary greatly in length
and, unlike the Northern *tsa-chü*, are not divided into acts.
The roles are quite different from those in the Northern
genre. Several characters have singing parts. The song titles
in the Southern plays are mostly different from those found
in the Northern drama (*tsa-chü*), and the songs do not form
a "song-suite" (*t'ao-shu*).[20] Although these Southern plays
may have been written at the same time that the Northern
drama began to flower, the two genres seem to have developed quite independently.

Puppet and Shadow Shows. Among the great variety of
theatrical entertainment that may have contributed to the
development of the new drama are puppet and shadow
shows.[21] Puppet productions existed as early as the Han

---

[18] The author of *Chang Hsieh chuang-yüan* is not given. These
three plays are found in *Yung-lo ta-tien* (completed in 1408), *chüan*
13,991, and collected in *Ku-pen hsi-ch'ü ts'ung-k'an* (hereafter referred to as *KPHC*), 1st series. Aside from these three complete plays,
a number of songs from Southern plays have been preserved in an-
thologies.

[19] Hu Chi, in his study of Southern drama, places *Chang Hsieh
chuang-yüan* in the Southern Sung period (*Sung Chin tsa-chü k'ao*,
Shanghai, 1957, p. 61); Chou I-pai, being more cautious, asserts that
the play is "a work at least not after the Yüan·period" (*Chung-kuo
hsi-chü shih chiang-tso*, Peking, 1958, p. 62).

[20] *T'ao-shu* is a unit consisting of songs in the same musical mode.

[21] For an argument of the influence of the puppet and shadow
shows on Yüan drama, see Sun K'ai-ti, *K'uei-lei-hsi k'ao-yüan*
(Shanghai, 1952), chapter 5.

dynasty.[22] In the Sung period, dramatic narratives enacted by puppets were immensely popular. According to contemporary records, the puppets were of various types: puppets hung from strings, puppets walking on ropes, puppets on sticks, puppets operated by controlled explosive charges, live puppets,[23] and water puppets. They "present stories of beauties and supernatural beings, of armored warriors and wise judges."[24] Names of well-known contemporary manipulators who could make the puppets come alive or move the audience to great emotions were also recorded.[25] Puppetry by this time must have attained a high artistic level.

The shadow play[26] is believed to have existed in the T'ang period. After Emperor Hsüan-tsung lost his favorite lady Yang Kuei-fei, a shadow play is said to have been produced to create an illusion of her presence. That the shadow play in the Sung period was already quite advanced may be seen from a description in *The Wonders of the Capital*: "Originally in the capital the figures were made of plain paper; later they are ingeniously cut from parchment, and colored. The script is like that of a narrator of histories, consisting of half truth and half fiction. The righteous and the loyal are given proper features, while the treacherous and the evil are given ugly looks. This is done in order to praise the virtuous and censure the wicked."[27]

[22] Ying Shao (fl. 178) in his *Feng-su t'ung* mentions the performance of "puppets" (*k'uei-lei-tzu*) at festivals in the capital (cited in Wang Kuo-wei, p. 35).

[23] A child sitting on a man's shoulder and manipulated by him.

[24] Kuan-p'u-nai-te-weng, p. 97.

[25] Chou Mi, *chüan* 6, pp. 461-62.

[26] Shadow plays as now performed in China consist of figures cut out of parchment, usually of sheep or ox skin, colored and varnished on both sides. A screen of white gauze is stretched between two poles on stage, and the figures, held by metal wires on bamboo poles, are manipulated behind the screen in front of lights. Since the figures' heads, arms, and legs are cut out separately, there is a sense of great motion, producing an animated, lifelike impression.

[27] Kuan-p'u-nai-te-weng, pp. 97-98.

The Oral Narrative Tradition

Although theatrical production of diverse kinds had existed before the Yüan period, the only dramatic literature extant that may possibly date from the pre-Yüan period is the three recently discovered Southern plays. It was the *pien-wen* (early popular literature)[28] and the oral storytelling of Sung times that had the greatest bearing on the emergence of Yüan dramatic literature.

Pien-wen. The development of *pien-wen* gained impetus in the early T'ang period when many stories found in the Buddhist canon were popularized as a means of explicating obscure scriptures. Buddhism, introduced into China during the Han dynasty (206 B.C.-A.D. 220), achieved maturity and wide influence in the T'ang through efforts on many levels. On the intellectual plane, devoted Buddhist disciples such as Hsüan Tsang (600-664) and I Ching (635-713) translated hundreds of Sutra texts into Chinese. On a more popular level, monastic priests converted esoteric scripture into appealing tales designed to attract a general and probably semiliterate or illiterate audience.

Lectures on Buddhist scripture for laymen (*su-chiang*) were quite popular in the T'ang period, as Han Yü (768-824), a leading scholar who was strongly opposed to Buddhism, notes with a tone of disapproval in one of his poems:

> *Clamouring on both sides of the streets are Buddhist lecturers;*

[28] *Pien* has been translated as "change" or "popularize"; and *pien-wen* as "changed writing" or "popularization," meaning "the changing of Buddhist scriptures into popularized versions." (See Cheng Chen-to, *Ch'a-t'u pen Chung-kuo wen-hsüeh shih* [1959], p. 449; J. Bishop, *The Colloquial Short Story in China*, 1956, pp. 3-4.) Other scholars prefer to translate *pien* as "unusual," and *pien-wen* as "writings of the unusual." (See Sun K'ai-ti, *Su-chiang shuo-hua yü pai-hua hsiao-shuo* [1956], p. 1; James J. Y. Liu, *The Chinese Knight-Errant* [1967], pp. 210-11.)

*The noise of bells and conch shells shatters the palace
    peace.
Attracted by exaggerated sermons on human sin,
A sea of people, like duckweed, surges forward to listen.*[29]

When the Japanese monk Ennin (793-864) visited the T'ang
capital of Ch'ang-an, he made several entries in his diary
about these lectures.[30]

Secular stories too were recited and became part of the
pien-wen tradition. The tragic story of the Han Court Lady
Wang Chao-chün, who was sent to a northern tribal chief,
was movingly narrated in the *pien-wen* style by a southern
entertainer. Chi Shih-lao, a late T'ang poet, depicted the
narration in his poem, "On Seeing a Szechwan Girl Perform
the *Pien* of Chao-chün" ("K'an Shu nü chuan Chao-chün
pien"):

*Before her days of the pomegranate skirt,
She lived, she says, by the bank of the Brocade River.
Her lovely lips can tell events of a thousand years,
Her clear words touchingly relate the sorrow of the
    autumn days.
By her arching brows hangs the southern moon,
But the moment she opens her painted scrolls,
She is amid the clouds beyond the northern pass.*[31]

Later the story of Chao-chün was celebrated in the Yüan
play *Autumn in the Han Palace* (*Han kung ch'iu*).

Existing texts of *pien-wen* recitations include both religious
and secular stories. Among the large collection of manuscripts
from Tun-huang, about 80 pieces are classified by Wang

[29] Han Yü, "Hua shan nü" ("A Girl of Hua Mountain") in *Chu
Wen-kung chiao Ch'ang-li hsien-sheng chi* (*SPTK so-pen*), *chüan* 6,
p. 61.

[30] Edwin O. Reischauer, *Ennin's Diary, The Record of a Pilgrimage to China in Search of the Law* (1955), pp. 298-99, 310-11, 316.

[31] *Ch'üan T'ang shih* (hereafter referred to as *CTS*), vol. 11, p.
8771.

Chung-min as in the *pien-wen* tradition.[32] In addition to the tale of the Lady Wang Chao-chün, several other *pien-wen* pieces also use stories from the folk tradition that later appear in Yüan drama: the story of Wu Tzu-hsü's escape from the State of Ch'u and his eventual revenge for his father's death ("Wu Tzu-hsü pien-wen"); the story of Meng Chiang nü's search for her conscript husband's remains beneath the Great Wall ("Meng Chiang nü pien-wen"); and the story of the amorous adventures of Ch'iu Hu ("Ch'iu Hu pien-wen"). Although some of the elements of these stories appear in earlier historical or semi-historical works, the original accounts are generally quite sketchy, and it is in the *pien-wen* version that they first take shape as imaginative and interesting popular stories.

In addition to enriching and expanding earlier stories, the *pien-wen* also introduced to the Chinese people tales from the rich storehouse of South and Central Asian folk literature. There is little doubt that the story of Mu-lien (Maudgalyāyana in Sanskrit) from Indian Buddhist scripture was first brought to China through *pien-wen*. The *pien-wen* narratives of Mu-lien's rescue of his mother, derived from the Avalambana Sutra, tell of a devout disciple who becomes an Arhat after his parents' death and succeeds in helping the ghost of his sinful mother to rise to Heaven from the Avici Hell.[33] The vivid description of the horrors of hell in these *pien-wen* writings, with grotesque demons and bloody torture, provides rich sources of melodramatic materials for the stage. One twelfth century author recalls in his memoirs that performances of "*Mu-lien Rescues His Mother* (*Mu-lien chiu mu*) *tsa-chü* were held each year in the North-

---

[32] See Wang Chung-min *et al.*, *Tun-huang pien-wen chi* (1957), 2 vols. The collection consists of 23 secular stories and 53 religious stories. Six of them contain the term *pien-wen* or *pien* in their original titles; and the editors, basing their choice on textual evidence, added 13 such titles containing the term *pien-wen* or *pien*.

[33] *Ibid.*, pp. 701-13, 714-55, 756-60.

ern Sung capital of Pien-liang from the seventh to the fifteenth day of the seventh month, at which time the audiences
were larger than usual."[34] A Yüan play entitled *Mu-lien
Rescues His Mother* is also known to us by name.[35]

Besides contributing to thematic material, *pien-wen* seems
also to have influenced the literary format of Yüan drama.
The alternating use of prose and verse, a prominent feature
of some *pien-wen* writings, became a marked feature in early
Chinese colloquial literature, including the Sung-Yüan stories, the Chin narratives (the "medley" or *chu-kung-tiao*),
and Yüan drama.[36] Although still rudimentary, these *pien-
wen* specimens represent some of the earliest extant Chinese
vernacular prose whose earthy colloquial language ushered
in the possibility of acting out, through dialogue, a long and
continuous story.

Sung and Chin Oral Narratives. Oral storytelling of the
Sung period was not only the immediate predecessor of the
Yüan drama, but also the most significant shaping force of
the new genre. By Sung times, oral storytelling had become
a regular profession. Contemporary accounts report that oral
narratives were of several types: (1) historical tales, relating
the rise and fall of states, wars, etc.; (2) popularization of
Buddhist scripture, meditation and enlightenment; and (3)
"small talk" (*hsiao-shuo*), dealing with love (*yen-fen*),
spirits (*ling-kuai*), marvels (*ch'uan-ch'i*), law suits (*kung-*

[34] Meng Yüan-lao, *chüan* 8, p. 49.

[35] Fu Hsi-hua, *Yüan-tai tsa-chü ch'üan mu* (1957), p. 351. A
drama version of the Mu-lien story from the Ming period, entitled
Mu-lien chiu mu ch'üan shan hsi-wen, is also preserved (in *KPHC*,
1st series, 1954). The Avalambana Festival (in Chinese, *Yü-lan-p'en*)
is still observed in Taiwan. For a few days, beginning on the fifteenth
day of the seventh month of the lunar calendar, prayers are offered
to rescue sinners from Hell.

[36] *Chu-kung-tiao*, a generic term, simply means "musical airs in
various modes," or "medley." Another earlier literary genre, the *fu*,
also involves alternation of prose and verse; it is questionable, however, whether the *fu* had any influence on colloquial literature.

an), combat with knives (*p'o tao*) or cudgels (*kan-pang*), immortals (*hsien*), and magic powers (*yao-shu*).[37] With their proved value as mass entertainment, oral narratives served as models for the emerging Yüan drama.

An outstanding Yüan play, *The Romance of the Western Chamber* (*Hsi hsiang chi*), offers an excellent example of the ways in which the dramatists borrowed from the oral narratives. This love story of Chang Chün-jui and the maiden Ts'ui Ying-ying originated in "Ying-ying chuan," a *ch'uan-ch'i* ("tale of the marvelous") written in the classical language by the T'ang author Yüan Chen (779-831). Later it became a favorite of the storytellers and survives in three versions in the few existing Sung and Chin recitative texts. In the "Flirtation Song" ("T'iao-hsiao ling chuan-t'a") by Ch'in Kuan (1049-1101), Ying-ying is one of ten beauties eulogized in ten sections of alternating poems and songs. In the drum song (*ku-tzu-tz'u*) written to the tune of "Tieh lien hua" in the *Shang* mode,[38] the author Prince Chao Ling-chih (c. 1110) tells the story of Ying-ying in alternating prose and song, with the prose sections taken almost verbatim from the original T'ang tale. The third version, *The Western Chamber Medley* (*Hsi hsiang chi chu-kung-tiao*), written by Tung *chieh-yüan* during the rein of Emperor Chang-tsung (1190-1208) of the Chin dynasty, is the script of an oral narrative in prose and songs sung to tunes in a variety of musical modes. This "medley" version is the immediate predecessor and main source of the Yüan play.

In the original T'ang story, the young girl Ying-ying is escorting the coffin of her late father to his home town for burial. On the way, she and her mother are alarmed when rebel soldiers besiege the monastery where they are staying.

---

[37] Contemporary sources agree on these three main categories, but differ on a possible fourth one. See Sun K'ai-ti, "Sung ch'ao shuo-hua jen te chia-shu wen-t'i" ("Problems of Classifying Oral Story-tellers of the Sung Dynasty"), *Ts'ang-chou chi* (1965), pp. 78-96.

[38] See p. 22, n. 2 and p. 181 below.

The girl's distant cousin, a student named Chang, also staying in the monastery, summons a friend of his, a general, to their rescue. After the defeat of the rebels, the student meets Ying-ying for the first time at a banquet given by the girl's mother Madame Ts'ui and is struck by her beauty. Ying-ying is at first indifferent to his attentions. Later, after an encouraging exchange of poems, she again frustrates his plan for a rendezvous. But when he is in utter despair, she suddenly appears one night at his chamber equipped with her pillow and quilt.

In the "medley" version, there is a marked improvement in character portrayal and significant elaboration in plot structure. Here Ying-ying is first attracted by the scholar's handsome appearance, and then moved by his skill in poetry and music. Finally, she is completely won over because of the unfair treatment he receives from her mother, who withdraws her earlier promise to give her daughter's hand to whoever might save them from the besieging enemy. The modification of the girl's actions reflects the narrator's improved handling of motivation. Not only do both lovers become far more alive and interesting, but the waiting-maid Hung-niang is transformed into one of the most remarkable characters in Chinese literature, whose name has since become a byword for a courageous and clever maid. The change of the ending—from the abandonment of the girl, in the literary T'ang story, to the lovers' eventual union in the "medley"—further reveals the storyteller's understanding of the psychology of a popular audience. The tragic ending of the T'ang story would have been too sophisticated and disappointing for a popular audience. In language, the concise classical writing of the T'ang story is transformed into a freer and livelier style, with many colloquial phrases scattered throughout the verse and prose sections adding vividness to both the expression of feelings and the description of scenes. With the expansion from the original 3,000-character T'ang tale into a "medley" of some 44,000 characters, the story of Ying-ying is greatly enriched in coloring and detail.[39]

In the Yüan play, all the expansions, innovations, and changes introduced in the "medley" were appropriated by the playwright Wang Shih-fu, who borrowed plot, characterization, language, and even whole passages from his model. Moreover, musical units in the "medley," consisting of tunes belonging to the same mode, became a basic structural element in this as in all Yüan plays. *The Romance of the Western Chamber* serves as a classic example of a Yüan dramatist's fundamental acceptance of this narrative source. Heavy borrowing from popular narratives can also be seen in the plays *The Deed* (*Ho-t'ung wen-tzu*) and *The Chicken Millet Dinner* (*Fan Chang chi shu*).[40]

In addition to the extant Sung-Yüan narratives and Yüan play scripts, there are a large number of works in both of these genres, the titles of which have survived, but the texts have not. The titles themselves give further indication of the close relationship between the genres, however. An examination of these titles shows that about forty plays are closely related to the "small talk" (*hsiao-shuo*) tales, and over two hundred plays to the historical tales.[41] Although it is possible that at certain stages of their development the borrowing between the two genres was mutual, it is unquestionable that the oral narratives exerted great influence on Yüan dramatic literature.

The favorable response to theatrical productions must have encouraged the poets to lay their hands on any appropriate dramatic material. Of the more scholarly of the playwrights,

[39] The character count of the "medley" is based on Tung *chieh-yüan, Hsi hsiang chi chu-kung-tiao*, Peking: Wen-hsüeh ku-chi k'an-hsing-she, 1955.

[40] See p. 38 and p. 88 below.

[41] See Tanaka Kenji, "Gen zatsugeki no daizai" ("The Subject Matter of Yüan Drama") *Tōhōgakuhō*, XIII, no. 4 (Sept. 1943), pp. 128-58.

some made use of the T'ang literary tales while others turned to the dynastic histories, the remarkable narrative prose of which was a rich source for such themes as loyalty and righteousness, virtues praised by the Confucians and by historians. The parallels between the well-known story *The Chao Family Orphan* (*Chao shih ku-erh*) and the original account in the *Records of the Historian* (*Shih chi*) illustrate the dramatists' success with this kind of source material.[42] Most Yüan playwrights, however, chose more popular sources; the common stock of oral narratives, offering an easily available supply of ready-made material with conventional situations and characters, were the favorites of all.

The Social Milieu

Under Mongol rule during the Yüan period, several factors combined to create a larger audience for entertainment presented in the spoken language and to stimulate the sort of experimentation necessary for the production of a written vernacular language. In the Sung period, economic developments gave rise to new urban centers populated by a growing mercantile class, people who had money and time for entertainment but were unschooled in the classical language. Adoption of the vernacular became necessary to hold such a popular theatre audience. By Yüan times, classical Chinese had become so divorced from the spoken language that it probably was comprehensible only to the small group of literati able to invest the time and money to gain a grounding in the Confucian classics. Thus greater demand for popular entertainment seems to have stimulated the flourishing of vernacular forms during this period.

The development of the vernacular genres, and particularly the flowering of the drama, was assisted significantly by Mongol rule, under which many of the links with the past

---

[42] See Liu Wu-chi, "The Original Orphan of China," *Comparative Literature*, V, no. 3 (1953), 193-212.

were broken. The Mongols' disregard for the traditional Confucian teachings and the classical language helped to stimulate experimentation with the spoken language, hitherto regarded as inappropriate for literary expression.

Moreover, in the production of a play the knowledge of the story and the dialogue must be shared by a number of performers, thus requiring a written script that was not necessary for a single narrator. This necessity may be considered a major reason for setting down the spoken lines on paper.

The prolonged suspension of the civil service examinations for seventy-eight years (1237-1314) deprived many Chinese scholars of the traditional privilege of holding public office, and consequently forced many of them to earn their living through practical professions.[43] Some tried their hand at writing plays in the hope of capturing fame and fortune. When they began to write in the vernacular, their ready facility with the classical language and their knowledge of the actual structure and substance of the living language must have combined to give them the energy and confidence that are manifest in the pages of the Yüan plays. Thus their entrance into this profession brought about the sudden flowering of the drama, producing a body of works qualitatively and quantitatively unequalled before or after in the Chinese theatre, and making Yüan drama one of the most brilliant genres in Chinese literary history.

[43] Civil service examinations were suspended in the North in 1237, soon after the conquest of the Chin by the Mongols, and in the South in 1274, just before the fall of the Sung. They were not reinstated until 1314.

For more information on the social milieu of the Yüan period, see Meng Ssu-ming, *Yüan tai she-hui chieh-chi chih-tu* (1938; reprint, 1967); Frederick W. Mote, "China Under Mongol Domination," in *Cambridge History of China*, forthcoming.

II

Conventions and Structure

Formal Conventions: The Heritage
of the Storyteller

CERTAIN conventions from the oral narrative tradition survived in the drama, making an important contribution to its form beyond actual stories and thematic material. It will be useful to begin by quoting a section of a Yüan play, *Autumn in the Han Palace*, by Ma Chih-yüan, to serve as a background for the discussion of the structural devices. The section quoted is from the beginning of Act I:

1 (Mao Yen-shou enters.)
MAO (recites):

> *Large pieces of gold I hoard and idolize;*
> *Seas of blood or royal commands cannot me jeopardize.*
> *I want to be rich when still alive,*
> *And mind not people's curses after my demise.*

I, Mao Yen-shou, am traveling all over the country with the Emperor's order to search out beautiful maidens for the palace. I have already selected ninety-nine of them. Each of
10 their families has given me gifts; the gold and silver I have thus amassed is quite considerable. Yesterday, I arrived at Tzu-kuei district in Ch'eng-tu, where I selected Wang Ch'iang, also called Chao-chün, daughter of Elder Wang, a dazzling beauty without peer. Unfortunately her father is a peasant without much money. I asked him for a hundred ounces of gold to have the girl placed at the head of the list. He at first pleaded poverty, and then, relying on her extraordinary beauty, rejected my offer completely. (Thinks.) No, if I do that, it would benefit her instead. As soon as I
20 knit my brow to think, a scheme comes up. I need only to

disfigure the girl's portrait a little, so that when she arrives at the capital, she will be sent to the "cold palace" for neglected ladies to suffer a whole life long. Truly it is said: He with only a little hatred is no man; he with but a little venom is no real wight. (Exit.)

(The principal female-role, playing Wang Ch'iang, enters leading two palace maids.)

WANG CHAO-CHÜN (recites):

> *One day I was summoned to enter Shang-yang,*
> *But I've not seen the Emperor ten years long.*
> *This lonely night, who will be by my side?*
> *Only the lute gives me joy in its song.*

30

I am Wang Ch'iang, also called Chao-chün, a native of Tzu-kuei in Ch'eng-tu. My father, the Elder Wang, has worked the land all his life. Before I was born, my mother dreamed that moonlight shone upon her breast and cascaded onto the ground. Soon afterwards, she gave birth to me. When I was eighteen years old, I was chosen for the rear women's palace. Who would have thought that when the minister Mao Yen-shou asked me for money and was refused, he would disfigure my portrait. I have never seen His Majesty, and now I am confined to live in this "Long Lane."[1] When I was at home, I acquired some little skill in music and learned to play several tunes on the lute. And now, at night in my solitude, I shall try to play a song to while away the time.

40

(Plays the lute. The Emperor enters attended by eunuchs carrying lanterns.)

EMPEROR (speaks): I am Emperor Yüan of the Han. Since the time maidens were selected for my palace, there are many I have never favored with my affections. They must be extremely unhappy. Today as I have a little leisure time from my ten thousand duties, I shall make a round in the palace. I shall see which one has the destiny to meet me.

50

(sings to the tune of "Tien chiang ch'un" in *Hsien-lii* mode):[2]

---

[1] Secluded quarters for palace ladies who have given offense to the Emperor.

[2] The meaning of a tune title is not always clear, and generally it

As my carriage rolls over the fallen flowers,
A beauty in the moonlight ceases playing her flute.
My ideal court lady I have not yet met—
How much the thought of this has added to my white hair.

(To the tune of "Hun-chiang lung")

60   *It seems she has not hung up her pearly curtains,*
        Gazing towards Chao-yang palace[3]—
            One step away is like the end of the earth.
        The bamboo shadows, though unstirred by wind, startle
            her;
        The moonbeams through the silken curtains grieve her.
        Each time she sees, amidst the trill of strings and pipes,
            The Jade-carriage making rounds,
        It is like the Spinning Girl,
            Looking for a raft at the banks of the Milky Way.[4]

70   (The female-role plays the lute.)
        EMPEROR: Is that a lute being played over there?
        EUNUCH: Yes, it is.
        EMPEROR (sings):

        Who is it that stealthily plays a tune,
        Sighing "alas, alack"?

        EUNUCH: I shall hurry to order her to come to your Majesty.
        EMPEROR: Stop.

        (sings): *Do not quickly announce to her the Imperial will;*
        I am afraid sudden favors would upset her,
80   *As a stir would startle nestling birds in the palace trees,*
            Or crows atop courtyard branches.

---

is not relevant to the song's content (see pp. 117-19, 185); thus, to avoid confusion, the tune titles are not translated. For information on musical modes, see p. 181 below.

3 Chao-yang palace is the residence of the Emperor's consort.

4 For the allusion, see p. 127, n. 22 below.

Attendants, see which palace lady is playing her lute. Bid her come to my presence, but do not alarm her.

EUNUCH: Which of you ladies played the lute? The Emperor is approaching. Be prepared at once to meet His Majesty. (The female-role quickly comes forward.)

EMPEROR (sings to the tune of "Yu hu-lu"):

> *You are forgiven, who are guilty of no crime.*
> *I personally ask you,*
> *Whose quarters are these?* 90
> *Don't blame me that I never came before,*
> *But only now suddenly appear.*
> *I have come to make amends for your tears,*
> *That have soaked your gossamer handkerchief,*
> *And to warm your embroidered stockings,*
> *Chilled through with icy dew.*
> *A natural born beauty,*
> *It is fit for me to love her.*
> *This night the painted candles on her silver stand*
> *Are sure to sputter forth auspicious signs.* 100

(speaks): Attendants! Look at the candle within the gauze lantern, how it now burns brighter! Lift it up so that I can see better!

(sings to the tune of "T'ien-hsia le")

> *It, too, strives to shine brightly under the red gauze;*
> *Just look, that slender shadow of hers delights me unto*
> *death.*

WANG CHAO-CHÜN (speaks): Had your handmaiden known that Your Majesty was coming, she would have gone farther out to meet you. Not meeting you in time, your handmaiden 110 deserves to die ten thousand deaths.

EMPEROR (sings):

> *Welcoming me, she calls herself "handmaiden",*
> *And greets me with the words, "Your Majesty";*
> *She must not be a girl from a common family.*

(speaks): I see such perfection in her features. She is truly a lovely girl.
(sings to the tune of "Tsui chung t'ien")

> *She paints her eyebrows after the palace fashion,*
120 > *And powders her lovely face;*
> *Scented pins and kingfisher flowers adorn her temples—*
> *One smile of hers is enough to topple a city.*
> *Had King Kou-chien seen her on the Soochow Terrace,[5]*
> *He would have rejected Hsi Shih*
> *And lost his kingdom ten years earlier.*

(speaks): You are indeed outstanding. Who are you?
WANG CHAO-CHÜN (speaks): Your handmaiden's family name is Wang, her given name is Ch'iang, and her style-name is Chao-chün, a native of Tzu-kuei district in Ch'eng-tu. Her
130 father is Elder Wang. Since my grandfather's time we have been working the land. We are common people and know nothing of royal etiquette.[6] (*YCH* 1, Act I, pp. 2-3.)[7]

The above passages, containing five songs intermingled with prose, constitute about half of Act I, which contains a total of nine songs.

Opening Verse. A Yüan play usually opens with a short verse recited by the first character to appear on stage, which sets the scene and reveals the identity and character of the speaker. When there is a prologue preceding the first act proper, this convention may be observed in both the prologue and the first act, as in *Autumn in the Han Palace*. In the prologue, the opening verse is delivered by the Tatar Khan:

---

[5] Ma Chih-yüan made a mistake in writing Kou-chien, when it should be Fu-ch'ai, the king who lost his kingdom because of Hsi Shih.

[6] Cf. Donald Keene's translation of the whole play in Cyril Birch, *Anthology of Chinese Literature* (1965), pp. 422-48.

[7] The number following *YCH* refers to the order in which the play appears in the *Yüan ch'ü hsüan* (see *Number of Extant Plays*, pp. 225-34 below); the page number refers to the modern edition by Chung-hua Book Co., 1958.

The autumn wind meanders in the grass by my tent;
A sorrowful flute sounds across the moonlit sky.
I am Khan to a million archers,
Yet my kingdom, a vassal state to the House of Han.

(*YCH* 1, Prologue, opening verse, p. 1.)

This verse identifies the Khan as a great and proud barbarian chieftain, while at the same time it conveys a vivid impression of the scene. In Act I quoted above, the opening verse by Mao Yen-shou provides us with an even more effective exposition of his thoroughly greedy and vicious character (ll. 3-6).[8]

In many other plays the opening verse is merely conventional, with no particular relevance to the story at hand. John Bishop, in his study of early Chinese stories written in the colloquial language, notes that in oral recitation the performer could conveniently postpone the story by citing verses or appropriate anecdotes until the audience reached a profitable size, while at the same time holding the interest of those who had arrived early. In some scripts, however, when the story begins just after the initial verse, such an opening appears to be a mere token observance of the literary convention.[9]

Self-Identification and Explanatory Monologue. The device of straightforward exposition of characters and events, occasionally used in the opening verse, is a conspicuous convention that also seems to have come from the oral tradition. In a Yüan play, when a character enters, he generally announces his identity and tells his background. In the Prologue to *Autumn in the Han Palace*, the Tatar Khan proceeds from the short verse cited above to an elaborate self-introduction: "I am Khan Hu-han-yeh, the denizen of the sandy waste, the sole ruler of the Northern regions. The wild chase is my trade, battle and conquest my chief occupation."[10]

---

[8] These numbers refer to the line numbers on pp. 20-24.
[9] Bishop, pp. 31-32.
[10] *YCH* 1, Prologue, opening scene, p. 1.

At this point, he briefs the audience on the facts it needs to know before the play gets underway, describing his own position and his tribe's historical association with China. The exposition over, he retires. Upon his heels enters the corrupt and ambitious Minister Mao, who, after identifying himself, proceeds to divulge his innermost secrets, outlining his scheme to alienate the Emperor from his wise counselors and thus enlarge his own influence over the monarch. Again in Act I, this same minister tells why he plans to disfigure the portrait of Wang Chao-chün (ll. 15-25). Just as it is the habit of storytellers to repeat the "who is who" in the interest of poor listeners and latecomers in the audience, so too, in drama, not only initially but upon subsequent entrances as well, a character announces himself, often in exactly the same words.

When dramatists first came to the theatre, they probably found this self-introduction a direct and economic way of exposition, and took over this labor-saving device without questioning its underlying principle. With the role system of Yüan drama, in which one actor who was adept at playing a certain role was engaged to play the parts of several characters, such self-introduction has its practical value. In *The Chao Family Orphan*, for example, the leading male actor in the singing role plays three different persons: a general in the first act, a retired court official in the second and third acts, and finally the grown-up orphan in the fourth and fifth acts. In such circumstances, self-identification is welcomed by the audience in order to keep track of the personages on stage.

The objective monologue, used extensively in Yüan drama, is quite different from the soliloquy employed on the Western stage for "thinking aloud" and thus revealing a character's innermost feelings. The explanatory monologue, in imparting objective information about the speaker himself and openly acquainting the viewer with his background and intentions, seems to lack psychological credibility. This direct and objective monologue is also used in Western plays, although infrequently. Richard's self-introduction in Shakespeare's *Richard III* is a soliloquy that has a large element of direct exposition. In *King Lear*, Edmund, Edgar, and the Earl of Kent all present some very primitive forms of self-introduction in their short monologues, stating who they are and why they conduct themselves as they do; they give expressly stated facts about themselves just as characters do in a Yüan play. Generally, however, in the Shakespearean plays a subtle and indirect exposition employing foreshadowing, hint, intimation, and suggestion is the rule. In Yüan, as in later Chinese drama, the direct method of simply having the character narrate the facts about himself prevails.

Direct Communication with the Audience. We tend to think that the verbal element of drama consists largely of characters addressing each other; but in Yüan drama, where monologues and soliloquies are frequent, actors often find themselves in the position of narrators or lyrical poets speaking directly to the audience. This technique, only occasionally seen in Western drama, is predominant on the Yüan stage. Direct communication with the audience is a long-standing practice of oral storytellers, for it is natural for them to address the audience even when speaking the parts of various characters. The Yüan playwrights' inadequacy in converting narratives such as the "medley" to drama, or in subordinating rhetorical or lyrical elements to dramatic form, may have contributed to the style of direct address so dominant in the plays. Probably the most important reason for the prominence of lyrical expression in the plays is the authors' preeminent interest in poetry. Of hundreds of Yüan plays, the ones that have survived are generally those of the highest poetic quality—products of the more learned dramatists, whose training in the traditional educational system emphasized poetry. A combination of all these factors created an atmosphere conducive to the assertion of lyrical elements in Yüan drama.

Alternating Prose and Verse. The use of alternating prose and verse throughout the Yüan plays is another feature possibly borrowed from the popular storytelling tradition, notably the "medley." A common device in the Yüan plays is the presentation of some informative lines in prose, followed by a song that may repeat what has been said in the prose passage; the reverse process is also used. In the scenes from *Autumn in the Han Palace* given above, for example, when the Emperor decides to make the rounds of the inner palace to visit his neglected beauties, he first expresses his intentions in prose (ll. 48-53), and then in song (ll. 55-58); later, he enjoins the eunuchs in song (ll. 78-81) not to alarm the lady and then repeats his caution in prose (ll. 82-83). This convention of stating the same idea first in one medium and then repeating it in the other is most noticeable on the Yüan stage.

Limitation to One Singing Role. Although there are a great number of songs in a Yüan play, the singing is limited to one character in each act, and normally one performer has the singing part throughout the four acts. In *Autumn in the Han Palace*, a play about the tragic love between Emperor Yüan and his consort, Chao-chün, the Emperor does all the singing. This convention is a determining factor in the structure of Yüan plays in that the development of the story often centers about the one singing character. Similarly, in *Injustice to Tou O* (*Tou O yüan*), the "leading woman" who plays the part of Tou O does all the singing in the play; even though Tou O is beheaded in Act III, her ghost appears and performs the singing in the final act. In *The Butterfly Dream* (*Hu-tieh meng*) the mother has the singing part. When her third son, a secondary character, bursts into song—evidently for comic effect—he is immediately reproved for this unexpected move.[11]

In a considerable number of plays, however, the singing

[11] *YCH* 37, Act III, Song "Tuan-cheng hao" and prose interpolation, p. 644.

part does shift to a different role (*e.g.*, from a male role to a female role).[12] Yoshikawa asserts that the assignment of the singing to more than one role represents a deviation from the convention, as such a practice is not found in plays of the leading dramatists.[13] The conventional practice seems to be that even when the singing part is assigned to several different characters, only one performer does all the singing. In *The Chao Family Orphan*, for example, although the singing in the five acts is assigned to three different characters (Han Chüeh, the general, in Act I; Kung-sun Ch'u-chiu, the official, in Acts II and III; and Ch'eng Po, the orphan, in Acts IV and V), the leading man does the singing for all these different characters.[14] Conventionally, however, songs in the "wedge"[15] could be sung by a second performer. This convention of limiting the singing to one performer is clearly a legacy of oral narrative, where only the narrator performed.

Recapitulation. Another feature that may well have been adopted from the oral narration is recapitulation, a device that is not in accord with the general principle of economy in drama. In a theatrical performance, where the audience gains an understanding of the story through both words and action, recapitulation of a simple situation becomes not only unnecessary but even cumbersome. In an oral recitation, on the other hand, the audience relies mainly on its ears, and an occasional summing up of the plot can be quite useful.

The device of recapitulation is used in almost all Yüan plays. When a character appears for the first time, he often

[12] There are 29 such instances in the *YCH*, consisting of a little over one-fourth of the corpus; for the list of the plays in which such instances occur, see Yoshikawa, *Yüan tsa-chü yen-chiu* (Chinese translation, 1960), pp. 193-94.

[13] *Ibid.*, p. 194.

[14] It is noted specifically in the text that "the leading man plays the part of Han Chüeh" (*YCH* 85, Act I, opening scene, p. 1479); "the leading man plays the part of Kung-sun Ch'u-chiu" (*ibid.*, Act II, opening scene, p. 1482); and "the leading man plays the part of Ch'eng Po" (*ibid.*, Act IV, opening scene, p. 1490).

[15] For the term "wedge," see p. 43 below.

reviews his background, and this same material may be repeated several times during the course of the play, sometimes
in both prose and verse. In *Autumn in the Han Palace*, in the
short space of the first half of Act I, the background of Wang
Chao-chün (a native of Tzu-kuei district in Ch'eng-tu from
a peasant family) is given three times (ll. 11-14, 33-35, 127-
31); and the scheme of Minister Mao to disfigure the portrait of Chao-chün is first outlined in Act I (ll. 20-23), repeated almost at once (ll. 39-41), and recapitulated again
in Acts II and III. In *Injustice to Tou O*, the young woman reviews her life at the end of a long prose section in the first
act. Again in the final act, she gives a lengthy summary of her
life story, including what has just taken place in the previous
acts. In this case, the report of the girl's ghost to her father-
official on what has befallen her and her plea for justice make
the recapitulation justifiable, in contrast to certain plays like
The Shirt (*Ho han-shan*), in which repeated plot summaries
appear unmotivated, clumsy, and obtrusive.

Concluding Couplets. At the conclusion of the text of a
Yüan play, there are always one or two couplets, usually in
seven-character lines headed by the labels *t'i-mu* (theme) and
cheng-ming (proper title), to sum up the story. The concluding couplet of *Autumn in the Han Palace* is translated
as follows:

THEME:
> *Drowned in the Dark River,*
> > *Ming Fei lies in the Green Mound in eternal grief.*

PROPER TITLE:
> *Breaking my sorrowful dream,*
> > *The solitary wild goose deepens the sense of autumn*
> > *in the Han Palace.*

> > > (*YCH* 1, Act IV, p. 13.)

And at the end of *The Chao Family Orphan*, the concluding
couplet appears as follows:

THEME:
> *Kung-sun Ch'u-chiu is ashamed of being questioned,*

PROPER TITLE:
> *The Chao family orphan soundly avenges his wrongs.*
> (*YCH* 85, Act IV, p. 1498.)

This "proper title" usually appears as the title at the beginning of the play as well. In the *Autumn in the Han Palace*, the line consists of eight characters:

P'o   yu   meng   ku   yen   Han   kung   ch'iu
Break sad dream, solitary wild-goose Han palace autumn.

And in *The Chao Family Orphan*, it contains seven characters:

Chao   shih   ku-erh   ta   pao-ch'ou
Chao   family   orphan   soundly   avenge-wrongs.

A shortened title of three or four syllables, however, such as *Han kung ch'iu* or *Chao shih ku-erh*, is conventionally used.

Scholars have yet to agree upon the nature of *t'i-mu* and *cheng-ming*. Aoki[16] and Yoshikawa[17] both believe that these couplets were lines written on banners or pieces of paper to advertise the plays, and thus are extraneous to the texts proper. Their evidence is that these couplets are sometimes printed after the term "play ends" (*san ch'ang*). Other scholars believe that these verses were indeed sung or recited as part of the play. Feng Yüan-chün cites passages in *Cutting Hair to Entertain* (*Chien fa tai pin*) to show that what a character says after the expression "the play ends" could still be a part of the play's text.[18] J. I. Crump further argues that if these lines were indeed extraneous to the texts proper, they would not have been included in the Yüan edition of the thirty plays, which contains only the songs, the most essential portion of the texts.[19] One recently discovered narrative

[16] Aoki, *Yüan-jen tsa-chü hsü-shuo* (Chinese translation, 1959), p. 29.

[17] *Genkyoku Kokukan tei* (*YCH* 58), translated by Yoshikawa, Tokyo (1948), p. 261.

[18] Feng Yüan-chün, p. 362.

[19] J. I. Crump, review of *Genkyokusen shaku*, in *Far Eastern Quarterly*, XII (May 1953), pp. 331-32.

text of the Sung-Yüan period, *Tripitaka of the Great T'ang in Search of Scriptures in Prose and Verse* (*Ta T'ang San-tsang ch'ü ching shih-hua*), includes a couplet-summary at the end of each of its seventeen selections.[20] This points to the possibility of the influence of oral narrative on the concluding couplet device in the plays.

Plot-Making

Not only are the formal conventions of the Yüan drama largely legacies of the early oral narratives, but its plot-making, a matter of structuring a story, also seems to have been considerably influenced by the earlier genres. The Yüan dramatists, although they did not aim at unity of plot, were not unmindful of its importance. *Kuan-mu*, a term sometimes used to refer to "plot," is mentioned five times by Chia Chung-ming[21] in a series of verses published in 1422, in which he praises certain plays in the following terms: the *kuan-mu* of *Both Without Success* (*Liang wu kung*) is striking;[22] the *kuan-mu* of *Exiled to Yeh-lang* (*Pien Yeh-lang*) is romantic;[23] the *kuan-mu* of *An Heir in Old Age* (*Lao sheng erh*) is truthful;[24] and the *kuan-mu* of *Wei Hsien of Han* (*Han Wei Hsien*) is splendid.[25] Playwright Yao Shou-chung is eulogized for his success in "arranging episodes and linking together separate items" (*pu-kuan ch'uan-mu*).[26] The context in the first four instances would indicate that *kuan-mu* may be used freely to mean either "plot" or "story," but the last example makes it apparent that this term refers more specifically to "plot."

A plot in a story or a play is mainly a matter of design. The order created by the dramatists out of a multitude of

---

[20] Section I is missing.   [21] See p. 206 below.

[22] *T'ien-i-ko lan-ke hsieh-pen cheng hsü Lu kuei pu*, 1422. Photo-lithographic reprint, 1960, *chüan* 1, p. 9a.

[23] *Ibid.*, p. 9b.   [24] *Ibid.*, p. 11b.

[25] *Ibid.*, p. 15b.   [26] *Ibid.*, p. 17a.

actions, personages, and feelings, and the selection and arrangement of incidents provide the dramatic framework of a play. The action in a drama initiates its own counter-action; it is the interaction of these two conflicting forces that engenders a sense of progression toward a solution. Whereas Western dramatists have consciously regarded the dramatic conflict and the dialectical process as crucial to all effective drama, the Yüan dramatists seemed only vaguely aware of plot-making, although a few masters achieved great success in adapting from their narrative sources plots that had stood the test of time.

Among the patterns of dramatic opposition found in the Yüan plays, as in earlier narrative art, three are most recurrent: conflicts between natural impulse and conventional morality; the motivation of action by self-interest or passion, with the resultant counter-action of revenge; and the conflict between good and evil, or right and wrong.

Conflict Between Natural Impulse and Conventional Morality. The dramatic opposition of natural impulse and conventional morality is most evident in the love stories. In *The Romance of the Western Chamber*, the mother embodies the values of organized society and conventional morality, while the young lovers, however great their intellectual or aesthetic refinement, represent the forces of natural inclinations. In recasting the story of Ying-ying in the rigid artistic medium of a play, the dramatist Wang Shih-fu managed to retain the original plot of the earlier oral narrative, *The Western Chamber Medley*, adopting the major incidents as related above. When the plot of the narrative source is good, as in this case, the dramatist's success is all but assured.

Similar patterns of conflict appear in many Yüan love stories. In *Looking Over the Wall* (*Ch'iang t'ou ma shang*), for instance, the heroine abandons her wealthy and prestigious family to elope with a young scholar-lover. In the play *A Disembodied Soul* (*Ch'ien nü li hun*), the mother, representing traditional values, disapproves of a poor student's engagement to her daughter, and the girl, in despair, falls ill as her soul leaves her body to follow the student.

Intrigue and Counter-action. The plot based on intrigue is most common in the plays about historical or fictional conspiracies, or about lawsuits (*kung-an*). Excessive ambition, greed, sensuality, or malice in the protagonist inevitably generates an opposing reaction of revenge, thus setting in motion a chain of crime and revenge, or of crime and justice.

Political intrigue, a favorite subject of the Chinese, abounds in plays dealing with historical material. The most popular setting is the colorful Three Kingdoms period (221-264), when the empire, after years of political maneuvering and military strife, was divided into three states: Wei in the north, Wu in the east, and Shu-Han in the southwest. A memorable figure of this period is Chu-ko Liang, a minister at the Shu-Han court of Liu Pei, with the triple role of scholar, diplomat, and above all military strategist. His almost supernatural wisdom and foresight fascinated story-tellers, playwrights, and audiences alike. By Yüan times, a fully developed narrative cycle, the *Romance of the Three Kingdoms* (*San kuo chih p'ing-hua*) was already in existence.[27]

The play, *The Duel of Wits Across the River* (*Ko chiang tou chih*), an outstanding example of the plot of intrigue and counter-action, describes how the statesman Chou Yü of the court of Wu tries repeatedly to trap Liu Pei, and how his plots are invariably thwarted by the strategist Chu-ko Liang. When Liu Pei occupies Ching-chou, Chou Yü persuades his lord, Sun Ch'üan of Wu, to offer his sister as Liu Pei's wife; she is to be escorted by two thousand soldiers who are actually to take over Ching-chou. Seeing through their scheme, Chu-ko Liang persuades Liu Pei to accept the offer, but when the bride arrives, only the bridal sedan and the maids are allowed into the city, and, before Chou Yü can re-

---

[27] See *Ch'üan-hsiang p'ing-hua wu chung*, dated 1321-1324. Photolithographic reproduction, 1956.

act, the wedding is performed. Prior to the bride's journey, her brother and Chou Yü charge her to murder her husband if the first plot should fail, but since she becomes very fond of her new husband, the second intrigue against Liu Pei's life is also frustrated. Resorting to a third strategy, Chou Yü persuades his lord to invite Liu Pei and his wife for a visit, and then to detain them. Having formulated a countermeasure, Chu-ko Liang advises Liu Pei to feign ignorance and accept the invitation to visit across the river. Later, Chu-ko Liang sends over a messenger with a package of clothing containing an embroidered bag, which Liu Pei, under the guise of drunkenness, allows Sun to examine. In it, Sun finds a message falsely reporting an impending attack on Ching-chou by Ts'ao Ts'ao, the general of the Wei state. Thinking that this is a good chance to have Ts'ao Ts'ao kill Liu Pei, Sun immediately releases his sister and Liu Pei and speeds them on their way home. Chu-ko Liang thus succeeds once again in rescuing Liu Pei. When Chou Yü hears of their departure, he immediately suspects something amiss and pursues them. Overtaking Madame Liu's carriage, he kneels in front of it, begging her to return, but to his surprise finds inside the carriage Liu's general Chang Fei, substituted for Madame Liu by Chu-ko Liang. Frustrated and disgraced, Chou Yü eventually dies from grief over his failure to defeat Chu-ko Liang. This story, under the new title *Chou Yü Thrice Foiled* (*San ch'i Chou Yü*), is still popular on the Peking opera stage.

An earlier political intrigue recorded in the *Records of the Historian* provides the background material for *The Meeting at Min Pond* (*Min-ch'ih hui*).[28] During the Warring States period (403-221 B.C.), the loyal strategist Lin Hsiang-ju of Chao exercises great courage and foresight to outwit the powerful Lord of Ch'in, first by safely restoring to Chao a national treasure, a piece of priceless jade, coveted by the Lord of Ch'in, and later by thwarting the Lord of Ch'in's attempt to kill the Lord of Chao at Min Pond. Here we see a

[28] In the biography of Lin Hsiang-ju, *Shih chi, chüan* 81, pp. 1a-5a.

clear example of the plot pattern of intrigue and counter-action. The Lord of Ch'in's scheme to pressure the State of Chao into delivering the jade to his court on the false promise of ceding fifteen cities in exchange is a clever one. However, it is defeated by Lin Hsiang-ju, who carries the jade to the Ch'in court and properly fulfills the demand made by Ch'in, but refuses to relinquish the jade before receiving a guarantee on the fifteen cities.

Plots based on intrigues and counter-actions are also employed in such historical plays as *The Double Bait* (*Lien-huan chi*), *Meeting at Hsiang-yang* (*Hsiang-yang hui*), *Yen-men Pass* (*Yen-men kuan*), *Carrying a Decorated Box* (*Pao chuang ho*), and *Burning the Po-wang Camp* (*Po-wang shao t'un*).

In addition to these stories based on historical events, some of the schemes in the Yüan plays are clearly fictional. In Kuan Han-ch'ing's *Rescued by a Courtesan* (*Chiu feng-ch'en*), Chou She plots to win a young courtesan from her student-lover. He succeeds, but soon after their marriage he tires of her and begins to treat her cruelly. In desperation, she appeals to a former friend, the clever courtesan Chao P'an-erh, who decks herself out with her finest jewelry and goes to see the young man in a fine carriage. Attracted by her charm and apparent wealth, he immediately loses his heart to her and demands a divorce from his wife. Once the divorce paper is safely in their hands, the two women run away. When Chou discovers the trick, he pursues them and regains the supposed divorce paper, which is actually a fake, but when he files a kidnapping suit against the clever courtesan, she produces the real divorce paper in court. Thus the case is cleared up, the heartless deceiver is flogged, and the young courtesan is wed to her former student-lover.

The most interesting presentation of the intrigue and counter-action plot structure is found in the lawsuit or "court case" (*kung-an*) plays,[29] based on traditional stories of ca-

---

[29] See Cheng Chen-to, "Yüan tai 'kung-an chü' ch'an-sheng te yüan-yin chi ch'i t'e chih" ("The Reasons for the Rise of the 'Court-Room

pable judges and their success in solving knotty cases of crime, a specialty in Sung oral storytelling (*shuo kung-an*). Among this group of plays *The Chalk Circle* (*Hui-lan chi*) by Li Hsing-tao is best known to Western readers through a number of translations based on that of Stanislas Julien.

In the Yüan play, a rich gentleman, Ma Chün-ch'ing, is murdered by his wife and her lover; the wife accuses the concubine Hai-t'ang of the murder and claims Hai-t'ang's child as her own, in order to assume all rights to the family fortune. Hai-t'ang is tried, convicted, and sentenced to death by a corrupt judge who has been bribed by the murderers, but her case fortunately comes to the attention of the great Judge Pao Cheng, to whom she pleads her innocence. When both women claim to be the child's mother, Pao Cheng orders that the child be placed within a chalk-marked enclosure and that the two women pull the child, one from each side; the one who pulls the child out of the enclosure is entitled to keep him. The first wife succeeds twice in the attempt, whereupon Judge Pao decides with Solomonic wisdom that Hai-t'ang must be the true mother, since she refuses to hurt the boy by pulling him too strongly. Her innocence is thus demonstrated, and she is awarded the young heir and the family property, while the first wife and her accomplice-lover confess their guilt and are punished.

The Deed provides another example of a wise judge ingeniously solving an intricate case of greed and crime. During a time of famine, a young man leaves his home in a village near the capital Pien-liang to seek a living elsewhere. Before setting out with his wife and three-year-old son, he and his older brother draw up a deed for the family property, and each keeps a copy of it. Soon after leaving home, however, the couple take ill and die. When the son, whom they have left in a friend's keeping, comes of age, he is told of his identity and is given the responsibility of transporting his parents'

Case' plays in the Yüan Dynasty and Their Characteristics"), *Chung-kuo wen-hsüeh yen-chiu* (1957), pp. 511-34.

coffins back to their native home. When the boy arrives at his uncle's house, his aunt, suspecting that the boy has come to claim his share of the property, refuses to recognize him, and deceives him into handing over the deed; thereupon the uncle hits the boy with a brick. When the uncle and aunt are brought before the judge, both vehemently deny that they have a nephew. In the course of the trial, a messenger reports the death of the boy and the judge promptly announces that those who kill deserve to die; if the dead are blood relations, then the matter is considered a family affair and not prosecuted; "if the dead are not blood relations, the killer must pay with his own life."[30] The aunt, fearful of the penalty, quickly admits that the dead boy was truly their nephew. The judge, feigning disbelief, orders the woman to show him both copies of the deed. At this point, the judge produces the boy, who has been only superficially injured, and the play ends with the punishment of the aunt and uncle. After seeing his parents properly buried in the family grave-yard, the boy and his childhood fiancée are married.

A comparison of this play with the narrative version of the same story in the *Ch'ing-p'ing-shan-t'ang Collection of Stories* (*Ch'ing-p'ing-shan-t'ang hua-pen*) reveals that in the dramatic version suspense is upheld through careful manipulation of the incident. Although the two versions are nearly identical in the first half, they differ considerably in the second part. In the narrative, the uncle and aunt refuse to have anything to do with the boy when he tries to show them the deed, and when they are brought to court they still deny having a nephew. Seeing the truth of the boy's claim through the deed presented to him, the judge threatens to beat the old couple, but the boy in turn entreats him to be merciful. Moved by the boy's filial piety, the judge pardons the criminals, and later the boy is rewarded by the Imperial Court for his virtuous act and is reunited with his aunt and uncle. In the play, the added trick of falsely reporting the death of the boy, in order to make the aunt confess to her crime, is

30 *YCH* 25, Act IV, prose speech following "Te-sheng ling," p. 434.

a complication that allows the action and counter-action to progress smoothly toward a more logical and satisfying solution.

Conflict Between Right and Wrong or Good and Evil. The dialectical opposition of right and wrong, or good and evil, are other familiar themes of earlier oral narrative that persisted in Yüan drama. For centuries Buddhist stories had vividly depicted the conflict between men and their evil enemies, sometimes in the form of ferocious demons, as in several *pien-wen* narratives. Notable among these are "The 'Overcoming the Wizard' *Pien-wen*" ("Hsiang mo pien-wen"), containing a long and lively account of a contest between a Buddhist disciple and a wizard; and the *pien-wen* narratives of Mu-lien, who has to fight his way through a host of adversaries to rescue his mother from hell.

An important narrative of Buddhist lore from the Sung-Yüan period, *Tripitaka of the Great T'ang in Search of Scriptures in Prose and Verse,* shows various elements in common with the plot of the Yüan play *A Pilgrimage to the West (Hsi yu chi).* This story is a romanticized account of the travels of the famous monk Hsüan Tsang, who, under the auspices of Emperor T'ai-tsung of the T'ang dynasty, traveled to India to obtain scriptures for the salvation of the people of China. The pilgrimage to India and back, lasting nearly eighteen years, gave rise to colorful legends and stories, which by Sung-Yüan times had developed into a narrative cycle of numerous adventures. This narrative text in prose and verse begins by relating how Hsüan Tsang and five followers are joined by the king of the monkeys. On their journey, the pilgrims must fight ferocious demons and overcome many obstacles; they often resort to magic, for instance, to extinguish a blaze in a mountain passage, or to subdue an obstinate tiger spirit and a vicious dragon. When they reach the "Kingdom of Women," they must resist the charms of beautiful young girls tempting them to give up their quest. Finally the pilgrims reach India and obtain over five thousand volumes of scriptures; upon returning to China, the monk is given the title "Tripitaka" by the T'ang emperor, whereupon the monk and his five followers ascend to Heaven.

The Yüan play *A Pilgrimage to the West* begins with the story of the miraculous birth of Hsüan Tsang and centers on his pilgrimage to India, escorted by three allegorical disciples: Monkey, Pigsy, and Sandy. Many tales, including those of the flaming mountain and the women's kingdom, found both in this play and in the narrative text, indicate the popularity of such stories, in which the element of religious propaganda, presented in terms of the conflict between good and evil, is prominent. They demonstrate the omnipotence of the Buddhist faith and the superior power of its followers, who are shown in triumph over ferocious ghosts and demons.

The concept of conflict between right and wrong in Taoist stories typically takes the form of the opposition of spiritual enlightenment to worldly desires. Fan K'ang's *The Bamboo-Leaf Boat* (*Chu-yeh chou*) tells the story of the scholar Ch'en Chi-ch'ing's conversion to Taoism after a struggle in the form of a debate with the Taoist Immortal Lü Tung-pin. After failing the Imperial civil service examination, Ch'en lingers in a temple and writes a poem on the wall expressing his homesickness and disappointment. At this point a Taoist appears, urging him to give up his ambition for an official career and to embrace the Tao. In the ensuing debate the Taoist sings of the joys of a life as free as the mountain breezes, and bemoans the burdens of rank and riches, while the scholar answers with an exaltation of the glories of official life. Finally, the Taoist sticks a bamboo leaf on the wall, which seems to turn into a magic boat. Ch'en falls asleep and in his dream boards the boat to make his way home. On his journey he loses his way, and is faced with great danger, before the Taoist appears again and successfully persuades him to give up his vain pursuit of worldly advancement. The same pattern of conflict between worldliness and spiritual enlightenment is also seen in Ma Chih-yüan's *The Dream of Yellow Millet* (*Huang-liang meng*). Its plot follows that of the original T'ang *ch'uan-ch'i* story, which celebrates the conversion of an aspiring Confucian scholar to Taoism.

The conflict between right and wrong, or good and evil, in Yüan drama, whether on the level of hand-to-hand combat or on the higher level of philosophical debate, is predominantly external, much like the collision of Macbeth's treasonous ambition with Macduff's unswerving loyalty in the Shakespearean play. The dimension of inner conflict, which we see within the soul of Macbeth himself, however, is largely lacking in Chinese drama. On the Yüan stage, inner conflict is not a necessary or an anticipated ingredient of tragedy. Although Hamlet's clash with his uncle fascinates the audience, it is the conflict within the prince's own mind that haunts them long afterward. Similarly, in *King Lear*, although there are fierce confrontations between man and man, or man and the elements, again the theme is inner struggle—a struggle between the old king's pride and his self-knowledge. In Greek tragedy, even with his destiny controlled by fate, the hero, torn by inner struggle, must at some point make a decision that will determine his future. Thus intense conflict within the mind of the protagonist is central in Western tragedy. The great Western tragedies are largely dramas of personality, while Yüan plays are dramas of events and their meanings.

Several theories have been proposed to explain this failure of Chinese drama to explore intense inner conflict. Ch'ien Chung-shu points out that modes of behavior in traditional Chinese society were so ordered that persons in all ranks of life knew how to act in any given situation.[31] A Chinese royal prince whose father was murdered and whose mother remarried the alleged murderer would have been expected to avenge his father; the prolonged wavering that paralyzes Hamlet's will would not have appealed to the Chinese mind.

[31] Ch'ien Chung-shu, "Tragedy in Old Chinese Drama," *T'ien Hsia Monthly*, I (1935), p. 44.

In *The Chao Family Orphan*, for example, twenty years elapse between the murder of the father and the final vengeance of the son, but as soon as Ch'eng Po is informed of the injustice to his family, he sets out to kill his father's murderer, even though the murderer is his own devoted foster father.

A second explanation is that the Chinese are always counseled to practice moderation in their social conduct; their major philosophies and religions—Confucianism, Taoism, and Buddhism—all advocate restraint.[32] The intense passions basic to Elizabethan tragedy, such as the all-consuming love of Othello, Anthony's obsessive passion for Cleopatra, and Macbeth's unbridled ambition, are irreconcilable with the Chinese ideal of moderation.

A further explanation could be that man, to the Chinese, is only a small part of nature, under a Heaven that is ultimately just and benevolent. He is consequently expected to accept his fate and remain in harmony with nature. Thus personal passions, doubts, desires, and scruples that generate intense unrest and conflict within the soul of a hero in his struggle against fate do not command admiration and awe among a Chinese audience. The same concept is constantly seen in Chinese painting, in which man is depicted as an inconspicuous figure set against the immense expanse of nature. For a single human being to pit himself against nature or fate—a scene familiar in Greek tragedy—is in the Chinese view a presumptuous and unnatural act. These three characteristic Chinese attitudes and beliefs militate against anything like the Western-style tragedy built on violent and intense conflict within the soul of the hero.

The Four-Act Division and the "Wedge"

Yüan drama's four-act division, which seems to have been derived from the four-act "variety play" of the Sung period,

---

[32] Cf. James J. Y. Liu, *The Art of Chinese Poetry* (1962), p. 155; C. T. Hsia, *The Classic Chinese Novel* (1968), Chapter I.

is not always closely correlated with the plot. It does constitute a prominent feature of the genre however, and is regular-
ly observed by the dramatists. Of the 171 extant Yüan plays,
165 consist of four acts, and only six of five acts.[33] An additional shorter unit called the "wedge" (*hsieh-tzu*) may be
placed before any of the regular acts, thus functioning as a
prologue or interlude.[34] The relation between the plot and
the four-act division varies considerably with individual
plays.[35]

In *Autumn in the Han Palace* the prologue, which provides
important background information, and Act I, which tells
of the Emperor's discovery of Wang Chao-chün and her
outstanding beauty, serve as an effective *exposition*. In Act
II the Tatar chieftain, instigated by Minister Mao, specifically demands the hand of this beauty. The Emperor, faced
with a choice between love for his favorite concubine and
duty to the state now under impending danger of foreign
invasion, decides to sacrifice his beloved. Here then is the
development by which the action builds to an eventful moment. The actual *climax* comes in Act III, when the Emperor
bids Chao-chün a moving farewell; soon after, she drowns
herself in a river at the frontier as an ultimate gesture of her
love and devotion towards the Emperor. In Act IV we have
the *denouement*, in which tension eases off from the climactic
action to the hero's final tranquil observation on the state of
affairs reached at the end of the play. Here in late autumn
in the Han palace, the Emperor mourns his loss and recalls
the tender love shared with his beautiful consort. The progress from exposition, to development, climax, and denouement correlates well with the four-act division.

[33] The plays with five acts are *YCH* 85, *WP* 109, 114, 117b, 126,
and 158. (While 117b consists of 5 acts in old editions, in *WP* one of
the 5 acts is labeled a *hsieh-tzu*.)

[34] See Cheng Chen-to, "Lun pei-chü te hsieh-tzu" ("A Study of the
'Wedge' in Northern Drama"), *Chung-kuo wen-hsüeh yen-chiu*
(1957), Vol. II, pp. 578-95.

[35] The correlation between the four-act division and music is discussed on pp. 193-94 below.

In a number of plays, however, such a correlation is lacking, as the action is mostly static. One good example of this type is the historical play *Lord Kuan Goes to the Feast with a Single Sword* (*Tan tao hui*), which celebrates the heroic act of Lord Kuan in the defense of Liu Pei's territory Ching-chou against the Kingdom of Wu. Lu Su, the crafty minister of Wu, who has formulated a three-stage scheme to lure Lord Kuan to a feast and then capture him, consults with the statesman Ch'iao Kung and a hermit, Ssu-ma Hui. Act I is mainly an account of Lord Kuan's outstanding strength and courage, by Ch'iao Kung, who warns against the scheme. Act II is a long description of Lord Kuan's superior power by Ssu-ma Hui, who also disapproves of the ambush. Not until Act III does Lord Kuan appear in person, fearless and self-confident. When warned of the superior force in the enemy's camp, he boasts:

> *I am Lord Kuan, hero of the Three Kingdoms,*
> *My valor knows no limit.*
>
> (*WP* 105, Act III, "T'i yin teng," p. 66.)

He then goes on to sing a number of songs recalling his past brave deeds. Only in the final act is there any actual confrontation with Lu Su. When asked to surrender Ching-chou, he grows furious and points to his sword, saying: "When it is happy, it rests at ease; when it is angry, it clangs in the scabbard."[36] By sheer defiance, he overpowers Lu Su and walks away unharmed. Even though the play is an interesting and effective portrayal of Lord Kuan, there is no action to speak of until the fourth act, and in this sense the course of development is essentially static.

While some Yüan plays evince a clear four-part dramatic structure, and some are mostly static, a considerable number are merely episodic, with a plot generally following a natural chronological order beginning at the beginning and moving along towards the conclusion. A classical Greek play, begin-

---

[36] *WP* 105, Act IV, following "Ch'en tsui tung feng," p. 69.

ning *in medias res*, follows an artificial order and usually commences at a critical point. An Elizabethan play, although also following a chronological sequence, is more selective in its presentation of details than a Yüan play and stands between the Greek classical drama and the Yüan drama in its narrative character. In the Yüan play, *The Chao Family Orphan*, the plot begins with a feud between two powerful households and the massacre of the Chao family; it then proceeds with the story of the Chao orphan, his growth to adulthood, and the final revenge of his father's death. Such a long-drawn-out presentation of events, beginning with the origins of the situation and proceeding chronologically towards the end, is typical of Yüan plays.

In a play, unlike a narrative, the sequential approach tends to create a somewhat loose and unstructured effect because of the limitations of space and time. For a modern Western reader, accustomed to tightly structured plots that demonstrate with compelling logic the inevitable course of cause and effect, the digressions and loose ends of a Yüan play can be disturbing. The Yüan audience, whose expectations were not geared to an Aristotelian concept of unity or an Ibsenian sense of logic, did not demand a well-unified story structure. There was no real problem if a few essential links in plot were omitted or a few extraneous details included. Even on the Chinese classical stage today an evening's performance generally consists of many scenes from different plays; only on rare occasions will a play be presented in its entirety. The main reason for this practice is to provide various actors and actresses with an opportunity to demonstrate their prowess in playing special roles. The emphasis is on performance rather than on story—on the theatrical rather than the dramatic—in the traditional Chinese theatre.

While many of the conventions discussed here had an important function in the earlier oral tradition, the fact that they are carried over into the drama with few significant alterations illustrates the conventionalism characteristic of the popular genres in Chinese literature. Just as the ancient Greek plays developed the unique convention of the chorus and as the Elizabethan plays are characterized by their frequent shift of setting on an open and fluid stage, Yüan drama too has its own unique structural features. The Yüan plays are narrative in nature because the dramatists, by force of tradition and by recognition of their value, adopted many storytelling devices that had become fixed as conventions in oral literature.

III

Characterization

Type Characters

In the Yüan plays, most characters are types: romantic figures, such as beautiful and accomplished maidens and talented scholar-lovers; and social types, such as corrupt officials, wise judges, rebels, defenders of order, and various quacks and rogues. Character portrayal in Yüan drama is based not on naturalism but on the presentation of universal traits, emphasizing the typical. Many Western dramatists, on the other hand, emphasize complexity in character portrayal, in the belief that the many-sided attributes of the subject are necessary to round out the character and to make him seem real. Because the standards and goals of Yüan theatre are different from those of Western drama, it is necessary to evaluate its characters and characterization with critical standards distinct from those applied to Western works. The prevailing use of type characters on the Yüan stage is to be understood within the framework of three traditions: the literary, the ethical, and the theatrical.

Literary Tradition. In developing their characters, the dramatists relied on a living literary tradition. The art of character portrayal was familiar in pre-Yüan prose writings, some of which depict men and women in terms of certain commonly shared social or personal characteristics, thus foreshadowing an interest in type characters. Ssu-ma Ch'ien's *Records of the Historian* includes a number of biographies grouped together under such headings as "Confucian scholars," "knights-errant" (*yu-hsia*), "merchants," and "assassins." Liu Hsiang's *Biographies of Illustrious Women* (*Lieh nü chuan*),[1] another well-known work, contains a gallery of portraits of women, with many of them sharing particular virtues or a certain range of habits, values, or emotions.

Later both the T'ang literary tales and the Sung oral narratives provided a repertoire of character types, which may be classified into two groups, "romantic" and "social." Whereas "romantic" types are always familiar in folk literature, the preoccupation with morals in Chinese storytelling called for the depiction of "social" types as well. Although often given great artistic vitality through realistic and concrete detail, most of these characters are marked by type features—the devotion to government service of a Confucian scholar, the carefree worship of nature of a Taoist, the craftiness of a scholar-strategist, and the chivalry of certain outlaws.

The method of giving certain distinct acts or feelings a general significance as marks of a type is prominent in both the sophisticated T'ang literary tales and the popular Sung and Yüan vernacular stories. Yüan dramatic literature, drawing on these prototypes, presents many categories of characters who possess the same qualities and are nearly indistinguishable in their actions. In some cases a proper name even turns into a common term, denoting the specific status, attributes, or virtues of the type; a wise and just judge is often called Pao Cheng or Pao-kung, while an official's servant is often called Chang Ch'ien. Thus both the literary and oral narratives offered rich source material and models for the depiction of type characters.

Ethical Tradition: Emphasis on Propriety. Drama, being essentially a mimesis of life, places a certain value on verisimilitude, even in romantic or stylized theatre. Successful dramatic portrayal, therefore, depends to a large extent on the appropriateness of represented behavior to the occasion, the person, and the purpose. Proper behavior in traditional

---

[1] Liu Hsiang (77-6 B.C.), *Lieh nü chuan* (1825: a facsimile edition by Yü Ching-an of the 1214 Sung version).

Chinese society is so well defined that there is little room for free individual action. This way of life, mirrored on the stage by characters who act according to prescribed rules of propriety, tends to result in type characters—loyal officials, filial sons, chaste wives, and devoted friends.

In traditional Chinese society, virtue resides not so much in individual achievement as in the proper fulfillment of one's role. Rulers are benevolent and subjects loyal; parents are loving and children filial. In the official histories, a person is often applauded or condemned because of the right or wrong way in which he plays his role. As mentioned above, the grand historian Ssu-ma Ch'ien many times classifies his subjects by their roles, and in some cases he further categorizes them according to their performance of these roles: Sun Shu-ao and Cheng Tzu-ch'an are called good officials, while Chih Tu and Ning Ch'eng are labeled together as bad officials.[2]

The teachings of propriety placed great emphasis on differences in sex, social class, and profession. Each person would be expected to act in certain ways under certain circumstances, according to his station in life. Distinctions were often expressed in style, color, and quality of dress, and in modes of everyday conduct. Since dramatists were required to identify characters by such class signs and specified conduct, the typical aspects of behavior were stressed, leading naturally to type characters.

Awareness of the Chinese concept of propriety and familiarity with the traditional concepts of correct conduct provide the frame of reference necessary to judge dramatic characters in action, and to appreciate and respond to their behavior. In *Injustice to Tou O*, the Confucian scholar Tou T'ien-chang, though destitute, is determined to pursue his career and become an official. In order to pay his debts and earn the few ounces of silver he needs to travel to the capital to take the state examination, he delivers his daughter to an old woman, Mistress Ts'ai, to be her daughter-in-law. Where-

[2] *Shih chi, chüan* 119 and 122.

as a Western audience would perhaps view such action as heartless, a Chinese audience may view it as a painful sacrifice that was morally justified in terms of Tou's duty as a scholar to try to achieve official position. His separation from his daughter in the Prologue is a touching scene, as is his meeting with his daughter's ghost in the final act of the play. The father emerges largely as a sympathetic character in the eyes of a Chinese audience. The wide acceptance of conventional ethical attitudes, along with the formalized approach to the code of behavior, tended to accentuate the propensity toward type characterization.

Theatrical Tradition: The Role System.[3] The role system, already a convention in the Sung "variety play" (*tsa-chü*), was adopted by Yüan drama and influenced its method of characterization. This system is reminiscent of the situation in American stock companies around the turn of the century, when each member of the company specialized in certain roles and was categorized accordingly: leading man, leading lady, juvenile, and the like. In the Yüan drama, a script may call for a given part to be played by the "leading man" (*cheng-mo*), "leading lady" (*cheng-tan*), "villain" (*ching*), or any of a number of other well-defined types. This system of roles is so important that a principal character's lines were generally marked by the role type rather than the name of the character in question, *e.g.*: "the leading man says. . . ." The types were not limited to one sex; there were many actresses who specialized in the male lead or the female lead role.[4]

The role system adds a measure of predictability to the nature of the stage character. In *Li K'uei Carries Thorns* (*Li K'uei fu ching*), when the bandit Li K'uei is played by the "leading man" (*cheng-mo*), a sympathetic role, the audience is predisposed to feel favorably toward him. On the other hand, when the *ching*, an unsympathetic role, plays the

³ See pp. 204-05 below.
⁴ See p. 201 below.

part of a doctor or an official, as in *Injustice to Tou O*,
the audience can expect the character to be vicious. When the
ching, playing Doctor Lu, first enters the stage, he identifies
himself as follows:

> *I diagnose disease with care,*
> *And prescribe according to the medicine book.*
> *I cannot bring dead men back to life,*
> *But the live ones by my doctoring often die.*[5]

In Act II, when the *ching* plays Prefect T'ao, he introduces
himself in similar fashion:

> *I am a better official than many another;*
> *Whoever comes to file a suit is asked to pay in gold*
> *　　and silver.*
> *If a superior official comes to investigate,*
> *I stay at home pretending to be under the weather.*[6]

The *ching* role is often made to appear comic and ludicrous,
even when involving a person of high position. In the same
way, when the "leading woman" (*cheng-tan*), a sympathetic
role, plays the part of a wife (as in *Ch'iu Hu Teases His
Wife* [*Ch'iu Hu hsi ch'i*]), she is kind and virtuous, but when
the "painted woman" (*ch'a-tan*), an unsympathetic role,
plays the part of a wife (as in *The Chalk Circle*) or of an aunt
(as in *The Deed*), the character is evil or even ludicrous.

The convention of the role system, which is discussed in
more detail below, partly explains what appears to be insufficient motivation in many of the Yüan drama characters.
A judge or a doctor in the *ching* role is plainly a villain, and
is therefore expected to be treacherous and avaricious. Villains were accepted as types, with or without motivation,
by the Yüan audience. Thus the role system provided
economy in characterization while at the same time stereo-
typing it.

[5] *YCH* 86, Act I, opening scene, p. 1500.
[6] *Ibid.*, Act II, following "Ko-wei," p. 1507.

Creative Vitality: Vignettes and Portraits

Literary models, the ethical emphasis on propriety, and the theatrical conventions of the role system all tended to stress the typical in characters. The Yüan dramatists, however, with their expressive vitality, created a number of dramatic figures that transcend the type and sparkle with life. Yüan drama is peopled not only with positive and negative types, but also with lifelike human beings, such as the resourceful and clever maid Hung-niang, the beautiful and coy maiden Ying-ying, the impetuous Li K'uei, the crafty and almost superhuman Chu-ko Liang, and the virtuous and tragic Tou O.

The dramatists bring these characters to life in several ways: by allowing them to express their feelings through poetry, by adding particular and realistic details to conventional types, by playing upon preconceptions grounded in popular tradition, and by skillfully presenting motivation and response.

Poetic Expressiveness. In embellishing their characterizations, the dramatists drew freely on a long tradition of lyric poetry. With its conciseness and range of connotation, Chinese lyric poetry offers an excellent vehicle for exploring various nuances of emotion and suggesting complex and often conflicting attitudes on the part of the characters in the plays. Poetic vigor lends animation and intensity to both speech and description, as illustrated by poetic passages from *Injustice to Tou O.*

Tou O loses her mother when she is a child of three. At seven, she is given by her father to Mistress Ts'ai to be her future daughter-in-law. The girl is married at seventeen and becomes a widow before two years are over. The central story of the play begins in Act I, when she is twenty years old. Appearing as a young widow, she recalls in her opening speech the hardships that have beset her childhood and youth:

Of my heart full of sorrow,
Of my years of suffering,
Is Heaven aware?
If Heaven only knew my situation,
Would it not also grow thin?
(YCH 86, Act i, "Tien chiang ch'un," p. 1501.)

At this time, the calm of her life is once again disrupted by the sudden arrival of two rogues, Old Chang and his son, "Donkey." Having accidentally saved Mistress Ts'ai from being strangled by one of her debtors, these two demand, as recompense, that the two widows become their wives. Mistress Ts'ai assents, but Tou O refuses, pleading with her mother-in-law not to remarry:

You are no longer young like a bamboo shoot, like a
   bamboo shoot;
How can you paint your eyebrows fine to make another
   match?
Your husband left you his property;
He made plans for you;
He bought fertile land to provide food for morning and
   evening
And clothing for summer and winter,
Fully expecting his widowed wife and orphaned son
To remain free and independent till old age.
Oh, father-in-law, you labored for nothing!
(Ibid., Act i, "Ch'ing-ko-erh," p. 1502.)

When the older woman counsels Tou O to compromise with the intruders and to accept their suit, as she herself intends to do, Tou O becomes indignant, pointing out the anomaly of the match:

You really can kill a person!
Swallows and orioles in pairs!

Mother-in-law, have you no shame?
My father-in-law worked in different prefectures and
    states;
He amassed a solid fortune, lacking in nothing.
How can you let the wealth he secured
Be enjoyed now by this "Donkey"?
(Ibid., Act i, "Chuan-sha," p. 1503.)

Frustrated by Tou O's steadfast refusal to his marriage proposal, "Donkey" reasons that when left alone the young woman will have to give in to his desires, and so he plots the death of the old woman. One day he secretly adds poison to some soup that Tou O has prepared for her mother-in-law. Unaware that the soup is poisoned, the old woman offers it to Old Chang, who drinks it and instantly dies. When Tou O still refuses marriage, "Donkey" accuses her of the murder and brings her to court. A corrupt magistrate has her severely flogged and threatens to do the same to the old woman. To save her mother-in-law from torture, Tou O makes a false confession and is condemned to die the following day. In utter despair she accuses Heaven and Earth of having failed in their duty to maintain justice (see lyrics on p. 153).

On the day of her execution, Tou O makes a final appeal to Heaven to prove her innocence by bringing to pass three wishes:

It is not that I, Tou O, make irrational wishes;
Indeed the wrong I suffer is profound.
If there is no miraculous sign to show the world,
Then there is no proof of a clear, blue Heaven.
(Ibid., Act iii, "Shua hai-erh," p. 1510.)

She prays that the blood from her wound will gush upward to stain a pennant flying high above the execution ground:

I do not want half a drop of my blood to stain the earth;
All of it will go to the white silk hanging on the eight-foot
    flagpole.

When people see it from four sides,
It will be the same as the blood of Ch'ang Hung turning
  into a green stone,
Or the soul of Wang-ti dwelling in a crying cuckoo.[7]

(*Ibid.*, Act III, "Shua hai-erh," p. 1510.)

Next, she prays that three feet of snow will fall, although it is midsummer, to cover her corpse; and, third, that a three-year drought will visit the district. She chides the incredulous guards:

You say that Heaven cannot be counted on,
It has no sympathy for the human heart.
You don't know that Heaven does answer men's prayers;
Otherwise, why did sweet rain fail to fall for three years?
It was all because of the wrong suffered by the filial
  daughter at Tung-hai.[8]
Now is the turn of your Shan-yang District!
It is all because officials care not for justice,
People in turn are afraid to speak out.

(*Ibid.*, Act III, "I-sha," p. 1511.)

Through these eloquent lyrics, the playwright suggests a great range of feelings, from grief and loneliness to indignation, despair, and then hope, giving the audience entry into her innermost thoughts and moving them to deep sympathy.

Particular and Realistic Detail. Characters often transcend their basic type by individualized behavior and speech. Originality and vividness are especially noticeable in the portrayal of courtesans, who appear frequently in Yüan plays. Young and beautiful courtesans, gifted in the arts of music, song, dance, and poetry, are products of a prosperous society, and serve to entertain and to provide companionship to young aspiring scholars, as well as to the rich and the powerful in the metropolis. Although it is often said that there are only

---

[7] For the legendary tales alluded to here, see Shih, *Injustice to Tou O* (*Tou O yüan*), 1972, p. 215, n. 847.

[8] *Ibid.*, pp. 4-5.

two kinds of courtesans—those who are heartless, squandering their lovers' money and then deserting them, and those who are true and sincere in their love, helping their scholar-lovers to achieve fame and honor—in the Yüan plays courtesans exhibit a wide variety of individual character traits. In *Rescued by a Courtesan*, Sung Yin-chang is a beautiful but empty-headed girl who loses her heart to the worthless Chou She, simply because of his sweet words and the little favors he showers upon her. Soon after the wedding, the husband is distressed to learn that his beautiful wife knows nothing about housekeeping. As reported by Chou She, one day when he returned home he found a quilt standing up as high as the bedposts. "When I put in the cotton, I sewed myself in by mistake," his wife shouted from inside the quilt. When he took up a stick to beat her, she cried, "But mind you don't beat our neighbor, Mistress Wang!"[9] Indeed, she had also sewed in a neighbor who came by to visit. The husband, tiring of her, treats her miserably and beats her at will. Chao P'an-erh, the courtesan who comes to her rescue, is just her opposite, being worldly, witty, and shrewd. She is cynical about men, and when thinking of marriage, reflects:

After all these years, I long to marry and settle down,
But who has ever heard of a man
Willing to clear a courtesan's debts and redeem her?
Intent on fawning on the rich in their splendid mansions,
Why should they care if they ruin the courtesans' quarters,
Floundering like fish escaping from a net,
Or squawking like wounded pigeons?
We girls are roadside willows;
Good families will not take us in.
The men seem sincere in the beginning,
But as they grow old they forget us.
            (*YCH* 12, Act II, "Chi hsien pin," p. 197.)

Which one doesn't take his pleasure
And swiftly go his way?

[9] *YCH* 12, Act II, opening scene, p. 197.

Which one doesn't disappear as quickly
As foam on a wave?
> (*Ibid.*, Act II, "Hsiao-yao le," pp. 197-98.)

When she learns of Sung Yin-chang's plight, she decides to use all her charms to save her:

First, I have no home of my own,
Second, I can sympathize with others,
Third, I, as a drinker, sympathize with drunkards.
> (*Ibid.*, Act III, "Kun hsiu-ch'iu," p. 200.)

She entertains no illusions about her position as a beautiful young courtesan:

A magistrate is always a magistrate,
A courtesan is always a courtesan.
I may play the part of a lady and enter my husband's
*   house,*
But I'll find it hard to fulfill all the household duties.
> (*Ibid.*, Act III, "T'ang hsiu-ts'ai," p. 200.)

Young ladies lightly dust their faces with powder,
They don't plaster it on the way we do.
> (*Ibid.*, Act III, "Kun hsiu-ch'iu," p. 200.)

When she goes to see Chou She, she unabashedly flatters him:

How clever and fortunate my sister is,
To be married to the handsomest man I've ever seen,
And so young too!
> (*Ibid.*, Act III, "Yao p'ien," p. 201.)

And when Chou She reminds her that she had objected to his marriage, she confesses that she was always in love with him herself, and was jealous. She plays the coquette, swears to him of her undying love, and wins his heart. But as soon as he gives the divorce paper to his first wife, Chao P'an-erh changes her mind. When he takes her to task about her vow, she simply says:

That was only to fool you;
We courtesans make a living by such oaths.

. . . .

Ask all the other girls in the courtesans' quarters;
Which one would not face candles and incense,
Which one would not call on Heaven and Earth to wipe
*   out her clan?*
If such oaths came true,
Why all of us would be dead!

                    (*Ibid.*, Act IV, "Ch'ing tung yüan," p. 204.)

In short, she makes a fool of Chou She, but she remains a
sympathetic character since Chou deserves the trick that she
plays on him. This portrayal of the courtesan Chao P'an-erh
is characterized by psychological acuity and realism.

Hai-t'ang in *The Chalk Circle* is another memorable courtesan who comes alive through her vivid behavior and speech.
The prologue establishes the fact that she has become a
courtesan only to relieve her family's poverty: "She knows
the arts of writing and drawing, can dance and play the lute
most delicately," says her mother. Although she comes from
a good family with ancestors who for seven generations held
high positions and achieved literary success, the wheel of
fortune has turned, and the family has lost everything. "And
now, pressed by necessity," laments her mother, "I have
to force my daughter to sell her beauty."[10] She goes on to
add that in the neighborhood there is a rich man named
Ma Chün-ch'ing, who has made proposals offering her daughter the rank of second wife.

When Hai-t'ang appears in Act I she is already married
and has a five-year-old son. Although formerly a courtesan,
she proves to be a virtuous and devoted wife and mother.
She is content and happy with her family, and thinks with
horror of her former way of life:

They shall see me no more
In the "abode of the wind and moon,"

10 *YCH* 64, Prologue, opening scene, p. 1107.

Seeking new paramours and seeing off old ones.

· · · · · · · · · · · · ·

Each day I happily keep my husband's company,
And sleep till the sun's shadow climbs up the gauze-
covered window.

>   (*YCH* 64, Act I, "Hun-chiang lung," pp. 1109-10.)

She acts prudently, even refusing to give her brother any money when he comes begging for help.

Later, when her husband is poisoned by his first wife, in tears she asks for nothing but her child. Although a concubine, she remains dignified, neither covetous of the family's fortune nor full of self-pity over her own ill-fate. In the ensuing fight for the child, she further demonstrates a sense of rightful anger and integrity. Her tender feeling for the child finally convinces Judge Pao Cheng of the truth of her claim. Here, then, we have a young courtesan who has entered the profession reluctantly in order to help support her family. Like her prototypes in T'ang literary stories, once she is married, she becomes an exemplary wife and mother.

Courtesans in *The Winding-River Pond* (*Ch'ü-chiang ch'ih*), *Tears on a Blue Gown* (*Ch'ing shan lei*), *Red Pear Blossom* (*Hung li hua*), and *Hundred-Flower Pavilion* (*Pai-hua t'ing*), although more sketchily drawn, all have certain individual touches that make them appealing. By the use of interesting, original, and realistic details, the dramatists succeed in making these characters, though of a basic type, come alive—sometimes for a moment, sometimes throughout a whole play.

Another successful use of realistic detail is seen in the portrayal of the Liang-shan heroes. The Liang-shan heroes of the late Northern Sung—some historical, some fictional—had established themselves in the popular imagination as noble bandits dedicated to furthering "Heaven's Way." Like Robin Hood of England, they were regarded as champions of justice, dedicated to righting the world's injustices and inequalities. Their ranks included all kinds of personalities,

from the valorous Lu Chih-shen to the shrewd Wu Hsüeh-
chiu, from the impetuous Li K'uei to the righteous and beloved Sung Chiang.

Sung Chiang, the leader of the group, illustrates the primary concept of the noble outlaw. Formerly a minor official,
he has been unjustly accused of insubordination and is forced
to flee to the rebel band. Endowed with no particular physical prowess, he is nonetheless chosen to be the bandit leader
because of his great sense of justice.

Spirited delineation of character is illustrated in the portrayal of Li K'uei in *Li K'uei Carries Thorns.*[11] He is a
rough, simple, and robust man, who enjoys the simple pleas-
ures of life. Impetuous and obsessed almost to a fault with
a desire to maintain justice, he is a memorable figure. When
he appears in Act I, he is already intoxicated, and his lyrical
soliloquy, interspersed with spoken monologue, offers us a
lively self-portrait:

(speaks): To drink without getting drunk is worse than being
sober. I am Li K'uei of Liang-shan-po. Because I am dark,
I am nicknamed "Black Whirlwind." On the orders of my
sworn brother Sung Kung-ming, I have a three-day leave to
enjoy the sights of spring. I, of course, have come down from
the mountain and am now on my way to old Wang Lin's place
to buy a few pots of wine and get rotten drunk.
(sings to the tune of "Tien chiang ch'un" in *Hsien-lü* mode):

> *The thirst for wine is hard to quench!*
> *This drunken spirit, as always,*
> *Seeks wine in the village.*
> *I've just inquired of Wang Liu about the matter.*

(speaks): I asked Wang Liu, "When can I find some wine?"
That rascal said nothing but started to walk away. So I
shouted, "Where are you going?" I chased him and seized
him by the whiskers. When I was about to hit him, Wang Liu
cried, "Don't hit me, sir. There is wine."

11 Synopsis and theme given on pp. 109-10 below.

(sings): *Wang Liu said,*
Ah, over there in that tavern, there is wine.

(To the tune of "Hun-chiang lung")

> *This is the time of the Ch'ing-ming festival,*
> *The wind and the rain grieve for the flowers;*
> *The mild wind gently rises,*
> *The evening showers have just ceased.*
> *I can see the wineshop, half-hid amidst the willows;*
> *Peach blossoms brightly reflect the fisherman's little boat.*
> *Blending with the ripples in the green waters of spring,*
> *The friendly swallows flutter back and forth,*
> *And seagulls wheel far and near.*

(speaks): If anyone says our Liang-shan-po has no scenery, I shall knock the rascal on the mouth.
(sings to the tune of "Tsui chung t'ien"):

> *Here are graceful mist-locked green mountains,*
> *And haze-covered willowy islets.*

(speaks): There is an oriole on that peach tree, pecking, pecking, pecking at the petals; and the petals are falling into the water. How beautiful! Who was it that said something about it? Let me think. Oh, I remember now. It was my brother, the scholar, Hsüeh-chiu.

> (sings): *He says these are the wanton peach blossoms,*
> *Chasing the water in its flow.*

(speaks): I pick up this peach petal to have a look. What a red peach petal! (Laughs.) Just look at how black my fingers are!

> (sings): *This petal is like red rouge,*
> *Glowing through a powdery lining.*

(speaks): I take pity on you, petal; I will let you join the others. Let's chase after them; let's eagerly chase after the peach blossom petals.

(sings): *Already I have arrived at this wineshop*
By the rustic bridge at the willow ford.

(speaks): This will not do. I am afraid to break my brother's order. I must return.

(sings): *If I don't drink,*
I'll be so tempted by the wineshop's flag,
Dancing in the east wind, on top of that bending pole.

(speaks): Hey, Wang Lin, have you any wine? I will not drink your wine for nothing. Here are some loose gold chips as wine money. (*YCH* 87, Act I, pp. 1519-20.)[12]

The interplay between Li K'uei's crude exterior and his delicate sensibility constitutes a large part of his appeal. His poetic exclamations on the scenery at Liang-shan-po, mixed with his threat to beat up all who fail to agree with him, reveal his honest but impulsive nature. Both speech and song have here a robust, racy quality that suggest the character of the man. The effectiveness of the portrayal is heightened by the fact that Li K'uei and everything around him are highly animated and charged with energy.

Popular Beliefs and the Audience's Preconceptions. On the Yüan stage, many characters undoubtedly seemed real and lifelike simply because they were already so well established in the popular imagination. In numerous plays, the characters are based on well-known historical prototypes, and when they appear on the stage there is no need to render them any more believable to the audience. Even when characters seem too superhuman to be real, they are so familiar to the audience that they can be accepted with a willing suspension of disbelief. The credibility of the characters depends not on plausibility of action or speech, but simply on the fact that they exist in the people's very modes of think-

---

[12] Cf. James Liu's translation in *The Chinese Knight-Errant* (1967), pp. 153-55; and Crump's in Cyril Birch, *Anthology of Chinese Literature* (1965), pp. 396-97.

ing and feeling. There are three predominant kinds of such
characters: characters around whom a whole body of legend
has grown up; characters whose deeds are little known but
whose names have become bywords for specific qualities;
and characters whose positions in society, independent of
their actions, elicit customary responses from the audience.

The figure who stands out immediately among the first
group is Chu-ko Liang. The Yüan play, *Burning the Po-wang
Camp*, tells of two famous incidents concerning Chu-ko: Liu
Pei's three visits to Chu-ko Liang's cottage to persuade him
to be his military commander; and Chu-ko's great victory at
Po-wang over Ts'ao Ts'ao's powerful army led by General
Hsia-hou Tun. In Chu-ko's biography in the official history
we find only the following references to these stories: "Lord
Liu Pei called on Liang three times before finally getting to
see him. . . . He and Liang became gradually more intimate
each day; Kuan Yü and Chang Fei [Liu Pei's sworn broth-
ers] were unhappy about the association. Liu Pei explained,
'My union with [Chu-ko] K'ung-ming is as natural as fish
and water!' "[13] About the second episode, the historian simply records that Liu Piao, Liu Pei's cousin, being jealous of
Liu Pei's popularity at Hsin-yeh, secretly planned to harm
him: "He sent Liu Pei to resist Hsia-hou Tun and Yü Chin
at Po-wang. After being there for some time, Liu Pei set up
an ambush; one day he himself burned the camp and pre-
tended to retreat. Chasing after Liu, Tun was trapped and
defeated."[14]

In the play, Chu-ko's part is greatly elaborated. He ap-
pears as a person of unusual wisdom and foresight, a shrewd
politician and military strategist. During Liu Pei's third visit,
Chu-ko suggests the brilliant idea of a three-way partition of
China, exploiting the rivalry between Wei and Wu to allow
Shu-Han to exist as an independent third power, which
would later, hopefully, bring about the restoration of the
Han dynasty. In the battle at Po-wang, Chu-ko anticipates

[13] *Shu chih, chüan* 5, pp. 2a-3a.
[14] *Ibid., chüan* 2, p. 6b.

his enemy's every move, as well as his own staff's weaknesses. Using both provocation and flattery, he gets his generals to give their best. By ordering his general Chao Yün to keep retreating, he succeeds in coaxing the enemy troops into a dense forest. When Hsia-hou Tun realizes his error and is about to turn back, Chu-ko's men set the woods on fire, and a strong wind fans the flames into a great blaze. Ts'ao Ts'ao's troops are thrown into great confusion and trample each other in their panic. In the meantime, the camp is burned and supplies are destroyed. Thus Chu-ko scores an easy victory over an army of great numerical superiority.

Another triumph in Chu-ko's career is dramatized in *The Yellow Crane Tower* (*Huang-ho lou*) by an anonymous author. Here he outwits his opponent Chou Yü, a shrewd adversary. With prophetic resourcefulness, he turns an ambush into a fortunate marriage for his lord Liu Pei. When he first comes on stage, he reminisces how, as an architect of victory at the battle of the Red Cliff, he conjured up an east wind to propel burning ships into Ts'ao Ts'ao's huge fleet. Chu-ko's prescience and skill with magic makes him, in the eyes of the audience, a man of exceptional wisdom and power; but he retains an aura of reality because of his personal identity in the folk mind. The story has a special atmosphere of credibility where he is concerned, for even when the plot is fantastic, his character is still essentially human.

The second category—characters whose names have become bywords for specific qualities—is represented by the upright judge Pao Cheng. Pao Cheng is a historical figure who symbolizes justice. The image of a savior who would relieve the people's suffering and rescue them from abusive authority was especially appealing during the late Sung and Yüan dynasties, when life was hard for the masses; legends and stories about Pao became very popular. Although given very sketchy presentation in Yüan plays, he must have appeared real to a Yüan audience because of their preconceptions about him.

In character study we tend to believe that characters manifest themselves through action and speech. In reading Yüan drama, however, we must sometimes reject the idea that people are only what they do or say; we must realize that sometimes they are what they are whether or not they do anything. This third group, the passive or inactive characters, is illustrated by the figure of Liu Pei in *The Yellow Crane Tower*; simply because he is a direct descendant of the Imperial Han house and future ruler of Shu-Han, one of the Three Kingdoms, he commands respect. The audience sees him as a real hero not because of what he does in the play, but simply because of who he is.

Motivation. The art of presenting compelling causes for a character's actions, although generally lacking in Yüan drama, is seen in the works of master playwrights like Kuan Han-ch'ing and Wang Shih-fu. *The Romance of the Western Chamber* by Wang Shih-fu provides a number of characters with convincing motivation and lifelike qualities. Of these, Ying-ying, a paragon of beauty, is more developed and better motivated in the play than in *The Western Chamber Medley* or the T'ang tale by Yüan Chen, although she was essentially Yüan Chen's creation. Even more vital and appealing is the character of the maid Hung-niang, whose personality shows considerable development in the course of the action. She is a sharp-tongued girl who at first is on the side of convention. Upon Scholar Chang's inquiry as to whether her young mistress is in the habit of going abroad, she enjoins him to be careful: "My mistress rules her family strictly and sternly, and is as cold as ice and frost. . . . If my mistress knew what you asked, how could the matter end here? In the future, ask only what is proper to ask and don't be so bold as to ask what you shouldn't ask."[15] Later, during the incense-burning ceremony in the courtyard at night, when Ying-ying and Chang indirectly address poems to each other, Hung-niang again warns of the danger of such action.[16] It is only

[15] *WP* 117a, Act II, following "Ssu pien ching," p. 265.
[16] *Ibid.*, Act III, following "Ma lang-erh," p. 268.

in Part Two, when Ying-ying's mother withdraws her promise to marry her daughter to her rescuer, that the maid grows indignant and becomes more sympathetic to the cause of her young mistress and the love-stricken student. After this she takes an active role in bringing the two together.

In her eagerness to assist the young lovers, Hung-niang becomes bold and decisive, seemingly willing to suffer any consequences. When Ying-ying's mother learns of the affair of the two lovers, she is incensed and gives the maid a sound beating, but Hung-niang is not intimidated. Overcoming her pain, she courageously and lucidly presents her argument that the union has already been consummated, and that if the mother refuses to recognize the fact she will suffer public criticism of her failure in maternal responsibility. Finally she succeeds in convincing her stern mistress to accept the inevitable.

Throughout the story, Hung-niang's actions are impelled by her sense of devotion to her young mistress, her matchmaking inclinations, her sympathy towards the wronged young man, and, most of all, her indignation at the double-dealing of Ying-ying's mother. As a result, Hung-niang is an extremely lively and well-developed character who acts as the catalyst for the dramatic action of the play. Although Ying-ying and Chang Chün-jui are the center about which all revolves, Hung-niang is the moving force. She chides and teases the young lovers, restraining them when they are too eager and encouraging them when they despair. She reacts with intuition, wit, and warmth to the foolishness of the lovers, to the occasional capriciousness of Ying-ying, and to the irrationality of her old mistress.

The success of Wang's play can be attributed largely to the masterful interplay of character and action in the person of Hung-niang. Not only are the resources of Hung-niang's character called into play by the various situations in which she appears, but the very action of the play evolves from her manipulation of various situations. Her wit and independence go considerably beyond what is called for by her role as a useful maid, and in some ways she resembles the clever and resourceful maid of neo-classical European comedy, well known in the works of Molière.

Yüan playwrights wrote poetic drama, and such drama is necessarily governed by pattern or design. Character, event, theme, language, imagery, and music are all only parts of a complex structure. This recognition of the essentially poetic nature of Yüan drama ultimately adds to our understanding of characterization. First of all, the poetic design of Yüan drama utilizes a primarily non-naturalistic mode, making characters either symbolic or typical. Second, even the few more realistically conceived characters do not remain consistently realistic. Finally, many characters are presented with no attempt at individuality. In *Injustice to Tou O*, for example, the central experience is expressed through the figure of Tou O, while most other characters, such as the doctor, the servant, and the prefect, are without personality and serve primarily in the dramaturgical function of unfolding the plot. But through individualized characters like Tou O, Yüan drama often makes a forceful statement on the complexities of the human mind.

IV

Themes

A GREAT majority of the plays known to have existed in Yüan times are now lost; however, the hundred and seventy-one extant plays cover a sufficiently wide range of subject and theme to give a fair indication of the total thematic spectrum of the genre. This range is exhibited in the twelve traditional categories listed in *The Sounds of Universal Harmony* (*T'ai-ho cheng-yin p'u*, 1398), by Chu Ch'üan, the son of the first emperor of the Ming dynasty and a playwright in his own right. The twelve categories are: (1) "becoming gods and immortals" (*shen-hsien tao hua*); (2) "living as recluses and enjoying the Way" (*yin-chü le Tao*), or "woods and springs, hills and valleys" (*lin ch'üan ch'iu-ho*); (3) "wearing robes and holding the official scepter" (*p'i p'ao ping hu*), that is, "plays about kings and ministers" (*chün ch'en tsa-chü*); (4) "faithful ministers and valiant warriors" (*chung ch'en lieh shih*); (5) "filial piety, righteousness, integrity, and chastity" (*hsiao i lien chieh*); (6) "admonishing the traitorous and denouncing the flatterers" (*ch'ih chien ma ch'an*); (7) "exiled officials and orphaned sons" (*chu ch'en ku tzu*); (8) "swords and clubs" (*p'o tao kan pang*), that is, "plays involving 'baring one's arms'" (*t'o-po tsa-chü*);[1] (9) "wind and flowers, snow and the moon" (*feng hua hsüeh yüeh*) [that is, plays about romantic love]; (10) "grief and joy, separations and reunions" (*pei huan li ho*); (11) "misty flowers, powder and eyebrow paint" (*yen-hua fen-tai*), that is, "plays with a flirtatious

---

[1] *T'o-po* is now an unfamiliar term. In translating it, I follow the interpretation of Aoki, *Yüan jen tsa-chü hsü-shuo*, pp. 34-35. Feng Yüan-chün believes that the term means "stripping down to the waist" (Feng, pp. 370-72).

female" (*hua-tan tsa-chü*); (12) "gods' heads and ghosts' faces" (*shen t'ou kuei mien*), that is, "plays about the gods and the Buddha" (*shen fo tsa-chü*).[2]

A Yüan source, Hsia Po-ho's *The Green Mansions* (*Ch'ing lou chi,* 1355), mentions several categories: (1) "plays about kings" (*chia-t'ou tsa-chü*); (2) "plays about melancholy ladies" (*kuei-yüan tsa-chü*); (3) "plays with females with painted faces" (*hua-tan tsa-chü*); (4) "plays about persons of the green-wood [outlaws]" (*lü-lin tsa-chü*); and (5) "soft *mo-ni*" (*juan mo-ni*).[3] These are evidently different labels for some of the same categories named by Chu Ch'üan. Plays about kings correspond to Chu Ch'üan's category 3; plays about melancholy ladies correspond to category 9; plays with painted-face women correspond to category 11; and plays about persons of the "green-wood" probably correspond to category 8. The nature of the last category (*juan mo-ni*), however, is not clear.

These classifications, although of historical interest, do not satisfactorily describe the extant corpus of Yüan drama. The present study based on the extant plays has isolated a number of themes that seem to be characteristic of the genre. Dominant among them is the love theme, which has many elements in common with the dramatic literature of other cultures and at the same time bears the unique stamp of the Chinese view. As in all drama, the playwrights are deeply interested in exploring problems involving the central values, both moral and religious, of the culture; thus various aspects of the individual's relation to Confucian, Taoist, and Buddhist teachings are dramatized in many of the plays. The problem of social justice has always been a particular concern in Chinese literature, but seems to have taken on a special urgency during periods of disorder such as the Yüan. The fact that justice is often effected through forces or in-

[2] Chu Ch'üan, *T'ai-ho cheng-yin p'u,* in *CKKT,* Vol. III, pp. 24-25.
[3] *Kuei-yüan tsa-chü* (Hsia Po-ho, p. 23); *lü-lin tsa-chü* (*ibid.,* p. 24); *chia-t'ou tsa-chü, hua-tan tsa-chü,* and *juan mo-ni* (*ibid.,* p. 19). For the term *mo-ni,* see pp. 204, 205 below.

dividuals who stand beyond the bounds of normal society reflects the personal dissatisfaction of both playwrights and audience with the conditions of life during these difficult times. A study of these representative themes of love, Confucianism, Buddhism, Taoism, the Taoist-recluse ideal, and social justice in the existing plays suggests that the playwrights dealt effectively with universal themes as well as those more particular to their time and place.

The Love Theme

Love, a dominant theme in Yüan drama, may be traced back to antiquity as a theme in Chinese poetry. The *Book of Poetry* (*Shih ching*) contains many songs professing open and unabashed love. The *yüeh-fu*—popular songs collected by the official "music bureau"—of the Han and Six Dynasties are also known for their love themes. Among the T'ang and Sung poets, Po Chü-i, Li Shang-yin, Wen T'ing-yün, Liu Yung and Chou Pang-yen all wrote enduring songs of love. However, in dealing with the subject of love, their works of lyrical poetry cannot compare in scope with the Yüan plays. In the T'ang literary tales and Sung colloquial stories, the love theme is popular but is generally presented under the guise of moral instruction. In the T'ang tale of Ying-ying, for instance, the student is saved in the end by realizing the dangers of sensual pleasure and abandoning the girl. Usually in such tales, an ostensible moral purpose is demonstrated both in the unhappy outcome of the young lovers' passion and in the narrator's or the "victim's" admonitions on the wages of sin. Such conventional moralizing, if it occurs at all, is slight and unobtrusive in the Yüan plays. In fact, one of Yüan drama's strongest claims to distinction is its resourceful and frank treatment of love, centering on physical fulfillment and including a stress on happy endings, often through the intervention of supernatural elements.

Physical Fulfillment. First and foremost, love is conceived of as an experience centering on physical fulfillment. The medieval Western concept of courtly love based on the hero's fervent adoration for his lady, and the idea of Platonic love based on spiritual transcendence, are both foreign to the values of the Yüan playwrights. The concept of love as physical fulfillment is best expressed in *The Romance of the Western Chamber*, where the eloquent depiction of sensual love assures the universality of the masterpiece. The love of Ying-ying and Chang Chün-jui begins with the delight of their first encounter. Upon seeing the girl in a monastery, the young man exclaims that his soul "soars to heaven":

Ah, who would have thought that I should meet an immortal here?
Whether pleased or distressed, she is a pleasing beauty.
> (*WP* 117a, Act I, "Shang ma chiao," p. 261.)

Her voice is like the oriole's singing o'er the flowers,
And every step she takes arouses love.
A dancer's waist, graceful and supple,
A thousand graces and ten thousand charms she displays,
Like a swaying willow in the evening breeze.
> (*Ibid.,* "Yao p'ien," p. 261.)

Not to mention the love shining in her eyes,
Her gait too reveals the feelings of her heart.
Walking slowly,
She reaches the gate;
After advancing one more step,
She faces me straight,
And I am beside myself.
> (*Ibid.,* "Hou t'ing hua," pp. 261-62.)

From that moment on, Chang claims that "love-sickness has penetrated the very marrow" of his bones.

Following his agonized yearning for his beloved (Pt. II,

Final Act) and an eternity of anticipation (Pt. III, Act IV),
the bliss of fulfillment finally arrives (Pt. IV, Act I):

> *Overcome with bashfulness,*
> *Ying-ying refuses to raise her head,*
> *But rests it on the love-bird pillow.*
> *Her golden hair-pins seem to fall from her locks,*
> *The more disheveled her hair, the lovelier she looks.*
>> (*WP* 117d, Act I, "Yüan-ho ling," p. 300.)

> *I unbutton the robe and untie the girdle;*
> *A fragrance of lily and musk permeates the quiet study.*
>> (*Ibid.*, "Shang ma chiao," p. 300.)

> *I hold close to me the soft jade and the warm fragrance;*
> *Like Juan Chao, I am in paradise.*[4]
>> (*Ibid.*, "Sheng hu-lu," p. 300.)

When the affair is discovered by Ying-ying's mother, a
separation is inevitable. The mother will consent to the marriage only if Chang Chün-jui passes the state examination
and obtains an official post. Chang Chün-jui leaves immediately for the capital, and the bitterness and despair of the
parting scene are expressed with great poignancy. To Ying-
ying the world looks desolate indeed, and the sorrow is more
than she can bear. When she bids farewell to her lover outside the city gate, she laments:

> *Dark is the cloudy sky,*
> *Yellow is the petal-strewn ground,*
> *Hard blows the west wind,*
> *Southward the wild geese fly.*
> *In the morning, who has colored the frosty forests*
> *   drunken red?*[5]

---

[4] "Soft jade and warm fragrance," two images appealing to many
senses, are used here to describe Ying-ying. Juan Chao and Liu Ch'en,
of the Han period, reputedly met two women immortals at the T'ien-
t'ai Mountain and lived happily with them thereafter.

[5] For discussion of this line, see James Liu, *The Art of Chinese
Poetry*, p. 120.

It must be parting lovers' tears.
> (*Ibid.*, Act III, "Tuan cheng hao," p. 304.)

So late we met,
And yet so soon we part.
Long are the willow branches, but they cannot stay his
*   steed.*
How I wish that autumn woods would detain the setting
*   sun.*
May his horse go slowly,
And my carriage follow it close.
Soon as our love is declared,
We are to be parted!
Upon hearing that he is to leave,
My golden bracelet at once becomes too large;
Upon seeing at a distance the Pavilion of Farewell,
My body withers away—
A sorrow no one can tell.
> (*Ibid.*, Act. III, "Kun hsiu ch'iu," p. 304.)

When the final moment of departure comes at the Pavilion, Chang tries his best to conceal his sadness, while Ying-ying professes openly:

My eyes shed tears of blood,
My mind turns to ashes.
> (*Ibid.*, Act III, "Shua hai-erh," p. 306.)

As the student fades into the distance, Ying-ying is overcome with a sense of solitude in an unsympathetic world:

The green hills prevent me from seeing him,
And the thin woods are of no help;
The light mist and evening haze too screen him from
*   my view.*
The afternoon sun falls on the old road,
Where no human voice is heard,
Only the rustling of the grain stalks in the autumn wind,
And the neighing of my horse.
Why am I so reluctant to mount the carriage?

How hurriedly I came,
And how slowly I return.

(*Ibid.*, Act III, "I sha," pp. 306-07.)

When she finally mounts the carriage, her heart is heavy indeed:

Now he is surrounded on all sides by the mountains;
His lonely whip flicks in the setting sun.
All the sorrows of the world have filled my heart;
How can a carriage of this size bear such a burden?

(*Ibid.*, Act III, "Shou-wei," p. 307.)

Although in its source in the T'ang tale their love concludes in everlasting separation and regret, in the Yüan play it ends on a different note. Chang's success in the official examination and the lovers' eventual marriage are anticipated in Part IV, which many consider to be the real end of the play. The actual reunion, however, takes place in Part V. Whether this last part was written by the same author Wang Shih-fu or added by his friend Kuan Han-ch'ing remains a controversial question.[6]

The play's presentation of youthful love through its stages of delight, impatience, ecstasy, and sorrow is reminiscent of familiar works in the West, particularly *Romeo and Juliet*. Because of its erotic scenes, *The Romance of the Western Chamber* has been considered by many Chinese as audacious and indecent. It has many admirers, however, among them the seventeenth-century critic Chin Sheng-t'an, who listed it as one of the six works of genius in Chinese literature along with *Chuang-tzu, Encountering Sorrow (Li sao), Records of the Historian*, poems by Tu Fu, and *The Water Margin* (*Shui-hu chuan*).

---

[6] C. T. Hsia, *e.g.*, feels that it is reasonable to assume "that some later hand, writing in the decadence of the *tsa-chü* tradition, wrote a sequel to meet popular demand for a complete cycle of plays based on Tung's poem." ("A Critical Introduction" to S. I. Hsiung's English translation, *The Romance of the Western Chamber*, 1968 edition, p. xxiii.)

The Happy Ending. Also characteristic of the love theme in the Yüan plays is its fundamental optimism. Although the thematic content of the Yüan love story largely follows the tradition of the T'ang literary tale, there is a marked difference in the denouement. Whereas the T'ang love story often ends in everlasting sorrow, the love story in Yüan drama almost always ends happily. The main line of the plot develops along a set pattern: a gifted young scholar and a beautiful girl fall in love, the girl usually being a daughter of a good family, a courtesan, or perhaps a supernatural being. After an initial period of courtship, obstacles arise, frequently in the form of parental objection, but in the end the lovers are generally united. This happy ending is often effected by the scholar's passing the state examination, securing an official position, or obtaining the help of an influential friend, thus causing the girl's family to acquiesce. Whereas in the Western tradition the hero of romantic literature is usually a person of outstanding physical prowess or bravery, in the Confucian tradition, with its great emphasis upon learning, the hero of romantic stories is usually an aspiring young scholar with no notable physical strength, and his passing the state examination and attaining official rank are considered the ultimate human achievements.

Before the Yüan period, stories about love frequently focus on an affair between a young scholar and a courtesan.[7] Since stories about love affairs involving girls of good family might meet with social censure, storytellers often found it expedient to cast women of little social status in the role of heroine in stories about such affairs. In the T'ang period, this type of story was very popular and attained great maturity as a sub-genre in T'ang fiction. True to the condition of these gay but pitiful women, many of the stories end tragically; desertion, unrequited love, and even death are their common lot.

In the hands of the Yüan playwrights, however, the courte-

[7] One of the exceptions is the well-known story of Cho Wen-chün and Ssu-ma Hsiang-ju, based on a historical event (see p. 192 below).

san love story, despite trials and tribulations, almost always ends happily for the lovers.[8] In utilizing the T'ang literary sources, the Yüan playwrights evidently either chose love stories that had a happy ending or modified the ending to provide a happy conclusion.[9] *The Winding-River Pond* is based on the well-known T'ang tale, "The Story of Li Wa" ("Li Wa chuan"). A young scholar from a prominent family is sent to the capital, Ch'ang-an, to take the state examination. Soon after arrival he falls in love with a beautiful and famous courtesan, Li Wa. Having impressed the girl and the procuress by his good looks and riches, he is readily accepted by the procuress as a "son-in-law" and willingly squanders his considerable fortune upon the two of them. When his funds are exhausted, they quickly abandon him. His plight becomes so desperate that twice he is on the threshold of death: once when he faints from starvation, and again when his father, during a brief visit to the capital, learns of his son's degradation and gives him such a thrashing that he is left for dead. But soon afterwards the wheel of fortune begins to turn in his favor. One snowy evening while he is begging in the street, his woeful cry is recognized by Li Wa. Greatly moved, she takes him in and nurses him back to health. Having freed herself from the procuress, she devotes all her time to the scholar and encourages him to pursue his studies. After two years of hard work, he takes the examination and passes it with high honors. Not only are he and the courtesan married, but he and his father are also reconciled. As in the T'ang story, the play has a happy ending.

A second play with a love theme derived from a T'ang literary tale with a happy ending is *Love Fulfilled in a Fu-*

[8] See *The Winding-River Pond, Love Fulfilled in a Future Life (Liang shih yin-yüan), Tears on a Blue Gown, Golden-Thread Pond (Chin hsien ch'ih), Red Pear Blossom, The Jade Vase and a Song in Spring (Yü hu ch'un), The Story of a Jade Comb (Yü shu chi), The Hundred-Flower Pavilion,* and *Hsieh T'ien-hsiang, the Courtesan (Hsieh T'ien-hsiang).*

[9] Plays based on historical incidents, such as *Han kung ch'iu* and *Wu-t'ung yü,* retain their tragic endings.

ture Life. In this play a courtesan named Jade Flute and her scholar-lover vow their love before the scholar embarks on his journey to the capital for the state examination. During their separation, her grief is so great that she finally takes ill and dies, although not before painting a portrait of herself for her lover. When her procuress goes to the capital in search of the scholar, she learns that he has passed the examination and has been sent to the frontier on an official mission. Later, when the scholar-general sends for his betrothed, he is told that she has died and her procuress is nowhere to be found. After his tour of duty is ended, he stops on his way back to the capital to visit an old friend. There he is greeted by his friend's eighteen-year-old adopted daughter and is struck by her resemblance to his former beloved, who had died eighteen years earlier. Unwittingly, he addresses her as "Jade Flute." The girl is equally moved and answers to the name, since it is also her own. The old friend is quite displeased by the scholar's imprudent attentions to the girl. It turns out that the courtesan's procuress is at this point also in the capital again. The old friend chances to see the portrait in the woman's possession and understands at once the reason for his visitor's unusual interest in his daughter. When the Emperor hears of this strange incident, he decrees that his scholar-general should marry the girl. Thus, although the love between the scholar and the courtesan is first thwarted by death, the lovers are finally united through reincarnation.

A third play deriving from a T'ang literary source is even more indicative of the playwrights' preference for a happy ending. *Tears on a Blue Gown* by Ma Chih-yüan is based on the celebrated T'ang poem, "The Lute Song" ("P'i-p'a hsing") by Po Chü-i. In the original, the poet meets a beautiful and talented lute player who has been left to herself on a boat in a remote area in the south by her absent merchant-husband. Her present sorrowful state, after her life of gaiety as a top courtesan in the capital Ch'ang-an, resembles the poet's situation as an official banished to this faraway place. Her mournful music so moves him that his tears drench his blue gown.

The Yüan play, while taking the last sorrowful line of the poem as its title, manages to create a happy conclusion. The poet Po Chü-i and a famous courtesan P'ei Hsing-nu of Ch'ang-an fall in love at first sight. After she has promised him marriage, Po is exiled to the south for official reasons. During his absence, the courtesan's procuress coerces her into marrying a rich merchant, after convincing her that the poet-official has died. Later, after accompanying her husband to the south, Hsing-nu is left alone on her boat and sadly plays her lute as she thinks of her former lover. Po, who happens to be seeing his friend off that evening at the river bank, recognizes the music and makes himself known. Po's friend persuades Hsing-nu to join her old lover. Later, through his intervention, Po is pardoned at court and summoned back to the capital. The merchant, moreover, is punished for having effected his marriage through false information.

In the Yüan plays, stories dealing with love between young scholars and girls of good families follow the same general plot pattern as those about love affairs with courtesans. The equal social standing of the young lovers, however, effects a certain degree of "moral" sanction, for the Chinese are firm believers in the idea that marriages are better contracted among families of comparable social position. While John Dryden asserts that "None but the brave deserve the fair," the Chinese prefer to see the talented scholar win the beautiful maiden (*ts'ai-tzu chia-jen*). In these stories love eventually leads to a happy ending, although in some instances the path is winding and digressive. In spite of modifications, the basic pattern of the happy ending is preserved.

Supernatural Elements. Interaction between the human and non-human worlds is characteristic of folk beliefs deeply embedded in the Chinese tradition, which tend to surface most dramatically in the more popular genres. In the colloquial narratives as well as the drama, devices such as *deus ex machina*, prophetic dreams, predestination, and transmigration occur frequently. These tend to be particularly prominent in the treatment of the love theme, with its special problems for the Chinese audience.

These devices conveniently allow the playwrights greater freedom in presenting intimate relations between young men and women that in a realistic context would violate the code of social behavior. Thus we see in the pages of the Yüan plays the wandering souls of love-lorn girls, the bewitching spirit of a willow tree, or the beautiful daughter of the dragon king, parading as seductive young women who give themselves readily to lonely students and poor scholars.

Love obstructed by parental interference, for example, can be fulfilled through a transmigration of the spirit, as in *A Disembodied Soul* by Cheng Kuang-tsu. In this play, a betrothal is arranged between Chang Ch'ien-nü and Wang Wen-chü before their birth—a common custom in traditional China. When the girl reaches the age of seventeen, Wang, by then poor and an orphan, visits the girl's family on his way to the capital for the state examination, only to be told that no marriage can be considered before he secures an official position. When he takes his leave, the girl is heartbroken and becomes seriously ill, whereupon her soul leaves her body and overtakes the young man in his boat. Swayed by her earnest entreaties, he finally ignores all propriety and takes her with him to the capital, not knowing, of course, that she is in fact a disembodied soul. After passing the official examination, he writes to his mother-in-law of his intention to return with his wife to visit. The sick girl at home, unconscious of the adventure of her own soul, is grieved by her fiancé's lack of faith. When the young scholar returns to the girl's house, he realizes at once that his "wife" is a spirit, and he strikes it with a sword. The spirit quickly returns to its body, and the sick girl, as if awakened from a dream, recovers immediately.

Whereas the daughter of a good family eloping with her

fiancé might meet with censure in Chinese society, the soul
of a love-lorn girl abandoning her body to pursue her love
would engender only sympathy. Although not displaying the
intense grief of Catherine's woeful spirit in *Wuthering
Heights*, the girl's spirit, a solitary wanderer in the vast expanse of nature, nevertheless presents an appealing figure
expressing the singlemindedness of true love:

> *I suddenly hear horses shrieking and men clamouring*
> *Under yonder willow trees;*
> *My heart leaps in fear.*
> *They turn out to be only the clapping of fishermen's*
>   *boards.*
> *Gradually the sound fades away in the west wind.*
> *On and on I walk through the glistening dew,*
> *And under the bright moon,*
> *Startling the wild geese to rise in fright.*
>   (*YCH* 41, Act II, "Hsiao t'ao hung," p. 710.)

The soul, with its hopes and fears, possesses emotions no different from those of a living person, but it offers the playwright greater freedom of expression.

In *Chang Yü Boils the Sea* (*Chang sheng chu hai*), a play
based on an old folktale, we are presented with the beautiful and solicitous daughter of the dragon king. While taking
a stroll along the seacoast, she is attracted by the student
Chang's zither-playing in a nearby temple. They meet and
fall in love. Using magic charms given to him by a divine
messenger, the student is able to secure the dragon king's
consent to marry his daughter. Soon after the wedding ceremony is celebrated, however, a messenger from heaven
comes to announce that the two are actually the "golden-
boy" (*chin-t'ung*) and the "jade-girl" (*yü-nü*), the page and
waiting maid of the Taoist immortals, and that their short
years on earth were meant to be a penalty for an offense
committed in their previous lives. The use of transmigration
of souls, predestination, and similar supernatural devices
adds a dimension of novelty to the stories that a Chinese

audience would very much expect and enjoy. To a Western audience, however, such supernatural devices may perhaps detract from the joy or pathos of a happy or tragic ending.

As a whole, the Yüan dramatists show considerable skill in dealing with the love theme. Their realistic emphasis on physical fulfillment, their preference for a happy ending, and their use of the supernatural stand out as the three striking characteristics of their treatment of the love theme.

Confucian Themes

While the treatment of love in Yüan drama is largely universal in nature, the moral and religious themes tend to involve values unique to Chinese culture. Various aspects of the individual's relation to Confucian, Taoist, and Buddhist teachings constitute the thematic nucleus of a great many plays, and the dramatists show a fair amount of adeptness in handling the difficult problem of fusing art and ethics.

The Chinese people, in spite of their predilection for the supernatural and the fantastic, are basically practical in outlook and attuned to order and propriety in human affairs. Confucianism, with its emphasis on correct conduct in personal relationships, was from ancient times a controlling force in Chinese society. Although under Mongol rule Confucianism was officially discredited, its system of ethics, with its long influence on Chinese life, remained ineradicable.

The influence of Confucianism is as pervasive in Yüan and later drama as it is in the Chinese literary tradition as a whole. From the Han dynasty on, the Confucian classics formed the core of the curriculum in the Chinese educational system and the basic discipline in the training of government officials, and as such large parts of them were committed to memory by the educated. The Yüan playwrights, many of whom had originally been trained for government service in the traditional manner, were thus well versed in Confucian doctrine. Moreover, drama, dealing as it does with men functioning in society, is perhaps more deeply concerned with ethical problems than are other literary genres. As a result, the Yüan dramatists naturally dwelt on these common moral beliefs while writing for an audience who understood and appreciated the Confucian ideals.

As an ethical philosophy, Confucianism teaches cultivation of the person and defines the social and familial relations that constitute an ideal moral order, extending peace and harmony from the individual to the family and thence to the entire empire. The core of the Confucian moral code is formulated in the "Five Relationships" (*wu-lun*): those between ruler and subject, father and son, husband and wife, elder brother and younger brother, friend and friend. Since the relationship between friends is comparable to that between brothers, while the relationship between ruler and subject is analogous to that between benevolent father and dutiful son, the entire social order is conceived of in terms of family relationships.

In the Yüan plays, the Confucian reverence for learning and the emphasis on government service normally appear as minor themes, while the celebration of *chung, hsiao, chieh,* and *i* are major themes. While the first two virtues can be translated as "loyalty" and "filial piety," the last two have no equivalents in English. *Chieh*, normally translated as "chastity," includes the idea of integrity. *I*, here translated as "fraternal fidelity," also embraces the concepts of righteousness, generosity, and chivalry. These four virtues, as defined by the advocates of Confucianism, evolved from the ideal qualities earlier set down by Confucius himself as the attributes of a gentleman (*chün-tzu*) and the proper attitudes governing the "Five Relationships." The virtues, of course, overlap in practice, but they will be separated here for convenience of discussion.

Loyalty. The theme of personal loyalty is perhaps best illustrated in *The Chao Family Orphan*. Based on a historical record of the state of Chin in the seventh century B.C.,[10] the play relates the story of an orphan whose life is saved through great sacrifices by loyal family acquaintances and who grows up to avenge the wrongs done to his family. In a power struggle at the court of the Prince of Chin, General T'u-an Ku attempts to seize power and rid himself of opposition by slaughtering all three hundred members of the rival family, the House of Chao, sparing only the mistress of the house, a daughter of the reigning prince. Later, when a son is born to her, the general issues a warning that anyone attempting to rescue the infant will suffer not only death but the extermination of his entire family as well. Anxious to preserve the continuity of the house, the mother persuades a faithful retainer, Ch'eng Ying, to save the baby, and in order to assure him that no one will learn of his deed, she commits suicide. The retainer tries to smuggle the baby out of the house in a medicine box, but is stopped by a guard. Impressed by the retainer's courageous act of devotion, the guard too commits suicide so that no one will learn the details of the rescue. Getting word of this escape, the incensed general orders the murder of all infants in the area under six months old. Fearful for the life of the Chao orphan, the loyal retainer decides, as a last resort, to sacrifice his own son. He places his own infant son in the hands of an old courtier, Kung-sun Ch'u-chiu, also a supporter of the Chao House, and arranges to falsely accuse the courtier of harboring the Chao orphan. When the baby and the old man are discovered, the latter commits suicide, and the baby is killed. The general, out of gratitude to the retainer for his information, adopts the Chao orphan, thinking that he is the son of the retainer.

When the boy reaches the age of twenty, the faithful retainer uses a painted scroll to inform the youth who he is and what has befallen his family. The boy immediately has the general arrested and delivered to the authorities, in whose

[10] *Shih chi, chüan* 43, pp. 3a-6b.

hands he meets a painful death. By following the course that Confucian tradition has laid down for sons to follow, the orphan thus avenges the death of his father and the calamity of his house.

In his efforts to protect his master's heir and to live up to the trust that has been placed in him, the loyal retainer not only sacrifices his own son but also moves others to offer their lives in service to his charge. While such sacrifice and devotion may perhaps seem to border on the fanatical, it indicates the high value placed on loyalty in traditional Confucian society.

Probably because of the universal appeal of the ideal of loyalty, this was the first of the Yüan plays to be introduced to the Western world. Translated into French by Father Joseph Prémare in 1735, it enjoyed considerable popularity and proved to be a model worthy of imitation by William Hatchett and Arthur Murphy in Great Britain, and by Voltaire in France.[11]

Filial Piety. Filial piety (*hsiao*) existed long before the time of Confucius as an important element in the Chinese family system. Since the dawn of history, the Chinese along the Yellow River had practiced ancestor worship. Exalted and elaborated by Confucian teachings since Han times, filial piety had come to be considered an unconditional duty of man, and unfiliality (*pu-hsiao*) a heinous sin.

This virtue of filial piety is the theme of *Chang, the Little Butcher* (*Hsiao Chang t'u*), in which a butcher and his wife decide to offer their son at a temple for the recovery of the man's sick mother. Moved by this act of filial piety, the gods rescue the boy and deliver him back to the family, while the mother also recovers. Irrational as the act may seem to us today, the sacrifice of one's own son for the sake of a beloved parent was no doubt esteemed in the same spirit as was Abraham's pious act.

[11] See Ch'en, Shou-yi, "The Chinese Orphan: A Yüan Play. Its Influences on European Drama of the Eighteenth Century," *T'ien Hsia Monthly*, III (Sept. 1936), pp. 89-115.

Another incident in which supernatural forces are moved to aid a devoted son occurs in *Mulberries from Heaven* (*Chiang sang-shen*), which presents Ts'ai Shun of the Han dynasty as a noted exemplar of filial piety. Unable, because it is winter, to obtain the mulberries his sick mother craves, Ts'ai Shun prays to the gods for help so piously that the gods are moved to hasten the springtime, and a whole nearby mountain becomes covered with mulberries. Such a miraculous phenomenon, prompted as it is by an act of filial love, would easily appeal to the Chinese audience's fancy.

Filial piety extends not only to the living but to the departed members of a family as well. According to Confucian teachings, one of the most unfilial acts is failure to provide an heir to preserve the family's name and to look after the needs of the ancestral spirits. The play *An Heir in Old Age*, by Wu Han-ch'en, reflects these deeply held values. In his old age, a well-to-do retired merchant named Liu regrets the lack of a son, although he has a married daughter whom his wife dotes upon and a nephew whom she dislikes. He also regrets the sometimes ruthless business dealings of his past and tries to make up for them by giving generously to the poor. On one Ch'ing-ming Festival day—the day on which the Chinese customarily visit the family graveyard to honor the dead—his poor nephew dutifully performs as well as he can the memorial rites around the ancestral graves, in the tradition of a true Confucian scholar. On his way to the family burial ground, he reflects:

"Today is the Ch'ing-ming Festival; sons from large and small households will all visit their ancestral graves. My uncle once said to me, 'Yin-sun, if you honor diligently our ancestral graves, in one or two years, you will be rich.' Could it be that my uncle has hidden some treasure there? My ancestors, including my father and mother, are buried in the family graveyard; it would be unthinkable for me to visit the burial ground only because my uncle tells me to do so. Although I am poor, I am a scholar and certainly would not want to neglect this duty. I have been to the papier-maché shop, where I obtained some spirit money[12] by begging. I have also secured half a jar of wine at the wine shop, and a loaf of steamed bread at the food shop. I have thus not forgotten my uncle's words. From a neighbor I have borrowed an iron hoe. Now I shall go to the family burial ground to offer the food, burn the spirit money, and add new earth to the mounds, thus fulfilling the duties of a son."[13]

When the uncle and aunt learn of the nephew's pious act, they are much moved. Their daughter, although diligent in performing the memorial rites at the ancestral graves of her husband's house, is tardy when it comes to visiting the Liu family graveyard. Madame Liu realizes at once that the nephew, although not her own offspring, truly belongs to the Liu family, and she shifts her affections. Taking back the authority over the family fortunes that she has entrusted to the daughter, she bestows it all upon the nephew.

Old Mr. Liu, as if rewarded for his charity to the poor, is surprised on his birthday with an heir, a son born to him by a concubine. The old man is grateful for his good fortune and divides his wealth among the daughter, the nephew, and the new heir. This simple and unaffected story is a faithful reflection of the primacy that the Chinese placed on filial piety and family identity.

Chastity. Many of the virtues advocated by Confucianism are no different from those valued by all cultures, except in the degree to which they are observed. This is as true of chastity as it is of filial piety. In Confucian society, although it was common for a widow from an uncultured family to remarry, it was deemed highly undesirable for a widow from a family with any scholarly standing to do so. On the other hand, it was socially acceptable and lawful for a man to have more than one wife. This double standard, such as exists in

---

[12] In Buddhist religious practice, the family of the deceased burns paper furniture, paper servants, and spirit money in the belief that the dead may receive these benefits in the other world.

[13] *YCH* 22, Act III, opening scene, p. 377.

almost every culture, was especially strong in a Confucian society. An observation made in reference to Japanese courtly love, that while "a man had the mobility of a bee, a woman was rooted like a flower in her house,"[14] is perhaps true of every Confucian household.

The play *Ch'iu Hu Teases His Wife* (*Ch'iu Hu hsi ch'i*) is a story of a frivolous husband and a chaste wife in the State of Lu during the "Spring and Autumn" period (722-481 B.C.). Earlier versions of this tale appear in *Biographies of Illustrious Women* by the Han author Liu Hsiang as well as in "Ch'iu Hu pien-wen." The extant portion of the *pien-wen* version corresponds in its general outline to the Yüan drama version, but it lacks the play's ending.[15] In the Han source, Ch'iu Hu leaves home soon after marriage to accept an official post abroad. He returns five years later, and just as he is about to reach home, he notices a woman of outstanding beauty picking mulberry leaves by the roadside. He tries to flirt with her and tempt her with gold, but is rebuffed. When he reaches home, he is embarrassed to learn that the beauty is his own wife. She rebukes him harshly for having offered his gold to a woman whom he thought to be a stranger: "Since you do not behave with righteousness in your private life, you cannot be principled in your official post. As you have acted contrary to filial piety and righteousness, I cannot stay with you."[16] Thereupon she drowns herself in a nearby river.

In the Yüan play, Ch'iu Hu is drafted into the army on the third day after his wedding. During his long absence, his wife diligently supports herself and her mother-in-law by raising silkworms and by performing odd jobs. Her father,

[14] Robert Brower and Earl Miner, *Japanese Court Poetry* (1961), p. 431.

[15] The extant portion concludes with the following unfinished remarks by the wife: "You are disloyal to the state and unfilial at home. I was married by my parents to you, and I have served your family for nine years in various ways and in strict propriety. My mother-in-law has wished that I . . ." (Wang Chung-min, p. 159).

[16] Liu Hsiang, *chüan* 5, no. 9.

convinced that his son-in-law has died, tries to coerce her into marrying a village landowner, but she is determined to remain faithful to her husband and forcibly resists her father and the suitor. Finally, after ten years of service on the frontier and in government posts, having won both fame and gold, the husband is granted leave to visit his old mother. When he has almost reached his house, he notices a beautiful woman resting in the shade of the family mulberry grove with her outer garment hanging from a tree branch. He catches her off guard and tries to force himself upon her by tempting her with offers of marriage and gold. She fights fiercely and staves off his advances. Upon entering his house, Ch'iu Hu is surprised and ashamed to discover that the young woman is his own wife. Angered at her husband's frivolous conduct, the wife asks for a divorce. In a variation from the Han source, the young couple are finally happily reconciled through the earnest entreaty of the mother-in-law.

Fraternal Fidelity. One Confucian virtue expected of all, regardless of age or sex, is *i*, which, as mentioned before, though translated as "fraternal fidelity," is much more comprehensive in nature. The play *The Chicken Millet Dinner* by Kung T'ien-t'ing, based on the biography of Fan Shih in the *History of the Later Han Dynasty (Hou Han shu),*[17] illustrates this comprehensive theme. The story of the Confucian scholar and his friend eventually gained such currency that by Yüan-Ming times there were at least two popular story versions in addition to the dramatic version.[18]

In the Yüan play, Fan Shih and Chang Shao become friends while members of the Imperial Academy in the capital. On the day they are to leave for home, Fan Shih

---

[17] *Hou Han shu, chüan* 81, pp. 13b-14a.

[18] One popular story version, more elaborate and more sensational than the historical source, and quite different from it in plot, is found in Feng Meng-lung, ed., *Yü shih ming yen* (1620-1621; reprint, 1947), *chüan* 16; see Bishop, pp. 88-97 for an English translation. Another popular version, which is incomplete, is in *Ch'ing-p'ing-shan-t'ang hua-pen*, pp. 280-83.

promises that two years hence, on the fifteenth day of the ninth month, he will visit Chang and his mother, and Chang agrees to prepare a chicken and millet dinner, a typical rustic treat. On the appointed day, Chang's mother has the dinner all ready, although she is doubtful that her son can rely on his friend to travel a thousand *li* to keep a promise made two years earlier. True to his word, Fan Shih arrives on time. After thoroughly enjoying their reunion, the two friends agree to meet again the following year at Fan's house. But before the year is over, Chang becomes seriously ill. As he lies dying, he instructs his family not to bury him until his good friend has come. In the meantime, Fan dreams of his friend's death and the impending funeral. He awakens deeply troubled and immediately makes preparations for the long journey to attend the last rites. Upon arrival, he finds that the mourners are unable to move the funeral carriage. Only after Fan Shih pours a libation of wine and begins to pull the carriage himself, does it start to move. Overcome with grief, he stays at the burial ground for a hundred days to keep vigil over his departed friend and to attend the grave. Such is the fame of his fidelity that it soon reaches the Emperor's ears, and for his great virtue Fan Shih is highly honored.

Another play that extols true friendship transcending even death is *The Old Man of Tung-t'ang* (*Tung-t'ang lao*). Yang-chou nu[19] is an undisciplined young man who indulges in wine and bad company. His father, on his deathbed, privately asks his friend Tung-t'ang lao to look after his son. When Yang-chou nu squanders the family fortune and turns to his own friends for help, they pretend that they do not know him. Deeply hurt, he repents of his old ways, and with money lent to him by his father's friend begins life anew as a vegetable vendor. When Tung-t'ang lao is convinced of the young man's sincere reform, he invites Yang-chou nu and the neighbors to his house and shows them the will that the young man's father entrusted to him. It states that he has

[19] "Tung-t'ang lao" and "Yang-chou nu" are nicknames.

secretly given the old friend five hundred ounces of silver to help his son when he is in need. The old friend had invested the money, and with the principal and interest had purchased, under a false name, the land, cattle, servants, house, and household property that Yang-chou nu had lost. True to the memory of his deceased friend, he thus helps not only to save the son but also to preserve the family name and fortune.

Altruism, another component of true friendship, is illustrated in the play *Hsieh T'ien-hsiang, the Courtesan*. When the scholar Liu Yung is about to leave for the capital for the official examination, he incurs the displeasure of his powerful friend, a governor, by repeated requests that the high official look after his favorite courtesan during his absence. When he is gone, the governor, convinced that the girl is a bad influence on his friend, summons her to his presence with the intention of penalizing her, thus disqualifying her from ever again keeping company with his scholar-friend. With this in mind, he tries to trap her into singing a song that contains a taboo word. The girl cleverly avoids saying the word, and instead uses a substitute word, for which she improvises a new chain of rhymes. Impressed with the girl's talent and charm, the governor establishes her as a concubine in his own household, although he never approaches her personally. Three years later, when Liu Yung passes the examination with highest honors, he shows open displeasure because the governor has appropriated his courtesan. At this point, the old friend explains that in order to encourage the young scholar to concentrate on his studies, and to protect the courtesan from falling into evil hands, he has taken the courtesan nominally as a concubine at the risk of losing a valuable friendship. The girl is then returned to Liu, to the lovers' eternal gratitude.

The play *Su Ch'in Gets the Cold Treatment* (*Tung Su Ch'in*) tells of another faithful friend who purposely incurs anger and displeasure in order to offer help. Su Ch'in of

Lo-yang, a famous personage of the Warring States period, is detained by a serious illness on his way to the state examination in the capital. When he returns home destitute, he is mercilessly rejected by his whole family. Thus spurned, he proceeds to the State of Ch'in with high hopes of help from his one-time fellow student and sworn brother, Chang I, who has attained the distinguished position of Prime Minister of Ch'in. When he is coolly received, served a cold meal, and sneered at for his wretched situation, he leaves the house deeply hurt, thinking of suicide. But he is overtaken by a stranger, who presents him with two pieces of silver, a suit of clothing, and a horse, gifts that provide him with both the means and the courage to continue on his way once again. When he finally attains the high post of Joint Minister of the six states, he refuses to see his family and Chang I when they come to the celebration. Only then is he told that Chang's icy treatment was meant to inspire him to hard study and success, and that the stranger who so opportunely supplied him with money and clothing was none other than a servant sent by Chang. Although Chang acted in an apparently heartless manner, he is indeed a genuine friend.

In varying degrees, all of these plays have a moral import in that they express the most prominent values in traditional Chinese society—values by which people in every station in life lived for centuries.

Taoist and Buddhist Themes

Taoist Themes. Taoism, both as a philosophy and as a religion, is in many ways the antithesis of Confucian teachings. To the Taoist, the ultimate principle of all existence, the Tao, is manifest in the natural state of things; man's essential task is simply to remain in harmony with the fundamental laws of nature, with the way the universe works. Unlike the Confucianists, then, the Taoists negate rather than affirm the artifices of civilization, seeing the bustle of everyday life, physical pleasure, fame, and material gain as only vain delusions.

A central metaphor for human existence is expressed in the famous passage of Chuang-tzu, in which he wakes from a dream wherein he appeared as a butterfly and exclaims: "I don't know whether I was then Chuang Chou dreaming I was a butterfly, or whether I am now a butterfly dreaming that I am Chuang Chou."[20] Thus, the realities of human existence and the values cherished by the Confucian thinker —filial piety, service to the state, and so forth—fade into the background for the Taoist, who seeks escape from this world of striving and activity into a kind of quintessential passivity, a oneness with the natural process. For the Taoist, to yield is to conquer, to grasp is to lose.

In the third century A.D., when Buddhism was introduced into China, the philosophy of Taoism began to take on many religious trappings in order to compete with Buddhism for a popular following. Ironically, many of the practices that came to be associated with the religious observances of Taoism, such as the search for elixirs to insure immortality and the worship of various saints in the pantheon, are actually in contradiction to Taoist philosophy, which attempts to eliminate striving for and attachment to worldly things.

In the Yüan plays, both religious and philosophical Taoism are represented, although the philosophical ideas are thematically dominant. Plays with Taoist themes generally emphasize a return to the simple life of nature and depict the Taoist as one who is carefree and happy through complete acceptance of natural law. Those who strive for success, particularly in government service or the accumulation of wealth, are often objects of scorn in such plays. The Taoist ideal of escape and withdrawal from organized society must have been an especially appealing philosophical attitude during times of great political and social upheaval such as

[20] Chuang-tzu, *Nan-hua chen ching* (*SPTK so-pen*), *chüan* 1, p. 26.

the Yüan era. This fact may account in part for the prevalence of Taoist ideals in these plays.

The most famous of the Taoist stories is Ma Chih-yüan's *The Dream of Yellow Millet* based on the equally famous T'ang tale by Shen Chi-ch'i, "The Story of the Pillow" ("Chen chung chi"). Employing exactly the same theme and story line, the play demonstrates, through the device of a dream, the evanescent, illusory quality of human existence. On his way to the capital for the state examination, the scholar Lü Tung-pin meets the immortal Chung-li Ch'üan, leader of the eight Taoist immortals, at an inn on the Han-tan road. While the keeper of the inn is cooking yellow millet, Lü is overcome by sleep. He dreams that he has passed the examination on the first try, is made a general, and becomes the son-in-law of the powerful official Kao. Later, his wife gives birth to a son and a daughter and his family enjoys great wealth, prestige, and power. When Lü is sent out to put down a rebellion, he is given a large amount of treasure by the rebel forces and returns without having suppressed them. Back home, he catches his wife having a liaison with another man. She, in turn, accuses him of having treasonous connections with the enemy and, as a result, he and his children are banished. During his exile he is caught in a storm and is taken in by an old woman. When the son of the woman returns home, he kills Lü's son and daughter and is about to kill Lü himself, when Lü awakens from his dream in fright. The cook of the inn is still cooking the same millet, but in the short space of his dream he has experienced eighteen years of life. Enlightened by his dream, Lü gives up all desires for worldly success and wanders off with Chung-li the Immortal.

This sort of Taoist enlightenment comes not only to intellectuals, but also to the lowly and uneducated. The play *Jen Feng-tzu, the Butcher* (*Jen Feng-tzu*), also by Ma Chih-yüan, describes the conversion of a small-town butcher to Taoism. In a small town by Chung-nan Mountain lives a

butcher named Jen Feng-tzu, who is predestined to be converted. The Immortal Ma Tan-yang realizes that if he asks
the butcher simply to stop killing, he will be ignored, so instead he converts all the other townspeople. When the people stop eating meat, the butcher is outraged, and decides to
kill the Taoist, but when he goes to the holy man's retreat he
himself is killed. When he asks the Taoist to give back his
head, the Immortal simply replies: "Your head is still on
your shoulders." The butcher feels for it and indeed the head
is there. Thereupon, he throws down his knife, bows down
to the Taoist, and asks to be his disciple. The Taoist gives
him simple chores to do and instructs him in the reading of
the scriptures. When the butcher's wife and children come
to persuade him to return home, the butcher is unmoved.
Under the direction of the Taoist, he eventually frees himself
of his desire for wine, sex, money, and all other worldly
things. After ten years he becomes an immortal himself.

The popularity of this theme of Taoist enlightenment is
seen in a great number of conversions of people from all
walks of life: the actor Hsü Chien in *Lan Ts'ai-ho, the Actor
(Lan Ts'ai-ho)*, the courtesan in *Liu hang-shou, the Courtesan (Liu hang-shou)*, the corrupt official Yüeh Shou in
"Iron Crutches" Li (T'ieh-kuai Li), and the teahouse proprietor Kuo Ma-erh in *Yüeh-yang Tower (Yüeh-yang lou)*.
Even the spirits of plants, such as those of the peach and willow trees in *A Dream of Immortality (Sheng-hsien meng)*, can
achieve enlightenment and become immortal.

Buddhist Themes. Like the moral and ethical teachings of
Confucianism and Taoism, various beliefs associated with
Buddhism play a significant role in the thematic structure
of Yüan drama. The Buddhist themes revolve around certain general ideas that had by Yüan times been thoroughly
assimilated into the folk beliefs of the Chinese people.
Among these the most important are the doctrines of karma,
predestination, transmigration of the soul, and enlighten-

ment. A thematic undercurrent in many plays is the belief that man is born into a continuous chain of reincarnations, each life being the fruit of seed sown in previous existences, with salvation attainable only through enlightenment—the realization of the pain of human existence and the cessation of earthly desires.

The problem of attaining enlightenment is treated in a number of plays, including *A Pilgrimage to the West, A Story of "Patience" (Jen tzu chi,) The Enlightenment of Liu Ts'ui (Tu Liu Ts'ui)*, and *A Monkey Hears a Sermon (Yüan t'ing ching)*. An example of this type of theme is found in *The Dream of Su Tung-p'o (Tung-p'o meng)*, which dramatizes the enlightenment of a courtesan as well as that of one of China's most famous poets. Su Tung-p'o, a scholar-official at the Sung court, has offended Prime Minister Wang An-shih by his protest against Wang's projects, and he is consequently banished. Along his exile route, he passes the Lute Pavilion at Hsün-yang and meets a courtesan who claims to be a descendant of the famous T'ang poet Po Chü-i. Struck by her beauty and intelligence, Su Tung-p'o invites her to visit the mountains with him. While staying at the Tung-lin Temple, Su Tung-p'o encourages the courtesan to use her charm in order to persuade the abbot to return to the "red-dust" world. The abbot, however, is unmoved, and the next day, while the abbot is lecturing on the scriptures, the courtesan becomes enlightened and decides to become a nun. At the same time, Su Tung-p'o comes to a deeper realization that the beauty of the material world is illusory.

Those plays which deal primarily with the themes of karma and transmigration of the soul include *Enemies and Creditors (Yüan-chia chai-chu)*, *The Miser (K'an ch'ien nu)*, and *Debts in a Future Life (Lai sheng chai)*. *Enemies and Creditors* describes the fate of Chang Shan-yu, a kind, honest Buddhist, and his wife. A monk entrusts ten pieces of silver to Chang's keeping. Later, a poor man named Chao T'ing-yü

steals five pieces of silver from Chang for his mother's funeral. Chang's wife is unhappy about the theft of their hard-
earned savings, and when the monk comes to ask for the
money she denies having it. She sends the monk away with
harsh words, keeping his silver to make up for her loss.

Sometime after this episode, the wife becomes pregnant
and gives birth to a son named "Begging Monk" (Ch'i-seng).
After the birth, the family's fortunes change, and the Changs
become richer and richer. Soon they move to another district, and the wife gives birth to another son, whom they
name "Lucky Monk" (Fu-seng). Years pass and the two
sons grow into young men. The elder son is wise and ac-
quires for the family much property and money. The second
son is foolish, indulges in sex and wine, and squanders the
family's fortune. One day the elder son suddenly dies of
sickness, and his death is soon followed by the death of his
mother and younger brother. While grieving over his overwhelming loss, Chang is visited by a good friend, Ts'ui
Tzu-yü, who knows of the affairs in the netherworld. Upon
Chang's entreaty, Ts'ui takes him to the underworld, where
he encounters his two sons. The first one complains: "I was
originally Chao T'ing-yü, who once stole five pieces of silver
from you. I have paid you back many-fold, so what do
you want of me now?" The second son reports: "I was
the monk who entrusted the silver to you but was denied
payment by your wife. Now you have paid me back; we
shall have nothing to do with each other any more." Later
Chang sees his wife, suffering great torments in Hell because
of the silver she stole from the monk. By the time he returns
to the world, Chang has become enlightened, realizing that
we reap in the after-life what we sow in the previous life.
He cuts his hair and becomes a monk.

The relationships between Confucian ethics, Taoist philosophy, and Buddhist religious ideas were complex, and
the different beliefs interacted constantly and modified one
another. Even the most moral and religious plays cannot
be considered solely as vehicles for the Confucian, Taoist,

or Buddhist teachings, but rather must be judged as artifacts created in a society in which these ethical and religious notions were sustaining ideals.

The Recluse Theme

Closely related to the Taoist and Buddhist outlook is the traditional idea of the recluse. Affirming Taoist withdrawal from public life and agreeing with the Buddhist stress on monastic existence, the idea of the recluse also finds support in Confucianism in times of political chaos. During the Yüan dynasty, Chinese resentment towards the Mongols forced many to embrace a recluse life as a kind of passive resistance. Disaffected with harsh alien rule, many men renounced state service and chose instead to withdraw, rejecting public office and turning away from society in order to devote themselves to self-cultivation, scholarship, or artistic pursuits. Nemoto Makoto's book *The Spirit of Resistance in Authoritarian Society*, a study of the Chinese recluse ideal,[21] describes this renunciation of official life and voluntary withdrawal from participation in public service. The author shows how the recluse, whether Buddhist, Taoist, or Confucian, dropped out of society and sought withdrawal in rural areas.

As the Yüan author Chu Ching mentions in his preface to *The Green Mansions*, when the Mongols first conquered China many persons from the Chin regime, such as Tu Shan-fu, Po P'u, and Kuan Han-ch'ing, "did not deign to take office; instead they devoted themselves to writing poetry about the wind and the moon."[22] Kuan and Po were two leading dramatists; they, as well as Ma Chih-yüan, may have seen withdrawal from society as a protest against the conqueror and his government. Although the ideal of the recluse had always existed in China, it became an alternative

[21] Nemoto Makoto, *Sensei shakai ni okeru teikō seishin* (1952).
[22] In Hsia Po-ho, *Ch'ing lou chi* (1355), p. 15.

way of life of particular importance in a time of disorder like the Yüan era, and therefore assumes prominence as a theme in the drama of the time.[23]

The recluse ideal, referred to as *yin-chü le Tao* ("living as a recluse and enjoying the Way"), is epitomized in the following two plays: *Life in Ch'i-li-t'an* (*Ch'i-li-t'an*) and *Ch'en T'uan Stays Aloof* (*Ch'en T'uan kao wo*). *Life in Ch'i-li-t'an,* consisting mainly of song-sequences with very little prose dialogue,[24] relates the story of the recluse Yen Tzuling, an intimate friend of Liu Hsiu during the usurpation of Wang Mang (A.D. 8-23). The two often visit taverns together, leading an apparently carefree life, although Liu, a direct descendant of the Emperor Kao-tsu, has his mind set on the restoration of the Han dynasty. When he eventually succeeds in overthrowing the usurper and ascends the throne as the Emperor Kuang-wu, he sends for his old recluse-companion. Yen goes to court but is not impressed by the jade and gold palaces or the court beauties. "Riches and fame are to me but dust," he explains, preferring the simple way of life at his thatched hut in Ch'i-li-t'an, "where deer bring flowers and wild monkeys offer fruit, where the sun and moon hang aloft as lanterns in the sky,"[25] and he spends his days quietly fishing or chopping wood. Realizing that it is futile to try to persuade him to change his mind, the Emperor lets him return to his life as a recluse.[26]

Ma Chih-yüan's *Ch'en T'uan Stays Aloof* is a more fully developed play on the same theme.[27] Ch'en T'uan, a Taoist

[23] On the importance of the ideal of the recluse in the Yüan dynasty, see Frederick W. Mote, "Confucian Eremitism in the Yüan Period," in Arthur Wright, ed., *Confucianism and Chinese Civilization* (1964), pp. 252-90.

[24] The extant text, consisting mainly of song-sequences, is from the Yüan edition, *Yüan k'an tsa-chü san-shih chung.*

[25] *WP* 127, Act IV, Song "Li-t'ing-yen-sha," p. 455, and speech following song "Ch'iao p'ai-erh," p. 454.

[26] The story of Yen Tzu-ling is found in *Hou Han shu, chüan* 83, pp. 8b-10b.

[27] Ch'en T'uan's biography appears in *Sung shih, chüan* 457, pp. 3b-6b.

recluse on Hua Mountain, occasionally goes down to the
city of Pien-liang to tell fortunes, "not for the money, but to
form friendships."[28] When Chao Hsüan-lang goes to have
his fortune told, Ch'en is startled by Chao's horoscope, as it
shows he is destined to become an emperor. He leads Chao
to a private corner in a tavern, and worships him as the
future ruler. When Chao goes on to become the first Emperor of the Sung dynasty, he invites the fortune teller to
come to court. "Leaving the crane to look after my abode,
and the clouds to lock my door,"[29] Ch'en proceeds to the
capital. The Emperor, delighted to see his old friend, bestows upon him an honorary title and pressures him to serve
in the new government. But Ch'en T'uan is uninterested in
fame or profit, and refuses to accept any official position,
professing his joy as a recluse in the mountains where life
is free and satisfying:

With a guest, I talk about the transient world,
At leisure, I ascend the cliffs to watch the sunset.
> (*YCH* 42, Act III, "Sha-wei," p. 728.)

He does things as he pleases and when he pleases. If, however, he should accept a government post, then

I shall have to review the laws of the Censorate,
And examine the affairs of the Six Departments.
Hurrying and hustling unwisely, I shall face troubles
  no end;
Fearful and trembling, I shall be unable to sleep well
  again.

> (*Ibid.*)

Ignoring the many beautiful ladies sent to wait upon him, he
falls into a sound sleep, and upon waking he repeats his intention to return to the mountains to spend his days planting
lotus flowers.

[28] *YCH* 42, Act I, opening speech, p. 720.
[29] *Ibid.*, Act II, Song "Huang-chung sha," p. 725.

Social Justice

Another prominent thematic category expressing values central to Chinese culture is that of social justice. The traditional Chinese concept of justice focuses upon retribution and the redress of wrongs, and this focus is pronounced in Yüan drama, where retribution is generally brought about by a wise judge or, ironically, through the intervention of outlaws. These stories about wise judges and outlaws reflect the people's basic trust in divine and social justice to punish villains in the end.

Wise Judges. The *kung-an* (courtroom) stories, relating the solution of a difficult case through the intervention of a wise and just judge, have long been favorites among the Chinese. A law-court setting, with its visible conflicts, became as effective on stage as a battlefield scene. The unraveling of a web of crime and fraud by a magistrate, as told in early short stories, such as "Censor Ch'en Solves the Secret of the Gold Hairpins" and "Master Shen's Bird Destroys Seven Lives,"[30] was especially popular in Yüan times under the corruption of alien rule.

Typical of the wise and just judges is Pao Cheng, who appears in eleven extant plays: *The Chalk Circle, The Deed, Selling Rice in Ch'en-chou (Ch'en-chou t'iao mi), A Miniature Raw-gold Pavilion (Sheng chin ko),*[31] *Flowers in the Rear Courtyard (Hou-t'ing hua), The Ghost of Shen Nu (Shen Nu-erh), Leaving the Shoes (Liu hsieh chi), The Butterfly Dream, The Execution of Lu Chai-lang (Lu Chai-lang),*

---

[30] "Ch'en Yü-shih ch'iao k'an chin ch'ai-tien," in Feng Meng-lung, *chüan* 2; "Shen hsiao-kuan i niao hai ch'i ming," *ibid., chüan* 26, the English translation of which is in Bishop, pp. 48-64, and C. Birch, *Stories from a Ming Collection* (1959), pp. 153-71. These two stories, first published in Ming times, are most likely from an earlier period.

[31] The term "Sheng chin ko" is now archaic, but the prose speech following the song "Te-sheng ling" in Act IV describes it as a miniature gold pavilion—a family treasure (*YCH* 99, p. 1734).

The Ghost of a Pot (*P'en-erh kuei*), and *Killing the Wife of
a Sworn Brother* (*T'i sha ch'i*).[32] Other extant courtroom
plays include *Injustice to Tou O, The Riverside Pavilion*
(*Wang-chiang t'ing*), *The Tablet at Chien-fu Temple* (*Chien-
fu pei*), *The Shirt, Mo-ho-lo Doll* (*Mo-ho-lo*),[33] *The Kerchief*
(*K'an t'ou-chin*), *Clues from a Dream* (*Fei i meng*), *The
Cries of Feng Yü-lan* (*Feng Yü-lan*), and *The Rescue of a
Filial Son* (*Chiu hsiao tzu*).

The theme of justice is well illustrated in *The Chalk
Circle, The Butterfly Dream*, and *The Execution of Lu Chai-
lang. The Chalk Circle* has been translated by Frances Hume
and is discussed above (pp. 36-37) in relation to plot patterns. The other two plays have been translated by Yang
Hsien-yi and Gladys Yang, the latter under the title *The
Wife Snatcher*. What appeals to the audience in these lawsuit stories is the triumph of justice in an unjust society,
brought about by the cleverness and wisdom of an upright
judge. By focusing on a single domestic incident, *The Chalk
Circle* exposes corruption in the society as a whole. As soon
as the governor of Cheng-chou enters the courtroom, he
confesses:

> *Though I occupy the post of a judge,*
> *I know nothing about the law;*
> *What I ask for is white silver,*
> *Which is enough to settle cases for one and all.*
> > (*YCH* 64, Act II, opening scene, p. 1116.)

He thus reveals not only his own corruption and his complete lack of interest in justice, but also the hopelessness of
the innocent Hai-t'ang's case. When the first wife lodges a
false charge against Hai-t'ang for poisoning her husband and
kidnapping her son, the judge does not bother to listen. "This
woman certainly can talk," he says, "I am sure she is ac-

---

[32] See George A. Hayden, "The Judge Pao Plays of the Yüan
Dynasty," an unpublished dissertation (Stanford University, 1971).

[33] *Mo-ho-lo* were figurines of clay or wood (Wu Tzu-mu, *chüan* 4,
p. 160).

customed to lawsuits. 'Yak, yak, yak,'—I have no idea what she is saying."[34] He then sends for the Clerk of the Court to handle the case for him. The Clerk is no other than the wife's lover, who hurls further invective at the accused and summarily forces a confession of murder from the innocent Hai-t'ang. The judge, without further ado, sentences Hai-t'ang to die. Before leaving the court, he reiterates his intent to leave all court affairs in the hands of his underling:

> *Henceforth whatever decisions he makes will not upset me,*
> *Neither will I care if the plaintiff's charge is true or false.*
> *He can beat, whip or exile the criminals as he likes,*
> *Only whatever money he obtains, he'd better share half with me.*

(*Ibid.*, Act II, concluding scene, p. 1120.)

As is well documented, corruption under Mongol rule was rampant,[35] and the alien conquerors were often negligent in

---

[34] *YCH* 64, Act II, following "Hsiao-yao le," p. 1117.

[35] The official history records that in 1303 the government discovered numerous cases of corruption among officials, involving bribes amounting to 45,865 pieces (*ting*) of silver, and 5,176 cases of wrong sentences (*Yüan shih, chüan* 21, p. 12a.) Two years earlier, in 1301, an Imperial inspector's report reveals in more specific terms the flagrant corruption of the time: "In many places, bureaux were established to help citizens to write bills of indictment, to make them more aware when they should or should not lodge complaints, and to help them eliminate superfluous words, and thus also relieve the court of a great deal of time and speed up official matters. In all these years, the persons appointed in these bureaux to write the bills of indictment were the court's own people. . . . The appointees knew nothing about the law and considered the bureaux as places for making profits. Those who lodged small complaints had to pay four or five taels of silver for a bill of indictment; those who lodged large complaints were forced to pay one or one-half *ting* of silver. . . . For those who had money, the clerk would use false words to twist the situation and make the plaintiff, though at fault, look right; for those who had no money to offer, though they were right, the clerk would omit an important point or not make a significant point clear. In a hundred ways, they manipulated the indictments, raising or eliminating issues as they wished.

dealing out justice to the Chinese people. The two plays translated by Yang Hsien-yi and Gladys Yang detail the corruption and the injustice suffered by the people during this time. *The Butterfly Dream* reflects the popular longing for righteous and wise judges who would uphold justice and defend the poor and innocent against the rich and the mighty. In this play, Old Wang, while on a shopping trip to town, is beaten to death by a bully, Kuo Piao. Aware of his own great strength and confident that he is beyond the reach of the law, Kuo Piao brags, "When I kill a person, I need not die for it!"[36] Wang's three sons, however, avenge their father's murder by beating the villain to death. They are immediately apprehended and imprisoned.

Judge Pao decrees that one of the three sons must pay for the murder with his own life. Each boy claims to be guilty in an attempt to spare the lives of the others. The mother selflessly decides to sacrifice her own son, the youngest of the three, in order to save her two stepsons. She pleads strongly for the first son's life because he is the most filial, and for the life of the second son because she needs him for support. Judge Pao suspects that the youngest son, whom the mother surrenders, is adopted, but when he learns the truth he is greatly moved by the mother's virtue. Earlier in the day he had dreamed that three butterflies were caught in a spider web. Another big butterfly flew by and rescued two of them but ignored the third and smallest, for which the judge felt compassion. Recalling the dream, he believes this is to be an omen for him to save the youngest boy.

As the mother goes to prison to deliver food to the sons, she sings plaintively of the misfortune that has befallen the family. She is pleased when her two stepsons are acquitted, but upon learning that her own son is to die, she recalls with bitterness that for ten months she carried this boy, and for

---

Consequently, lawsuits have increased." (*Yüan tien-chang*, 1322; reprint, 1972, Chapter 12, p. 37b.)

[36] *YCH* 37, Act I, opening scene, p. 632.

three years nursed him. Later she and the two stepsons go to claim the corpse. Seeing what she thinks to be her son's body outside the prison wall, she bursts into tears and calls him by name. To her amazement, the boy walks onto the scene. To the distraught mother who mistakes him for a ghost, the boy explains that Judge Pao has hanged a horse thief in his place, and the corpse is that of the thief. In the end justice is rendered; the good judge commends the virtuous mother and filial sons to the Emperor, and the whole family is rewarded with titles and positions.

It is interesting to note that the treatment of this serious theme of justice is lightened by touches of coarse humor. When the play opens, the father complains that all three of his sons prefer studying to farming. The first son says, "Father and mother above, what good is it to practice farming?" ("Above," *tsai shang*, is an honorific expression used in addressing one's superiors.) The second son also argues in his own defense. When it comes to the youngest son's turn to speak, he blurts out: "Father above, mother below." The father asks what he means by "mother below," and the boy replies: "When I was small, I saw father above and mother below—in bed."[37]

In the second play, *The Execution of Lu Chai-lang*, Judge Pao displays great wisdom and courage in combatting the mighty and maintaining justice for the common citizen. Lu Chai-lang, a powerful figure who served the Emperor for many years in court, is now transferred to Hsü-chou, where he leads a debauched life. Conscious of his great power, he appropriates people's horses and possessions as he wishes. One day, while wandering in the street, he notices the beautiful wife of a silversmith named Li. Accompanied by his servant, he goes to the shop next day on the pretext of having his silver kettle mended, and then makes off with the silversmith's wife. Because of the villain's position, the silversmith can do nothing.

[37] *Ibid.*

Chang Kuei, an official, warns the silversmith not to mention the incident because of Lu's great influence. Intoxicated with his own power, Chang sings of the glories of being a magistrate. On the day of the Ch'ing-ming Festival, while he and his family are visiting their ancestral graves, his little boy is struck by a pellet. Chang and his wife are terrified when they learn that the offender is none other than Lu Chai-lang. To complicate matters still more, the villain sees Chang's pretty wife and secretly demands that the husband deliver her to his household the next day. "If you are late, you will pay double for it," he warns Chang.[38]

The next morning before dawn, Chang hurriedly takes his wife to Lu's house, pretending that they are going to see an aunt. The villain takes Chang's wife from him and gives him Li's wife in return, professing that the woman is his sister. Later, Li the silversmith happens to visit Chang and discovers his wife there. Learning who she really is, Chang returns her to Li, gives Li all his possessions, and decides to become a hermit.

In the final scene, after a lapse of many years, Judge Pao appears. Fully aware of the criminal acts of Lu Chai-lang, he contrives a way to dispose of him. The Judge reports to the Emperor that a certain Yü Ch'i-chi had been harming good citizens, kidnapping women, and committing all manner of crimes. The Emperor is outraged and issues an order for Yü's execution. Later when the Emperor summons Lu Chai-lang, he is told that Lu has been executed. Greatly puzzled, the Emperor asks for an explanation. The Judge replies that the Emperor himself had sentenced Lu to death and shows him the decree. Since the characters "Yü Ch'i-chi" have been changed to "Lu Chai-lang" by the addition of a few strokes, the decree now reads: "The criminal Lu Chai-lang, oppressor of good citizens, is to be executed." Thus the wise Judge rids the people of a bully.

Not only were officials apt to engage in corrupt practices,

[38] *YCH* 49, Act I, speech following "Ch'ing-ko-erh," p. 846.

but the laws themselves were often unjust. In *The Butterfly Dream*, for instance, when Kuo Piao kills Old Wang, he brags that he need not die for murder. The old man's sons are forced to take the law into their own hands and punish the villain themselves. But when they kill Kuo, they are immediately arrested and are expected to pay for Kuo's life with their own. Moreover, while the judge feels it is unjust for Old Wang's youngest son to die, he cannot do anything to spare his life in the name of the law. It is only after he has a chance to report the case to the Emperor that he is able to save the Wang family by means of a special imperial favor. In *The Execution of Lu Chai-lang*, even though Judge Pao is convinced of Lu's criminal deeds, he is unable to do anything in the name of the law and must resort to a ruse to dispose of him.

Pao Cheng, therefore, stands as a symbol of justice in the minds of the people. Usually appearing in plays as a scholar and a prefect of K'ai-feng, he was in fact an historical personage from Anhui province, whose biography appears in the official Sung history. After receiving the *chin-shih* degree, he served in the government in a number of high official positions, where he won a reputation for being just and firm. Royal relatives and personages of high rank were in awe of him; corrupt officials feared him. His fame was so great that children and women knew his name, as in the popular saying: "If one doesn't behave properly, he will have to answer to Yama and Lord Pao."[39] He is a favorite subject in stories as well as plays.

In addition to Judge Pao, the following historical figures also appear frequently in Yüan plays as pillars of justice: Chang Ting, Ch'ien K'o, Wang Hsiu-jan, and the Sung Emperor Kao-tsung. These stories of crime and fraud often blend the historical with the fictional, or the human with the supernatural, adding interest and complexity to the plots and reflecting the strong desire of the people for the triumph of justice.

[39] *Sung shih, chüan* 316, p. 3a.

Outlaws. In addition to wise judges, outlaws also appear in the Yüan plays as indirect agents of justice. The outlaw stories were referred to in Yüan times as "green-wood plays" (*lü-lin tsa-chü*); the most notable ones are the stories about the Liang-shan heroes, which number more than thirty plays.[40] Although Sung Chiang is the uncontested leader of the group, Li K'uei, the "Black Whirlwind," must have had a special appeal to the Yüan audience. His name features in fourteen plays by six dramatists, and he plays a major part in four of the six extant outlaw plays: *Li K'uei Carries Thorns, The "Black Whirlwind's" Double Feat (Shuang hsien-kung), Yellow-flower Valley (Huang-hua yü),* and *Twice Imprisoned (Huan lao mo).* The other two plays about outlaws are *Repaying Favors (Cheng pao-en),* and *Yen Ch'ing Bets on a Fish (Yen Ch'ing po yü).*

The general theme of justice in these outlaw plays—the righting of wrongs imposed by an unfair system and corrupt men—is very similar to that of the novel *The Water Margin.* It is this theme that elevates the stature of Sung Chiang and his group above that of common thieves and highwaymen. Although the outlaw stories derive from traditional sources, the circumstances of the time seem to have stimulated a special interest in the theme. Since law had become a tool of injustice in the hands of evil men, who could better represent the cause of right than the men who set themselves against the law and its administrators? The ferocity of the bandits gains some justification from their role as heroes of the people, champions of the victims of misfortune and oppression. In the Yüan plays, we see them administering a very basic sort of justice, robbing the rich to feed the poor, confounding the wicked, and easing the lot of the oppressed common man.

Because they are outside the law, the Liang-shan band are the freest spirits in the land. Unlike the rest of the population, they live unbound to the soil or the whim of any master.

---

[40] Listed in Chung Ssu-ch'eng's *Lu kuei pu*; many of them are no longer extant.

They make their own laws, belong to a society of their own, and talk on equal terms with anyone they may encounter.

Although several major episodes in these plays are not found in the extant version of *The Water Margin*, in general the Liang-shan heroes of the plays are identical with their counterparts in the novel, with the exception of Li K'uei, whose portrayal at times is at variance with the narrative version. Li K'uei's description in the play *Twice Imprisoned* as a person of large stature, dark in complexion, and with a face full of whiskers, and again in *Yellow-flower Valley* as a man "impetuous as fire, and straight as a string on a bow,"[41] accords well with his portrayal in the narrative. In many episodes in the plays, however, he is shown with a sensitivity and ingenuity which are not associated with his character in the novel.[42]

Of the eight plays about the "Black Whirlwind" written by Kao Wen-hsiu (fl. 1264), only one is extant. In *The "Black Whirlwind's" Double Feat*, Li K'uei is sent by Sung Chiang in the guise of a farmer to protect a friend, Sun Yung, and his wife on a journey. On the way the wife runs away with a clandestine lover. When Sun reports the mishap to an official, he is sent to jail, because the official is actually the wife's lover. Li K'uei, claiming to be Sun's bond-brother, visits the prison, poisons the guard, and saves Sun. Later he kills both the wife and the official. Carrying their heads to the robber's lair, Li K'uei presents them as a double tribute. Here, he is depicted not only as a person of great physical strength, as in the novel, but also as one who uses his head.

The theme of chivalrous outlaws is clearly seen in the play *Yellow-flower Valley*. Liu Ch'ing-fu, a young scholar, is on a pilgrimage with his wife and stops at a tavern for a drink. When his wife entertains him with a song, she is heard by an official, Ts'ai, who takes a fancy to her and commands that she serve him wine. Liu denounces him and is in turn

[41] *WP* 156, Act II, following "Liang-chou," p. 939.

[42] See pp. 60-62 above for a discussion of Li K'uei's character portrayal.

bound and beaten, and his wife is taken by force to Ts'ai's stronghold. As a final recourse to justice, Liu goes to Liang-shan to lodge a complaint with Sung Chiang. Li K'uei, volunteering to rescue the young woman, goes to the stronghold and gives Ts'ai a sound beating. Seeking a place to hide, Ts'ai flees to a monastery in the Yellow-flower Valley, where Lu Chih-shen, another outlaw from Liang-shan, happens to be staying. Together the two outlaws capture Ts'ai and take him to Liang-shan. Before executing him, Sung Chiang announces that because the official Ts'ai took advantage of his power and influence to abduct a good woman, he is to die, for "although we are outlaws, we are dedicated to 'Carrying out the Way of Heaven' (*t'i t'ien hsing tao*)."[43]

The outlaw play most familiar to Western readers is *Li K'uei Carries Thorns* by K'ang Chin-chih, primarily because of Professor Crump's translation. Here Li K'uei's passion for justice verges on fanaticism. During the Ch'ing-ming Spring Festival, he is given a three-day leave from the mountain to visit his ancestral graves. When he makes a stop at Wang Lin's tavern, a favorite spot of the Liang-shan band, he learns from the tearful proprietor that his daughter has been abducted. Two impostors have convinced the half-blind father that they were Sung Chiang and Lu Chih-shen and have carried away the girl. Li K'uei is incensed, and vows that he will avenge the father for this wrong. He rushes back to the lair, cuts down the symbolic yellow flag of the band, and swears that he will kill Sung Chiang and his guilty associate.

When Sung denies any knowledge of the abduction, Li K'uei is not convinced. Sung and Li then take an oath that if Sung is guilty he will commit suicide, and if he is innocent Li will be beheaded. When the party goes to Wang Lin's shop and the old man realizes that Sung and Lu are not the guilty ones, Li K'uei becomes frightened and later carries thorns on his back seeking forgiveness. Because thorns can be made into a whip, carrying thorns is a gesture of guilt and repentance. At first Sung is determined to carry out his

[43] *WP* 156, Act IV, last scene, p. 948.

oath, but later he relents and agrees to spare Li's life if he can capture the real villains. The impostors return to the tavern, and the old man secretly notifies the Liang-shan heroes. Li K'uei rushes to the scene, captures the two villains, and brings them to Liang-shan. Sung Chiang executes them on the spot, and a feast follows to celebrate the good deed of Li K'uei in returning the daughter to the old man and redressing the wrong.

Li K'uei avenges the wrongs of another husband in the play *Twice Imprisoned*. Here, Li K'uei accidentally kills a person on one of his visits down the mountain. Recognizing that Li K'uei is a man of courage, the court officer, Li Yung-tsu, lessens his charge and spares his life. As a token of thanks, Li K'uei leaves a pair of golden rings at the officer's door. The officer's concubine, who has a lover and wants to get rid of her husband, informs on him for receiving gifts from a robber. After the husband is arrested, the concubine bribes the prison guard to murder him. The prison guard, thinking Li Yung-tsu dead, throws him over the wall, but the concubine finds him still alive and reports to the guard, who drags Li Yung-tsu back to his cell. When Li K'uei hears of Li Yung-tsu's troubles, he returns to the scene and succeeds in rescuing him. Later, after killing both the woman and her lover, he displays the mutilated corpses as a warning to others.

Since in Yüan times the concept of justice was retributive rather than merciful, the callousness and brutality of the men in the outlaw stories was not considered excessive. They saw nothing lamentable in the downfall (no matter how brutal) of the wicked. To shed the blood of one who had done wrong was merely to perform an act of retributive justice. The death of hundreds was of no consequence provided that the cause had absolute justice. In *Injustice to Tou O*, Heaven brings three years of drought upon the land to show its displeasure at the injustice suffered by a young innocent woman at the hands of an ignorant and corrupt magistrate. To the Chinese there was nothing incongruous about justice and

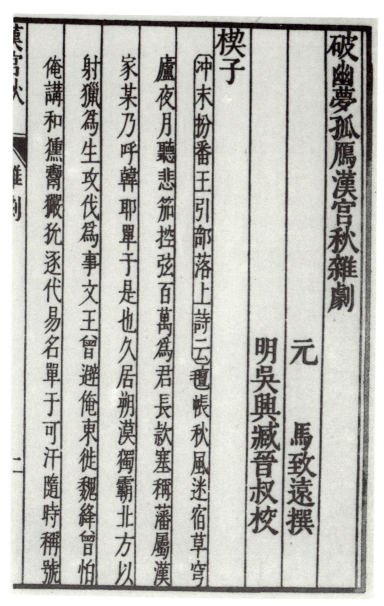

破幽夢孤鴈漢宮秋雜劇

元

馬致遠撰

明吳興臧晉叔校

楔子

〔冲末扮番王引部落上詩云〕氈帳秋風迷宿草穹
盧夜月聽悲笳挖弦百萬爲君長款塞稱藩屬漢
家某乃呼韓耶單于是也久居朔漠獨霸北方以
射獵爲生攻伐爲事文王曾避俺東徙魏絳曾怕
俺講和獯鬻獫狁逐代易名單于可汗隨時稱號

1. Text of *Autumn in the Han Palace* (*Han kung ch'iu*). From *Selected Yüan Plays* (*Yüan ch'ü hsüan*), 1616.

2. Text of *Lord Kuan Goes to the Feast with a Single Sword* (*Tan tao hui*). From *A Yüan Edition of Thirty Plays* (*Yüan k'an tsa-chü san shih chung*). Yüan Period. Facsimile edition in *KPHC*, 4 series.

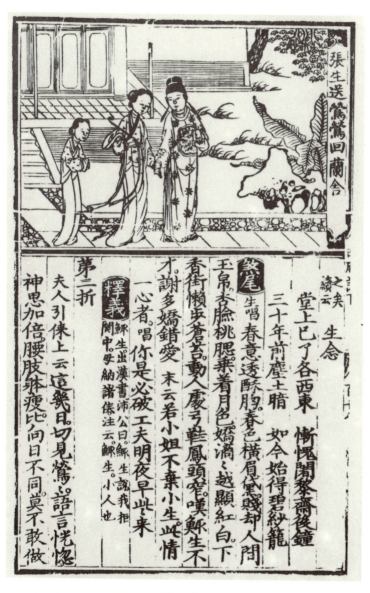

神思加倍腰肢体瘦比向日不同莫不敢做

夫人引俅上云這幾日切見鴬鴬語言恍惚

第二折

【擇義】鰥生出漢書沛公曰鰥生說我拒
關中心毋納諸俟注云鰥生小人也

一心者。唱你是必破工夫明夜早些來

才。謝多嬌錯愛　末云若小姐不棄小生此情

香街懶步蒼苔動人麼弓鞋鳳頭窄嘆鰥生不

玉帛杏臉桃腮乘着月色嬌滴々越顯紅白下

【煞尾】生唱春意透酥胸香色橫眉代黛慼却人問

三十年前塵土暗　如今始得碧紗籠

（續云） 生念 堂上巳了各西東　慚愧闍黎齋後鐘

之夫

3. Illustrated Text of *The Romance of the Western Chamber* (*Hsi hsiang chi*). From *A New Marvelous Fully-Illustrated and Annotated Edition of The Romance of the Western Chamber* (*Hsin k'an ch'i-miao ch'üan-hsiang chu-shih Hsi hsiang chi*), 1498. In *KPHC*, 1st series.

醉汪集

孤兒

十一

趙氏孤兒大報仇

4. *The Chao Family Orphan* (*Chao shih ku-erh*).
From *Selected Famous Plays Old and New* (*Ku chin
ming chü ho-hsüan*), 1633.

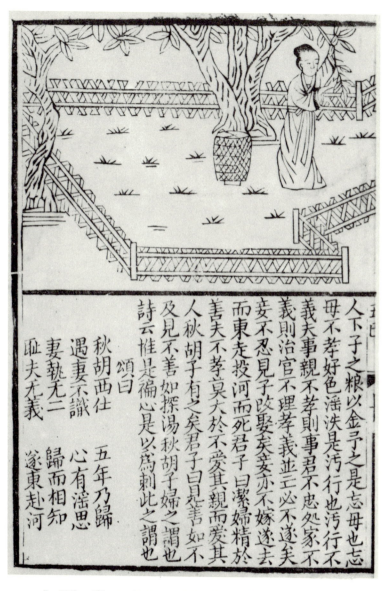

人下之粮以金予之是忘母也忘
母不莘好色淫泆是汚行也汚行不
義夫事親不莘則事君不忠処家不
義則治官不理孝義並亡必不遂矣
妾不忍見子改娶矣妾亦不嫁遂去
而東走投河而死君子曰潔婦精於
善夫不孝莫大於不愛其親而愛其
人秋胡子有之矣君子曰見善如不
及見不善如探湯秋胡子婦之謂也
詩云惟是褊心是以為刺此之謂也
頌曰
秋胡西仕　五年乃歸
遇妻不識　心有淫思
妻執無二　歸而相知
耻夫无義　遂東赴河

5. "The Chaste Wife of Ch'iu in the State of Lu" (*Lu Ch'iu chieh fu*). From Liu Hsiang (77-76 B.C.), *Biographies of Illustrious Women* (*Lieh nü chuan*).

梁山泊李逵負荊

酹江集　負荊　大

6. *Li K'uei Carries Thorns* (*Li K'uei fu ching*). From *Selected Famous Plays Old and New*, 1633.

7. *Autumn in the Han Palace*. From *Selected Yüan Plays*, 1616.

曉風楊柳赤欄橋〔韻〕放詩豪〔韻〕一半兒行

書讀一半兒草〔韻〕

又一體

我見他涙漫漫讀不住點兒流〔韻〕情脈脈

讀常懷鬱悶憂〔韻〕我這裏連忙迎接慌問

元人百種

候〔韻〕他那裏要說緣由〔韻〕則見他一半兒

徘徊讀一半兒羞〔韻〕

8. Song to the Tune of *I pan-erh*. From *Scores of Northern and Southern Songs in the Nine Musical Modes (Chiu kung ta-ch'eng nan pei tz'u kung-p'u)*, 1746.

violence going hand in hand. In fact, this violence does not dampen the gay mood that often prevails in the stories of the outlaws, a mood that abounds in stories of the impetuous "Black Whirlwind" Li K'uei.

An examination of these themes shows that the Yüan dramatists painted a broad and vivid picture of life in thirteenth- and fourteenth-century China. Both the drama and the colloquial tales present a much more comprehensive picture than is found in traditional classical literature. From the Han dynasty on, Confucian literati had fostered an outlook towards the problems of human society that emphasized the cultivation of certain moral values, and they had attempted to govern society in accordance with these values. The role of literature was conceived of as an essentially didactic one; its function was to influence people's behavior and emotions in conformity with Confucian ideals. The incorporation of Confucianism into the institutional structure of the Empire, and the great emphasis on Confucian classics in the civil service examinations, resulted in the strong Confucian cast so characteristic of much of traditional literature.

The popular genres, on the other hand, celebrate these values in the breach as well as in the observance. Not only do they incorporate materials such as Buddhist and Taoist mythology, legend and folklore customarily excluded from serious consideration by most Confucian literati, but they also frequently deal in a frank if not irreverent way with many of the cardinal Confucian virtues. The panoramic view presented by the Yüan dramatists encompasses activities of the common people, local events, strange or supernatural occurrences, and minor incidents not usually found in the official histories. They offer a realistic picture of the inner workings of society, such as fights between wives and concubines and intrigues among beautiful and shrewd courtesans. They portray the colorful life of those who live on the fringes of society, particularly the outlaws who take upon themselves the maintenance of justice in the land. They spare no details in delineating malfunctions in the body politic, especially in the administration of justice: the corrupt courts, the unjust sentences, the inhuman treatment that are the lot of the lowly. The picture of society painted in Yüan drama is replete with intimate and candid details most likely derived from firsthand knowledge; it represents facets of life not often explored in the official histories.

Although the dramatists do not consistently celebrate Confucian ideals, they nevertheless share in the emphasis on the moral and ethical, even when their stories center on outlaws or people ostracized from society. This emphasis, which is so typical of Chinese thought, tends to modify or subordinate the individual passions that are the center of interest in Western drama. Their bold treatment of love as a theme, however, as discussed above, remains a distinctive feature of Yüan dramatic literature.

V

The Language

Poetry

WHEN Voltaire adapted Father Prémare's translation of the Yüan play *The Chao Family Orphan* for the French stage, he observed that, in spite of the improbability of the plot, interest is maintained throughout the play and, in spite of the multiplicity of episodes, everything is of the most brilliant clarity. He added that notwithstanding the fact that the play lacked passion and eloquence, it was more brilliant than anything written in France during the same period.[1] Had Father Prémare not omitted from his translation of 1735 virtually all the forty-three songs that were in the original play, Voltaire probably would not have lamented the play's lack of passion or eloquence. Whatever else Yüan drama may be, it is certainly eloquent and poetic. The art of Yüan drama is not only expressed in poetry, but is actually conceived in terms of poetry.

To understand Yüan dramatic poetry, we must view it against the background of the Chinese culture of its time. Poetic training was one of the distinctive and essential features of the traditional humanistic education. Poetry was not only an expression of emotion and thought but also a necessary accomplishment of an educated man. As early as the "Spring and Autumn" period, poetry, with the accompaniment of music, was quoted on diplomatic missions in order to exchange views between states without causing affront or embarrassment.[2] Poetry, believed both to embody an image of

[1] Voltaire, *Oeuvres complètes de Voltaire* (1819), Vol. IV, pp. 381-82.

[2] See "27th Year of Duke Hsiang," *Tso chuan* (in James Legge, ed., *The Chinese Classics*, Vol. V), Book IX, p. 530; trans., pp. 533-34.

the ideal man and to teach the means of moving men toward virtuous ends, was a partial requirement of the state examination. As scholars brought up in the traditional educational system, many of the Yüan playwrights were well versed in Chinese poetry.

The Yüan dramatic and non-dramatic lyrics, called *ch'ü*, originated in songs composed for the popular tunes of the time; the non-dramatic lyrics are referred to more specifically as *san-ch'ü*. Throughout the literary tradition, Chinese poets have often turned to popular songs in their search for greater license in prosody and freshness of expression. This resulted in the emergence of such new poetic genres as the Han *yüeh-fu*, Sung *tz'u*, and Yüan *ch'ü*. In the late T'ang period, poets who wanted to experiment with new verse forms began to write lyrics for the folk tunes and foreign music current among popular entertainers of the time. This new form of verse, written to musical patterns and employing varying numbers of lines of unequal length, became a recognized poetic genre, the *tz'u*. During the Sung period, *tz'u*, in turn, lost its original connection with popular music and became increasingly formal and literary. With the occupation of northern China by Chin and the eventual conquest of the country by the Mongols, poets again adopted the refreshing popular melodies of the time as the model for more expanded lyrics, known as *ch'ü*.

The greatness of *ch'ü* lies in its vitality, the quality that ultimately defines a work of art. The vitality of the Yüan *ch'ü* is easily observable in its resourceful use of the Chinese language, with a large number of fresh colloquial expressions, as well as in its introduction of a host of arresting images, symbols, and associations.

Versification of Ch'ü

The poetics of *ch'ü* were codified by Chou Te-ch'ing in his *Sound and Rhymes of the Central Plains* (*Chung-yüan yin yün*; hereafter referred to as *CYYY*), dated 1324. Invaluable for the study of the genre, it is essentially a handbook of technique for *ch'ü* writers. It consists of two sections. The first is an extensive list of rhyming words; the second, entitled "Beginner's models in the composition of songs[3] according to the standard pronunciation of the *CYYY*," contains a discussion of the ten rules for writing such songs, some forty contemporary *ch'ü* songs as illustrations, and a listing of 335 titles of melodies.

Chou Te-ch'ing states that in writing songs "one must use the correct language; and in the choice of correct language, one must follow the pronunciation of the Central Plains,"[4] and that the perfection of *ch'ü* has arrived with the new creation of Kuan Han-ch'ing, Ma Chih-yüan, Cheng Kuang-tsu, and Po P'u, "whose rhymes sound natural and whose words are of the universal language."[5] These four writers were all from North China, and it is clear from Chou's statement that they were writing in the living language of that area in the Yüan period.

Since the conventions of *ch'ü* versification are based on the sound system of the spoken language of the Yüan capital area around Peking, a knowledge of both this language and its use in the *ch'ü* is essential to our understanding of the genre.

Tone. In prosody, the sound structure uses such features and embellishments as suit the unique nature of the language involved. In Chinese prosody, the tones of the words play a crucial role in meter and rhyme. The Chinese characters are predominantly monosyllabic and each is pronounced in a fixed tone. In ancient Chinese, there are four tones: *p'ing* or "level," which is relatively long and remains at constant pitch; *shang* or "rising," which slides upward in pitch; *ch'ü* or "fall-

---

[3] For "songs," Chou used the term "*tz'u*," which in his time was interchangeable with "*ch'ü*". Generally *tz'u* is used to designate a specific poetic genre that flourished during the Sung dynasty.

[4] Generally the Central Plains refers to the plains around the lower reaches of the Yellow River.

[5] Chou Te-ch'ing, *Chung-yüan yin yün* (in *CKKT*, Vol. I), p. 175.

ing," which moves downward; and *ju* or "entering," which is cut off abruptly and is thus relatively short. Whereas the sound variation in pitch in Chinese verse is comparable to variation in stress in English verse, the variation in the duration of the pitch is reminiscent of the variation in the length of syllables in Latin verse.

In both T'ang and Sung prosody, a distinction of the *p'ing* and *tse* (oblique) tones is made, by which the *p'ing* (level) tones are contrasted with the other three tones—*shang, ch'ü,* and *ju*—grouped together as the *tse* tone. In *ch'ü* prosody, the "level," "rising," and "falling" tones are regarded as three distinct types, though sometimes only the level-oblique distinction is observed. In the Yüan Northern dialect, while the "level" tone evolved into two groups (the *yin*-level and *yang*-level), the "entering" tone in all probability had disappeared.[6] In the rhyme section in *CYYY*, the old "entering" tone graphs are redistributed into the other tone groups, but listed separately, as follows:

"*yin*-level"
"*yang*-level":
   "falling" tone as "*yang*-level" tone
   "entering" tone as "*yang*-level" tone
"rising":
   "rising"
   "entering" tone as "rising" tone
"falling":
   "falling"
   "entering" tone as "falling" tone.

Although the tonal value of these four categories cannot be fully ascertained, they are believed to correspond roughly to the four tones in modern Mandarin.[7]

  [6] For the controversy on the *ju* tone, see Shih, pp. 10-12.

  [7] For a discussion of the tones in the Yüan dialect, see Schlepp, *San-ch'ü Its Technique and Imagery* (1970), pp. 16-17.

Meter. The *ch'ü* were originally lyrics composed for current popular tunes. As the poetic genre developed, the arrangement of lines and tones in the original songs formed the basis for later metrical patterns. Chou Te-ch'ing gives two specific examples to illustrate that music strongly affects the choice of words by requiring certain tones to be used in certain positions of a melody: in the melody "Tien chiang ch'un," the syllable at the end of the first line calls for a *yin*-level tone; thus *huāng* (deserted) can be used, but not *huáng* (yellow), which is of a wrong tone; and the fifth syllable of the last line of the melody "Chi-sheng ts'ao" requires a *yang*-level tone; thus *huáng* (yellow) can be used, but not *hūn* (dark), which is of an incorrect tone.[8] It is important to note that music helped to create the pattern for the tonal structure of a *ch'ü* song. Today the music is lost, but records of the meters (line lengths and tonal arrangements) of many of the original songs have been preserved.

The choice of tones in a *ch'ü* is as follows:

1. *p'ing* only: P
2. *shang* only: S
3. *ch'ü* only: C
4. *tse* (either *shang* or *ch'ü*): T
5. ( ): to enclose an alternative

The tonal pattern and rhyme scheme of the song to the tune of "Hsiao t'ao hung" is given on p. 118. This song has 42 prescribed syllables in 8 lines of unequal lengths comprising 7, 5, 7, 3, 7, 4, 4, and 5 characters respectively. Rhymes in lines 6 and 7 are optional, but in the other 6 lines, rhymes are required.[9] (See lyrics on p. 123.)

[8] Chou Te-ch'ing, pp. 235-36.

[9] The meter here is based on the analysis in Wang Li's *Han-yü shih-lü hsüeh* (1962), p. 819. Cf. the meter in Chu Ch'üan's *T'ai-ho cheng-yin p'u* (1398, pp. 174-75), which disagrees with Wang's only in the first syllable in l. 7 (Chu Ch'üan's is a P).

Tones of Characters							End Rhyme	Line
P(T)	P	T(P)	T	T	P	P	R	1
T(P)	T	P	P	C			R	2
T(P)	T	P	P	T	P	C	R	3
T	P	P					R	4
P(T)	P	T(P)	T	P	P	C	R	5
P	P	T	S(P)				(R)	6
T	P	P	C				(R)	7
T(P)	T	T	P	P			R	8

The *ch'ü* writer could draw upon a large supply of popular melodies as music for his verses; over 500 metrical patterns bearing titles of these melodies have come down to us. *The Sounds of Universal Harmony* of 1398 by Prince Chu Ch'üan, containing 335 songs with a notation of metrical patterns, provides the earliest extant models. In the Ch'ing period a number of similar studies appeared, including *The Standard Metrical Patterns of the Northern Songs (Pei tz'u kuang cheng p'u)* by Li Yü *et al.*, containing 445 songs and patterns, and *Formularies of the Ch'ü-songs Compiled under Imperial Auspices (Ch'in ting ch'ü p'u)* by Wang I-ch'ing *et al.* Among recent works, Wang Li's *Chinese Poetics (Han-yü shih-lü hsüeh)* is most thorough, containing 151 formularies of *ch'ü* tonal patterns and rhyme schemes.

These books of metrical patterns include non-dramatic songs (*san-ch'ü*) as well as songs from plays. The cited lyrics bearing the same tune titles vary a great deal in the length of their lines or phrases. This phrase-length variance could be due to the mutation of verse forms, the use of *ch'en-tzu* ("non-metric words"), or the filling of the same rhythmic space with one or more notes of the same duration. Cheng Ch'ien in his article "Changes of Form of Northern Songs" suggests some general principles of the mutation that might have taken place in the songs in Yüan drama.[10] Dale John-

[10] Cheng Ch'ien, "Pei ch'ü ke-shih te pien-hua," *Ta-lu tsa-chih*, I, no. 7 (1950), 12-16.

son's study of the prosody of *ch'ü* further substantiates and defines these principles of mutation; he describes them as a system of variations that could be super-imposed on nuclear melodies, thus often altering the melodies, but probably without erasing their distinctive features. In addition to the underlying mechanism of mutation, there is the utilization of the *ch'en-tzu*, which Johnson thinks probably represents the embellishment of the melody.[11]

Rhyme. Various patterns of rhyme have always been a part of the sound structure of Chinese poetry, but the *ch'ü* presses the rhyming capability of the Chinese language to its furthest limits by using the same rhyme throughout an entire act, with sometimes more than a hundred rhyming words. In *Autumn in the Han Palace*, the nine songs in Act I, using the *chia-ma* rhyme (the thirteenth rhyme in *CYYY*), utilize 62 rhyme words in a total of 68 lines:

Song No.	Tune Title	Total No. of Lines	Total No. of Rhymes (end/internal)
1	"Tien chiang ch'un"	5	5/–
2	"Hun-chiang lung"	10	8/–
3	"Yu hu-lu"	9	8/–
4	"T'ien-hsia le"	6	5/1
5	"Tsui chung t'ien"	7	7/–
6	"Chin chan-erh"	8	6/1
7	"Tsui fu kuei"	6	6/–
8	"Chin chan-erh"	8	6/–
9	"Chuan-sha"	9	8/1

Of the 62 rhymes, 59 are end-rhymes and 3 are internal rhymes. Because of its euphonic effects, internal rhyme is used frequently in *ch'ü*, sometimes excessively. In a "six-

[11] Dale Johnson, "The Prosody of Yüan Drama," *T'oung Pao*, LVI, nos. 1-3 (1970), 96ff.

word, three-rhyme" (*liu tzu san yün*) line, rhyme occurs in
every other word, as in the following:

Wo hu t'ing i sheng meng ching.[12]

I, suddenly hearing a sound, am startled.

(*WP* 117a, Act III, "Yao p'ien," p. 268.)

This extensive use of rhyme would have led to monotony
if another practice—the freeing of tone restrictions in rhymes
—had not been introduced into the *ch'ü* form at this time. In
the *ch'ü*, syllables within the same rhyme group could rhyme
regardless of tone—a license not allowed in *shih* and only
rarely in *tz'u*. In the first song in *Autumn in the Han Palace*,
for example, the five rhyme words, *huā* (flower), *hsià* (below), *pà* (finished), *wá* (girl), and *fă* (hair), are of *p'ing,*
shang, and *ch'ü* tones. In the *shih* poetry, *huā* and *wá*, being
of the *p'ing* tones, may rhyme with each other, but not with
hsià, *pà*, and *fă*, the three *tse* tones. In *ch'ü* the double inno-
vation of admitting a large number of rhymes while freeing
the rhyme words from tone restrictions allows variation within a consistent rhyme, and thus adds great liveliness to the
new verse form. Because of the close association of sound and
mood, a recurring rhyme, in the hands of a most discerning
playwright, may be played for additional effect.[13]

In the *CYYY* Chou Te-ch'ing divides all syllables into 19
groups according to the finals in the Northern dialect. Since
its appearance, the *CYYY* has been the orthodox guidebook
for technique in the Northern *ch'ü* rhymes. The 19 groups of
characters in the *CYYY*, classified according to the finals in
the Northern dialect, are listed in their original order as follows (the pronunciation is Tung T'ung-ho's reconstruction):[14]

[12] *T'ing, sheng*, and *ching* are listed in the same rhyme group in
CYYY (Chou Te-ch'ing, p. 204).

[13] See Wang I, *Tz'u ch'ü shih* (1960), p. 283.

[14] For a discussion of these 19 groups, see Tung T'ung-ho, *Chung-
kuo yü-yin shih* (1954), pp. 27-34.

(1) 東鍾 uŋ, iuŋ   (11) 蕭豪 ɑu, au, iau, (uau)

(2) 江陽 aŋ, iaŋ, uaŋ   (12) 歌戈 o, io, uo

(3) 支思 ï   (13) 家麻 a, (ia), ua

(4) 齊微 i, iei, uei   (14) 車遮 ie, ye

(5) 魚模 u, iu   (15) 庚青 əŋ, iəŋ, uəŋ, yəŋ

(6) 皆來 ai, iai, uai   (16) 尤候 ou, iou

(7) 眞文 ən, iən, uən, yən (17) 侵尋 əm, iəm

(8) 寒山 an, ian, uan   (18) 監咸 am, iam

(9) 桓歡 on   (19) 廉纖 iem

(10) 先天 ien, yen

These 19 groups consist of over 1,500 syllables with a total of more than 5,800 homonyms. The large number of entries in each group are accepted as rhymes in *ch'ü.*

Ch'en-tzu (*"Non-metric Words"*). In *ch'ü,* aside from the prescribed syllables, additional words may be inserted. These are known as *ch'en-tzu,* translated alternatively as "padding," "additional," "foil," "extra-metric," or "non-metric" words. The use of non-metric words in *ch'ü* prosody enhances the feeling of freedom and vitality. In *ch'ü,* the non-metric words in a single interpolation can amount to as many as twenty syllables, as in Kuan Han-ch'ing's lyric composed to the tune of "Ch'u ch'iang hua to-to." In some lyrics, the number of syllables of non-metric words exceeds the number of prescribed syllables. Wang Ho-ch'ing's short lyric to the tune of "Autumn, in a Song of 100 Characters" ("Pai tzu chih ch'iu ling") is an interesting illustration, as it is written in exactly 100 characters, of which 39 are prescribed syllables and 61 are non-metric syllables. Normally, in singing, words inserted between musical notes are to be pronounced "trippingly on the tongue" (to borrow Hamlet's words), and not mouthed or stressed. In fact, Wang Chi-te (Ming dynasty) asserts that "the use *of ch'en-tzu* began with the Northern and Southern *ch'ü*. Northern *ch'ü* is accompanied by string music; thus the extra-metric words can be easily carried over (*yin-tai*). Southern *ch'ü* is accompanied by percussion instruments; the beat is definite, and the extra-metric words cannot be easily carried over."[15] Wang Li also believes that these extra-metric words are unstressed and are to be sung quickly and lightly.[16] In a performance or in silent reading, these unstressed words, occurring as single syllables or in strings of up to 20 syllables, could easily lend a sense of airiness and briskness to the lines.

The *tz'u* with its lines of unequal length gains an air of naturalness over the T'ang *shih* with its uniform five- or seven-character lines. With *ch'ü* this irregularity of line length is further amplified by the insertion of non-metric words, as the verse below illustrates (the non-metric words are underlined). The romanization follows Tung T'ung-ho's reconstruction of the pronunciation of the Yüan period:[17]

	Rhyme	Line
I è ʃiɘm xiāŋ ăi sàn k'ūŋ t'iɘŋ	R	1
L iém mò̤ tūŋ fūŋ tsiɘŋ	R	2
P ài pà i<u>ĕ</u> sié tsiāŋ k'iŭ lán p'iɘŋ	R	3
T <u>ʃ'iáŋ xiū liău</u> liăŋ sām ʃiɘŋ	R	4
T '<u>ĭ</u> t'ón lón miɘŋ yè ʒiú xién kiɘŋ	R	5
I <u>òu pŭ ʃì</u> k'iɘŋ yón pó vù	–	6
T<u>ū tsăi ʃì</u> xiāŋ iēn ʒiɘn k'ì	–	7
L<u>iăŋ pān ʒí</u> iɘŋ yɘŋ *tĕi* pŭ fɘŋ miɘŋ	R	8

[15] Wang Chi-te, *Ch'ü lü* (in *CKKT*, Vol. IV), p. 125.

[16] Wang Li, pp. 715-16.

[17] The pronunciation of graphs follows Tung T'ung-ho's reconstruction as given in Liu Te-chih, *Yin chu Chung-yüan yin yün* (1962), pp. 1-55. For a discussion of the pronunciation of the Yüan Northern dialect, see Shih, pp. 7-12.

夜深香靄散空庭

簾幕東風靜

拜罷也斜將曲欄凭

長吁了兩三聲

剔團圞明月如懸鏡

又不是輕雲薄霧

都則是香煙人氣

兩般兒氤氳得不分明 [18]

The night is deep, wisps of incense float in the empty court-
yard;
The curtains hang still, the eastern breeze has ceased.
Her worship completed, she leans against the winding
balustrade;
Long and deep, more than once she sighs.
The full, bright moon shines like a hanging mirror.
It is neither light cloud nor thin fog;
All is but incense smoke and the maiden's breath—
The two like vapors are fused indistinguishably.

(*WP* 117a, Act III, "Hsiao t'ao hung," p. 268.)

The irregularity of line length and rhythm effected through
the use of non-metric words enhances the naturalness that is
the hallmark of the *ch'ü* as a poetic genre. The three-syllable
colloquial utterances in the form of non-metric words, as in
the above passage, have a brisk, unstable, and fluid rhythm.
As noted by Professor Yoshikawa, the Chinese language normally forms two-syllable or four-syllable expressions; these

[18] Tones of four characters (*pó* and *vù* in l. 6. *xiāŋ* in l. 7, and *yǝn*
in l. 8), do not agree with Wang Li's meter (see p. 117, n. 9 and p. 118
above). The variation could be because of the freedom the Yüan
playwrights frequently asserted in the handling of poetic components
within a framework of carefully defined form; the mutation of verse
forms; or the inadequacy of meters provided in books such as
Wang Li's.

unusual three-syllable colloquial phrases, used repeatedly as
adverbs or adjectives throughout the songs, not only enliven
the lines but also endow the plays with a spontaneous air and
vitality.[19]

Figurative Language

In addition to developing their new metrical structure, the
Yüan playwrights seem to have enjoyed experimenting with
figurative language as well. All of the standard poetic devices
of the long literary Chinese tradition—simple and complex
imagery, symbolism, parallelism and allusion—are used with
ingenuity, endowing many plays with an extraordinary richness of texture. Poetic imagery, because of its unique and
profound effect in Yüan drama, is the focus here for discussing the figurative language in the genre.

Imagery serves a variety of functions in Yüan drama. Perhaps the most important of these is the creation of atmosphere, suggesting the context of action on a stage essentially
devoid of scenery. Given the weight of tradition and the conciseness of the language, even the apparently simple nature
images can carry a whole complex of connotations. In some
plays, images functioning primarily to set the scene are developed in such a way as to suggest the tone of the play as a
whole, thus underlining the theme and often taking on symbolic overtones. The dramatists also employ images in establishing character and relating the characters to their milieu.
These various functions are discussed in detail below, particularly as seen in the work of such leading dramatists as Wang
Shih-fu, Kuan Han-ch'ing, Ma Chih-yüan, Cheng Kuang-tsu,
and Po P'u.

Creating Atmosphere. In the absence of scenery on the
Yüan stage, as on the Elizabethan, poetic passages play a
primary role in suggesting atmosphere. The stage of *Macbeth*

[19] Yoshikawa, p. 281.

cannot be darkened, but the hero's words, "Light thickens, and the crow makes wing to the rooky wood,"[20] immediately invoke an atmosphere of foreboding darkness. On the Yüan stage, heroes and heroines sing of moonlit spring gardens and rain-drenched autumn palace grounds to create moods and settings for their actions.

The opening songs of Chang Chün-jui in the first act of *The Romance of the Western Chamber* serve as an example. Arriving in Ho-chung prefecture, Chang strolls along the Yellow River and is struck by the magnificent view:

The snow-white waves reaching to the void on high:
    Autumn clouds rolling in the sky.
The floating bridge of bamboo-ropes:
    A giant dragon crouching on waves.
From east to west, it runs through nine states,
From north to south, it cuts across a hundred streams.
How fast or slow do the home-bound junks appear?
They are like speeding arrows shot from a bow.

雪浪拍長空

天際秋雲捲

竹索纜浮橋

水上蒼龍偃

東西潰九洲

南北串百川

歸舟緊不緊如何見

卻便似弩箭乍離弦[21]

(*WP* 117a, Act I, "Yu hu-lu," p. 260.)

[20] *Macbeth*, Act III, Scene ii, lines 50-51.

[21] The inclusion of Chinese characters here in the discussion of imagery should be helpful for those who have a knowledge of Chinese, for the translation cannot convey adequately the connotations that are in the original.

Appearing as if the Milky Way has tumbled down from the
  Ninth Heaven,
The River hides its source high beyond the clouds.
Following an undivided course, it enters the Eastern Sea;
Its water nourishes thousands of flowers in Lo-yang,
And bathes countless acres of Liang park.
Once it even carried a raft to the land of the sun and moon.

只疑是銀河落九天

淵泉雲外懸

入東洋不離此巡穿

滋洛陽千種花

潤梁園萬頃田

也曾泛浮槎到日月邊

(*WP*, 117a, Act I, "T'ien-hsia le," p. 260.)

The leisurely pace characteristic of Chinese plays fosters a type of imagery that allows for elaboration. The expansive image above, in addition to presenting a beautiful natural scene, also reflects the romantic temperament of the young scholar and evokes an atmosphere of wild nature with its billowing waves reaching upward to the sky and eastward to the sea—an atmosphere in keeping with the love story of impetuous youth about to unfold. This river scene in Ho-chung prefecture (now Yung-chi, in Shansi), where the Yellow River and the Fen River meet, is masterfully painted. The images of beating waves and the infinite stretch of cloudlike water suggest dynamic movement on a grand scale and convey an overpowering impression of beauty, sound, and motion. The hanging bridge undulating over the river and the scudding, arrow-like junks add a human touch and movement to the picture.

The comparison of the river to the Milky Way not only underlines again the gigantic size of the river, but also reflects the thoughts of the student at the moment. The Milky Way has been established in the Chinese popular mind as a symbol of romantic love through its association with the legend of the Spinning Maid and the Cowherd, two devoted lovers in Chinese folklore.[22] One version of the legend states that the Milky Way is connected to the sea, and a raft from the Milky Way appears by the seashore every year in the eighth month. Once a man caught the raft, and sailed away on it. When he reached a city, he saw a woman and a man leading a cow to drink at a river. Later, upon his return, he was told by an astrologist that he had visited the Milky Way, where the Cowherd dwells.[23] The word "raft" (*fu-ch'a*) in the last line of the above lyric is thus an additional allusion to these legendary lovers.

The first line of the second song, "Appearing as if the Milky Way has tumbled down from the Ninth Heaven," is borrowed from the T'ang poet Li Po:

> *The flying stream plunges three hundred thousand feet,*
> *Appearing as if the Milky Way has tumbled down from the*
> *Ninth Heaven.*[24]

Appropriate borrowing from the classical poets, demonstrating scholarship and ingenuity, is an accepted and esteemed practice in the Chinese literary tradition. When the borrowing is apt and striking, as it is here, it is obviously a literary achievement. Similarly, the simple image "thousands of flow-

---

[22] The Spinning Maid, a granddaughter of the King of Heaven, is banished from Heaven because of a misdemeanor. On Earth, she falls in love with and marries a Cowherd. When she returns to Heaven, he follows her, but is stopped by the Milky Way ("Silver River," Yin-ho). Once a year on the seventh day of the seventh month they are permitted to meet when celestial magpies form a bridge for the Cowherd to cross. A Peking opera entitled "Meeting at the River of Heaven" (*T'ien ho hui*) is still staged yearly during the seventh month.

[23] Chang Hua (232-300), *Po wu chih* (*Ssu-pu pei-yao* edition), p. 3a.

[24] Li Po, "Wang Lu shan p'u-pu" ("Gazing at the Waterfall on Mount Lu"), *CTS*, vol. III, p. 1837.

ers in Lo-yang" recalls the lines of the Sung poet Su Ch'e, addressed to his friend Ssu-ma Kuang:

Now you are returning to attend your farm and garden,
Again to plant the thousand species of flowers of Lo-yang.[25]

Such borrowings enrich the texture of the poems by adding a historical dimension. Although the images fulfill several dramatic functions, their primary role is to provide a vivid scene for the action.

From the broad river scene, the poet moves within the walls of the Monastery of Universal Redemption (P'u-chiu ssu), where Chang Chün-jui falls in love at first sight with Ying-ying on a beautiful and provocative spring day:

The east wind tosses the hanging willow branches,
The trailing strands playfully tug at the peach petals,
And the beaded curtain half reveals her lotus-blossom face.

東風搖曳垂楊綫

遊絲牽惹桃花片

珠簾掩映芙蓉面

(*WP*, 117a, Act I, "Chi-sheng ts'ao," p. 262.)

The term "tug and tease" (*ch'ien je*), normally used for people but here attributed to the willow and peach blossoms, paints a charming scene of spring, when all forms of life come alive, and not only the fancy of young men but that of all elements in nature seems to turn to love. The east wind tossing the willow branches in the air, the trailing strands playfully tugging at the peach blossoms, and the beaded curtain (probably moved gently by the same east wind that blows the willow), half revealing the lovely lotus-like face of Ying-ying —all these set a mood that makes the girl seem a natural

[25] Su Ch'e, "Ssu-ma Chün-shih tuan ming tu le yüan" ("Ssu-ma Chün-shih Enjoying His Garden"), in *Luan ch'eng chi* (*SPTK so-pen*), *chüan* 7, p. 107.

object of love in springtime. Moreover, the image of the spring willow, often used in descriptions of courtesans and young girls of easy virtue, hints at the nature of the girl and the love story that is to develop.

These lines also illustrate the effective use of parallelism in Yüan dramatic verse. In addition to the two-line parallel, which is a popular device in Chinese poetry, a great variety of parallelisms are used in the *ch'ü*-songs. The three-line parallel, as shown here, is rarely found in *shih* or *tz'u*; but in the *ch'ü* this device, known as "tripod" parallelism (*ting-tsu tui*), is often used to bring out a greater richness in the thought and language of the poetry.[26] The syntactical parallelism of the verbs "toss," "tug," and "half reveal"; the repetition of the plant images of "willow branches," "peach petals," and "lotus blossom"; and the resonances produced by the sound and meaning of the geometrical terms *hsien* ("lines"), *p'ien* ("slices"), and *mien* ("surface"), all give the student's lyric

[26] The "tripod" parallelism here is one of the seven types of parallelism in *san-ch'ü* mentioned by Chu Ch'üan (the annotations are his): (1) *ho-pi tui* ("united jade" parallelism), two parallel lines; (2) *ting-tsu tui* ("tripod" parallelism), three parallel lines, usually referred to as *san-ch'iang* ("three spears"); (3) *lien-pi tui* ("joined jade" parallelism), four parallel lines; (4) *lien-chu tui* ("string of pearls" parallelism), parallelism in several lines; (5) *ko-chü tui* ("alternating lines" parallelism), parallelism in alternating lines of different lengths; (6) *luan-feng-ho-ming tui* ("harmonizing phoenixes" parallelism), parallelism in the beginning and concluding lines of a stanza, as in the "Tao-tao ling"; (7) *yen-chu-fei-hua tui* ("swallows chasing flying petals" parallelism), three parallel phrases in one sentence. (Chu Ch'üan, pp. 14-15.)

In his brief discourse on parallelism, Chou Te-ch'ing mentions three unusual types that are used in *ch'ü*: (1) *shan-mien tui* ("fan-cover" parallelism), as in "T'iao-hsiao ling," where alternating lines are parallel, *e.g.*, line four with line six and line five with line seven; (2) *ch'ung-tieh tui* ("piling" parallelism), as in the song "Kuei san t'ai," in which line one is parallel with line two, and line four with line five, but at the same time, lines one, two, and three are parallel with lines four, five, and six, respectively; (3) *chiu-wei tui* ("save the ending" parallelism), as in the song "Hung hsiu hsieh," in which the last three lines—four, five, and six—are parallel. (Chou Te-ch'ing, p. 236.)

a symmetry that is striking in its re-echoing of sounds and vivid images.

Later, as Ying-ying suffers the pangs of unfulfilled love, she finds affirmation of her anguished feelings in the fading spring scene:

> *The powdered butterflies' wings lightly touch the snow-like*
> *   catkins;*
> *The swallows' mud turns fragrant, mixed with the fallen*
> *   petals.*
> *I wish to tie my spring heart, my feelings being ephemeral,*
> *   though the willow branches are long;*
> *Heaven seems near compared to the man separated from*
> *   me by these flowers.*

蝶粉輕沾飛絮雪

燕泥香惹落花塵

繫春心情短柳絲長

隔花陰人遠天涯近

(*WP*, 117b, Act I, "Hun-chiang lung," pp. 271-72.)

Although the willow floss, the falling peach petals, and the darting butterflies create a scene dazzling with color and fragrance, they nevertheless presage the quick passing of spring, as echoed in the third line. The images vividly reveal the complex emotions of the young maiden. The ironic comparison of the inaccessibility of her lover with that of Heaven further emphasizes the depth of Ying-ying's feeling of hopelessness.

Spring is frequently introduced in its different aspects as the background of romance. In the play *Maid "Plum-Fragrance"* (*Tsou Mei-hsiang*) by Cheng Kuang-tsu, the young mistress, who has determined to grant her affections to her despairing lover, strolls with her maid "Plum-Fragrance" in the family garden looking for a chance to deliver a love-token to the study, where he is temporarily staying. The spring evening, aglow with moonlight, provides a perfect atmosphere for the budding romance, while at the same time foretelling a happy ending. The shimmering cherry-apple blossoms, the shiny young grass, the sparkling dewdrops on the willow branches, the reflected stars in the pond, and the bright moon suspended above the pine tree all help to create the magic of the scene.

> *The wind swaying the cherry-apple blossoms—*
> *A loom weaving a piece of cold shimmering brocade;*
> *The vapor over the grass—*
> *Green gauze spread on a sheet of clear glass;*
> *The dewdrops clinging to the willow branches—*
> *Pearls strung on green silken threads.*
> *The stars in the pond*
> *Are like crystals scattered in a jade plate;*
> *And the moon over the top of the pine tree*
> *Is as a mirror held by a dark dragon.*[27]

海棠風錦機搖動鮫綃冷

芳草煙翠紗籠罩玻璃淨

垂楊露綠絲穿透珍珠迸

池中星有如那玉盤亂撒水晶丸

松稍月怡便似蒼龍捧出軒轅鏡

(*YCH* 66, Act I, "Chi-sheng ts'ao," pp. 1151.)

These lines have a remarkable unity of imagery. The cherry-apple blossoms in the wind, mist, dewdrops, stars in the pond, and moon in the sky, presented as cool brocade, silken gauze, clear glass, pearls on green threads, crystals in a jade plate, and a shiny mirror, yield a unified visual effect, suggesting a cold, crystal purity and extraordinary brilliance and color—the shimmering dark greens and blues of nature. The play on light and color is subtle and effective. The unmistakable coldness is, however, physical rather than psychological. The presentation of the moonlit garden in terms of articles and ornaments with which the girl is familiar succeeds in fusing the exterior and the interior world and in evoking a

[27] Cf. James Liu, *The Art of Chinese Poetry*, p. 117.

feeling of intimacy. The unity of imagery is further strengthened by the auditory effect achieved through internal rhyme and the repetition of closely associated end-sounds. The seventeen -*ng* endings account for roughly one-third of all the syllables in the lyric. The sound -*ng* may not be onomatopoeic; it nevertheless gives an effect similar to the clinking of pearls against each other or crystals in a jade plate.

Much of the content of the above images displays the passion for adornment characteristic of T'ang and Sung poetry. The image of crystals scattered in a jade plate in line 8 illumines a case of imaginative borrowing by the Yüan dramatist; where the T'ang poet Po Chü-i uses the image of pearls falling on a jade plate for auditory effect in his description of a lady's magnificent lute playing,[28] the use here is visual in the description of the twinkling stars reflected in a pond. Although many of these images illustrate the Yüan dramatists' dependence on traditional poetry, their use in creating a fairyland atmosphere so conducive to youthful love clearly belongs to the individual talent of the playwright Cheng Kuang-tsu. Images like these provide not only scenery and lighting but also the synesthetic effect of a lovely moonlit night. They also act as subtle means of influencing the imagination and attitudes of the audience. Much of the success of the scene is achieved through this creative use of visual, tactile, and auditory effects.

Onomatopoeia, an especially effective device for auditory effect, is frequently used by the Yüan dramatists. Chiefly an imitation of sound or action, it is the type of verbal imagery that comes closest to the reproduction of the subject. The most popular form generally entails alliteration in two neighboring words or syllables (*shuang-sheng*); double-rhyme (*tieh-yün*), the rhyming of the vowels in a pair of syllables with identical finals; and reduplication (*tieh-tzu*).[29] While all these three poetic devices, found in as early a work as the

---

[28] Po Chü-i, "P'i-p'a hsing" ("The Lute Song") in *Po shih Ch'ang-ch'ing chi* (*SPTK so-pen*), *chüan* 12, p. 64.

[29] For a discussion of these devices, see James Liu, *The Art of Chinese Poetry*, pp. 34-36.

Book of Poetry, have been favorites of Chinese poets, reduplication is especially popular with the Yüan poets and is sometimes carried to extremes. One example with excellent dramatic auditory effect is found in *The Songstress* (*Huo-lang tan*):

> *All I see is a dark gloom, with clouds covering the sky;*
> *How are we to bear this pouring, pelting rain?*
> *The roads all along have been twisting, narrow, and rough;*
> *Where shall we turn?*
> *I am glad that the rain seems to slacken—pausing now and*
> *then.*
> *Ch'u-ch'u lü-lü hu-hu lu-lu—as the dark clouds open,*
> *I see nothing but lightning flash and strike.*
> *What can one do? The swishing wind and the dripping rain*
> *Make the whole place—up and down, all around—a foggy*
> *mist.*
> *Shaking in the wind and drenched by the rain,*
> *We have become travellers in a bare forest—*
> *All this helps to form a dismal black-inked landscape of the*
> *Hsiao and Hsiang Rivers.*

	Number of Reduplications	Lines
我只見黑黯黯天涯雲布	1	1
更那堪濕淋淋傾盆驟雨	1	2
早是那窄窄狹狹溝溝塹塹路崎嶇	4	3
知奔向何方所	0	4
猶喜的消消灑灑斷斷續續	4	5
出出律律忽忽嚕嚕陰雲開處	4	6
我只見霍霍閃閃電光星炷	2	7
怎禁那颯颯飀飀風點點滴滴雨	4	8
送的來高高下下凹凹凸凸一搭模糊	4	9
早做了撲撲簌簌濕濕淥淥疏林人物	4	10
倒與他粧就了一幅昏昏慘慘瀟湘水墨圖	2	11
Total:	30	11

(*YCH* 94, Act IV, "Liu chuan," p. 1652.)

With its stark visual picture of the storm-darkened chiaro-scuro landscape, accentuated by the profusion of images that evoke all the sounds of a blinding rain, this lyric has an unusual richness and complexity.

While here the downpour is overpowering, the rainfall in Po P'u's *Rain on the Wu-t'ung Trees* (*Wu-t'ung yü*) is faint and wistful, evoking a painful memory for the Emperor in the quiet of the night. The play tells the love of the T'ang Emperor Ming Huang and his favorite consort Yang Kuei-fei. After the An Lu-shan revolt, the Emperor lives in retirement in the Western Palace. One night while dreaming of his late consort he is awakened by the rain beating on the *wu-t'ung* trees, under which they have sworn undying love to each other. The changing rhythm of the rain recalls for the Emperor many familiar scenes—it is "fast as ten thousand pearls falling on a jade plate," or "loud as a band of musicians playing before a banquet," or "clear as a cold spring splashing on verdant mossy rocks," or "violent as battle drums rolling under embroidered banners."[30] The use of onomatopoeia in the following lines adds further vividness to the rain images:

> *Ch'uang-ch'uang—like propitious animals spurting fountains over twin ponds;*
> *Shua-shua—like spring silkworms consuming leaves all over the mulberry frames.*[31]

咻咻似噴泉瑞獸臨雙沼

刷刷似食葉春蠶散滿箔

(*YCH* 21, Act IV, "Erh-sha," p. 363.)

The unceasing rain on the *wu-t'ung* trees, reminding the Emperor of his happier days and accentuating his present loneliness, provides an effective dramatic background for the situation. Eloquent presentations of rainfall in other Yüan plays, *Rain on the Hsiao and Hsiang Rivers* (*Hsiao Hsiang*

---

[30] *YCH* 21, Act IV, "Tao-tao ling," p. 363.
[31] Cf. James Liu, *The Art of Chinese Poetry*, p. 37.

yü) and *The Tablet at Chien-fu Temple*, give further evidence of the Yüan dramatists' great skill in creating vivid and suggestive scenes and atmosphere appropriate to the stories.

Delineation of Emotions. As the examples in the above section illustrate, an image, charged as it is with intense thought and feeling, stimulates an emotional response even when used primarily for painting a scene. Nature images, in fact, are often used more for delineation of feelings than for providing atmosphere. For example, in the difficult task of representing an experience of a deeply personal nature, Scholar Chang in *The Romance of the Western Chamber* resorts to skillful use of spring imagery. Dazzled by his first rendezvous with Ying-ying, he sings out:

Spring is here and flowers flaunt their beauty;
Her willow-like waist is supple.
The heart of the flower is now gently plucked,
And the dewdrops make the peony unfold.

春至人間花弄色

將柳腰款擺

花心輕折

露滴牡丹開

(*WP*, 117d, Act I, "Sheng hu-lu," p. 300.)

I am like a fish delighting in water,
Or a butterfly gathering the sweet nectar of a bud.
Half pushed back and half welcomed,
I am filled with surprise and love.

魚水得和諧

嫩蕊嬌香蝶恣探

半推半就

又驚又愛

(*Ibid.*, "Yao p'ien," p. 300.)

In the songs immediately following this scene, Chang repeatedly uses images of spring to express youthfulness and passion:

The spring-like white silk handkerchief,
Is now lightly stained with red perfume.

春羅元瑩白
早見紅香點嫩色

(Ibid., "Hou t'ing hua," p. 300.)

When he steals a glance at Ying-ying's body by lamplight, he feels a surge of elation:

I do not know where this feeling of spring comes from.

不知春從何處來

(Ibid.)

And again he sings:

The feelings of spring have permeated her bosom,
The expression of spring is seen in her eyebrows,
Making treasures of jade and silk poor in comparison.

春意透酥胸
春色橫眉黛
賤卻人間玉帛

(Ibid., "Sha-wei," p. 301.)

The use of such spring imagery demonstrates the suggestive power of the metaphorical language with which the poet-dramatist successfully portrays the student's passionate response to Ying-ying's loveliness. The use of figurative language in dealing with the taboo subject of sensual love not only enriches the texture of the lyrics but also helps avoid social censure. Sometimes it may be the sole means of expressing thoughts which are otherwise impossible to convey.

In contrast to the spring imagery, autumn imagery traditionally conveys a sense of desolation and sadness. In *Autumn in the Han Palace*, the autumn imagery is used effectively to express a deep sorrow. After sending his favorite consort, Lady Chao-chün, to the Tatar chief, the Emperor returns to his autumnal palace grounds, dejected and overwhelmed by a sense of solitude. The images chosen to reflect his feeling of sorrow come from the season's sights and sounds—a wild goose flying southward and the chirping cicadas. When the Emperor returns to his palace, he finds that

The cicadas are crying
Under the green curtained window.

泣寒螿
綠紗窗

(*YCH* 1, Act III, "Mei hua chiu," p. 10.)

Later, while dozing off, he is awakened by the cry of a wild goose, which sounds to him like

. . . the soughing of a forest wind,
And the murmuring of a mountain stream.

…似林風瑟瑟
嵓溜泠泠

(*Ibid.*, Act IV, "Man t'ing fang," p. 12.)

It is fairly conventional for Chinese poets to resort to what John Ruskin termed "the pathetic fallacy," and to ascribe human qualities to nature. In this passage, the Emperor attributes to the cicada a grief as deep as his own; the emotional effect is intensified by the suggestion that nature itself shares and reflects these feelings. The simile likening the cry of the wild goose to the soughing of the wind expresses the same sense of chill solitude. Both images reflect the heart of the tired, aging Emperor, alone with his sadness. For him autumn is symbolic as well as real. His next words again establish a connection between the cold world outside and what takes place within himself.

My hair has turned white, my body, sick and feeble.
Indeed I feel disconsolate.

暗添人白髮成衰病

直恁的吾家可也勸不省

> (*Ibid.*, Act IV, "Sui-sha," p. 13.)

The absence of Lady Chao-chün creates such a void that he compares her to the "Bamboo Grove Temple" (Chu lin ssu),[32] which has disappeared completely. The Bamboo Grove Temple often mentioned in Yüan poems comes from a story about a Buddhist pilgrim who, after visiting the temple, could find no sign of it when he turned his head to have a second look.

The images of fallen leaves, the empty imperial couch, and the cold jade staircase in the moonlight further intensify the sense of bleakness and solitude and sharpen the poignancy of the Emperor's grief. The nature of the poetic effect becomes clearer if we compare these images to those used in some famous love stories of the West. After Desdemona's death, Othello cries out:

> *. . . Had she been true,*
> *If heaven would make me such another world*
> *Of one entire and perfect chrysolite,*
> *I'd not have sold her for it.*
> > (Act V, Scene ii, ll. 143-46.)

Pitching such a gigantic image as "another world of one entire and perfect chrysolite" against the image of his deceased

[32] *YCH* 1, Act IV, "Tsui ch'un feng," p. 11.

wife reflects the Moor's intense feeling for her. Antony, upon deciding to give up the world for Cleopatra's love, proclaims:

Let Rome in Tiber melt, and the wide arch
Of the ranged Empire fall! Here is my space.

(Act I, Scene i, ll. 33-34.)

Later, upon receiving the mistaken news of her death, he bids his heart to

Crack thy frail case!

(Act IV, Scene xiv, l. 41.)

In contrast to these violent and disruptive images, those employed in suggesting the Han Emperor's state of mind have the soft, blurred quality of a Chinese painting of a forlorn autumnal scene, merging the human being with the world around him and achieving an identity between the two. For a Chinese Emperor, who theoretically stands as a harmonizing force between the human and the cosmic spheres, it would have been highly inappropriate to express his love in such violent images as those of Antony and Othello.

The effectiveness of images in depicting emotions is further seen in a comparison of the above images, reflecting the Emperor's despondent and desolate feelings after his humiliating appeasement and the death of Chao-chün, with the images showing his confidence, his romantic spirit, humor, and buoyancy in the early part of the story. When the Emperor first appears on the stage, he proclaims that the world is at peace, the harvest is rich, and there seems to be no more need for fighting men and horses. Even as the traitorous minister Mao Yen-shou is persuading the Tatar chieftain to demand Chao-chün as a wife, the Han Emperor seems unaware of the shaky condition of his state and sings confidently:

The rain and dew of the four seasons are timely,
Thousands of miles of rivers and mountains are beautiful;

My loyal ministers all prove themselves useful men;
And I on my high pillow have no more cares.

四時雨露勻

萬里江山秀

忠臣皆有用

高枕已無憂

(*Ibid.*, Act II, "I chih hua," p. 5.)

The "high pillow," a familiar image in Chinese, stands for sound, restful sleep and an absence of worries.

Another example of the happy mood of the Emperor at the beginning of the play can be seen in his joy at having discovered a lute-playing beauty, for years neglected in his huge harem. He compares her to the immortals—the Goddess of Mercy (Kuan-yin) of Lo-chia Mountain, and the Goddess of the Moon—showing his extreme appreciation of her loveliness and grace. When Chao-chün, as any filial daughter would do under the circumstances, asks his Majesty to show some favor to her parents, poor commoners, the Emperor teases her, saying:

My rank is almost as high as a village chief,
This house is as big as a magistrate's court,
Thank Heaven and Earth! What a nice poor son-in-law—
Now who would dare again to insult my father-in-law?

俺官職頗高如村社長

這宅院剛大似縣官衙

謝天地可憐窮女婿

再誰敢欺負俺丈人家

(*Ibid.*, Act I, "Chin chan-erh," p. 4.)

The utter understatement in the similes in the first two lines reveals the Emperor's conviviality and extreme good humor. This lighthearted humor is again seen when he bids good night to Chao-chün after their first encounter. Since he has discovered her through her lute playing, he enjoins her to wait quietly for his arrival the following evening. "I fear that the beauties of my six palaces will soon all be plucking their lute strings,"[33] he confides.

The Emperor's happiness, however, is short-lived. When the Tatar chieftain demands Chao-chün for his wife, the ministers of the Han Court, fearful of defeat, pressure the Emperor to give her up. Embittered, the Emperor asks sarcastically why in time of peace his civil and military officers boast of their achievements, but now when trouble threatens they have nothing to suggest:

Like wild geese with arrows sticking through their bills,
None of you dare even cough.

似箭穿着雁口

沒個人敢咳嗽

(*Ibid.*, Act II, "Tou ha-ma," p. 6.)

A sharp image indeed of the now mute officials at court! He berates them bitterly, trying to shame them into action:

Henceforth it's no use to expect dragons and tigers to fight;
All I can depend on will be my friends, the phoenixes.

枉以後龍爭虎鬥

都是俺鸞交鳳友

(*Ibid.*, Act II, "K'u huang-t'ien," p. 7.)

The generals and fierce warriors, traditionally compared to mighty dragons and tigers, are no more to be counted on to defend the land; only the palace ladies, compared to royal birds, can be his defenders. In pointing out the uselessness of his civil and military leaders, the Emperor clearly betrays his own weakness and that of the country; he is no doubt a be-

---

[33] *YCH* 1, Act I, "Chuan-sha," p. 4.

nevolent but ineffectual ruler. After bidding farewell to Chao-chün at the border and seeing her taken away by the foreign envoy, he rightly bewails:

> How am I an Emperor of the great Han!
> (*Ibid.*, Act III, following "Tien ch'ien huan," p. 9.)

It is worthwhile to note here that the suggestion by some modern scholars that the Yüan playwrights were committed to social protest or satire, on the whole, cannot be substantiated. But in *Autumn in the Han Palace*, there seems to be an implied censure of the inefficiency and weakness of the Chinese Emperor and the central government—a weakness that eventually led to their humiliation by a threatening foreign force. But it must be understood that this exposure of his weakness did not destroy his dignity in the eyes of the Yüan audience. The traditional Chinese attitude toward their emperors was much like the Elizabethans' attitude toward the English kings: while the monarch depicted in the drama may have been inept or inefficient, the audience never lost their respect for the ideal of kingship—the representation of divine power or the symbol of order and harmony. The Elizabethans' ability to distinguish the essence of kingship from its understandable aberrations in mortals enabled them to view with composure the pleasure-seeking indulgence of monarchs upon the stage without any lessening of their devotion to them. Here, even though the Han Emperor does not live up to the ideal of kingship, he is still the man who holds the mandate of Heaven. In some instances in this play, the symbolic is given greater emphasis than the actual situation. The fact that many incidents here, notably the suicide of Chao-chün, differ greatly from history further indicates that the playwright's interest in this love story goes beyond the mere telling of a historical event.[34]

[34] In history, Wang Chao-chün, a Han palace lady of outstanding beauty, was given to the Tatar chieftain in marriage, and later bore him two sons (*Hou Han shu, chüan* 89, pp. 3a-3b). However, minor errors, such as using Cheng-yang Gate (Cheng-yang *men*) of the Sung

In the course of the play, the Emperor's changing mood, from gaiety and good humor to sarcasm and eventually sadness, is reflected in the imagery. An organic relation between images and the narrative is manifest, especially in the last act, where poetic images grow out of the external situation: the autumn season. Through the effective use of autumnal images, the poet succeeds in vividly conveying the complex emotions of a kindly, weak, and lonely emperor.

Characterization. Imagery can also be used effectively as a means of characterization. *The Chao Family Orphan* provides a good example of the dramatic use of recurrent animal-images to underline villainy, and to create a pervading atmosphere of brutality and viciousness in keeping with the action. The tone of the play is set with the first entrance of the villain, T'u-an Ku, chanting:

> *A man seldom wants to harm a tiger,*
> *But a tiger is intent on harming man.*
> *If one does not satisfy his desires when occasions arise,*
> *He will afterwards live in vain regret.*

(*YCH* 85, opening quatrain, p. 1476.)

Thus hinting at his own ferocious nature, he relates his scheme to destroy Chao Tun, his enemy at court.

The reaction of the other characters to the villain is reflected in the repeated beast-imagery of their speeches. The son of Chao Tun, being forced to suicide, laments the sorry state at court where power is in the hands of a

kingdom-gnawing traitor.

蠹國的奸臣

(*Ibid.*, Prologue, "Shang hua shih," p. 1477.)

He thus compares his enemy to a termite. Later, when a faithful retainer tries to smuggle the orphan from the heavily

---

dynasty in a story of the Han dynasty, may be due to an oversight of the playwright. Yoshikawa believes that such an error could be due to the dramatist's poor scholarship (Yoshikawa, p. 75).

guarded house, he is warned by a sentinel that it would be futile to try to escape from this

air-tight lair of tigers and leopards

不通風虎豹屯

> (*Ibid.*, Act I, "Ho hsi hou t'ing hua," p. 1480.)

Kung-sun Ch'u-chiu, an old friend of Chao Tun who is instrumental in saving the orphan's life, views his own retirement from court as

an early escape from this group of vicious, hungry tigers.

早跳出傷人餓虎叢

> (*Ibid.*, Act II, "Liang-chou ti-ch'i," p. 1483.)

He is relieved that he will

never again be expected to follow after the hawks and leopards.

再休想鵰班豹尾相隨從

> (*Ibid.*)

He is also aware that his attempt to save the orphan is like

challenging a scorpion and stinging bees.

剔蝎撩蜂

> (*Ibid.*, Act II, "San-sha," p. 1485.)

When arrested, he tells the villain that he is

a stormy sky-whirling vulture.

狂風偏縱撲天鵰

> (*Ibid.*, Act III, "Chu ma t'ing," p. 1487.)

And finally, when the grown orphan is informed of the tragedy that has befallen his house, he voices his determination to destroy the murderer and *to haul him away like a dead dog.*

死狗似拖將去

(*Ibid.*, Act IV, "Shua hai-erh," p. 1495.)

The audience, though not necessarily conscious of it, sees the nature of the murderer T'u-an Ku in the images of different beastly shapes, and his brutal character is thus repeatedly underlined. Although symbolic animal images had appeared often in folklore, here they are unusually effective in suggesting the villain's character.

In contrast to the fierce animals that characterize the traitorous minister, delicate birds are used repeatedly to represent the famous and beautiful dancer, the Imperial consort Yang Kuei-fei, in the first two acts of *Rain on the Wu-t'ung Trees*. The Emperor Ming Huang thinks of her as a divine bird, and their happy life together,

a perfect harmony of male and female phoenixes;

鸞鳳和鳴

(*YCH* 21, Act I, "Pa sheng Kan-chou," p. 350.)

and her sweet voice

as that of an oriole beyond the willow tree.

似柳外鶯

(*Ibid.*, Act I, "T'ien-hsia le," p. 351.)

In dancing, she displays appealingly

her bee-like slender waist, her swallow-like whirling body.

蜂腰細燕體翻

(*Ibid.*, Act II, "Hung shao-yao," p. 355.)

The audience's unconscious imagination is influenced by these images to see Yang Kuei-fei as a graceful and airy dancer.

The effectiveness of the bird-imagery is the more apparent when we see that the consort, after her death in Act III, is compared no more to birds, but instead to flowers: quiet, delicate, and transient. Formerly a patron of the now rebellious An Lu-shan, she is accused by many of ruinous influence over the Emperor and the state. The Imperial guards who escort the Emperor in his escape to Szechwan during the rebellion refuse to proceed unless the consort is put to death. The Emperor is greatly bewildered and asks:

> *She is such a delicate lovely cherry-apple blossom,*
> *How could she be the root of the destruction of the state?*

他是朵嬌滴滴海棠花

怎做得閙荒荒亡國禍根芽

> (*Ibid.*, Act III, "Tien ch'ien huan," p. 359.)

After she is strangled at the foot of Ma-wei Mountain, her clothes are brought in; upon seeing them, the Emperor laments:

> *How cruelly the land-sweeping fierce wind stormed;*
> *Why of all things should it blow down*
>   *This renowned flower of my Imperial garden!*

恨無情捲地狂風刮

可怎生偏吹落我御苑名花

> (*Ibid.*, Act III, "T'ai ch'ing ko," p. 359.)

After the rebellion is suppressed, the Emperor returns to the capital to live in retirement in the Western Palace, where he is haunted by regret for the cruel death of his consort:

> *How unfortunate that a cherry-apple blossom has been*
>   *swept away!*

可惜把一朵海棠花零落了

> (*Ibid.*, Act IV, "Tai ku to," p. 361.)

The familiar sights in the garden constantly remind him of her:

Looking at the lotus, I think of her beautiful face,
Facing the willows, I recall her slender waist.

見芙蓉懷媚臉

遇楊柳憶纖腰

(*Ibid.*, Act IV, "Yao," p. 361.)

The "lotus" and the "willow," taken from the T'ang poet Po Chü-i's "Song of Unending Sorrow" ("Ch'ang hen ke"), upon which this play is based, have since been established in the popular imagination as a special allusion to the tragic beauty of this famous Chinese love story. The use of bird and flower images for Yang Kuei-fei in this play, and of weeping cicadas, soughing winds, and other autumnal sounds and sights to reflect the grief of the aging Emperor in *Autumn in the Han Palace*, illustrates a subtle function of imagery: by their instinctive choice of objects which reflect their thoughts, the characters reveal their own personalities and moods as well as the relation between object and theme. This highly dramatic use of imagery is prominent in Shakespeare's tragedies: Macbeth, Othello, and Hamlet all have their characteristic imagery. Although rare in the Yüan plays, the same subtle function is seen in the speeches of the two Emperors and even more notably in the words of the recluse in *Ch'en T'uan Stays Aloof*. In this latter play, images obviously function to reveal the nature of the speaker while underlining the Taoist theme.

Underlining a Theme. Although nature images are used to reproduce a setting, their potency often derives from the fact that they are called forth not by the immediate need to report the scene, but primarily by the poet's perception of the fundamental identity between the scene and his theme. In Ma Chih-yüan's *Ch'en T'uan Stays Aloof*, Taoist recluse Ch'en rejects the repeated invitation of the Emperor to serve at court. When asked for an explanation, he responds with an

idyllic description of a life of serenity and freedom in nature
—the quintessence of the ideal of the Taoist recluse:

Resting serene in the quiet of the dwelling,
A cicada newly emerged from its shell.
Appearing in the dream of Chuang-tzu,
A butterfly flies free.
I sleep on a bed of gentle breeze,
And gaze at the disk of the moon.
A white cloud is my cover;
A stone, my pillow.
I shall sleep till mountains move and valleys change,
Rocks decay and pine trees wither,
Planets turn and stars shift.
My way shall remain forever the same,
Seeking after the mysterious scheme of things.

身安靜宇蟬初蛻

夢遶南華蝶正飛[35]

臥一榻清風

看一輪明月

蓋一片白雲

枕一塊頑石

直睡的陵遷谷變

石爛松枯

斗轉星移

長則是抱元守一

窮妙理造玄機

(*YCH* 42, Act III, "San sha," p. 728.)

[35] Nan-hua refers to Chuang-tzu.

Although many of the nature images here are conventional, they are used creatively in the presentation of the recluse's character and the Taoist ideal. In the first two lines, the comparison of embracing Taoism—discarding one's old self and beginning a new life—with the emergence of a cicada from its old shell, effectively sums up the poet's theme.[36] The cicada casting off its old shell is a symbol for one's removal from the mud of the world. The next two lines, referring to the butterfly dream of Chuang-tzu, are an apt illusion to the Taoist concept that there is no distinction between dream and reality. Lines 5 through 8 use concrete images—a bed of gentle breeze, the disk of the moon, the white cloud cover and the stone pillow—to express closeness to nature and oneness with the universe. The white clouds, the moon, and the pine trees are visible symbols of freedom, peace and contentment in nature. Here the mountain or the forest is not simply a place where the Taoist hermit resides, but a state of mind as well. These images are used to reveal spiritual experiences that could not have been as richly expressed in the language of abstract statements, and are closely related to the underlying mood of the play. Images such as the following, found also in earlier recluse-poetry, are scattered throughout this play:

I, this Taoist, in a yellow cap and rustic gown,
Am company to two idle fellows—the gentle breeze and the bright moon.

則這黃冠野服一道士

伴着清風明月兩閒人

(*YCH* 42, Act II, "Ho hsin-lang," p. 724.)

You are tied down by the human affairs of a thousand years,

---

[36] The number of lines here refers to the English version. A seven-character line in Chinese, normally with a caesura after the fourth syllable, is often rendered into two lines in English.

I, busy only in a game of chess under the pines,
Regard riches and rank as but floating clouds.

您那人間千古事

俺只松下一盤棋

把富貴做浮雲可比

(*Ibid.*, Act III, "T'ang hsiu-ts'ai," p. 726.)

I am a leisurely cloud wandering free in the sky.

俺便是那閒雲自在飛

(*Ibid.*, Act III, "Kun hsiu ch'iu," p. 726.)

Here the Taoist recluse can be totally oblivious to the hustle and bustle of the world, for his is a life of inaction and serenity.

Another well-known play, *The Dream of Yellow Millet*, also by Ma Chih-yüan,[37] similarly describes the beauty and calm that is found in the life of a Taoist recluse:

Where I live, dust gathers not on the ground,
Grass remains forever young;
In all four seasons flowers bloom tenderly,
And the jade-screen mountains face my thatched gate.

俺那裏地無塵

草長春

四時花發常嬌嫩

更那翠屏般山色對柴門

(*YCH* 45, Act I, "Chin chan-erh," p. 779.)

Such calm repose in nature, though seldom seen in Western drama, is aptly expressed by the Duke in Shakespeare's *As You Like It*. Living in exile in the forest of Arden, he exclaims:

37 He co-authored the play with Hua Li-lang and Hung-tzu Li-erh.

And this our life exempt from public haunt
Finds tongues in trees, books in the running brooks,
Sermons in stones, and good in everything.

(Act II, Scene i, ll. 15-17.)

The rolling mountains, the breeze, and the pine shadows are both scenery and forces in nature. The Chinese scholar-recluse feels at one with nature, and his lyrics constantly express this. Here in these Yüan plays, nature images act as trenchant reflections of emotions and thought.

Images are also used to expand the scope of plays and thus to add to their thematic significance, as in *Injustice to Tou O*. The vastness of the issues involved—chastity versus lust, justice versus corruption—of which the action of the play is but a part, is kept constantly before us by imagery. The introduction of the cosmic images of heaven and earth, the whirling snow, the three-year drought, and other supernatural phenomena lead the imagination to another world. Through these images the immediate human domain of the play seems limitlessly extended, and the personal events of an individual's life are related to the fate of all men. Here men and nature stand in a continuous relationship. Tou O's situation flashes before us in separate images of the surrounding universe; we are never long without a reminder of the universal nature of her calamity. In the first scene, we find a series of cosmic images connected with her, or spoken by her, that unobtrusively convey her sorrow. When Tou O first appears as a widow in mourning for her late husband, she wonders if Heaven is aware of her years of suffering:

If Heaven only knew my situation,
Would it not also grow thin?

天若是知我情由

怕不待和天瘦

(*YCH* 86, Act I, "Tien chiang ch'un," p. 1501.)

The use of the term "thin" (*shou*) presents Heaven in human form and shape, perhaps sympathetic to what is occurring on earth. She is puzzled by all the misfortunes that have been heaped upon her since childhood:

Is it my fate to bear life-long sorrows?

莫不是八字兒該載着一世憂

(*Ibid.*, Act I, "Yu hu-lu," p. 1501.)

The word "bear" (*tsai*) customarily used in connection with a vehicle, makes Tou O's ill fate, weighed down by a load of lifelong grief, appear concrete and vivid. One tragic event after another is more than she can bear, because, as she observes,

the human heart cannot be like water flowing forever onward!

人心不似水長流

(*Ibid.*)

The force of her statement is that "My grief just can't go on and on like this; it can't be like the water flowing endlessly; and yet, it seems there is no end to it!" In comparing her endless sorrow with permanence in nature, she makes it apparent that the misfortunes that have been a continuous drain on her emotions and energy are unbearable. This series of images evoked within the space of a few lines in her opening speech conveys her sorrows more quickly and forcefully than would direct comments by her or another character.

In Act II, when a corrupt and stupid magistrate has her cruelly beaten, she asks:

Why don't the sun's rays shine under an overturned tub?

怎麼的覆盆不照太陽暉

(*Ibid.*, Act II, "Ts'ai ch'a ko," p. 1508.)

The two images comparing justice to sunlight and a corrupt court to an overturned tub are familiar ones, an overturned tub meaning a court without justice.

In Act III, after Tou O has been condemned to die and stands alone and forsaken, she makes a direct apostrophe to Heaven and Earth, challenging them to assert themselves and mete out justice as it is their responsibility to do:

> *Even Heaven and Earth have come to fear the strong*
> *and oppress the weak.*
> *They, after all, only push the boats floating with the cur-*
> *rent.*
> *O Earth, if you fail to discriminate between good and evil,*
> *How can you be called Earth?*
> *O Heaven, in mistaking the sage and the fool,*
> *You are called Heaven in vain!*

天地也做得箇怕硬欺軟

却元來也這般順水推船

地也你不分好歹何爲地

天也你錯勘賢愚枉做天

> (*Ibid.*, Act III, "Kun hsiu ch'iu," p. 1509.)

By using the image of pushing a boat with the current, Tou O pointedly accuses Heaven and Earth of simply going along with things in the human world, thus failing in their categorical duties of discriminating between the good and the evil, the wise and the foolish. Nevertheless, on the execution ground she appeals to Heaven to right her wrongs and send down snow to indicate Heaven's displeasure over the injustice that has been heaped upon her:

> *If my breast is full of wronged feelings that spurt like fire,*
> *It will move six-sided snowflakes to tumble down like*
> *cotton.*

若果有一腔怨氣噴如火

定要感的六出冰花滾似綿

(Ibid., Act III, "Erh-sha," pp. 1510-11.)

In Act IV, having convinced her father of the injustice that has befallen her, the ghost of Tou O bids him farewell, lamenting that

> *my everlasting sorrow flows on like the long Huai River.*
> 悠悠流恨似長淮

(Ibid., Act IV, "Shou chiang nan," p. 1517.)

In all these scenes, Tou O invokes gigantic images in which the cosmic forces and the elements rage in whirling movement. Not only does she feel herself to be closely related to the elements, but nature's forces actively participate in the action of the play. Imagery here reveals the presence of a surrounding or accompanying universe of thought and feeling. The play is not merely the story of a single woman fighting for her life; the cosmic images transform the confrontation between her and her enemies into a confrontation between the powers of good and evil.

In spite of the dramatist's success in presenting Tou O's wrongs with clarity and force, the action in the play does not generate a passionate conflict within the soul of the heroine. The three principal reasons for this failure to explore internal conflicts in Chinese drama, as discussed in Chapter II,[38] define the difference between *Injustice to Tou O* and Western tragedy. First, in a Confucian society the modes of behavior are so regulated that the course of conduct for a young widow like Tou O is well defined; she is to remain loyal to the memory of her late husband and filial to her widowed mother-in-law. In her opening speech in Act I, after bemoaning her unkind fate, she immediately asserts that she will obey and serve her mother-in-law, observe mourning for her late husband, and live up to her vows. Even when she is offended by Mis-

[38] See pp. 41-42 above.

tress Ts'ai's plan to marry Old Chang and berates her violent-
ly, her devotion to the old woman never falters. Eventually,
in an effort to protect her from suffering, Tou O sacrifices
her own life. As the daughter of a Confucian scholar, she
knows how she is expected to act, and she follows this course
unswervingly, in spite of an occasional desire to deviate. Had
she come from a family of Mistress Ts'ai's stock, her behavior
might very well have been different. But the presentation of
her father as a true Confucian early in the play makes Tou
O's self-sacrificing conduct later in life credible, and makes it
unlikely that she will suffer any strong doubts or inner conflicts regarding her chaste widowhood and filial piety.

Secondly, the Chinese ideal of moderation makes undesirable and unappealing the representation of intense and sustained passion. Tou O may feel bitter about the cruel events
that have befallen her, and she may be outraged by the un-
reasonable demands of "Donkey" Chang or by her mother-in-
law's unseemly conduct, but these strong feelings are never
sustained. On the whole, Tou O is seen as a gentle person of
great sensibility and restraint. Even on her way to the execution ground, she pleads with the guard to take her by a back
street so as to spare her mother-in-law the pain of seeing her
as a condemned convict.

Thirdly, the fundamental Chinese belief in a benevolent
Heaven tends to modulate the personal passions and doubts
that would generate intense conflict within the soul of the
protagonist. When such passions and doubts do occur, as in
Tou O's denunciation of Heaven and Earth in Act III, neither
the passion nor the conflict is enduring. Tou O's vehement
protest is understandable under the circumstances. Though
she has followed religiously the Confucian teaching of chastity and filial piety, she has been convicted of a crime. The
lust of "Donkey" and the foolishness of Mistress Ts'ai are
comprehensible to her, but that the court of justice should
have sentenced her to die is beyond her belief. Thus she cannot help feeling wronged by Heaven and Earth as well as by
her fellow men. At the execution ground, however, her three

prophecies demonstrate clearly her restored faith in a just Heaven. She is convinced that Heaven will cause unnatural events to happen to show its displeasure and to prove her innocence. She reminds the world that Heaven also sent a three-year drought to indicate the injustice suffered by the filial woman of Tung-hai and caused frost in June to prove the innocence of Tsou Yen.[39] Confident her innocence will be vindicated, she is in the end at peace with herself and with Heaven.

This view of a benevolent Heaven is reinforced in the last scenes of the play. Although the two most cited versions, *Plays of Former Famous Playwrights* (*Ku ming chia tsa-chü*) of 1588 and *Selected Yüan Plays* (*YCH*) of 1616, differ greatly in their presentation of the last part of the story, the basic theme is the same in both versions.[40] In the *YCH* version, all three prophecies of Tou O are fulfilled—the blood from Tou O's wound flies upward to stain the white pennant on the execution ground, snow begins to fall in midsummer at her decapitation, and later a severe drought of three years descends upon the land. In the 1588 version, the three-year drought also comes to pass, and the falling snow is hinted at by the executioner just before Tou O's beheading; but there is no mention of blood from the wound except when the ghost of Tou O recapitulates the story to her father. The omission of this most unnatural event on stage may make the 1588 version more realistic in its presentation, but the fundamental belief in both versions is clearly that a just Heaven will send omens to insure that wrongs in the human world will be rectified.

This basic view of a benevolent Heaven consequently makes improbable a sustained, intense conflict in the soul of the heroine in a struggle against Heaven or fate. The final justice rendered by a fair Heaven eliminates the likelihood of

---

[39] For the stories, see Shih, pp. 4-5.

[40] For a comparison of the two versions, see *ibid.*, p. 279, n. 1160-1383.

the kind of tragic conclusion that carries everything to its bitter end, common in Western tragedy. In this way, *Injustice to Tou O* illustrates the basic difference between Chinese and Western tragedy in their conceptions of the universe. Viewed within its own cultural context, the play is immensely successful in endowing the tragic events of Tou O's life with cosmic scope and significance.

Recurrent imagery, another device for underlining the theme or mood of a play, is used effectively in all great poetic drama. Of all the Yüan plays, the use of this device is most noticeable in *The Romance of the Western Chamber*. Here the moon is a recurrent image, and almost all of the significant action occurs in moonlit scenes. Something lovely in itself and an object of romantic longing, the moon is a universal symbol of beauty, solitude, loftiness, and the beloved. In Chinese literature there is no association of the moon with lunacy or witchcraft as in the West; it is traditionally associated with love and homesickness. The moon has always been a favorite of the Chinese poets, who are especially fond of comparing its purity and enchantment with that of a fair maiden. In this play, it provides symbolic significance beyond simple stage lighting: a full moon with its brilliance and magic quality bespeaks romance and union, and the waning moon reminds one of inconstancy in human affairs. References to the moon occur at least fifty-four times in *The Romance of the Western Chamber*. Because of its symbolic nature and its power to evoke rich associations, the recurrent imagery diffuses an atmosphere of romance throughout the entire play.

When Chang Chün-jui is first struck by Ying-ying's divine beauty, he calls her:

the moon-gazing Goddess of Mercy of the Southern Sea.

南海水月觀音[41]

(*WP* 117a, Act I, "Chi-sheng ts'ao," p. 262.)

[41] *Shui-yüeh*: "gazing at the moon in the water"—the idea evoked is the illusoriness of all phenomena.

Watching her surreptitiously as she burns incense in the court-yard, he finds the scene deeply moving, as

the full bright moon shines like a hanging mirror.

剔團圝明月如懸鏡

(*Ibid.*, Act III, "Hsiao t'ao hung," p. 268.)

In order to sound out her feelings towards him, he recites the following poem in thinly disguised figurative language:

The moonlight is soft and mellow;
The shadows of flowers lie in the quiet spring.
How is it that I now face the bright moon,
But see not the person in the moon?

月色溶溶

花陰寂寂春

如何臨皓魄

不見月中人

(*Ibid.*, Act III, following "Hsiao t'ao hung," p. 268.)

Later, he sends her a poem through the maid; it brings an immediate reply—a daringly explicit invitation in metaphorical language:[42]

I wait for the moon in the Western Chamber;
Facing the breeze, the door stands ajar.
Along the wall the shadows of flowers move;
Perhaps the man of jade is coming.

待月西廂下

迎風戶半開

隔牆花影動

疑是玉人來

(*WP* 117c, Act II, following "Man t'ing fang," p. 291.)

[42] A poem borrowed verbatim from the source, the T'ang tale by Yüan Chen. The only difference is the first character in line 3; in the T'ang text, it is *fu* ("to brush against").

On the evening when the lovers are finally united,

*The bright moon, like water, floods the Pavilion and
terrace.*

月明如水浸樓臺

(*WP* 117d, Act I, "Hun-chiang lung," p. 298.)

The ensuing separation, enforced upon the couple by Ying-
ying's mother, breaks Chang's heart, and he likens the occasion to

the fading flowers and the waning moon.

花殘月缺

(*Ibid.*, Act IV, "Che kuei ling," p. 308.)

At the conclusion of the story, Chang heads the list of successful examination candidates. When Ying-ying's cousin, to
whom she is betrothed, comes to claim her hand, the maid
Hung-niang asserts that this man is no match for his rival, the
brilliant student Chang, for,

How can a firefly compare with the disk of the moon?

螢火焉能比月輪

(*WP* 117e, Act III, "T'iao-hsiao ling," p. 317.)

The effect of the moon image throughout this poetic drama is
clear: the play is richer in its texture and meaning because we
are continuously in the presence of an element of nature, itself
the reflection of the romantic mood in which the play is
presented. In all three plays discussed here, *Ch'en T'uan Stays
Aloof, Injustice to Tou O,* and *The Romance of the Western
Chamber,* we see the effectiveness of imagery in reinforcing
the themes.

Poetic eloquence is the strength of Yüan drama. The above
passages amply demonstrate how the dramatists used images
not merely to add to the richness of poetic quality, but also

to serve several other dramatic purposes: to create scenery, reflect and intensify emotions, strengthen characterization, and support the themes of the plays. In all these roles the poetic images function naturally and organically.

Not only the Yüan dramatists, but also the early critics of the drama, focused their attention on poetry. This emphasis is reflected in the frequently cited criticism by Prince Chu Ch'üan in the early fifteenth century. Couching his critical remarks in imagistic language, he praises the dramatists for their poetic achievement alone: Ma Chih-yüan's poetry, not to be compared to the ordinary, is like "a phoenix gliding and singing in the highest clouds"; Po P'u's poetry, of great strength, is like "an eagle, which, arising over the arctic, soars to the highest heaven"; Kuan Han-ch'ing's poetry, showing uneven talent, hovering between the excellent and the inferior, is like "a drunken guest at a banquet"; Cheng Kuang-tsu's poetry, of an extraordinary quality, is like "precious pearls and jade of the Ninth Heaven"; and Wang Shih-fu's poetry, appealing and romantic, is like "beautiful women amidst flowers."[43] These comments reflect an emphasis on poetry, an emphasis perhaps as characteristic of the Yüan playwrights as of later Chinese scholar-critics of Yüan drama.

The Yüan dramatists gained great success through their indirect, poetic, and subtle means of expression. There are, however, many poetic passages in the Yüan plays containing conventional images and descriptions unrelated to the plot. The dramatic structure is sometimes obscured by the proliferation of lyrics with their often extraneous detail. There is much that could be described as digressive. But as we have seen, in the hands of master dramatists such as Kuan Han-ch'ing, Ma Chih-yüan, Cheng Kuang-tsu, Po P'u, and Wang Shih-fu, the poetic images are carefully worked into the texture of the plays. Through their lyrics, they were able to explore the depths of mood and feeling of the characters and the significance of a variety of themes.

[43] Chu Ch'üan, pp. 16-17.

Prose

Prose passages representing both monologue and dialogue are a significant part of the Yüan drama. While the lyrics are usually sung by only one actor or actress, the prose speeches are spoken by all the characters. The Yüan dramatists used both colloquial and semi-classical language to good effect in the prose monologues and dialogues. Writing primarily in one Northern dialect, they helped to establish a tradition that later prose narratives followed. They used puns for humor and for making a point; they used vulgar language for comic effect. Prose served these and a variety of other functions in the Yüan drama.

The Northern dialect adopted by the dramatists is that of the capital region of Ta-tu and adjacent areas. Three types of evidence support this identification. First, in the early stage of the development of the genre, the majority of prominent playwrights were natives of Ta-tu (Cambaluc or Khanbalik), in the region of present-day Peking.[44] Chou Te-ch'ing names especially four Northern playwrights as the masters whose sound and rhymes are to be followed in the composition of *ch'ü*.[45] Second, historical linguistic studies point to evidence that the sound and rhyme system found in the Yüan plays was that of Old Mandarin.[46] Finally, the prose speeches in the Yüan drama, except for some occasional expressions, are quite similar to the dialect in the Peking area of today.

Grammatically, Old Mandarin differs in certain ways from modern Mandarin.[47] Some of the particles in the Yüan plays have functions similar to those in modern Mandarin; others have gone out of use, but can be understood by examination of their use in non-dramatic writings of the period. The oc-

---

[44] See pp. 207-08 below. [45] See p. 115 above.

[46] See Shih, pp. 7-12.

[47] See, for example, the comparative study of the usage of grammatical particles in Yüan drama and modern Mandarin in Shih, pp. 14-21.

currence of many now unfamiliar expressions in a wide variety of Yüan writings makes it clear that they are a part of the colloquial language of the period; it appears that the playwrights adapted the colloquial mode of expression to dramatic use without altering it to any great extent. If some of the language of the drama is incomprehensible to us today, this is the natural result of the seven centuries of change and development that have elapsed since the Yüan period. The surprising thing is how little of the language has lost its intelligibility.

The Problem of Authorship. There has been a persistent tendency among critics since the Ming period, including Tsang Mao-hsün and Wang Chi-te, to insist that while the lyrics were composed by the learned, the prose monologues and dialogues were works of actors, or staff members of the Music Academy.[48] Tsang asserts that in Yüan times writing *ch'ü* was an important part of the state examinations and thus was a natural accomplishment for scholars. Modern scholarship refutes such a theory of dual authorship; although the prose parts are not always as artfully wrought as the verse, and some passages are even crude, scholars such as Wang Kuo-wei have shown that there is an unmistakable continuity between the two forms of writing. He asserts that in a play like *An Heir in Old Age* it is the prose dialogue that gives the play its dramatic interest. Although many of the plays in *A Yüan Edition of Thirty Plays* (*Yüan k'an tsa-chü san-shih chung*) do lack prose dialogue, Wang Kuo-wei argues that these texts were probably intended as a sort of libretto, assisting the audience in understanding the songs. Since the prose parts would have been easily comprehensible, they required no printed texts. Wang further points out that the plays of Chu Ch'üan during the early Ming period include

----

[48] Tsang Mao-hsün believes that the prose dialogues were works of the actors (Preface to *YCH*, p. 3); Wang Chi-te asserts that they were products of the staff members of the Music Academy (Wang Chi-te, p. 148).

both lyrics and dialogue; thus, it is reasonable to assume that their prototypes during the Yüan were of essentially the same format.[49] Yoshikawa, reaching conclusions similar to those of Wang Kuo-wei, refutes the assertion of Tsang Mao-hsün that the state examinations during the Yüan times included writing of *ch'ü* lyrics; he points out that neither the *Yüan Code* (*Yüan tien-chang*) nor the official history mentions anything about composing such lyrics as part of the requirements.[50]

It must be admitted that the passages of prose on the whole are not sophisticated, and often do not equal the literary excellence of the verse. Nevertheless, even a cursory reading of the plays makes clear that the prose passages, in fulfilling various important functions such as character portrayal or development of the action, form a necessary and organic part of the Yüan drama.

Quality of the Prose. In addition to the successful blending of prose and verse asserted by scholars such as Wang Kuo-wei and Yoshikawa, many plays contain prose passages characterized by a lively use of the colloquial language, showing a vigor, simplicity, directness, and expressiveness seldom found in earlier vernacular writings. A comparison of the prose in the Yüan plays with that of the earlier *pien-wen* and Chin "medley," or the later prose of Ming drama, makes apparent the unique achievement of the Yüan dramatic prose.

The *pien-wen* and the "medley" are the embryo from which Yüan prose writing developed. In the *pien-wen*, there is an attempt to use dialogue and direct address as an integral part of the narrative, enhancing the quality of realism and lending dramatic interest, as well as offering relief from the monotony of indirect narrative. In "The Story of Shun in *Pien-wen*" ("Shun-tzu pien-wen"), for instance, Shun's wicked stepmother tries her best to hurt him. When his father returns from a three-year journey and addresses her, asking why she is staying in bed, the woman bursts into tears and says:

[49] Wang Kuo-wei, p. 120.   [50] Yoshikawa, pp. 200-05.

"Since you went away to Liao-yang, leaving me to take care of the household, your child by your previous marriage has behaved in an unfilial way. Seeing that I was picking peaches in the back garden, he placed sharp thorns under the trees. They pricked my feet, causing wounds, the pain of which goes straight to my heart. At the time, I thought of going to the magistrate, but I didn't, on account of our relation as husband and wife. If you don't believe me, look at the pus on the soles of my feet."[51]

Passages such as this have an air of homely realism about them. On the whole, however, the prose passages in the *pien-wen* are quite stiff and crude and tend to be rather heavily burdened with semi-classical constructions. The prose dialogue in the "medley" of the Chin period shows little advance in the art of representing actual speech. Thus the Yüan dramatists had very little in the way of prototypes for the use of the written vernacular.

It is interesting to note that the new prose medium created during the Yüan quickly came under pressure from the classical tradition. The process of classicization that began in the theatrical world of the Yüan reached its height in the Ming period, with the result that in the Southern drama of the Ming, prose speeches are almost entirely in the classical language, except for those spoken by lower-class characters. The prose dialogues and monologues of the Yüan drama, therefore, are by far the most natural and vigorous in all Chinese traditional drama.

Function of the Prose. The prose passages in the Yüan plays fulfill a number of important functions, such as introducing and defining characters, carrying forward the action, and creating the mood or tone. They may also have functioned as a "translation" of the poetic passages, which may not have been understood by the whole audience. Perhaps the most important overall function of the prose, and its success as a medium, lies in its contribution of realism to the

51 Wang Chung-min, vol. I, p. 130; cf. A. Waley, p. 66.

dramatic form, exploiting to good effect the medium's earthy quality and comic potential. Although realistic vernacular prose prevails, semi-classical prose and poetic prose are also used. In discussing these functions, I shall focus on *The Chalk Circle* and *Injustice to Tou O*.

Prose contributes significantly to character portrayal by creating a realistic effect, strengthening the credibiltiy and vividness of the characters. The exchange of invective between Hai-t'ang and her brother in *The Chalk Circle* illustrates such an unmistakably earthy quality. Incensed that his sister is a courtesan, Chang Lin berates her fiercely and accuses their mother of indiscretion:

CHANG LIN: When you let the wretch follow this disgraceful trade, how do you expect me to stand up before people?
MOTHER: What's the use of such idle talk? Since you fear that your sister disgraces you, why don't you earn money to provide for me?
HAI-T'ANG (enters and sees them): Brother, since you want to be a man, why don't you provide for mother?
CHANG LIN: Wretch, following this kind of trade! If you are not afraid of people's sneers, I am. I shall beat you, you depraved creature! (He strikes her.)
MOTHER: Do not beat her, beat me![52]

The above seems to be a mere transcription from the diction of ordinary life and is a notable example of dialogue at its most realistic level.

After the brawl, Hai-t'ang decides to become the concubine of a Mr. Ma who has been good to her. He turns out to be a kindly, generous husband, but his first wife is shrewd, vicious, and jealous. The first wife's monologue following the murder of her husband reveals her extreme cunning, contrasting with the stupidity of her lackluster lover, the court clerk. Reflecting vividly the perversity of this grasping woman, blinded by lust and greed, her words carry the conviction of living speech:

[52] *YCH* 64, Prologue, p. 1107.

MRS. MA: How about it! Hai-t'ang has fallen into my trap. I can see that the entire fortune as well as the child will soon be mine. (She thinks.) Hah, all undertakings need to be thought over three times if one wishes to be spared later regrets. Let me think. This child was not borne by me; in order to prove that she is the real mother, Hai-t'ang is going to call as witnesses the women who received the baby at birth and the woman who gave the first shave to the baby, as well as the neighbors who have watched the child grow. If these witnesses make statements unfavorable to me before the judge, I will lose everything. I have an idea. No one can help craving for white silver when the black pupil of his eye catches its glint. I shall give each of these witnesses a piece of silver and win them over beforehand. They will surely speak in my favor. Moreover, I must also win over the court officials. When the clerk Chao comes, I shall ask for his advice. How very nice!

CHAO (enters): Speaking of Chao, Chao is here![53] I am clerk Chao. It has been several days since I last visited Mrs. Ma. My heart itches for her, and I am unable to get her out of my mind. Now I am already before the door of her house. As there is no master now inside, I have nothing to fear anymore. I shall go straight in. (Sees Mrs. Ma.) Madam, I have almost died from thinking of you.

MRS. MA: Mr. Chao, you are perhaps unaware that I have poisoned Mr. Ma. Now Hai-t'ang and I are going to court to fight for the family fortune and the child. You had better go back to the court to prepare things. Be sure to win over the judge as well as those below him. I have counted on your help in this matter. Afterwards, we can live as man and wife for a long, long time.

CHAO: All this is easy. What I cannot understand is why you even want to keep this child when he is not your own. It would be better to let go of him.

MRS. MA: You are a clerk of the court for nothing. So igno-

---

[53] Here Chao seems to speak directly to the audience: "You people are speaking of me, and here I am."

rant of the situation! If I let Hai-t'ang keep the child, the heirs of the family will fight for the family wealth, and I shall not be able to get any of it. Hai-t'ang can count only on having the midwives and some of the neighbors as witnesses. But I have bought them all with silver. The things outside of the court you need not worry about; you need only take care of things inside the court.

CHAO: What you say is true. Since this is so, come to court early to make your accusations. I will go back to court and arrange everything. (Exit.)[54]

The effectiveness of prose speech in character portrayal is particularly clear if we compare the case of Tou T'ien-chang and "Donkey" Chang, two debtors to Mistress Ts'ai in *Injustice to Tou O*. Tou, a Confucian scholar, is reduced to a difficult situation by poverty:

TOU: I am as poor as if I had been cleaned out; now I have drifted aimlessly to Ch'u-chou to live. Around here is a Mistress Ts'ai, who is quite well off. Lacking traveling money, I once borrowed from her twenty taels of silver. Now I should repay her forty taels including interest. She has asked for the money several times, but with what am I supposed to pay her back? Who would have thought that she would often send people over to say that she wants my daughter to be her daughter-in-law? Since the spring examinations will soon start, I should be going to the capital. However, I have no traveling money. I have no other choice; I just have to send my daughter Tuan-yün to Mistress Ts'ai to be her future daughter-in-law. (He sighs.) How can one say that this is marrying her off to be a daughter-in-law? It is clearly the same as selling the child to her. If Mistress Ts'ai would cancel the forty taels she has lent me, and if I can get a little something extra for my expenses while taking the examination, it would be more than I can hope for.[55]

[54] *YCH* 64, Act I, concluding scene, p. 1115.
[55] *YCH* 86, Prologue, p. 1499.

Caught between his obligations as a scholar and as a father, he is visibly distressed, and his few parting words to the daughter and to the old woman give a moving portrayal of him as a loving parent and a man with dignity, humility, and warmth:

TS'AI: Now you are my in-law. As to the forty taels you owe me, including the interest, here is your promissory note, which I am returning to you. In addition, I am presenting you with ten taels of silver for your traveling expenses. In-law, I hope that you do not find this too little.

(Tou T'ien-chang thanks her.)

TOU: Many thanks, Madam. Not only have you cancelled the amount I owe you, but you have also presented me with traveling money. Someday I shall greatly repay you for your kindness. Madam, if my little girl acts foolishly, please look after her for my sake.

TS'AI: In-law, you need not worry. Now that your worthy beloved daughter has come to my family, I shall look after her just as though she were my own daughter. You may leave with your mind at ease.

TOU: Madam, when Tuan-yün deserves a beating, please, for my sake, only scold her. When she deserves to be scolded, please just speak to her. My child, now it won't be like staying with me any more. I, as your father, can be tolerant of you. Now if you are naughty here, you will be asking for a scolding and a beating. My child, I do what I do because there is no other way.[56]

Dr. Lu, on the other hand, presents a totally different picture.

LU: My name is Lu. People say that I am good at doctoring, and call me "Sai Lu-yi."[57] I keep an apothecary shop at the South Gate of Shan-yang District. In town there is a Mistress Ts'ai from whom I borrowed ten taels of silver. With interest I now owe her twenty taels. She has come several times for

56 *Ibid.*, Prologue, pp. 1499-1500.
57 For the meaning of "Sai Lu-yi," see Shih, p. 59, n. 105.

the money, but I have none to repay her. If she doesn't come again, then there's an end to it. If she comes, I have a scheme. Now I'll just sit down in the apothecary shop here and see who will come.[58]

Even as he is talking of Mistress Ts'ai, the old woman appears and calls through the door.

LU: Come in, lady.

TS'AI: You have kept my few pieces of silver for a long time. How about paying them back to me?

LU: Madam, I have no money at home. Come with me to the village,[59] and I shall get the money for you.

TS'AI: I shall go with you.

(They start walking.)

LU: Well, here we are—nobody to the east, nobody to the west. If I don't do her in here, what am I waiting for? I have some rope with me. Hey, Mistress, who is calling you?

TS'AI: Where?[60]

As the unwitting old woman turns to look for the person who is calling her, he tries to catch her unawares and strangle her. His villainy comes through vividly in these prose speeches.

In addition to illuminating character, realistic prose is especially effective in advancing action, often at a brisk pace. Caught in the murder attempt by two men who suddenly appear on the scene, Dr. Lu quickly makes his retreat. The two men, "Donkey" Chang and his father, succeed in reviving the old woman, whose story immediately interests them.

"DONKEY": Father, did you hear what she said? She has a daughter-in-law at home. We have saved her life; she will have to reward us. The best thing would be for you to take this old woman, and I'll take her daughter-in-law. What a convenient deal for both sides! Go and talk to her.

[58] *YCH* 86, Act I, p. 1500.

[59] The term *chuang-shang* ("village") may also mean *ch'ien-chuang* ("a money exchange shop").

[60] *YCH* 86, Act I, p. 1500.

OLD CHANG: Hey, old woman, you have no husband and I have no wife; how about you being my wife? How does that strike you?

TS'AI: What talk is this? Wait till I get home; I shall get some money to reward you.

"DONKEY": You must be unwilling and want to bamboozle me with money. Doctor Lu's rope is still here; perhaps I had better strangle you after all. (Takes up rope.)

TS'AI: Brother, how about waiting till I think it over slowly?

"DONKEY": Think what over? You go with my old man, and I'll take your daughter-in-law.

TS'AI (aside): If I don't go along with him, he will strangle me. All right, all right, all right, you two, father and son, come home with me.[61]

Thus begins the incident that sets in motion the central story of the play. The success of telling these and other incidents clearly and interestingly is due largely to the straightforward, fast-moving narrative prose.

Because of its freer syntax, prose is also a better means for conveying comic mood or tone than verse. Yüan drama abounds in prose passages of both high and low comedy. Although comic scenes also appear in verse, most of them are in prose. Humorous interludes in prose occur in various kinds of situations, even in serious plays. In *Injustice to Tou O*, for instance, Dr. Lu's attempt to strangle Mistress Ts'ai—leading her to the deserted countryside, observing clownishly, "nobody to the east, nobody to the west,"[62] and then trying to catch her unawares—is a combination of humorous and villainous behavior, typical of the *ching* role. Clerk Chao in *The Chalk Circle,* also a *ching*, epitomizes this combination of humor and villainy. In the final scene, when the judge asks Chao about his relations with Mrs. Ma, he replies: "My Lord, do you not see that the woman's face is completely covered with powder? If this powder were washed off, all that would be left would be a face that no man would even bother

[61] *Ibid.*, p. 1501.   [62] *Ibid.*, p. 1500.

with if found in the street. How could I have been willing to have an affair with her?" To this, Mrs. Ma retorts: "When we were alone you often assured me that I was as beautiful as the Goddess of Mercy, and now you talk of me as if I were nothing. You false-hearted man!"[63] The very idea of comparing herself to the Goddess of Mercy is ludicrous and comical.

In the Yüan plays, the *ching*, the painted female role (*ch'a-tan*), and the *ch'ou*, are all comic roles, and they lend comedy to all the scenes in which they appear. Coarse humor, slapstick comedy, extravagant fantasies, and villainy are their trademarks. Although their speeches are occasionally interposed with short rhyming lines or doggerel verse, these comic characters speak primarily in prose, since singing in Yüan drama is conventionally limited to the leading male or female role.

The play on words, which occurs frequently in the Yüan plays, reveals a special linguistic consciousness. Possibilities for word play are very extensive in a language so rich in homophones as Chinese, and the dramatists exploited them to good effect. Extended word plays are carried through in both prose and poetry, in serious as well as comic situations, but the characteristic medium for word play is prose, and the predominant mode is comic.

The dramatists use puns to give a lively humor to the plays. In *The Winding-River Pond*, when courtesan Li asks her sworn sister why she keeps company with a rustic fellow, the girl replies: "My older sister, I am like a blind fellow jumping across a stream; I only 'look at what's ahead' (*k'an ch'ien mien*),"[64] by which she means "for the sake of money" (*k'an ch'ien mien*), as these two phrases are homophonous. Later when courtesan Li's lover has squandered all his money and

---

[63] *YCH* 64, Act IV, p. 1128.

[64] *YCH* 16, Act I, speech following song "Hun-chiang lung," p. 264. For this and other examples, see Wang Chi-ssu, "Yüan chü chung hsieh-yin shuang-kuan-yü ("Puns in Yüan Drama"), in *Kuo-wen yüeh-k'an*, no. 67 (May 1948), pp. 15-19.

is forced to make a living by singing at funerals, the procuress wants her to give him up. She takes the courtesan to see the young man in his destitute situation, singing at a funeral. Pointing at him, the old woman says, "Look at him leaning on that coffin (*k'ao ting kuan-han*)." The courtesan replies, "He is from a family 'of official position and influence' (*i kuan hsia shih*)."[65] Here the courtesan turns the old woman's sneer into a less derogatory remark by playing on the sound *kuan*, which means both "coffin" and "official position." When the young man's father discovers his wretched state and tries to beat him to death, he calls him a "disgraceful son" (*ju tzu*); thereupon the servant remarks: "He does not now even have a mat, why speak of a mattress (*ju-tzu*)."[66] When the son seems dead, the father calls out his name, "Yüan-ho!" Thereupon, the servant feels the young man's nose and says, "Alas, he is dead! How could you say *yüan huo*?" The term *yüan huo*, meaning "alive," is a pun on the young man's name.[67]

Plays on words that sound alike but have different meanings are sometimes purposely adopted as a veiled means of communication, and their intent can be serious. An interesting instance of this use is found in *The Chao Family Orphan*. In the beginning of the story, the loyal retainer Ch'eng Ying, who has hidden the baby in a medicine box, is being searched by the guard, who says: "You told me you have only orange branches, licorice roots, and mint leaves; I have found, however, ginseng."[68] Ginseng in Chinese is *jen-shen*, which is homophonous with a phrase meaning "human body"; so the guard is saying that he has found a baby. Since the guard is moved by the loyalty of this retainer and decides to sacrifice his own life to protect him and the baby, he simply wants the retainer to know that he knows what is in the medicine box, but conceals his knowledge from others by punning on the word *jen-shen*.

---

[65] *Ibid.*, Act II, interpolated in "Mu yang kuan," p. 268.
[66] *Ibid.*, following "Mu yang kuan," p. 269.
[67] *Ibid.*, p. 269.
[68] *YCH* 85, Act I, following "Hou t'ing hua," p. 1480.

To play upon the various meanings of a word represents an intellectual exercise, and a personal application sometimes has its special appeal. In the play *The Dream of Su Tung-p'o*, Su Shih (styled Tung-p'o) recalls a pun referring to the well-known personal feud between him and Prime Minister Wang An-shih. One day when the Emperor was in the Imperial garden, he came upon a piece of broken stone by Lake T'ai. (Since there was a Lake T'ai in Soochow, the stones of Lake T'ai were also called "Soochow stone.") The Prime Minister remarked to the Emperor, "This is what one means when he says that 'Soochow stone' (Su *shih*) is not strong," punning on the scholar's name. Another official then told the Emperor: "This is not a case of the 'Soochow stone' not being strong; this is 'An-shih' (firm stone) not being firm," making a pun on the Prime Minister's name. This rejoinder greatly delighted the Emperor.[69]

In the same play, when Su Shih asks his abbot friend a question about the Buddhist religion, the abbot says: "Breaking an earthen pot, the crack goes to the bottom (*Ta p'o sha kuo, wen tao ti*),"[70] meaning, "You indeed inquire about things to the bottom [of the matter]." Here the fifth character is a pun, as *wen* (crack) is a homonym of *wen* (to inquire). "To inquire to the bottom" (*wen tao ti*) sounds like "a crack [from top] to bottom"; therefore the abbot's words can be applied to one who questions to the limit or is too inquisitive. This saying is still current today in the Northern dialects, but the origin of the pun probably is lost to many, as the word *wen* (crack) is seldom used now in the spoken language.

Punning is a popular stock-in-trade in the theatre. In the West, puns have enjoyed an uneven fate. Praised by Aristotle, practiced by the great Greek dramatists, beloved by Renaissance preachers in their sermons, and considered as rhetorical ornaments by the Elizabethans, they have often been regarded as trivial wit since the eighteenth century. Puns, in

[69] *YCH* 71, Act I, opening scene, p. 1234.
[70] *Ibid.*, Act IV, following song "Hsin shui ling," p. 1247.

Chinese *shuang-kuan-yü*, existed in ancient writings and were
sometimes employed as an effective instrument of indirect
persuasion. Many T'ang and Sung theatrical sketches are
based on puns.[71] Punning is a marvelous tool of clowning,
often based on the corruption of words or turning sentences
inside out, and quips or quibbles produce excellent comical
effects. Punning, involving a keen sensitivity to semantic distinctions, is an imaginative use of language, particularly in enhancing humor. This use is well demonstrated in Yüan dramatic prose.

In addition to punning, the dramatists, like the writers of
other vernacular genres, resort to earthy language when it
heightens the comic potential of a scene or when it is appropriate to a character's status. In *A Pilgrimage to the West*, for
instance, there is plenty of vulgar language used to create
coarse humor, even though the motivating force of the play is
Tripitaka's holy mission to India to secure sacred scriptures.
After leaving the Kingdom of Women, Tripitaka congratulates
himself on his narrow escape from disaster. He then asks his
disciples, "How did you three escape?" Monkey (a *ching*
role) replies:

"Master, listen to me tell my story. I was pinned down by a
wench, and my desires were about to be aroused. Unexpected-
ly, the gold ring on my head began to tighten. My whole body
ached, and the ache reminded me of several kinds of vegeta-
bles. My head ached so that my hair stood up like chives, my
face was green like smartweeds, my perspiration was like
pickled eggplants, my penis was soft like a salted cucumber
. . . and so she set me free."[72]

Language representing the speech of the lower classes is
also used effectively to heighten the credibility of characters
and events and the quality of realism in the plays. In *The*

[71] See examples cited in Wang Kuo-wei, pp. 17-33.
[72] *WP* 140e, Act I (or *WP* 140, Act 17), following "Wei," p. 679.

Chalk Circle, when the midwife, Dame Liu, is summoned to court to identify the true mother, she says: "Let me think. That day the room of the woman in labor was closed tight and dark; I could not see her face, but when I felt with my hand, I could tell the cunt was Mrs. Ma's."[73] Dame Chang, another witness who has been bribed by Mrs. Ma, also speaks in her favor: "That day when I was asked to shave the baby's head, it was certainly the first wife who was holding him. I saw her two white feedbag-shaped breasts. Only one who has borne a son can have feeding breasts like that. The baby is indeed Mrs. Ma's."[74] S. Julien, in translating the play, expurgated the latter part of the two women's speeches, noting that "it has been necessary in the interests of decency to suppress certain details."[75]

In reproducing everyday speech, particularly of lower-class folk, the dramatists employ a natural diction, with plenty of striking illustrations and current metaphors of familiar speech. Used to especially good effect are proverbs, which abound in Chinese tradition. They appear frequently in Yüan drama and carry great conviction, expressing what generations have regarded as true and lending an aura of folk wisdom. Proverbs are generally introduced by such phrases as "isn't it said" (*k'o pu tao*), "it is true that" (*cheng shih*), "the proverb says" (*ch'ang yen tao*), or "indeed it is said" (*kuo yen tao*). In *The Chalk Circle*, a neighbor who has received Mrs. Ma's bribe tries to justify his attempt to defend her by arguing, "The proverb says: If you take one's money, you are to ward off his trouble."[76] Proverbs are often used as potent arguments. In *Injustice to Tou O*, the heroine, resisting the pressure exerted by both her mother-in-law and "Donkey" Chang to marry,

[73] *YCH* 64, Act II, following "Yao p'ien," p. 1119.

[74] *Ibid.*

[75] Cited in Frances Hume, *The Story of the Circle of Chalk*, p. 74. Hume makes the same omission in her English translation of the play, based on Julien's French version.

[76] *YCH* 64, Act II, following "Ts'u hu-lu," p. 1118.

quotes the proverb: "A good horse should not have two saddles; a chaste woman will not serve two husbands."[77] She would rather die than marry again. Her words serve to clothe her personal conviction and argument in the universally intelligible language of a proverb.

In the study of the realistic quality of the prose of Yüan drama, the question of the Mongolian language is one of interest. Many of the officials in the plays are Mongolians, the conquerors of the land, but their speeches include very few Mongolian words. It is clear that the dramatists sometimes pay great attention to the subtle distinctions in speech differentiating the speaker's social class, but they do not exploit individual or regional peculiarities of speech. The occasional use of the Mongolian language is more for novelty than for depicting characters or creating atmosphere. The most prominent instance is in the beginning of *Weeping for Ts'un-hsiao* (*K'u Ts'un-hsiao*) by Kuan Han-ch'ing. When general Li K'o-yung's no-good son, Li Ts'un-hsin, first appears, he brags about his decadent way of life, using many Mongolian words (the meanings of which are given below in parentheses):

I eat *mi-han* (meat) by the catty,
But *mo-lin* (horses) I cannot ride;
As to *nu-men* (bows) and *su-men* (arrows), how does
    one use them?
Wherever I see *sa-yin* (good) *ta-la-sun* (wine), I gulp it
    down;
Once *sa-t'a-pa* (drunk), I fall asleep.
As to our names, I cannot remember;
We are a pair of *hu-la-hai* (thieves)—sons of bitches.[78]

Here the use is clearly playful and for comic effect. The inclusion of such expressions as *ha-la* (to kill) in the Tatar chieftain's speech in *Autumn in the Han Palace*,[79] and *ha-sa-erh*

---

[77] *YCH* 86, Act IV, following "Ch'iao p'ai-erh," p. 1514.
[78] *WP* 104, Act I, opening speech, p. 42.
[79] *YCH* 1, Act III, closing speech, p. 11.

(a kind of dog) in the Mongolian official's parlance in *Yellow-flower Valley*[80] may lend a touch of realism, but their effect is negligible.[81]

Although realistic and vernacular prose prevails in the Yüan plays, semi-classical prose or poetic prose is also used. Semi-classical prose is usually spoken by dignified persons, such as high government officials, to indicate their lofty position and education, although in some plays semi-classical prose is used by lesser characters indiscriminately.[82] In *The Chalk Circle*, the renowned judge Pao Cheng expresses himself in semi-classical prose that is more clearly elevated in style than the speech of any other character in the play, a style that suits his background and position. His speech is dignified, and the arrangement of words, pauses, and cadences has a measured rhythm that contrasts with the prose speeches of other characters, especially in his self-introduction in the beginning of Act IV; again at the end, where he sentences the criminals, his semi-classical prose heightens the solemnity of the scene and adds impact to the punishments that are meted out.[83] The use of this kind of semi-classical prose is illustrative of the dramatist's awareness that characters of different social origins speak in styles compatible with their stations in life.

Prose raised to the pitch of poetry is a mode of expression not uncommon in Yüan drama. In *The Chalk Circle*, the most obvious illustration of this kind of prose is to be found in the speech of Hai-t'ang, on the way to the capital K'ai-feng for

[80] *WP* 156, speech following "Tsui fu kuei," p. 937.

[81] For miscellaneous notes on the use of the Mongolian language in Yüan drama, see Tai Wang-shu, "T'an Yüan ch'ü te Meng-ku fang-yen" ("Notes on Mongolian Dialects in Yüan drama"), *Hsiao-shuo hsi-ch'ü lun-chi* (1958), pp. 87-90; and Ho Ch'ang-ch'ün, "Yüan ch'ü te yüan-yüan chi ch'i yü Meng-ku yü te kuan-hsi" ("The Sources of Yüan Drama and the Latter's Relation to the Mongolian Language"), in *Yüan-ch'ü kai-lun* (1930), pp. 73-92.

[82] *E.g.*, the maid Hung-niang in *The Romance of the Western Chamber*.

[83] *YCH* 64, Act IV, p. 1129.

the death sentence. Weighed down by a cangue,[84] escorted by a prison guard, and trudging in the snow, she moans:

"When shall I be cleared of the crimes that have been attributed to me? To whom may I speak of the grievances of my heart? Having robbed me of my child, she falsely accused me of poisoning my husband. I could hardly endure the torture of being suspended, beaten, bound, and stretched, and I am unable to meet with a righteous and incorrupt judge."[85]

Impatient over her complaint, the guard chides her for her words. Hai-t'ang, despairing over the hopeless situation, asks:

"Where is the man who would uphold justice and take pity on me? Soaking wet, my wounds inflicted by the rod are killing me with pain. With a thousand groans and ten thousand cries I fill the air. Where could I, starved and faint, beg for a meal? Thin and inadequate, my garments are in rags. Heavy and clumsy, my iron lock and brass cangue are crushing me. A weak and helpless woman, whom, alas, no cruel guards can understand. Brother, I am truly wronged and suffer injustice."[86]

This piece of prose is excellent in every respect: the arrangement of the words, the cadence, and the sentiment. A translation obviously cannot do justice to the richness of the language; it can merely suggest the quality. It is poetical, impassioned prose. Of such prose the Yüan dramatists have left us many specimens, even though they usually expressed themselves in verse whenever the subject required a more elevated style.

Yüan dramatic prose is a phenomenon almost as remarkable as its verse. Many of the conventions of *tsa-chü* combine to create a highly stylized form. The colloquial prose, on the other hand, with its simplicity and naturalness of diction, suc-

---

[84] "Cangue" is a frame used to confine the neck and hands: an old Chinese punishment (see Shih, p. 181, n. 692).

[85] *YCH* 64, Act III, opening scene, p. 1121.

[86] *Ibid.*, p. 1121.

ceeds in attaining considerable realism in depicting human passions and manners, and in telling a story. The Yüan dramatists contributed considerably to the emergence of vernacular prose by inventing new written forms for many colloquial expressions and by making new adaptations. They made the colloquial prose plastic, taught it to assume with propriety every tone, be it realistic, comic, or poetic. They showed its capacity for exposition, for portrayal of characters, and for narrative.

The influence of Yüan dramatic prose extended beyond the theatre; it offered a valuable vocabulary for the emerging prose narrative fiction. Although there were many dialects in North China, a fairly standard spoken language had developed by the early fourteenth century. The evidence for this is provided by the Yüan scholar Chou Te-ch'ing, who advises poets to use the correct language, that is, the language popularized by the master dramatists.[87] Thus, Yüan dramatic prose contributed significantly to the success of the genre, to the development of the written vernacular, and to the popularization and growth of the Northern dialect around Ta-tu as a standard spoken language.

[87] Chou Te-ch'ing, p. 175.

VI

Music

CHINESE traditional theatre is inextricably associated with music. In Yüan drama, songs appear in every scene. To achieve a workable artistic unity of poetry, narrative, stagecraft, and acrobatics requires a framework allowing each element adequate scope, so that the aesthetic effect of each can be appreciated. In a Yüan play, music seems to be a significant part of such a framework.

Since there are no surviving musical scores from the Yüan period, studying the nature of the music employed and its value as a dramatic element becomes an extremely difficult problem. However, some information can still be gleaned from a careful evaluation of available evidence, such as the names of musical modes used in the plays, the titles of tunes composed in these modes, and the surviving printed texts of the lyrics. Stage directions and dialogue also suggest some of the habits and conventions governing the use of vocal and instrumental music. Even brief notations that indicate which character sings are informative because they testify to the unique practice of limiting the singing to one actor or actress in a single play.

In addition to the internal evidence in the plays themselves, several Yüan works, including (Yen-nan) Chih An's *Discourse on Singing* (*Ch'ang lun*), Chou Te-ch'ing's *Sound and Rhymes of the Central Plains*, and T'ao Tsung-i's *Jottings During Intervals of Farming* (*Ch'o keng lu*), as well as a number of Ming accounts and treatises, such as Chu Ch'üan's *The Sounds of Universal Harmony* and Hsü Wei's *Notes on Southern Songs* (*Nan tz'u hsü-lu*), also serve as sources of information.[1] Some musical notation, possibly

---

[1] These works by (Yen-nan) Chih An, Chou Te-ch'ing, Chu Ch'üan,

dating from the Yüan period, is found in a number of Ch'ing dynasty collections of musical scores, the best known of which is *Scores of Northern and Southern Songs in the Nine Musical Modes* (*Chiu kung ta-ch'eng nan pei tz'u kung-p'u*), published in 1746.[2] It contains excerpts of about one hundred plays labeled as from the Yüan period, and these texts have a musical notation written alongside the lyrics. In these libretti there is also information on aria titles and prosody. Their authenticity as genuine Yüan works, however, has not been established.

The Musical Modes (Kung-tiao)[3] *in Yüan Plays*

As a basis for investigating the musical activity in Yüan drama, some understanding is needed of the basic technical conventions that govern musical performance in the plays. In Yüan drama the songs in each act belong to a single mode or key. The musical modes used in extant Yüan plays are known by their traditional popular names, as follows: *Cheng*

---

and Hsü Wei, together with writings by the following authors on music in traditional Chinese drama, are collected in the *Chung-kuo ku-tien hsi-ch'ü lun-chu chi-ch'eng* (*CKKT*): Ts'ui Ling-ch'in, Tuan An-chieh, Hsia Po-ho, Ho Liang-chün, Wang Shih-chen, Wang Chi-te, Shen Te-fu, and Hsü Fu-tso. For titles and dates, see the individual entries in the bibliography.

Discussions in English on the nature of the music in Yüan drama are found in E. Bruce Brooks, "Chinese Aria Studies" (Seattle: University of Washington, 1968), a doctoral dissertation; and Dale Johnson, "The Prosody of Yüan-*ch'ü*" (Ann Arbor: University of Michigan, 1968), a doctoral dissertation.

[2] Compiled by Chou Hsiang-yü *et al.* It is the largest repository of what purports to be Sung *tz'u*, *chu-kung-tiao*, *san-ch'ü*, and *tsa-chü* music. For other collections, see pp. 196-97 below.

[3] *Kung-tiao* may not correspond exactly to the Western concept of "mode" or "key"; for more information on the subject see Rulan Pian, "The Basic Definition of a Mode," *Sonq Dynasty Musical Sources and Their Interpretation* (1967), pp. 43ff., and James Liu's note on "The meanings of *kung-tiao*," in *The Chinese Knight-Errant*, pp. 213-14.

kung, Chung-lü, Hsien-lü, Huang-chung, Nan-lü, Shang tiao, Shuang tiao, Ta-shih tiao, Yüeh tiao.

A tenth mode, *Pan-she tiao,* which was used a great deal in the "medley," is almost extinct in Yüan drama, appearing only three times.[4] In his *Jottings During Intervals of Farming,* T'ao Tsung-i limits his tally of musical modes used in Yüan plays to the nine listed above. Chou Te-ch'ing, another contemporary author, adds in his list *Pan-she tiao* and two other modes: *Hsiao-shih tiao* and *Shang-chüeh tiao.*[5] These musical modes, known as *kung-tiao,* are defined by the pitch on which the basic scale is constructed, and by the choice of the cadencing note, as discussed below.

The Scale and Pitch-keys. Ancient Chinese music can be considered both pentatonic and heptatonic. The five notes of the pentatonic scale are known by their ancient names— *kung, shang, chüeh, chih,* and *yü.* The heptatonic scale has two additional notes known as *pien-kung* ("modified kung") and *pien-chih* ("modified chih"), each being a half-tone lower than the note from which it derives its name. The heptatonic scale thus consists of the following notes: *kung, shang, chüeh, pien-chih, chih, yü,* and *pien-kung.* The two scales are as follows:

kung   shang   chüeh   chih   yü

[4] In the extant plays no single entire act is written in the *Pan-she tiao.* Each time this mode is used, it is only in one song in an act where the rest of the songs are in the *Chung-lü* mode, and each time in a song to the tune "Shua hai-erh." The plays in which this occurs are: *Hsi yu chi* (*WP* 140a, Act II, p. 638; *WP* 140d, Act II, p. 670); and *Fu Chin-ting* (*WP* 160, Act III, p. 993).

[5] Chou Te-ch'ing, pp. 225 and 229-30.

kung   shang   chüeh   pien-chih   chih   yü   pien-kung

The absolute pitch-keys, known in Chinese as *lü-lü*, are standardized by bamboo pipes, according to traditional theory.[6] The sound produced in a bamboo pitch pipe of nine "inches" (*ts'un*) was called *Huang-chung* ("Yellow bell"), and was taken as the basic note. The higher notes were obtained by sounding on shorter lengths of bamboo. The Chinese thus evolved the note-series through a set of bamboo tubes differing in length. The second tube, which measured two-thirds the length of the first tube, rendered a note a perfect fifth higher (*e.g.*, $C \rightarrow G$). From G the next note thus rendered would be the D beyond the first octave; the producing tube was doubled in length to obtain the D that is within the octave. Repeating the process eventually gave all 12 semi-tones of an octave. These notes, with their traditional names and corresponding Western notes, are as follows: *Huang-chung*, E; *Ta-lü*, F; *T'ai-ts'ou*, F#; *Chia-chung*, G; *Ku-hsien*, G#; *Chung-lü*, A; *Jui-pin*, A#; *Lin-chung*, B; *I-tse*, C; *Nan-lü*, C#; *Wu-i*, D; *Ying-chung*, D#.[7]

The System of Twenty-eight Popular Musical Modes. A seven-note scale can be constructed on any one of the twelve pitches within the octave. On *C*, the following scale can be produced: *C, D, E, F#, G, A, B*; or on *D*: *D, E, F#, G#, A, B, C#*; etc. Each note in the seven-note scale theoretically can be used as the cadencing note of a melody. Since there are seven modes in each basic scale and twelve absolute pitches, eighty-four modes (or keys) are theoreti-

[6] *Lü shih ch'un-ch'iu*, compiled under the patronage of Lü Pu-wei (ca. 239 B.C.), contains one of the earliest accounts of the making of pitch pipes (see *SPTK so-pen* edition, *chüan* 5, pp. 32-33).

[7] Ch'en Wan-nai, *Yüan Ming Ch'ing chü-ch'ü shih* (1966), pp. 112-13; Pian identifies *Huang-chung* as C (Pian, p. 92).

cally possible.[8] A musical mode is labeled jointly by the name
of the pitch-key on which this basic scale is constructed, and
by the cadencing note, *e.g., Huang-chung kung, Huang-
chung shang.* In addition to such theoretical names, these
musical modes also were referred to by a separate set of
popular names.[9]

By the later T'ang period, a system of Twenty-eight Popular Modes had been organized; except for some details, this
series is not structurally different from the Eighty-four
Modes.[10] In the course of time, some of these 28 modes
ceased to be used. In the Yüan plays, as has been pointed out,
only ten modes appear in the extant plays, though Chou
Te-ch'ing mentions the use of twelve.

Musical Notation in the Yüan Plays. A system of notation
used as early as the Sung times was popular in the Yüan
dynasty under the Mongols. It consists of the characters *ho,
ssu, i, shang, kou, ch'e, kung, fan, liu, wu;* and they correspond to the staff notation as follows:

Like Chinese writing, these characters are printed from the
top to the bottom of the page, from right to left, and between the song text. Dots and small squares are sometimes

---

[8] Pian, p. 43; Chang Yen (1248 to ca. 1315), *Tz'u yüan* in *Tz'u
hsüeh ts'ung-shu,* ed. by Ch'in En-fu, 1810, pp. 6b-11a.

[9] *Ta-shih tiao* or *Hsiao-shih tiao* and *Pan-she tiao,* for instance, are
adaptations of the Sanskrit names *Kaiśika* and *Pañcama* (K. Hayashi,
Sui T'ang yen yüeh tiao yen-chiu, Chinese translation by Kuo Mo-jo,
pp. 44-46). In most cases, however, the derivation of the names can
no longer be ascertained. Some names, such as *Huang-chung kung,*
appear to be of classical origin, but no longer necessarily correspond
to their original technical meanings (Pian, p. 50).

[10] Pian, p. 45.

added to indicate the basic beat. The song from *Injustice to Tou O* (see Figure 8), appears on a book of musical scores compiled in the Ch'ing period.

Songs and Song-Sequences

The individual songs sung on the stage are generally the same in form as the non-dramatic songs (*san-ch'ü*) and bear the same tune titles. A single tune, once adopted, is used for a number of lyrics in a play. At present, the songs in print are considered primarily as lyric poetry, but it must be kept in mind that they were originally songs drawn from and performed in a lively and popular musical milieu. The playwrights adopted melodies from various popular sources; they usually did not compose original music. Contemporary accounts provide names of 335 tunes current in the Yüan period.[11] In the extant plays, about 270 different tunes in ten musical modes are used:[12] *Shuang tiao*, 66; *Chung-lü*, 39; *Cheng kung*, 35; *Hsien-lü*, 31; *Yüeh tiao*, 25; *Nan-lü*, 23; *Shang tiao*, 21; *Ta-shih tiao*, 15; *Huang-chung*, 12; *Pan-she tiao*, 1.

Popular songs that were not part of plays existed either individually or in sequence. Songs on stage, however, except for the prologue, always came in sequences known as *lien-t'ao*. Songs in the extant plays indicate that certain standards governed the ordering of individual songs in a song-sequence as well as the ordering of the song-sequences in an act. By the time Yüan drama had reached its height, song-sequence patterns must have been conventionalized. Ts'ai Ying's *Song-Sequences in Yüan Drama* (*Yüan chü lien-t'ao shu-li*), writ-

---

[11] Chou Te-ch'ing, pp. 224-30; Chu Ch'üan's list is the same as Chou Te-ch'ing's, pp. 54-62; T'ao Tsung-i lists only 230 tune titles (*chüan* 27, pp. 4-7).

[12] For information on the tunes found in the extant plays and the frequency of their appearance, see Dale Johnson, "The Prosody of Yüan-*ch'ü*," Vol. II.

ten in 1933, represents the first serious study of the subject. Working with 119 plays,[13] the total number of plays known to him at that time, he detects a limited number of combinations of tunes in a certain order, and patterns that repeat themselves throughout the plays. Tabulating all the tune titles in each act as a unit and arranging these units under the headings of the nine musical modes, Ts'ai Ying makes clear that each unit consists of a number of song-sequences rather than a number of single songs. He notes further that the shortest act in a Yüan play consists of three songs, while the longest act consists of as many as twenty-six songs.[14]

Extending his study to include the plays discovered since Ts'ai Ying's time and confining it to one musical mode, Hugh Stimson makes a far more thorough analysis of the song-sequence patterns.[15] The *Hsien-lü* mode, which he examines, is the most frequently used mode of all, appearing in 170 out of the 171 extant plays; except for two plays in which it is in the second act, it always appears in the first act. From the tabulations, patterns of five song-sequences become clear. With one exception, the *Hsien-lü* act always begins with the following sequence of four tunes, arranged in a fixed order (*a b c d*) with only slight variations: (*a*) "Tien chiang ch'un," (*b*) "Hun-chiang lung," (*c*) "Yu hu-lu," (*d*) "T'ien-hsia le."

A second sequence, occurring in about half the *Hsien-lü* acts (87 times), consists of the three following tunes in a fixed order, with the last tune sometimes repeated (*e f g* or *e f g g*): (*e*) "Na-cha ling," (*f*) "Ch'üeh t'a chih," (*g*) "Chi-sheng ts'ao."

The third sequence, which appears about thirty times, consists of two arrangements: it contains five tunes in a fixed

[13] He counted *Hsi hsiang chi* and *Hsi yu chi* each as one play.

[14] Act II of *Chui Han Hsin* has 3 songs (Ts'ai Ying, p. 20a); and Act II of *Mo-ho-lo* has 26 songs (*ibid.*, p. 31b).

[15] Hugh Stimson, "Song Arrangements in Shianleu Acts of Yuan Tzarjiuh," *Tsing Hua Journal of Chinese Studies*, New Series, V, no. 1 (July 1965), pp. 86-106.

order, of which the fourth may be left out and the last re-
peated (*h i j k l*, or *h i j l l*): (*h*) "Ts'un-li ya-ku," (*i*)
"Yüan-ho ling," (*j*) "Shang ma chiao," (*k*) "Yu ssu men," (*l*)
"Sheng hu-lu."

The fourth sequence, which occurs about twenty times,
consists of simply two lyrics to the same tune (*m m*): (*m*)
"Liu-yao ling."

Following the fourth sequence appear a number of independent tunes, sometimes in no particular order and sometimes in a kind of cyclical arrangement.

The fifth sequence consists of three tunes (*n o p*): (*n*)
"Hou t'ing hua," (*o*) "Ch'ing-ko-erh," (*p*) "Liu yeh-erh."
Sometimes, however, only one or two of these tunes appear.
The last unit, a coda ("Sha-wei"),[16] appears in almost all the
Hsien-lü acts.

The patterns of the recurring song-sequences illustrate the
structural consistency and complexity of Yüan drama. While
the dramatist had considerable freedom in positioning song-
sequences within the acts and interspersing them with independent songs, he was limited by the requirements of convention. The overwhelming majority of the plays have one
or two standard melodies in the prologue, and an opening
song-sequence consisting of four tunes in the first act. The
prologue songs are usually set to one of two tunes, "Shang-
hua shih" and "Tuan-cheng hao"; and in Act I, of the four
tunes that make up the first sequence, only the tune "Tien
chiang ch'un" has an alternative: "Pa sheng Kan-chou."
These opening songs must not only observe the complicated
and rather closely defined meter of the tunes, and the rhyme
uniformity of the genre; they must also provide significant
background information, establish the mood, and introduce
major characters. Although the formal device of the song-
sequence may have been a restriction on the dramatist, the
very conventionality of the music may also have helped by
providing him with ready melodies for diverse situations.

[16] Other titles of the codas are "Chuan-sha," "Chuan-sha wei,"
"Wei-sheng," or simply "Wei."

The origin of the song-sequence patterns may be traced to earlier forms, such as the *ch'an-ta* of the Sung[17] and especially the "medley" of the Chin period, the influence of the latter being particularly clear. The combination of songs and a coda is a predominant structure in the *Liu Chih-yüan Medley* (*Liu Chih-yüan chu-kung-tiao*) and *The Western Chamber Medley*; in these, some sequences consist of as few as one song and a coda, and some of as many as fifteen songs and a coda.[18] The song-sequence patterns in *A Medley on Events in the T'ien-pao Era* (*T'ien-pao i shih chu-kung-tiao*) composed by Wang Po-ch'eng in the Yüan period are especially similar to the patterns in the Yüan drama.[19] In general, however, the song-sequences in Yüan drama have greater variety and complexity than the earlier genre.

That musically there is a close and organic relationship between the songs in a sequence is emphasized by Hsü Wei, a Ming musician whose comments on Southern drama throw some light on the conventions of song-sequences in general:

"It is true that Southern drama does not confine the

[17] Wang Kuo-wei, p. 86.

[18] See Feng Yüan-chün, pp. 254-55. The use of the coda is a distinctive convention in Northern drama seldom found in Southern plays.

[19] The similarity in the song-sequence patterns in the two genres is illustrated by this medley's song-suite entitled "Shih mei jen shang yüeh" in the *Hsien-lü* mode containing sixteen songs (in *Yung-hsi yüeh-fu* [*SPTK so-pen*], *chüan* 4, pp. 75a-77a). Its first sequence of four tunes ("Tien chiang ch'un," "Hun-chiang lung," "Yu hu-lu," "T'ien-hsia le") is the same as the standard first sequence in the *Hsien-lü* act in Yüan drama. In fact, the first nine tunes, including these four and tunes Nos. 5 to 9 ("Na-cha ling," "Ch'üeh t'a chih," "Chi-sheng ts'ao," "Liu-yao hsü," and "Yao p'ien") occur in the same order in the Yüan plays *K'an ch'ien nu* (*YCH* 91, Act I, pp. 1586-88) and *Chieh Tzu-t'ui* (*WP* 124, Act I, pp. 394-96). Its next sequence of tunes Nos. 10-12 ("Tsui fu kuei," "Chin chan-erh" and "Tsui chung t'ien") occurs in the plays *Chin hsien ch'ih* (*YCH* 72, Act I, p. 1254), and *Yü-ching t'ai* (*YCH* 6, Act I, pp. 86-87). Its last sequence of tunes, Nos. 15-16 ("Hou t'ing hua" and "Chuan-sha"), is found in *Mo-ho-lo* (*YCH* 79, Act I, pp. 1371-72). See Feng Yüan-chün, pp. 263-64.

songs in each act to one mode; however, there is a fixed order of songs and there are conventions about the connecting sounds. Between the songs, there are certain relations which are not to be confused. For instance, the tune 'Huang-ying-erh' is followed by 'Ts'u yü lin,' and 'Hua-mei hsü' is followed by 'Ti-liu-tzu.' The songs themselves have their fixed places; a composer may look at the old drama and follow the convention."[20]

Instruments

Instruments were used in Yüan drama in two ways. First, instrumental accompaniment was added to accentuate the melodies of the songs. For this purpose there is evidence that three types of instruments were used, classified as string, wind, and percussion; they included the *p'i-p'a* or lute, flute, and drums and wooden clappers. Second, an instrument sometimes appeared in the play as part of the story; often this was a *ch'in*, or zither. Since there is very little description of instrumental music in Yüan drama, it will be helpful to examine the instruments themselves in order to determine how they were capable of being used, and to seek out references to music in the plays themselves.

Accompaniment. For musical accompaniment, the Northern school used predominantly string instruments. Northern drama is sometimes referred to as *hsüan-so tiao* (string music). *The Romance of the Western Chamber*, for instance, is sometimes called *A Stringed Version of the Romance of the Western Chamber* (*Hsüan-so Hsi-hsiang*).

The lute was played like a guitar or mandolin with fixed

[20] Hsü Wei, *Nan tz'u hsü-lu*, p. 241. The observation by Ho Liang-chün, another Ming connoisseur of drama, that "the melody 'K'uai-huo-san' in the *Chung-lü* mode slows down in order to ease into the melody 'Ch'ao t'ien-tzu'" (*Ch'ü lun*, in *CKKT, IV*, p. 12) again indicates the relationship of the closing sounds of one melody and the initial sounds of the succeeding melody.

frets. Introduced into China around the Han period, it was used in popular music. There were many types of lutes. The four-stringed, pear-shaped, bent-neck lute originated in Persia and arrived in China around the Han period; the five-stringed, straight-neck lute, developed in India, arrived in China through Gandhara during the fifth century; a third type, with a round body, was developed in China.[21] A flexible instrument, the lute can supply much of the volume of sound in instrumental groups. Because its tone is soft, it can provide much of the accompaniment for singing as well.

Of the wind instruments, there is evidence that the flute (*ti-tzu*) was used. A Yüan dynasty wall painting discussed in Chapter VII shows a group of players performing on a Yüan stage.[22] One man in the last row plays a horizontal flute, a fixed-pitch instrument similar in appearance to the traditional Chinese flute, which is still often used to accompany the voice.

The wall painting also includes two percussion instruments: a large drum and a pair of sizable wooden clappers. Both instruments were important in providing the rhythm for singing and movement. The fact that drums and clappers were used in the "medley," the immediate forerunner of Yüan drama, further indicates that they were probably used on the Yüan stage.[23]

Part of the Plot. In addition to serving as an accompaniment, music sometimes constitutes an integral part of the play, and the instrument becomes a prop on stage. In *Autumn in the Han Palace*, for example, the lute is played by

[21] Kishibe, "The Origin of the *P'i-p'a*, with Particular Reference to the Five-stringed *p'i-p'a* Preserved in the Shô-sô-in," *Transactions of the Asiatic Society of Japan*, ser. 2, XIX (December 1940), 259-304.

[22] See Frontispiece, and reference on p. 199 ff.

[23] Hung Mai (1123-1202) records that once he saw "a girl, while singing a 'medley,' suddenly stop the drum and say . . ." (*I-chien chih*, Section *Chih-i, chüan* 6, p. 5a). In the Yüan play *Tzu-yün t'ing*, the female protagonist, a singer of "medley," is referred to as a "lovely woman with an ivory clapper and a silver gong" (*WP* 120, Act IV, p. 354).

a character to advance the plot. In the opening scene, the Emperor is attracted by the doleful strains from a *p'i-p'a* in his harem and asks:

> Who is it that stealthily plays a tune,
> Sighing "alas, alack"?

(YCH 1, Act I, "Hun-chiang lung," p. 2.)

Thus it is the lute that first draws the Emperor's attention to the previously neglected beauty Wang Chao-chün.

The *ch'in* or zither, another string instrument, is used even more prominently in the Yüan plays to forward dramatic action. In both *Chang Yü Boils the Sea* and *The Romance of the Western Chamber*, it is the students' zither playing which helps them to attract and win their ladies. The *ch'in* is especially significant because of its conventional association with the literati. With origins extending far back into the past, this instrument is still played today. In its present form, it has seven strings of equal length stretched over a wooden sounding board about four feet long. The sound of the *ch'in* is produced by plucking the strings with the fingers of one's right hand, while the pitch can be controlled by stopping the string at various lengths with the fingers of the left hand. The quality and the appeal of its music are movingly described by the lovers in *The Romance of the Western Chamber*. In the following passage, Ying-ying is profoundly touched by the music of Scholar Chang's zither:

> The sound is forceful,
> Like the swords and spears of armored horsemen;
> The sound is soft,
> Like flowers falling into flowing streams;
> The sound is high,
> Like the cry of a crane under the moonlight in the pure
> breeze;
> The sound is low,
> Like the whispers of young men and maidens by the
> small windows.

(WP 117b, Act IV, "T'u ssu-erh," p. 284.)

He has not yet finished his song,
My feelings are fully aroused.
What can one do when the love birds are so separated?—
All is expressed without words.

(*Ibid.*, Act iv, "Sheng yao wang," p. 284.)

Unaware that the lady has been so affected by his playing, the young man sighs and hopefully compares himself to a famous successful lover of the past: "I shall play and sing the song 'The Phoenix Seeks His Mate.' Formerly Ssu-ma Hsiang-ju through this song succeeded in wooing Cho Wen-chün. Although I cannot compare myself to Hsiang-ju, I hope the young lady will be like Wen-chün."[24]

Ying-ying, moved to tears, sings of the quality and expressiveness of the zither music:

Word follows word like the endless dripping of a water-
*   clock,*
*   Marking the night watches;*
Sound after sound is enough to make one waste away,
*   Finding her robe too wide and girdle too loose.*
The sorrows of parting and the grief of separation—
*   All are expressed in his playing.*

(*Ibid.*, Act iv, "Lo-ssu-niang," p. 285.)

Here the music of the zither is part of the ritual of courtship; it increases the emotional impact of the scene on the lovers as well as the audience. The scene thus illustrates the Yüan playwright's creative use of music to intensify the feelings that lie behind the words of the two lovers.

Dramatic Significance of the Music

In order to understand the general dramatic function of music in Yüan drama, it is necessary to discuss more fully the modal system already mentioned. While the principles underlying the modal system in a play are not yet clear, it

---

[24] *WP* 117b, Act IV, following "Sheng yao wang," p. 284.

is apparent from statistical analysis that the mode usage signifies a certain type of structure.

Modes	Acts					
	I	II	III	IV	V[25]	Total
Hsien-lü kung	168	2	0	0	0	170
Shuang tiao	0	6	20	121	4	151
Chung-lü	0	31	53	19	0	103
Cheng kung	1	43	34	14	1	93
Nan-lü	0	66	10	2	0	78
Yüeh tiao	0	12	34	7	0	53
Shang tiao	1	9	15	1	0	26
Huang-chung	0	1	3	7	1	12
Ta-shih tiao	1	1	2	0	0	4
Total	171	171	171	171	6	

Statistics of the 171 extant plays thus reveal a tendency to use certain modes in certain acts. The *Hsien-lü* mode is used in Act I in 168 out of the total of 171 plays. In Act II, *Nan-lü* is used 66 times, and *Cheng kung*, 43 times. In Act III, *Chung-lü* appears 53 times. The *Shuang tiao* mode appears in the last act in 121 plays. There clearly is a preference for a certain musical mode for each of the four acts.

(Yen-nan) Chih An of the early Yüan period, in his *Discourse on Singing*, characterizes the emotional quality of each of the twelve modes as follows:[26] *Cheng kung*, sorrowful and powerful; *Chung-lü kung*, abrupt and swift; *Hsiao-shih*, lovely and flirtatious; *Hsien-lü tiao*, refreshing and far-reaching; *Huang-chung kung*, rich and clinging; *Nan-lü kung*, wistful and sad; *Pan-she*, sharp and staccato; *Shang-chüeh*, grief-stricken and convoluted; *Shang tiao*, sorrowful and

[25] Conventionally, Yüan plays conclude with Act IV. In only six plays are there five acts. The "last act" refers to Act IV unless stated otherwise. Cf. Stimson, "Song Arrangements in Shianleu Acts of Yuan Tzarjiuh," p. 93.

[26] (Yen-nan) Chih An, pp. 160-61.

longing; *Shuang tiao*, energetic and agitated; *Ta-shih*, romantic and suggestive; *Yüeh tiao*, sarcastic and cynical. His comments indicate that the mode chosen in each act does relate
to the emotional quality of the play's dramatic action.

Music can create the atmosphere or emphasize the direction of the action in a particular act. It is reasonable to assume that since only one musical mode is used in an entire
act, the mode sets the overall mood for the act, although the
mood of individual scenes may diverge considerably. The
predominant use of the *Hsien-lü* mode for the opening act
and the *Shuang tiao* mode for the last was perhaps based on
the emotional atmosphere of the two modes: the "refreshing
and far-reaching" sound of the former would be well suited
to the setting of a scene and the introduction of characters,
while the "energetic and agitated" nature of the latter would
accord well with the final resolution of the dramatic action;
such use, however, could often have been merely conventional.

Using the collection *A Yüan Edition of Thirty Plays* as
his source, E. Bruce Brooks demonstrates that the song-sequence within a given mode, as well as the sequence of the
modes themselves, is correlated with stages in the plot development. This correlation is the main factor in influencing
the playwrights' choice among the available groups of songs
within the key or mode. The song-sequence chosen would be
one that acted for listeners as a symbolic guide to plot development.[27]

Earlier, the *ta-ch'ü* ("song-and-dance suite") in the T'ang
period and the "medley" in the Chin times, both of which
used only one musical mode in one song-suite, probably
depended to a certain degree on musical modes for their
unity. In a Yüan play, the division of acts seems to be based
largely on the music rather than on the action of the play.
The unifying pattern of the modal systems must have helped
to remedy the episodic nature of many a plot.

---

[27] Brooks, p. 24.

Yüan Music in Later Drama

Music that was used in the Yüan theatre may not have been written down, and it is even less likely to have been published, since it came out of the popular and oral tradition. In observing the present system of setting words to music in the Peking opera, one may make some intelligent guesses as to what might have been possible in earlier dramatic practice. In the case of the Peking opera, one of the procedures is as follows: a story is selected, the character-roles are decided upon according to the story, or even according to the talents of a certain performer, and then lyrics are composed in the prevailing verse forms with rhyming couplets of 5, 7, or 10 syllables in each line. Next, the composer decides upon the type of melody to be used with reference to the dramatic situation or mood, *e.g.*, the Lyric Aria (*man-pan*) of slow tempo for pensive moments, the Narrative Aria (*yüan-pan*) for telling a story, the Animated Aria (*liu-shui*) or (*k'uai-pan*) for scenes of excitement, and the gradually slowing Declamatory Aria (*san-pan*) for the conclusion. Highly conventionalized and yet flexible (in the sense that a melody can be slightly altered here and there upon repetition, without losing its identity), the music is easily adapted to new words and yet still recognized and appreciated by the general public.[28]

It is quite possible that in Yüan drama the situation was generally comparable to the Peking opera today: highly conventional and yet flexible music that was easily adaptable to new dramatic pieces was used. Indeed, the music need only be labeled by tune titles, *e.g.*, "Tien chiang ch'un," instead of completely written out. If such were the case, one should not be surprised by the absence of any contemporary written music of Yüan drama.

[28] See Rulan Pian, "Text Setting with the *Shipyi* Animated Aria," in *Words and Music: The Scholar's View*, ed. by Laurence Berman, 1972, pp. 237-70.

Traces of the Yüan dramatic music, however, are preserved in *K'un-ch'ü*, a Southern drama that attained great
popularity in the Ming period, as pointed out by Aoki
Masaru.[29] A brief review of the development and interplay
of Southern and Northern drama throws some light on the
nature of Yüan dramatic music. When Yüan drama flourished under the Mongol rule, it overshadowed Southern
drama. From the end of the Yüan dynasty, however, Southern drama gradually reasserted itself. During the early six-
teenth century, Wei Liang-fu of K'un-shan in Kiangsu,
absorbing the best there was in the different schools of Southern style music,[30] created a new music style known as the
"music of K'un-shan" (*K'un-ch'ü*). Soft, refined, and romantic, the music attained immediate fame on the stage when
Liang Ch'en-yü used it in his play, *Washing Yarn* (*Huan
sha chi*). The fortunate union of the genius of the musician
and dramatist started a new school of drama, which domi-
nated the Chinese stage for almost three hundred years.

When *K'un-ch'ü* spread to the North, it adopted Northern
tunes, and these have been preserved as a part of *K'un-ch'ü*,
for which we do have musical scores. In Liang Ch'en-yü's
Washing Yarn, some acts are composed of Northern songs.[31]
In *A Thousand Pieces of Gold* (*Ch'ien chin chi*) by Shen
Ts'ai, Act XXII contains nine songs that have the same tune
titles and texts as those in Act II of the Yüan play *In Pursuit
of Han Hsin* (*Chui Han Hsin*). Collections of essentially
K'un-ch'ü song scores also include Northern songs. Both the
Na-shu-ying Collection of Musical Scores (*Na-shu-ying*

[29] On this subject, I rely essentially on Aoki Masaru's study "Hokkyoku no ikyo," *Tōhōgakuhō* (Kyoto), VIII (Oct. 1937), 1-10.

[30] Chiefly the Hai-yen, I-yang and Yü-yao music, named after their
locales in the Kiangsi and Chekiang areas in Southern China. Wei
Liang-fu achieved his great success through the cooperation of musicians in the K'un-shan region, chiefly Yüan "Hu-tzu," Yu "T'o-tzu,"
and Wei's son-in-law Chang Yeh-t'ang, who was well versed in both
Southern and Northern music.

[31] *Huan sha chi*, Act XIV (*KPHC*, 1st series), Fascicle I, pp. 43a-
46a; Act XXXIII, Fascicle II, pp. 38a-42b.

ch'ü p'u) published in 1784 and 1792 and the *Chi-ch'eng Collection of Musical Scores* (*Chi-ch'eng ch'ü p'u*) published in 1925 contain a considerable number of lyrics from Yüan with musical notations.[32] Hsü Ta-ch'un (fl. 1750) points out that Northern songs sung after mid-Ming were in fact rendered largely in *K'un-ch'ü* music.[33] Modification of the Northern music in the course of time is to be expected, especially if musicians traditionally played by rote. However, the works that have been set aside by later music experts as Northern music should represent to some extent the spirit or essence of that genre, and this spirit was vividly noted by Hsü Wei (1521-1593), who claimed that listening to Northern melodies gave him a surge of courage, "making his spirit rise like a hawk," since the Northern music was remarkably different from the flowing, refined, and meandering Southern melodies.[34]

From the scant information pertaining to the dramatic function of music in Yüan drama, one may draw a few general conclusions. It is clear that music in Yüan drama is integral to the form, and is not used simply to mark or signify the presence of a critical or climactic situation in the plot. The fact that the musical modes are almost always noted before the title of the first song in each act indicates that music was not merely inserted at specific intervals in the action of the plays. It is likely that music in Yüan drama not only contributed to the structure of the play, but also, as in *K'un-ch'ü* and Peking opera today, served as an accompaniment for lyrical speeches, as a background for stylized movement, and as a creator of atmosphere.

[32] Yeh T'ang, *Na-shu-ying ch'ü p'u*, 1784-1792, and Wang Chi-lieh and Liu Fu-liang, *Chi-ch'eng ch'ü p'u*, Shanghai, 1925. In these collections, additional marginal notes are provided for the Northern lyrics to indicate that the characters pronounced in the *ju* tone in the Southern dialect are pronounced in *p'ing*, *shang*, or *ch'ü* tones in these Northern lyrics because of the absence of *ju* tone in the Northern dialect.

[33] Hsü Ta-ch'un, *Yüeh-fu ch'uan sheng*, in *CKKT*, Vol. VII, p. 157.

[34] Hsü Wei, p. 245.

VII

The Stage

Yüan Performance

As in the case of music, any attempt to study the Yüan stage is hampered by the scarcity of available information. Scattered and fragmentary references must be gathered from many sources. The following are most significant to an understanding of Yüan theatrical performance.

"A Peasant Unfamiliar with the Theatre" (*"Chuang-chia pu shih kou-lan"*). "A Peasant Unfamiliar with the Theatre," a song-suite (*t'ao-shu*) by the thirteenth-century author Tu Shan-fu, gives valuable information about a performance in a town theatre in the Yüan period. Although it is not known for certain that the presentation was a *yüan-pen* or *tsa-chü*, the peasant's description indicates that it was a simple performance in the nature of a comic skit, probably a *yüan-pen* that served as a prelude to a *tsa-chü* presentation. Written in the first person, the song-suite tells about the country bumpkin's bewilderment at the theatre and his great enjoyment of the performance:

I came to town to buy some spirit money and incense.
As I walked down the street I saw a colorful paper notice;
Nowhere else was there such a bustling throng.

I saw a man leaning with his hand against a wooden gate,
Shouting loudly, "Step right up, step right up,"
Warning that latecomers would find the place full and
*   no more benches.*
He said that the first part would be a yüan-pen *called*
Chasing and Wooing,

*And the second part would be a junior lead playing Liu
   Shua-ho.*[1]

*He demanded two hundred in cash and then let me pass.
A fter entering the gate, I went up a wooden ramp;
I saw row after row of people all seated around.
Lifting my head I saw a bell-like tower;
Looking down I saw a whirlpool of people.
I saw a few women sitting on the platform.
Though it was not a festival honoring the gods,
They kept beating the drum and striking the gongs.*[2]

The colorful paper notice about the performance, the barker
shouting vigorously to draw in customers, the milling crowd
inside the theatre, and the noise of drums and gongs paint a
vivid picture of the festive atmosphere. The "wooden ramp"
was probably a staircase. The audience, looking like a "whirlpool of people" from the country bumpkin's vantage point
on the "ramp," was evidently seated in circles. The nature
of the "bell-like tower" is not clear. It may have been a place
for the audience, or it may have been the stage.

Yüan Wall Painting. A significant source of information
on the physical stage is a wall painting preserved from the
Yüan period. In Ming-ying-wang (Dragon King) Temple in
the complex of the Kuang-sheng Monastery (about twelve
miles southeast of the small town of Chao-ch'eng and nine
miles northeast of the town of Hung-tung in Shansi Province), there is a series of wall paintings, which came to the

---

[1] Liu Shua-ho is listed in *Lu kuei pu* as the son-in-law of actor
Hung-tzu Li-erh (Chung Ssu-ch'eng, p. 15). If this is not the same
man, it is at least clear that this is a man's name.

[2] Tu Shan-fu, "Chuang-chia pu shih kou-lan" in Yang Chao-ying,
ed., *Ch'ao-yeh hsin sheng t'ai-p'ing yüeh-fu* (*SPTK so-pen*), p. 80.
For a translation of the whole poem, see James I. Crump, "Yüan-pen,
Yüan Drama's Rowdy Ancestor," *Literature East and West*, XIV, no.
4 (1970), pp. 481-83; David Hawkes, "Reflections on Some Yuan
Tsa-chü," *Asia Major*, XVI, parts 1-2 (1971), pp. 75-76.

attention of scholars in the 1930's.[3] The Hung-Chao district, known in Yüan times as P'ing-yang, was probably a center of Yüan drama, since it produced a number of well-known dramatists, including Shih Chün-pao and Cheng Kuang-tsu.[4] The Ming-ying-wang Temple was built in 779 during the T'ang dynasty and rebuilt from 1201 to 1204. Among its murals is one painted in 1324, at the height of Yüan drama, which depicts a Yüan theatrical performance (Frontispiece).

On top of the painting in a horizontal line from right to left are the words: "A performer from T'ai-hang, Chung Tu-hsiu, acted here. Fourth Month, 1324 A.D." (T'ai-hang *san-yüeh* Chung Tu-hsiu *tsai tz'u tso-ch'ang. T'ai-ting yüan nien ssu yüeh*). T'ai-hang is a place name; *san-yüeh* means "performer";[5] and *tso-ch'ang* means "to give a performance." A comparable reference, "A performer from Tung-p'ing, Wang Chin-pang, acted here," in an early Southern play[6] indicates that this kind of announcement may have been customary for a performance. The inscription in the painting, mentioning the main performer, is clearly a star-billing device to attract spectators.

It is evident that specific actors and actresses enjoyed considerable popularity, and that the success of a performance often rested on the fame and skill of the leading player. This is supported by the Yüan play *Lan Ts'ai-ho, the Actor*, in which the main character portrays an actor who is the leader of a troupe, and during whose absence business drops drastically.[7] In *The Green Mansions*, which contains a series of brief anecdotal biographies of Yüan courtesans and actresses written by Hsia Po-ho in 1355, 117 courtesans are mentioned as being outstanding in some way. Many of them,

[3] See L. Sickman, "Wall-Paintings of the Yüan Period in Kuang-Sheng-Ssu, Shansi," *Revue des Arts Asiatiques*, XI (1937), pp. 53-67.

[4] Chung Ssu-ch'eng, pp. 111 and 118; dramatists Yü Po-yüan (*ibid.*, p. 112), Chao Kung-fu (*ibid.*, p. 114), Ti chün-hou (*ibid.*, p. 116), and K'ung Wen-ch'ing (*ibid.*, p. 117) were also from P'ing-yang.

[5] *San-yüeh* has several meanings; here, "performer."

[6] *Huan-men tzu-ti ts'o li-shen* (in *KPHC*, 1st series), p. 55a.

[7] *WP* 159, Act III, prose interpolation in "Kun hsiu ch'iu," p. 977.

such as Chu Lien-hsiu, Chao P'ien-hsi, Chu Chin-hsiu, and Yen Shan-hsiu, known for their outstanding beauty and talent, enjoyed great fame and popularity as *tsa-chü* performers as well.[8]

The wall painting itself measures 3.11 metres in width and 4.11 metres in height. It shows a group of eleven colorfully costumed personages, ten of whom appear to be taking a "curtain call." The costumes, make-up, stage properties, and back-curtain give an idea of the stylization of a Yüan dramatic performance. From the painting we can see that plays were performed on a tiled stage, backed by an elaborately painted curtain. Costumes were ornate and of great variety. The front middle figure in the picture wears a rather official-looking red Sung-dynasty robe and a black hat with long narrow wings. The other figures in the front wear robes embroidered with colorful floral patterns, flying birds, cranes, and dragons (front, far left); several of the figures in the back row are clad in Mongolian costumes, with wide-brim, flat Mongolian hats. Many of these articles of clothing are probably symbolic, enabling the audience to make immediate associations when the characters enter.

Especially noticeable in the mural is the highly stylized use of make-up. Two characters are made up with heavy black eyebrows underlined with white. Because this kind of

---

[8] Chao P'ien-hsi, Chu Chin-hsiu, and Yen Shan-hsiu are known "to be good in both the male lead role and the female lead role" (Hsia Po-ho, pp. 28, 29, and 39); Chu Lien-hsiu "is superb in *chia-t'ou*, *hua-tan*, and *juan mo-ni* roles" (*ibid.*, p. 19. For references to these terms, see pp. 68-69 above): T'ien-jan Hsiu "is the best in love drama, excelling in playing two different roles, including the *hua-tan* role" (*ibid.*, p. 23); Li Chiao-erh "is especially good in the *hua-tan* role" (*ibid.*, p. 31); Kuo Yü-ti and P'ing-yang nu are good in outlaw drama (*ibid.*, pp. 24 and 28); Mi-li-ha, who is probably a Tatar, has a pure singing voice and "specializes in the *t'ieh-tan* role, even though she is not goodlooking" (*ibid.*, p. 34); Wei Tao-tao "does a certain solo dance to the tune 'Partridge' ('Che-ku'), which no one in the present dynasty can imitate. She has no rivals in playing a female role" (*ibid.*, p. 24).

make-up is similar to a clown's make-up of white eye circles and nose, or a villain's make-up of black and white lines as found in traditional Chinese drama since Yüan times, it may be assumed that the make-up on the characters in the mural indicates one of these types. Black and white make-up was also used on a mischief-maker, as Tu Shan-fu's song-suite, "A Peasant Unfamiliar with the Theatre," indicates:

> *A girl made a few turns,*
> *And soon led out a troupe of others.*
> *In the middle was a mischief-maker,*
> *His head wrapped in a jet-black scarf, stuck with a*
> *   writing brush.*
> *His face was covered with white powder,*
> *With black lines painted on top.*[9]

References to painted faces are found also in the Yüan drama texts. In *Cold Pavilion* (*K'u-han t'ing*), the leading male character Chao Yung refers disparagingly to the *ch'a-tan* in the part of a courtesan: "Her painted face is in some spots blue, some spots purple, some spots white, some spots black; she truly appears like a multi-colored ghost."[10] A female role with a painted face (the *hua-tan* or *ch'a-tan*) usually plays a woman of questionable character.

The figures in this wall painting also indicate that beards are sometimes highly stylized and possibly symbolic. In one case (front, second from right), the actor's beard consists of a long, thin front whisker and two side whiskers strung together with a wire; there clearly was no attempt to make the beard seem real.

Lan Ts'ai-ho, the Actor and Other Yüan Plays. The Yüan play *Lan Ts'ai-ho, the Actor*, about a family of theatrical performers, is especially helpful for information concerning the Yüan stage. Hsü Chien plays the lead male role under

---

[9] Tu Shan-fu, p. 80.
[10] *YCH* 58, Act II, speech following "Sheng yao wang," p. 1007.

the theatrical name Lan Ts'ai-ho and also leads the troupe, consisting of his wife Hsi Ch'ien-chin, his son Little Ts'ai-ho, his daughter-in-law Lan Shan-ching, and his brothers-in-law Wang Pa-se and Li Po-t'ou. Their speech and conduct give insight into the life of a theatrical troupe, and the play provides a lively account of the actor's world.

Many stage terms are used here. For example, Lan Ts'ai-ho often refers to the theatre as *kou-lan* ("railings"), to the stage itself as *hsi-t'ai*, and to the place on the stage where the female players sit as *yüeh-ch'uang* ("music-bed"). The day before the performance Lan Ts'ai-ho asks that colored-paper notices (*hua chao-erh*) be hung; on the day of the performance, he asks his brother-in-law to hang flags, bunting, and back-curtains (*shen-cheng k'ao-pei*).[11]

The play also indicates that one could make a decent living in the theatre, and that actors had a certain pride in their profession. Referring to the art of acting, Lan Ts'ai-ho says, "To learn this humble skill is better than owning thousands of acres of good land."[12] When too old to act, the players sometimes assisted with the music. In the final act, Lan Ts'ai-ho's brother-in-law comments: "It has already been thirty years since Lan Ts'ai-ho followed the footsteps of the Taoist and left home. I, Wang Pa-se, am now eighty years old; Li Po-t'ou is seventy, and our sister-in-law is ninety; we have all become old. We can no longer make a living. When the young ones perform, we beat the drums for them."[13]

Although the players were self-supporting, they were under obligation to answer calls from officials and were subject to severe punishment when tardy. In the second act, when an attendant from the magistrate calls Lan Ts'ai-ho, he is not willing to go because it is his birthday. He suggests that either his brother-in-law or the *tan* role act as his substitute, but

[11] For many comparable citations of these terms from Yüan plays, see Feng Yüan-chün, pp. 1-120.

[12] *WP* 159, Act I, "Hun-chiang lung," p. 971.

[13] *Ibid.*, Act IV, opening scene, pp. 978-79.

the attendant does not agree. At last he reluctantly consents: "All right, all right, I will go to the magistrate."[14] He arrives late and is threatened with forty strokes, which almost frightens him out of his wits.

Lan Ts'ai-ho is often referred to by his role, *mo-ni* ("the male lead"), a title that he used with pride. When involved in an argument with an officious old man, he reminds himself: "People call you a *mo-ni*, a stage personality; why should you argue with this crazy old fool?"[15]

Another source of information on Yüan theatre is the notations in the playscripts. Beyond necessary "entrances" and "exits," Yüan plays print very few stage directions; there are no elaborate descriptions of setting such as modern dramatists use, and only rarely are there references to stage properties, furniture, sound effects, or movements.[16] However, the cumulative information of all the plays is valuable. Although no description of the *dramatis personae* is given in the Yüan plays, mention is always made of the proper roles of the more important characters. In *Autumn in the Han Palace*, for example, upon the entrance of the heroine, it is stated: "The principal female-role, playing Wang Ch'iang, enters leading two palace maids."[17]

The roles in Yüan drama, as on the later Chinese stage, are divided into several main categories: male (*mo*), female (*tan*), villain (*ching*) and clown (*ch'ou*). In each Yüan play there is one leading male or female role and a multiplicity of minor roles. Among the male roles are: *cheng-mo*, the principal male role; *fu-mo, ch'ung-mo, wai*, supporting male roles; *hsiao-mo*, a child or youth; *po-lao*, an old man. Among the female roles are: *cheng-tan*, the principal female

[14] *WP* 159, Act II, speech following "Tou ha-ma," p. 975.

[15] *Ibid.*, Act II, prose interpolation, "Ho hsin-lang," pp. 974-75.

[16] Some of the handwritten texts in *Mo-wang kuan ch'ao-chiao pen ku chin tsa-chü* compiled by Chao Ch'i-mei contain more information on costumes, properties, and stage directions than is available in other editions. Feng Yüan-chün has compiled a list of such costumes and properties from 15 of these texts (Feng Yüan-chün, pp. 342-60).

[17] *YCH* 1, Act I, opening scene, p. 2; see p. 21 above.

role; *wai-tan*, supporting female role; *se-tan*, *ch'a-tan*, *hua-tan*, a female with a painted face;[18] *hsiao-tan*, a little girl; *lao-tan*, *pu-erh*, an old woman; *hun-tan*, ghost of a female. Among the *ching* and *ch'ou* roles are: *ching*, usually a villainous person; *fu-ching*, a secondary *ching*; *ch'ou*, a clownish person.

The origin of the term *mo* to denote a male role is not clear. It probably comes from the term *mo-ni*, used in the Sung "variety play" (*tsa-chü*). Another possibility is that the word *mo*, meaning "the last," was used by a male to indicate humility. *Tan*, denoting a female role, is believed to have been derived from the word *tan*, a "female monkey," a term thought applicable to a courtesan.[19] The classification of players into types or roles is in harmony with the symbolic nature of the Chinese stage.

Individual theatres must have varied considerably in their physical setup. When Lan Ts'ai-ho returns to his home town after a long absence and encounters a great deal of commotion, he remarks:

> It's a traveling troupe
> Moving around in the public square,
> Carrying spears and swords,
> Gongs, castanets, drums, and flutes,
> And curtains and streamers as well.
> Who are these actors?—
> They must be newcomers.
>
> (*WP* 159, Act IV, "Ch'ing tung yüan," p. 979.)

They turn out to be none other than his family and relatives. The performing ground and the staging here are apparently crude and makeshift. On the other hand, the stage scene in the Yüan mural appears quite elaborate.

Some of the stages may have been built permanently on temple grounds, some set up temporarily in ancestral halls,

---

[18] According to *Ch'ing lou chi*, an actress who uses black color on her face is a *hua-tan* (Hsia Po-ho, p. 40).

[19] Chu Ch'üan, p. 53.

and some, makeshift constructions in the towns and country-side. Nevertheless, the conditions of staging seem to have had certain general similarities, and some theatrical practices were probably common to all theatres. Tu Shan-fu's song-suite, the wall painting, and the play *Lan Ts'ai-ho, the Actor* give evidence of at least a partially consistent stage tradition.

Dramatists

For the study of Yüan dramatists, there is fortunately an informative and reliable source, *A Register of Ghosts*, by Chung Ssu-ch'eng, himself a playwright.[20] Written in 1330, it includes 152 Yüan writers, with brief biographical notes and elegiac verses for 19 of them. In 1422 Chia Chung-ming, also a playwright, added more elegiac verses on several authors whom Chung Ssu-ch'eng had failed to include.[21] Around the time Chia Chung-ming's work appeared, an anonymous writer published *A Supplement to A Register of Ghosts* (*Lu kuei pu hsü-pien*), extending the list to include a few more Yüan dramatists as well as some from the early Ming period.[22] Brief as they are, these works provide the major source of information on the Yüan playwrights.

Chung Ssu-ch'eng's *A Register of Ghosts* consists of seven sections divided into two large categories and arranged in chronological order. The first two sections refer mainly to celebrated men and non-dramatic *ch'ü* composers, and the next five sections are on dramatists, with the following headings:

[20] For information on Chung Ssu-ch'eng as a playwright, see *Lu kuei pu hsü-pien* (*CKKT*, II, p. 281).

[21] This enlarged version is found in *T'ien-i-ko lan-ke hsieh-pen cheng hsü Lu kuei pu*, with a preface by Chia Chung-ming dated 1422. The *Lu kuei pu* cited here is the *CKKT* variorum edition, using the Ch'ing period writer Ts'ao Lien-t'ing's 1706 edition as the basic text. For information on the various versions, see *CKKT*, II, pp. 87-102 and p. 141.

[22] See *Lu kuei pu hsü-pien*, in *CKKT*, II, p. 277.

I. 1. Celebrated men of previous generations who have died and have left songs [31 persons];

   2. Celebrated men of present times [10 persons];

II. 3. Celebrated men and dramatists of previous generations who have died and whose plays are current today [56 persons];

   4. Celebrated men and dramatists of present times who have died and whom I knew . . . [19 persons];

   5. Dramatists of present times who have died and whom I did not know [11 persons];

   6. Dramatists of present times whom I know [21 persons];

   7. Dramatists of present times whom I have heard of but do not know personally [4 persons].[23]

The 111 dramatists belong to roughly two periods: those who lived before the author's time, and those contemporary with the author. Chung Ssu-ch'eng's date of birth is believed to be around 1280; however, this cannot be conclusively established.[24] Kuan Han-ch'ing, listed first among the dramatists, is believed to have lived between 1220 and 1324, but the dates of his birth and death have also remained a matter of controversy.[25]

Wang Kuo-wei, a foremost scholar on the subject of Yüan drama, asserts that the development of the genre occurred in three stages: the first period of about fifty years started with the conquest of the Chin in 1234 and lasted until the unification of China by the Emperor Shih-tsu in 1279; the second period of about sixty years began in 1280 and ended around 1340; and the third period covered the reign of Chih-cheng (1341-1368) at the end of the Yüan dynasty.[26]

Places of origin of the playwrights make it apparent that Yüan drama first flourished in the North around Ta-tu and later moved its center of activity to the South. In the genre's

[23] Chung Ssu-ch'eng, pp. 104-37.
[24] See Feng Yüan-chün, p. 65, and n. 95 on pp. 104-05.
[25] See p. 209 below.   [26] Wang Kuo-wei, p. 93.

first stage of development, the outstanding playwrights were
all northerners. There were nineteen playwrights from Ta-tu,
including Kuan Han-ch'ing, Ma Chih-yüan, and Wang Shih-
fu. In the second period, in addition to the sixteen playwrights from Hangchow, seven were relocated to the south;
famous playwrights like Cheng Kuang-tsu and Ch'iao Chi
were among those who moved from the north to Hangchow.
In the third period, the majority of the playwrights were
southerners, and there were no important playwrights remaining in the north.[27]

Dramatists were referred to by their contemporaries as
ts'ai-jen,[28] and had their own organizations known as *shu-hui*
(writing societies). Some with proper names such as the
"Nine-mountain Writing Society" (Chiu-shan shu-hui), were
known to have existed in Hangchow and Ta-tu.[29] Apparently
there was competition among the various writing societies.
In the play *Chang Hsieh, the First-place Graduate*, for instance, the actor says: "*Chang Hsieh chuang-yüan* has been
performed by you people in the past. This time our writing
society will win the first prize."[30]

While the collective energy of the literati helped to generate the great popularity of drama during the Yüan period,
the creative genius of a few poets established the genre as a
unique achievement in Chinese literary history. Kuan Han-
ch'ing, Ma Chih-yüan, Cheng Kuang-tsu, and Po P'u are ac-
knowledged by Chou Te-ch'ing, author of *Sound and Rhymes
of the Central Plains*, as outstanding among *ch'ü* writers. To-

[27] For places of origin, see Chung Ssu-ch'eng, pp. 104-37.

[28] For a discussion of the term *ts'ai-jen*, see Feng Yüan-chün, pp.
15-22 and 57-72.

[29] For information on the history and nature of *shu-hui*, see Feng
Yüan-chün, pp. 17-18, 57-58, and 99 (n. 58 and n. 59); and Sun
K'ai-ti, *Yeh-shih-yüan ku chin tsa-chü k'ao* (Shanghai, 1953), pp. 388-
95. Both Feng and Sun use as their source *T'ien-i-ko lan-ke hsieh-pen
cheng hsü Lu kuei pu*, in which the supplementary elegiac verses associate many playwrights with the *shu-hui*.

[30] Opening scene in *Chang Hsieh chuang-yüan* (KPHC, 1st series),
p. 13b.

gether with Wang Shih-fu and Ch'iao Chi, they are traditionally regarded as the six master playwrights of the Yüan
era.

Of these six men, Kuan Han-ch'ing and Ma Chih-yüan
are the ones about whom we can make more conclusive
generalizations regarding their philosophies and personalities. Kuan Han-ch'ing is perhaps the best known of the
Yüan dramatists. Although there are no precise dates available, we can ascertain his approximate chronological position from several passages in *A Register of Ghosts*. It places
him at the head and Po P'u fourth in the first section on the
dramatists, indicating that he was likely a contemporary of
Po P'u, who lived from 1226 to 1285, and whose birth date
is one of the very few of Yüan dramatists to be known with
certainty. Kuan Han-ch'ing must have died before 1324, as
A Register of Ghosts listed him first among the deceased
dramatists "of previous generations," and Chou Te-ch'ing's
Sound and Rhymes of the Central Plains of 1324 indicates
that he was no longer alive.[31] The *Register of Ghosts* also
informs us that he was a man of Ta-tu, and a member of
the Medical Academy (*t'ai-i-yüan-yin*); he was known as
"the old man of I Study" (*I-chai sou*), after the name of his
studio.[32]

---

[31] Chou Te-ch'ing, p. 175. It is to be noted that *Lu kuei pu*, first
completed in 1330, must have been revised later, as 1345 is given as
the death of Ch'iao Chi (Chung Ssu-ch'eng, p. 126). For a discussion
on the dates of Kuan Han-ch'ing, see A. W. E. Dolby, "Kuan Han-
ch'ing," *Asia Major*, XVI, parts 1-2 (1971), pp. 17-33 (Dolby places
his date of birth around 1220-1230 and his death before 1324); Sun
K'ai-ti, "Kuan Han-ch'ing hsing-nien k'ao" in *Kuan Han-ch'ing yen-
chiu lun-wen chi* (1958), pp. 11-15 (Sun asserts that the playwright
was born between 1241 and 1250 and that he died between 1320 and
1324).

[32] Chung Ssu-ch'eng, p. 104. The exact nature of the post *t'ai-i-
yüan-yin* is not clear since it is not listed among the official posts in the
Chin shih or *Yüan shih*. As to the nickname, it was originally *I-chai
sou*, but since Wang Kuo-wei used *Chi-chai sou*, the mistake has often
been repeated by others (*Kuan Han-ch'ing yen-chiu lun-wen chi*,
p. 33).

Kuan Han-ch'ing's extraordinary success as a dramatist
may perhaps be partly attributed to the fact that he himself
had acted in plays and was intimately familiar with the stage,
the audience, and the skills of the profession. He is known
to have "appeared on the stage himself with his face painted
black and white. He considered this his profession and had
no objection to the company of actors."[33] An elegy by Chia
Chung-ming states that Kuan Han-ch'ing was "the forerunner of the theatre . . . the leader of the *tsa-chü* drama" (*li-
yüan ling-hsiu . . . tsa-chü pan-t'ou*).[34] His popularity was
such that another successful dramatist, Kao Wen-hsiu, was
nicknamed by people in the capital "Little Han-ch'ing."[35]

Kuan Han-ch'ing's copious output (sixty-three plays in all)
includes seventeen or eighteen plays that have survived to
the present day,[36] and eight of these have been translated
into English: *Injustice to Tou O, The Butterfly Dream, The
Execution of Lu Chai-lang, Rescued by a Courtesan, The
Jade Mirror Stand, The Riverside Pavilion, Lord Kuan Goes
to the Feast With a Single Sword,* and *Weeping for Ts'un-
hsiao.*[37] Even this limited number of titles indicates the dramatist's broad scope of artistic concern, ranging from courtroom drama and domestic comedies to re-creations of historical events on the stage.

A number of his songs seem highly personal and offer information that is consistent with the scanty information we
have of him from other sources, such as his association with
courtesan-actress Chu Lien-hsiu;[38] however, in any attempt to

---

[33] Tsang Mao-hsün, Second Preface of 1616 to *YCH*, p. 3.

[34] *T'ien-i-ko lan-ke hsieh-pen cheng hsü Lu kuei pu, chüan* 1, p. 3.

[35] *Ibid., chüan* 1, p. 6.

[36] See "A Complete List of Kuan Han-ch'ing's Plays" ("Kuan Han-
ch'ing tsa-chü ch'üan-mu") and the postscript in *Kuan Han-ch'ing
hsi-ch'ü chi* (1958), pp. 1003-52 and 1053-70. On the authorship of
some plays, scholars do not agree (see p. 225 below).

[37] See Yang Hsien-yi and Gladys Yang, translators, *Selected Plays
of Kuan Han-ch'ing* (1958); and pp. 273-79 below.

[38] Kuan Han-ch'ing wrote several song-suites in the *Nan-lü* mode
for Chu Lien-hsiu. (See *Shuo-chi* version of *Ch'ing lou chi*, cited in

gather information about a poet's life from his poetry, one must be aware of the equivocal nature of such an approach. In his song-suite "Never Say Too Old" ("Pu fu lao"), Kuan Han-ch'ing says:

> *I picked flowers growing beyond the walls,*
> *And plucked twigs of willows along the road.*
> *With flowers, I pick the tender red buds;*
> *With willows, I pluck the green supple twigs—*
> *A romantic, free and gay.*
> *With my willow-plucking, flower-picking hands,*
> *I shall go on till flowers die and willows wither.*
> *For half a lifetime I have been plucking willows and*
> *   picking flowers;*
> *For a whole generation I have slept with flowers and*
> *   lain with willows.*[39]

"Flowers" and "willows" here are metaphors for "courtesans"; the "mist and flowers" quoted below refers to "the world of pleasure." In another song in the same song-suite, he claims that he is a man of many talents and that he is not ready to give up his pursuits of pleasure until the end:

> *I can play go, kick a ball,*
> *   Hunt and do comic parts;*
> *I can sing and dance,*
> *   Play stringed and wind instruments;*
> *I can perform at parties,*[40]
> *   Compose poems and play the "Double Six."*[41]

Hsia Po-ho, p. 48, n. 97. The *Shuo-chi* version contains the oldest text of *Ch'ing lou chi.*)

[39] Sui Shu-sen, ed., *Ch'üan Yüan san-ch'ü* (1964), p. 172.

[40] *Yen-tso*, translated here as "to perform at parties" ("to entertain"), is an unfamiliar term; perhaps *yen* is the same as *yen*, "feast," and *tso* is *tso-ch'ang*, "performance" (see p. 200 above).

[41] "Double Six" (*shuang-lu*) is a board game like backgammon. (The game is illustrated in a painting entitled "Court Ladies Playing Double Six" [Nei-jen shuang-lu], attributed to the eighth-century painter Chou Fang, now at the Freer Gallery of Art.)

Even if you knocked out my teeth, twisted my mouth,
  Lamed my legs and broke my arms—
Since Heaven bestowed upon me these weaknesses,
  I still would not give up.
Not until Yama himself summons me,
  Spirits and demons come to catch me,
My three souls are brought to the Underworld,
  And my seven spirits are lost in oblivion,
O Heaven!
  Only then shall I cease to travel the road
    of "mist and flowers."[42]

Conscious of his talents and disillusioned with his times, Kuan Han-ch'ing seemed to have had neither the desire nor the opportunity to achieve a satisfying life in public service. Instead, he sought to lose himself in a life of love, pleasure-seeking, and writing for the theatre. This type of escapism was common among Chinese intellectuals, especially in times of trouble.

Whereas Kuan Han-ch'ing abandoned himself to women and song, Ma Chih-yüan, a representative of the type of the disillusioned scholar-poet recluse of his time, tried to take comfort in nature, and he distinguished himself as a song writer as well. Also a native of Ta-tu, Ma Chih-yüan served for some time as a minor official of the Chiang-che provincial administration. The emotions expressed in his lyrics correspond with the basic thought of his plays: the longing for a life remote from the meaningless hurly-burly of this world. The following lines of his renowned "Autumn Thoughts" ("Ch'iu ssu") are reminiscent of Shelley's "Ozymandias" in their expression of the futility of worldly power:

Consider that the palace of Ch'in and the halls of Han
Have all become wild pastures for sheep and cows;
If not so, the fishermen and the woodsmen would have
  nothing to chat about.

[42] Sui Shu-sen, p. 173.

> *Upon the deserted graves lie broken monuments*
> *Distinguishing not the dragon from the snake.*[43]

Realizing the emptiness of power and fame, he seeks retirement from the world of earthly gains:

> *Profit and fame concern me not,*
> *Right and wrong are excluded from my life;*
> *The "red-dust" cannot draw me outside the gate.*
> *Verdurous trees lean to shield the corner of the house,*
> *Green mountains fill the gap within the wall;*
> *What is as fine as a bamboo fence and a thatched hut?*[44]

He finds comfort and satisfaction in the simple things in life:

> *Picking chrysanthemums wet with dew,*
> *Opening purple crabs covered with frost,*
> *And burning red leaves for heating wine.*[45]

Often we detect a sense of serenity and a feeling of fulfillment in his communion with nature; sometimes, however, a note of sadness, a sense of resignation to fate, is unmistakable. Retirement from officialdom and escape to nature were often brought about by circumstances as well as by temperament. The following song by Ma Chih-yüan depicts through a series of images in only twenty-eight characters the pervading desolation symbolized by fading autumn, reflecting the subdued mood of the poet-scholars of the time.

> *Withered vines, old trees, twilight crows;*
> *A little bridge, flowing river, a homestead;*
> *Ancient road, west wind, a lean horse.*
> *The evening sun sinks westward—*
> *A heartbroken man stands at the edge of the sky.*[46]

---

[43] *Ibid.*, to the tune "Ch'iao-mu-cha," p. 269.
[44] *Ibid.*, to the tune "Po pu tuan," p. 269.
[45] *Ibid.*, to the tune "Li-t'ing-yen-sha," p. 269.
[46] "Ch'iu Ssu" to the tune "T'ien-ching sha," *ibid.*, p. 242.

Ma Chih-yüan, like many of his contemporaries, sought something enduring and satisfying in Taoism and the world of nature.

Information leading to any understanding of the other four master Yüan playwrights is scarce. Yoshikawa, in his chapter on Yüan dramatists,[47] and T'an Cheng-pi, in his book *Brief Biographies of Six Master Yüan Playwrights* (*Yüan ch'ü liu ta-chia lüeh-chuan*), do provide some insight into the lives of these men, but very little is actually known about them. At this point, one can only offer some brief biographical sketches.

Cheng Kuang-tsu, singled out by Chou Te-ch'ing, the author of *CYYY*, as a leading playwright in Yüan times, was from P'ing-yang in present-day Shansi. According to *A Register of Ghosts*, he served as a minor official in Hangchow and was known all over the country for his integrity. Actors always referred to him reverently as "teacher." He died in Hangchow and was cremated in a temple by West Lake. Of his eighteen plays that are known by title, only eight are extant. His *A Disembodied Soul* and *Maid "Plum-Fragrance"* are considered his best.[48]

Po P'u (1226-1285) is known to have come from a distinguished literary and official family, his father being a prominent official in the Chin court and a lifelong friend of the literary giant Yüan Hao-wen (1190-1257), who also held office under the Chin court. As noted above, Po P'u is one of the few dramatists whose date of birth can be identified with certainty.[49] Yüan Hao-wen recognized his talent even when he was a boy and encouraged his literary pursuits. Because of his fame, Po P'u was recommended for

[47] Yoshikawa, pp. 71-162.

[48] Chung Ssu-ch'eng, pp. 118-19; see also T'an Cheng-pi, *Yüan ch'ü liu ta-chia lüeh-chuan* (1957), pp. 268-309.

[49] See biography of Po Hua, Po P'u's father, in *Chin shih, chüan* 114 下下, 1a-12b. Po P'u's date of birth is mentioned in Wang Po-wen's preface to Po P'u's *T'ien-lai chi*: In the year of *Jen-ch'en* (1232) Po P'u was 7 years old (cited in Yoshikawa, p. 79).

service in the Mongol court, but he refused, perhaps partly because of feelings of loyalty to the defunct Chin court, and partly because of his distaste for official life. Later, he moved to Nanking, where he associated with other survivors of the Chin court and lived as a recluse, devoting himself to poetry. When his son attained prominence in public life, he was awarded high official rank. Sixteen titles of his plays are recorded in *A Register of Ghosts*, and three are extant. Of these three, *Rain on the Wu-t'ung Trees* is considered his best work. He also left two volumes of poetry.[50]

Wang Shih-fu, author of *The Romance of the Western Chamber*, lived in the thirteenth century and was a native of Ta-tu. He wrote at least fourteen plays, but only three are extant. His *The Romance of the Western Chamber*, the longest and perhaps the best of the Yüan plays, consists of five parts, each part comparable in length to a regular Yüan play. According to one tradition, only the first four parts were written by him.[51]

Ch'iao Chi was from T'ai-yüan, Shansi, and later moved to Hangchow. Of his eleven known plays, the three extant are all love stories: *Love Fulfilled in a Future Life, Dream of Yang-chou* (*Yang-chou meng*), and *Story of a Golden Coin* (*Chin ch'ien chi*). Ch'iao Chi enjoyed contemporary fame on the strength of his lyrics and his unusual good looks. According to *A Register of Ghosts*, "Ch'iao was handsome, of good bearing, and dignified. He excelled in poetry. People were respectful and in awe of him. He lived across from T'ai-i Palace in Hangchow. Many people wrote prefaces for his volume entitled *Wu-t'ung Leaves on the West Lake* (*Hsi-hu wu yeh-erh*). He was active for forty years, traveling widely. He had hoped to have his work printed, but before his desire was realized, he died of sickness in the second month of the fifth year of the Chih-cheng period [1345]."[52] His poems cover a wide variety of subjects, but he is best known for his

---

[50] Chung Ssu-ch'eng, p. 107; also see T'an Cheng-pi, pp. 176-219.

[51] On Wang Shih-fu, see T'an Cheng-pi, pp. 119-73.

[52] Chung Ssu-ch'eng, p. 126.

delicate descriptions of feminine beauty and charm. He is also known to have associated with courtesans and to have dedicated to them many of his songs and poems. He left behind him nearly two hundred poems and ten song-suites, second only to Chang K'o-chiu as the most productive of the Yüan song writers.[53]

Biographical material relating to some one hundred other known dramatists is either fragmentary or nonexistent. Many of them were evidently men of education whose public lives as civil servants were not distinguished. None of the Yüan dramatists attained the prominence of having his biography included in the official histories. Among the civil servants listed in *A Register of Ghosts*, Shih-chiu San-jen held the highest post as a military commander over ten thousand households (*wan-hu*).[54] There was also a commander over one thousand households (*ch'ien-hu*),[55] three magistrates,[56] one prefect,[57] one supervisor of education,[58] and several persons in insignificant posts.[59] Besides the civil servants, there were also men from other professions who wrote plays. Shih Hui was a merchant[60] and Hsiao Te-hsiang was a doctor,[61] while there were several from the acting profession.[62]

The Yüan playwrights seem to have been a fairly varied group, including scholars, civil servants, merchants, doctors, and actors. Versed in poetry and trained in the classics, many

[53] On Ch'iao Chi, see T'an Cheng-pi, pp. 312-40.

[54] Chung Ssu-ch'eng, p. 115.

[55] Commander Wang T'ing-hsiu (*ibid.*, p. 112).

[56] Magistrate Li Tzu-chung (*ibid.*, p. 114); Magistrate Li Wen-wei (*ibid.*, p. 108); and Magistrate Li K'uan-fu (*ibid.*, p. 116).

[57] Prefect Liang Chin-chih (*ibid.*, p. 114).

[58] Supervisor Chao Kung-fu (*ibid.*, p. 114).

[59] Yü Chi-fu (*ibid.*, p. 108); Shang Chung-hsien (*ibid.*, p. 111); Tai Shan-fu (*ibid.*, p. 112); Chao T'ien-hsi (*ibid.*, p. 114); Ku Chung-ch'ing (*ibid.*, p. 115); Liu T'ang-ch'ing (*ibid.*, p. 117), and Chang Shou-ch'ing (*ibid.*, p. 117).

[60] *Ibid.*, p. 123.   [61] *Ibid.*, p. 134.

[62] Chao Wen-yin, Chang Kuo-pao, and Hung-tzu Li-erh (*ibid.*, pp. 113 and 117).

of them probably would have served, or served with more distinction, in government posts, had they not been under the alien Mongol rule. Some of them were forced to depend on the theatre and other practical professions as a means of support. They wrote to please themselves, the actors, and the audience. Even the least of them had a sense of the beauty of language, for the Yüan theatre was chiefly a school of poets.

Audience

The omission of Yüan dramatists in official histories and the critical silence concerning the Yüan drama indicate that the Yüan theatre's primary function was popular entertainment. The richness of this drama, however, suggests the heterogeneity of the audience, and other evidence supports the impression that the Yüan theatre audience included all classes of people.

The description of the whirlpool-like crowd in the Yüan song-suite "A Peasant Unfamiliar with the Theatre" shows that the audience at a theatre ground was large. In the complete absence of statistical data, it is unwise to attempt to estimate the actual size of a Yüan audience, especially when the capacity of the entertainment grounds must have varied a great deal. But fragmentary contemporary evidence fortunately gives some clue to the social composition and aesthetic and intellectual capacities of the Yüan audience.

The Common People. Many accounts of the Sung capitals testify to an already thriving popular audience for entertainment. During the Yüan period, Marco Polo's descriptions, while exaggerated, show that there was substantial wealth in the country, particularly in the capital. These accounts suggest that the people of the middle and lower classes could afford to pay for various forms of entertainment such as theatre and puppet shows. The country bumpkin in Tu Shanfu's song-suite, who paid 200 cash (*erh pai wen*) as admission to the theatre, is one obvious instance of a peasant spectator. (To translate this price into monetary values familiar to us is, however, difficult.) It is quite probable that the Yüan audience to a large degree consisted of peasants, artisans, and merchants—the middle and lower middle classes.

While Mongols and titled officials knew little Chinese and generally remained out of touch with the lives of the Chinese people, the Yüan playwrights were attuned to the troubles of their countrymen. Corrupt judges and overbearing officials are often treated harshly in the satires of these dramatists. The great popularity of this drama under the alien rule attests to the playwrights' close rapport with the audience.

The tastes and values of a middle-class audience are well reflected in the stories, which are filled with courtesans ambitious to marry officials, attractive wives abandoned by heartless fortune-seeking husbands, beggars, quacks, and outlaw heroes. The attempted strangling of Mistress Ts'ai for twenty ounces of silver, the rogues "Donkey" Chang and his father forcing their way into the widows' household, the corrupt judge's sentencing of an innocent woman to death—all these scenes in *Injustice to Tou O* probably mirror the realities of life among the lower middle class. The content of the plays reveals that the audience sought after moral instruction as well as diversion. The viewers enjoyed both stories that purported to be true and stories that were apparently fictitious. They insisted only upon a triumph of virtue, often with tangible rewards. While virtue usually does triumph in the end, nevertheless the moral of the story is sometimes obscured by sensationalism and interest in the salacious, indicating the playwrights' awareness of the psychology of a popular audience.

The Yüan stage was crowded with plays based on historical events that reflect patriotism and interest in the national past. The popular audience would have looked back on the years preceding the Mongol invasion with nostalgia and pride. The Three Kingdoms period in particular was brought to life with emotional impact in these plays. Only to an audience with great interest in its history could the world of intrigue of the Three Kingdoms have a thrilling reality, even for the illiterate.

The popular audience also welcomed stories about the life of the traditionally respected figure of the scholar, as reflected in the preponderance of tales about the literati, their successes in love affairs, and their scholarly and official achievements. The shopkeepers, the peasants, and the artisans offered a receptive ear to the popularization of the lore of scholars; they shared a basic admiration for those men who pursued a life of study. It is not only the themes that suggest the demands of a middle-class audience, but also the use of the common vernacular language, especially in its often coarse and ribald details, which expresses the tastes and humor of the common people.

The Literati. The scholars, although generally deprived of their honored positions during the Yüan rule, continued to be a special class. The fact that they were an important part of the audience of Yüan drama can be seen in the writings of these men themselves. Hu Tzu-shan (1227-1293), whose name appears in the official Yüan history, was a scholar specializing in the Sung philosopher Chu Hsi and served as an Imperial inspector of Chiang-nan and Che-hsi circuits. In his "Preface for Miss Sung" ("Tseng Sung shih hsü"), he shows a high esteem for *tsa-chü* and admiration for the talents of the actress:

"Recently, *yüan-pen* plays have evolved into the *tsa-chü* genre. Since they are called 'variety' (*tsa*) plays, they deal with emperors and officials, as well as with life in the markets, and the affairs of fathers, sons, brothers, husbands, wives and friends. They cover themes of medicine, fortune-telling, Buddhism, Taoism, and commerce. They deal with the customs and languages of different places. They describe superbly people's feelings and behavior. For one woman to be able to do what ten thousand others do, and in such a way as to be pleasing to the eye and ear, is not an art that former actresses could emulate. All these qualities I see in Miss Sung."[63]

In his two poems entitled "To Actor Chao Wen-i" ("Tseng ling-jen Chao Wen-i"), Hu praises another performer:

> *The rich, the noble, the wise, the foolish all coexist in this world;*
> *A thousand purples, ten thousand reds together compete in fashion;*
> *Who of these will in the end be fed the meal of yellow millet—*
> *All is won by the actors on the stage.*

> *Painted with mud and ashes, his whole face is covered with dust;*
> *It is hard to predict the lawsuit, which is so strange.*
> *Of the myriad things in this world, which ones are real, which false—*
> *One needs to learn from the traveler in Ch'ang-an.*[64]

Yoshikawa asserts that the poem may refer to the play *The Dream of Yellow Millet*, and the actor to whom the poems are addressed may be Chao Wen-yin mentioned in *A Register of Ghosts*.[65]

Hu's friend Wang Yün (1227-1304) was also interested in the theatre. He was a member of the Imperial Academy of Letters (Han-lin) and was well known for his writings. Like his friend, he was also mentioned in the official Yüan history. In addition to addressing poems to Chu Lien-hsiu,[66] a famous actress, he wrote an essay for the singer, Ts'ao

---

[63] Hu Tzu-shan, *Tzu-shan ta-ch'üan chi*, *chüan* 8, pp. 43b-44a. On the subject of the literati and Mongol audience, I am indebted to Yoshikawa Kōjirō for directing my attention to this and several other Yüan and early Ming sources. (See Yoshikawa, *Yüan tsa-chü yen-chiu*, pp. 44-70).

[64] *Ibid.*, *chüan* 7, pp. 49a-50b.

[65] Yoshikawa, p. 66.

[66] *Ch'iu-chien hsien-sheng ta-ch'üan wen-chi* (*SPTK so-pen*), *chüan* 77, pp. 745-46.

Chin-hsiu, entitled "Preface to the Poems of Actress Ts'ao" ("Yüeh-chi Ts'ao shih shih yin").[67] Another contemporary source of information about the literary men's interest in and patronage of the theatre is *The Green Mansions*, which mentions a number of men of letters in connection with the lives of courtesan-actresses. Moreover, the artistic emphasis on exquisite poetry in Yüan drama itself undeniably indicates the interests of the literary class.

The Mongols. That *tsa-chü* drama reached the ruling Mongol class as well as the conquered Chinese masses can hardly be doubted. References to theatrical performances at the Chin court and later at the Mongol court reflect the Mongols' interest in music and dramatic arts.[68] Such performances are also mentioned in the writings of Marco Polo, when he describes the feasts of the Great Khan: "When the repast is finished, and the tables have been removed, persons of various descriptions enter the hall, and amongst these a troupe of comedians and performers on different instruments, as also tumblers and jugglers, who exhibit their skill in the presence of the grand Khan, to the high amusement and gratification of all the spectators."[69]

Specific reference to *tsa-chü* drama is found in the poem "Palace Song" ("Kung tz'u") by the Yüan author Yang Wei-chen (1296-1370):

> *Music of the last era remains popular in the new dynasty—*
> *The "White Plume" flew onto the thirteen strings;*[70]
> *The dramatist, Kuan Ch'ing of the great Chin, was present,*
> *And the play* I Yin Assists T'ang *was performed.*[71]

[67] *Ibid., chüan* 43, pp. 438-39.   [68] See Yoshikawa, pp. 51-55.

[69] Marco Polo, *The Travels of Marco Polo, the Venetian,* p. 186.

[70] "White plume" (*pai-ling*) is probably the same as *pai-ling-ch'üeh.* The latter is the name of a "song-and-dance suite" (*ta-ch'ü*), current in the Yüan period—of slow tempo in the beginning, but fast toward the end (T'ao Tsung-i, *chüan* 20, p. 14b).

[71] Yang Wei-chen, "Kung tz'u," in *T'ieh-ya san chung, chüan* 8, p. 6b. *I Yin fu T'ang* is listed in *Lu kuei pu* as a play by Cheng Kuang-tsu (Chung Ssu-ch'eng, p. 119).

Prince Chu Su (d.1425) makes a reference to the same play-wright in his "Yüan Palace Song" ("Yüan kung tz'u"):

> *The first to compose the music was Kuan Ch'ing,*
> *A tsa-chü* I Yin Assists T'ang *was presented.*
> *Brought to the Forbidden City, it was enjoyed within*
>   *the palace,*
> *For a time, all listened to the singing of the new music.*[72]

The dramatist Kuan Ch'ing mentioned in these two poems may well be the leading Yüan dramatist Kuan Han-ch'ing, and the use of a contracted form of the name may have been called for by prosody, or the limitation of a seven-character line. However, this specific play, *I Yin Assists T'ang*, is not listed as one of Kuan's plays in *A Register of Ghosts*. Even though the dramatist cited in the poems and the one listed in *A Register of Ghosts* may not be identical, it is quite certain that *tsa-chü* were presented in the Yüan palace.

The Yüan theatre audience must have been a variegated group including poor laborers and Mongol princes, illiterates and scholars, the conquered and the conquerors. It was an audience to which the playwright had been conditioned and for which he wrote. Since the Yüan audience was educationally, socially, racially, and economically mixed, it forced the most observant of all authors to address themselves to all men and not to any specific class or rank. Yüan plays were consequently a people's literature, and they became, like folk tales, a part of the people's lore. The universality achieved in the Yüan plays perhaps resulted from the interplay between the dramatist and his audience. As living theatre, Yüan drama was the product of the dynamic process in which the creative mind is nourished by the life and spirit of the people.

[72] Chu Su, "Yüan kung tz'u," collected in Chang Hai-p'eng, *Kung tz'u hsiao-tsuan* (in *Chieh-yüeh-shan-fang hui-ch'ao ts'ung-shu*), *chüan* 1, p. 12a.

Epilogue

THIS study of Yüan drama, drawing attention to various relevant and modifying elements, has touched upon diverse aspects of the genre. The poet's script is our main source of information about the sundry ingredients of the drama, but the script itself cannot be considered to be the play. In a study of Yüan drama, it is essential to remember that the script is only one aspect of a play; the narrative tradition, language, and music, as well as the dramatists and audience, must all be taken into consideration in an attempt to understand the genre.

Judging this literature by universal human standards, but also within its own conventions and against the background of the traditions that shaped it, we can see Yüan drama as an artistic success, blending elements of storytelling, poetry, acting, singing, and music. The best of the Yüan plays are indeed great literature, outstanding both in the beauty of their poetry and in their insight into human psychology.

Yüan drama exerted a tremendous influence on the drama that followed it. The juxtaposition of song and prose, symbolism and naturalism, tragedy and comedy, has become conventional on the Chinese stage. The basic techniques of presentation and the established characters—the long-suffering heroine, the scholar-lover, the crafty general, the devoted son, the loyal servant, the wise judge, the corrupt magistrate, and the beautiful and talented courtesan—have persisted on the traditional Chinese stage to the present time.

For centuries Yüan drama has been considered by the literary elite to be an outstanding poetic genre, comparable to T'ang *shih* and Sung *tz'u*; it is now claimed in the People's Republic of China as one of the most representative types of "people's literature."[1] Many editions of Yüan plays appeared in China in the late 1950's, and dramatists such as Kuan Han-ch'ing have been singled out as the champions of the oppressed masses. Because of its roots among the people, Yüan drama continues to have its appeal alongside revolutionary social change.

This book, offering an overview of the genre and at the same time exploring more deeply its several central values, is presented in the hope that it will not only help to give Western students a greater appreciation of the achievements of Yüan drama, but also stimulate specialized studies in areas that are still essentially virgin territory. Such studies could evaluate the various ways in which the dramatists exploited the earlier literary tradition, in terms of sources, conventions, and themes. They could make a critical analysis of sustained patterns of imagery in the dramatic poetry, as has been attempted in this study, showing how the lyrics are integrated into the very fibre of the plays and how the imagery enhances the plays' dramatic significance. They could explore methods of characterization and the playwrights' ways of establishing and sustaining the interplay between the characters. They could investigate the possible influence of foreign drama or the effect, however great or small, of traditional performances at religious festivals upon the secular Yüan theatre. A particularly productive study would be a detailed analysis of a single play, such as *The Romance of the Western Chamber*, as an artistic entity; after all, this play has been singled out by the famous seventeenth-century critic Chin Sheng-t'an as one of the six wonders of Chinese literature. Studies such as these would do much to shed light on the rise of Yüan drama under the alien Mongol rule and on the plays themselves, which are unquestionably a brilliant achievement in Chinese literary history.

[1] Except during the period of the Cultural Revolution in the late 1960's, when all traditional literature, vernacular and classical, was repudiated.

Appendix

Extant Yüan Plays and Their Authors

Number of Extant Plays. There are 162 titles. For the convenience of statistical analysis, they are counted as 171 plays, since two titles (117, 140) have more than one part, and each part is comparable in length and form to a conventional play. Of the 100 plays in the *YCH,* six (27, 63, 68, 78, 81, 88), however, are believed to be of the early Ming period (Wang Kuo-wei, p. 99); some plays in *WP* may also belong to the same period.

Authorship. The authorship attributed here to the extant plays corresponds to what is found in *YCH* and *WP.* For differences of opinion on authorship, see Ch'en Wan-nai, *Yüan Ming Ch'ing chü-ch'ü shih* (pp. 248-58), which provides a comparative list of the playwrights and their works, as identified by Wang Kuo-wei (*Sung Yüan hsi-ch'ü shih*), Yoshikawa (*Yüan tsa-chü yen-chiu*), and Lo Chin-t'ang (*Hsien ts'un Yüan-jen tsa-chü pen-shih k'ao*). On this subject, consult also Yen Tun-i, *Yüan chü chen i,* and William C. C. Hu, *"A Bibliography for Yüan Opera (tsa-chü)"* in *Occasional Papers* (The University of Michigan), no. 1 (1962), pp. 1-37. Several lists of Yüan plays, including one by the contemporary author Chung Ssu-ch'eng of 452 titles, have been preserved. (Chung Ssu-ch'eng, pp. 104-37; see also Chu Ch'üan, pp. 26-44).

The numbers in the following list refer to the order in which the plays appear in *YCH* and *WP.*

Play Number	Short Title	Author
YCH		
1	*Han kung ch'iu* 漢宮秋	Ma Chih-yüan 馬致遠
2	*Chin-ch'ien chi* 金錢記	Ch'iao Chi (Meng-fu) 喬吉（孟符）
3	*Ch'en-chou t'iao mi* 陳州糶米	— : anonymous
4	*Yüan-yang pei* 鴛鴦被	—
5	*Chuan K'uai T'ung* 賺蒯通	—
6	*Yü-ching t'ai* 玉鏡臺	Kuan Han-ch'ing 關漢卿
7	*Sha kou ch'üan fu* 殺狗勸夫	—
8	*Ho han-shan* 合汗衫	Chang Kuo-pin 張國賓
9	*Hsieh T'ien-hsiang* 謝天香	Kuan Han-ch'ing 關漢卿
10	*Cheng pao-en* 爭報恩	—
11	*Chang T'ien-shih* 張天師	Wu Ch'ang-ling 吳昌齡
12	*Chiu feng-ch'en* 救風塵	Kuan Han-ch'ing 關漢卿
13	*Tung-t'ang lao* 東堂老	Ch'in Chien-fu 秦簡夫
14	*Yen Ch'ing po yü* 燕青博魚	Li Wen-wei 李文蔚
15	*Hsiao Hsiang yü* 瀟湘雨	Yang Hsien-chih 楊顯之
16	*Ch'ü-chiang ch'ih* 曲江池	Shih Chün-pao 石君寶
17	*Ch'u Chao kung* 楚昭公	Cheng T'ing-yü 鄭廷玉
18	*Lai sheng chai* 來生債	—

19	*Hsüeh Jen-kuei* 薛仁貴	Chang Kuo-pin 張國賓
20	*Ch'iang t'ou ma shang* 牆頭馬上	Po P'u (Jen-fu) 白　樸（仁甫）
21	*Wu-t'ung yü* 梧桐雨	Po P'u 白　樸
22	*Lao sheng erh* 老生兒	Wu Han-ch'en 武漢臣
23	*Chu sha tan* 硃砂擔	—
24	*Hu t'ou p'ai* 虎頭牌	Li Chih-fu 李直夫
25	*Ho-t'ung wen-tzu* 合同文字	—
26	*Tung Su Ch'in* 凍蘇秦	—
27	*Erh nü t'uan-yüan* 兒女團圓	Yang Wen-k'uei 楊文奎
28	*Yü hu ch'un* 玉壺春	Wu Han-ch'en 武漢臣
29	*T'ieh-kuai Li* 鐵拐李	Yüeh Po-ch'uan 岳伯川
30	*Hsiao Yü-ch'ih* 小尉遲	—
31	*Feng-kuang hao* 風光好	Tai Shan-fu 戴善夫
32	*Ch'iu Hu hsi ch'i* 秋胡戲妻	Shih Chün-pao 石君寶
33	*Shen Nu-erh* 神奴兒	—
34	*Chien-fu pei* 薦福碑	Ma Chih-yüan 馬致遠
35	*Hsieh Chin-wu* 謝金吾	—
36	*Yüeh-yang lou* 岳陽樓	Ma Chih-yüan 馬致遠
37	*Hu-tieh meng* 蝴蝶夢	Kuan Han-ch'ing 關漢卿
38	*Wu Yüan ch'ui hsiao* 伍員吹簫	Li Shou-ch'ing 李壽卿

39	*K'an t'ou-chin* 勘頭巾	Sun Chung-chang 孫仲章
40	*Shuang hsien-kung* *(Hei hsüan-feng)* 雙獻功（黑旋風）	Kao Wen-hsiu 高文秀
41	*Ch'ien nü li hun* 倩女離魂	Cheng Kuang-tsu (Te-hui) 鄭光祖（德輝）
42	*Ch'en T'uan kao wo* 陳摶高臥	Ma Chih-yüan 馬致遠
43	*Ma-ling tao* 馬陵道	—
44	*Chiu hsiao tzu* 救孝子	Wang Chung-wen 王仲文
45	*Huang-liang meng* 黃粱夢	Ma Chih-yüan *et al.* 馬致遠
46	*Yang-chou meng* 揚州夢	Ch'iao Chi 喬 吉
47	*Wang Ts'an teng lou* 王粲登樓	Cheng Kuang-tsu 鄭光祖
48	*Hao t'ien t'a* 昊天塔	—
49	*Lu Chai-lang* 魯齋郎	Kuan Han-ch'ing 關漢卿
50	*Yü ch'iao chi* 漁樵記	—
51	*Ch'ing shan lei* 青衫淚	Ma Chih-yüan 馬致遠
52	*Li-ch'un t'ang* 麗春堂	Wang Shih-fu 王實甫
53	*Chü an ch'i mei* 舉案齊眉	—
54	*Hou-t'ing hua* 後庭花	Cheng T'ing-yü 鄭廷玉
55	*Fan Chang chi shu* 范張鷄黍	Kung T'ien-t'ing (Ta-yung) 宮天挺（大用）
56	*Liang shih yin-yüan* 兩世姻緣	Ch'iao Chi 喬 吉
57	*Chao li jang fei* 趙禮讓肥	Ch'in Chien-fu 秦簡夫
58	*K'u-han t'ing* 酷寒亭	Yang Hsien-chih 楊顯之

59	*T'ao-hua nü* 桃花女	—
60	*Chu-yeh chou* 竹葉舟	Fan Tzu-an 范子安
61	*Jen tzu chi* 忍字記	Cheng T'ing-yü 鄭廷玉
62	*Hung li hua* 紅梨花	Chang Shou-ch'ing 張壽卿
63	*Chin t'ung yü nü* *(Chin An-shou)* 金童玉女（金安壽）	Chia Chung-ming 賈仲明
64	*Hui-lan chi* 灰闌記	Li Hsing-tao 李行道
65	*Yüan-chia chai-chu* 冤家債主	—
66	*Tsou Mei-hsiang* 㑳梅香	Cheng Kuang-tsu 鄭光祖
67	*Tan pien to shuo* 單鞭奪槊	Shang Chung-hsien 尙仲賢
68	*Ch'eng nan liu* 城南柳	Ku Tzu-ching 谷子敬
69	*Sui Fan Shu* 誶范叔	—
70	*Wu-t'ung yeh* 梧桐葉	—
71	*Tung-p'o meng* 東坡夢	Wu Ch'ang-ling 吳昌齡
72	*Chin hsien ch'ih* 金線池	Kuan Han-ch'ing 關漢卿
73	*Liu hsieh chi* 留鞋記	Tseng Jui-ch'ing 曾瑞卿
74	*Ch'i Ying Pu* 氣英布	—
75	*Ko chiang tou chih* 隔江鬭智	—
76	*Liu hang-shou* 劉行首	Yang Ching-hsien 楊景賢
77	*Tu Liu Ts'ui* 度柳翠	—

78	*Wu ju t'ao yüan* 悮入桃源	Wang Tzu-i 王子一
79	*Mo-ho-lo* 魔合羅	Meng Han-ch'ing 孟漢卿
80	*P'en-erh kuei* 盆兒鬼	—
81	*Yü shu chi* (*Tui yü shu*) 玉梳記（對玉梳）	Chia Chung-ming 賈仲明
82	*Pai-hua t'ing* 百花亭	—
83	*Chu wu t'ing ch'in* 竹塢聽琴	Shih Tzu-chang 石子章
84	*Pao chuang ho* 抱粧盒	—
85	*Chao shih ku-erh* 趙氏孤兒	Chi Chün-hsiang 紀君祥
86	*Tou O yüan* 竇娥冤	Kuan Han-ch'ing 關漢卿
87	*Li K'uei fu ching* 李逵負荊	K'ang Chin-chih 康進之
88	*Hsiao Shu-lan* 蕭淑蘭	Chia Chung-ming 賈仲明
89	*Lien-huan chi* 連環計	—
90	*Lo Li-lang* 羅李郎	Chang Kuo-pao [*sic*] 張國寶 [*sic*]
91	*K'an ch'ien nu* 看錢奴	—
92	*Huan lao mo* 還牢末	Li Chih-yüan 李致遠
93	*Liu I ch'uan shu* 柳毅傳書	Shang Chung-hsien 尙仲賢
94	*Huo-lang tan* 貨郎旦	—
95	*Wang-chiang t'ing* 望江亭	Kuan Han-ch'ing 關漢卿
96	*Jen Feng-tzu* 任風子	Ma Chih-yüan 馬致遠

97	*Pi t'ao-hua* 碧桃花	—
98	*Chang sheng chu hai* 張生煑海	Li Hao-ku 李好古
99	*Sheng chin ko* 生金閣	Wu Han-ch'en 武漢臣
100	*Feng Yü-lan* 馮玉蘭	—
101	*Hsi Shu meng* 西蜀夢	Kuan Han-ch'ing 關漢卿
102	*Pai-yüeh t'ing* 拜月亭	Kuan Han-ch'ing 關漢卿
103	*P'ei Tu huan tai* 裴度還帶	Kuan Han-ch'ing 關漢卿
104	*K'u Ts'un-hsiao* 哭存孝	Kuan Han-ch'ing 關漢卿
105	*Tan tao hui* 單刀會	Kuan Han-ch'ing 關漢卿
106	*Fei i meng* 緋衣夢	Kuan Han-ch'ing 關漢卿
107	*T'iao feng yüeh* 調風月	Kuan Han-ch'ing 關漢卿
108	*Ch'en mu chiao tzu* 陳母敎子	Kuan Han-ch'ing 關漢卿
109	*Wu-hou yen* 五侯宴	Kuan Han-ch'ing 關漢卿
110	*Yü shang-huang* 遇上皇	Kao Wen-hsiu 高文秀
111	*Hsiang-yang hui* 襄陽會	Kao Wen-hsiu 高文秀
112	*Min-ch'ih hui* 澠池會	Kao Wen-hsiu 高文秀
113	*Chin-feng ch'ai* 金鳳釵	Cheng T'ing-yü 鄭廷玉
114	*Tung ch'iang chi* 東牆記	Po P'u 白　樸
115	*I ch'iao chin lü* 圯橋進履	Li Wen-wei 李文蔚
116	*Chiang shen ling-ying* 蔣神靈應	Li Wen-wei 李文蔚

117a-d	*Hsi hsiang chi* 西廂記	Wang Shih-fu 王實甫
117e	*Hsi hsiang chi* 西廂記	Kuan Han-ch'ing 關漢卿
118	*P'o yao chi* 破窰記	Wang Shih-fu 王實甫
119	*San to shuo* 三奪槊	Shang Chung-hsien 尙仲賢
120	*Tzu-yün t'ing* 紫雲亭	Shih Chün-pao 石君寶
121	*Pien Huang-chou* 貶黃州	Fei T'ang-ch'en 費唐臣
122	*Pien Yeh-lang* 貶夜郎	Wang Po-ch'eng 王伯成
123	*Chuang Chou meng* 莊周夢	Shih-chiu Ching-hsien 史九敬先
124	*Chieh Tzu-t'ui* 介子推	Ti Chün-hou 狄君厚
125	*Tung ch'uang shih fan* 東窗事犯	K'ung Wen-ch'ing 孔文卿
126	*Chiang sang-shen* 降桑椹	Liu T'ang-ch'ing 劉唐卿
127	*Ch'i-li-t'an* 七里灘	Kung T'ien-t'ing 宮天挺
128	*Chou-kung she cheng* 周公攝政	Cheng Kuang-tsu 鄭光祖
129	*San chan Lü Pu* 三戰呂布	Cheng Kuang-tsu 鄭光祖
130	*Chih yung ting Ch'i* 智勇定齊	Cheng Kuang-tsu 鄭光祖
131	*I Yin keng hsin* 伊尹耕莘	Cheng Kuang-tsu 鄭光祖
132	*Lao chün t'ang* 老君堂	Cheng Kuang-tsu 鄭光祖
133	*Chui Han Hsin* 追韓信	Chin Jen-chieh 金仁傑
134	*Yen-men kuan* (*Ts'un-hsiao ta hu*) 雁門關（存孝打虎）	Ch'en I-jen 陳以仁
135	*Chien fa tai pin* 剪髮待賓	Ch'in Chien-fu 秦簡夫

136	*Huo Kuang kuei chien* 霍光鬼諫	Yang Tzu 楊　梓
137	*Yü Jang t'un t'an* 豫讓吞炭	Yang Tzu 楊　梓
138	*Ching-te pu fu lao* 敬德不伏老	Yang Tzu 楊　梓
139	*Feng yün hui* 風雲會	Lo Kuan-chung 羅貫中
140a-f	*Hsi yu chi* 西遊記	Yang Ching-hsien 楊景賢
141	*Sheng-hsien meng* 昇仙夢	Chia Chung-ming 賈仲明
142	*T'i sha ch'i* 替殺妻	—
143	*Hsiao Chang t'u* 小張屠	—
144	*Po-wang shao t'un* 博望燒屯	—
145	*Ch'ien li tu hsing* 千里獨行	—
146	*Tsui hsieh Ch'ih-pi fu* 醉寫赤壁賦	—
147	*Yün ch'uang meng* 雲窗夢	—
148	*Tu chiao niu* 獨角牛	—
149	*Liu Hung chia pei* 劉弘嫁婢	—
150	*Huang-ho lou* 黃鶴樓	—
151	*I ao ch'e* 衣襖車	—
152	*Fei tao tui chien* 飛刀對箭	—
153	*Wang chiang t'ing* 望江亭	—
154	*Ts'un le t'ang* 村樂堂	—
155	*Yen-an fu* 廷安府	—

Abbreviations

CKKT *Chung-kuo ku-tien hsi-ch'ü lun-chu chi-ch'eng*
中國古典戲曲論著集成

CTS *Ch'üan T'ang shih* 全唐詩

CYYY *Chung-yüan yin yün* 中原音韻,
(See Chou Te-ch'ing 周德清)

KPHC *Ku-pen hsi-ch'ü ts'ung-k'an* 古本戲曲叢刊

SPTK so-pen *Ssu-pu ts'ung-k'an so-pen* 四部叢刊縮本 (In the
case of standard histories, references are to *SPTK Po-na*
百衲 edition.)

YCH *Yüan ch'ü hsüan* 元曲選

WP *Yüan ch'ü hsüan wai-pien* 元曲選外編

Selected Bibliography

A. PRIMARY SOURCE: YÜAN DRAMA TEXTS

1. COLLECTIONS

(i) Yüan Editions

Ch'ao-yeh hsin sheng t'ai-p'ing yüeh-fu 朝野新聲太平樂府.
Edited by Yang Chao-ying 楊朝英 (ca. 1324). 9 *chüan*. In
SPTK so-pen. Contains songs from Yüan drama.

Yang ch'un pai hsüeh 陽春白雪. Compiled by Yang Chao-
ying 楊朝英. Shanghai: Commercial Press, 1936. 10
chüan. Facsimile of Yüan edition. Contains songs from
Yüan drama.

Yüan k'an tsa-chü san-shih chung 元刊雜劇三十種 (*A
Yüan Edition of Thirty Plays*). A wood-block edition, this
is the oldest extant text of Yüan drama. The thirty plays in
the collection consist mainly of song-sequences and very
scanty prose dialogue. Modern editions include the following: (1) an improved wood-block facsimile, published by
Kyoto University in 1914; (2) a photo-reprint edition of
the original Yüan copy, in the *Ku pen hsi-ch'ü ts'ung-k'an*,
4th series; (3) *Chiao-ting Yüan k'an tsa-chü san-shih
chung* 校訂元刊雜劇三十種. Edited by Cheng Ch'ien
鄭騫. Taipei: Shih-chieh Book Co., 1962.

(ii) Ming Editions

Ku chin ming chü ho-hsüan 古今名劇合選 (*Selected Famous
Plays Old and New*). Edited by Meng Ch'eng-shun 孟稱舜,
1633. A wood-block edition.

This collection of 56 Yüan plays originally existed in two
separate editions: *Liu-chih chi* 柳枝集 of 26 plays, and
Luo-chiang chi 酹江集 of 30 plays, both dated 1633. Reprint in *KPHC*, 4th series, vols. 101-20.

Ku ming-chia tsa-chü 古名家雜劇. (*Plays of Former Famous Playwrights*). Compiled by Ch'en Yü-chiao 陳與郊, 1588.

A Mr. Hsü 徐 of Lung-feng 龍峯 is thought to be the engraver of this edition (see *Kuan Han-ch'ing hsi-ch'ü chi* 關漢卿戲曲集, ed. Wu Hsiao-ling 吳曉鈴 *et al.*, Peking, 1958, pp. 1956-57). It consists of at least 78 Yüan and Ming plays: 55 of these are included in the *Mo-wang kuan ch'ao-chiao pen ku chin tsa-chü;* 13 are not extant; and 10 are included in the photo-reprint edition of *KPHC*, 4th series, vols. 93-95 (see note to the table of contents vol. 93, pp. 1a-1b).

Mo-wang kuan ch'ao-chiao pen ku chin tsa-chü 脈望館鈔校本 古今雜劇 (*Plays Old and New in the Mo-wang kuan Library Collection*). Compiled by Chao Ch'i-mei 趙琦美 (1563-1624).

The collection consists of 242 Yüan and Ming plays (some of which are only excerpts; 55 plays are from *Ku ming-chia tsa-chü*, 15 are from Hsi Chi-tzu's *Tsa-chü hsüan*, and the remaining 172 plays exist as handwritten copies). *Mo-wang kuan* was the name of the library of the compiler. A photolithographic reprint is in *KPHC*, 4th series, vols. 9-92.

Some of the plays in this collection contain more information on costumes, properties, and stage directions than is available in other editions.

Sheng shih hsin sheng 盛世新聲 (*New Sounds in a Prosperous Era*). Anonymous editor. Preface dated 1517. 12 *chüan*. Photo-reprint by Peking: Wen-hsüeh ku chi k'an-hsing-she, 1955.

Contains songs from Yüan drama.

Tsa-chü hsüan 雜劇選 (*Selected Plays*; also known as *Yüan jen tsa-chü hsüan* 元人雜劇選 or *Ku chin tsa-chü hsüan* 古今雜劇選). Compiled by Hsi Chi-tzu 息機子, with a preface dated 1598.

It consists of 30 plays; 15 of these are in *Mo-wang kuan ch'ao-chiao pen ku chin tsa-chü*, 4 are not extant, and 11 are included in a photo-reprint edition of *KPHC*, 4th series, vols. 96-98.

Yang-ch'un tsou 陽春奏. Compiled by Huang Cheng-wei 黃正位, with a preface dated 1609.

A Ming dynasty wood-block edition, it consists of 39 Yüan and Ming plays. Three of the Yüan plays are included in a photo-reprint edition of the *KPHC,* 4th series, vol. 99 (see note to the table of contents, vol. 99, p. 1a).

Yüan ch'ü hsüan 元曲選 *(Selected Yüan Plays).* Edited by Tsang Mao-hsün 臧懋循 (Chin-shu 晉叔), 1616. A woodblock edition.

Used as the basic text in my study, this collection of 100 plays has enjoyed great popularity through the centuries. Modern editions include the following: (1) Shanghai: Commercial Press, 1918 (a photo-reprint of the 1616 edition; this collection, originally known as *Yüan jen pai chung ch'ü* 元人百種曲, was given its present title in this 1918 edition, now known as the Han-fen-lou edition); (2) Shanghai: Chung-hua Book Co., 1936 (a block-print edition, in the *Ssu-pu pei-yao* collection); (3) Shanghai: Shih-chieh Book Co., 1936 (a typeset edition); (4) Peking: Chung-hua Book Co., 1958 (a revised edition of the 1936 Shih-chieh Book Co. edition), 4 vols. References are made to this last edition of 1958 (see p. ix).

Yung-hsi yüeh-fu 雍熙樂府. Edited by Kuo Hsün 郭勛. Printed between 1522 and 1566. 20 *chüan.* In *SPTK sopen,* 2nd series.

(iii)   Modern Editions

Genkyokusen shaku 元曲選釋 *(An Annotated Edition of Selected Yüan Plays).* Edited by Aoki Masaru 青木正兒, Yoshikawa Kōjirō 吉川幸次郎, Iriya Yoshitaka 入矢義高, and Tanaka Kenji 田中謙二. Kyoto: Kyoto University, 1951-52.

The annotations in Chinese are copious, including citations from other plays, poems, and notes by Chinese commentators. Vol. I contains three plays: *Han kung ch'iu* 漢宮秋, *Chin ch'ien chi* 金錢記, and *Sha kou ch'üan fu* 殺狗勸夫 (*Yüan ch'ü hsüan* nos. 1, 2, and 7). Vol II contains: *Hsiao Hsiang yü* 瀟湘雨, *Hu t'ou p'ai* 虎頭牌, and

Chin hsien ch'ih 金線池 (*Yüan ch'ü hsüan* nos. 15, 24, and 72).

Ku-pen hsi-ch'ü ts'ung-k'an 古本戲曲叢刊 (*A Collection of Old Texts of Traditional Drama*). Compiled by Ku-pen hsi-ch'ü ts'ung-kan pien-chi wei-yüan-hui. Shanghai and Peking: 1st series, 1954. 2nd series, 1955. 3rd series, 1957. 4th series, 1958.

Facsimile reproduction of traditional dramatic texts, some in handwritten and some in printed versions. The 4th series is in 120 volumes as follows: *Yüan k'an tsa-chü san-shih chung* 元刊雜劇三十種 (vols. 1-3); *Ku tsa-chü* 古雜劇, compiled by Wang Chi-te 王驥德 (vols. 4-8); *Mo-wang kuan ch'ao-chiao pen ku chin tsa-chü* 脈望館鈔校本古今雜劇, compiled by Chao Ch'i-mei 趙琦美 (vols. 9-92); *Ku ming-chia tsa-chü* 古名家雜劇, compiled by Ch'en Yü-chiao 陳與郊 (vols. 93-95); *Tsa-chü hsüan* 雜劇選, compiled by Hsi Chi-tzu 息機子 (vols. 96-98); *Yang-ch'un tsou* 陽春奏, compiled by Huang Cheng-wei 黃正位 (vol. 99); *Yüan Ming tsa-chü ssu chung* 元明雜劇四種 (vol. 100); *Ku-chin ming-chü ho-hsüan* 古今名劇合選, consisting of *Liu-chih chi* 柳枝集 and *Luo-chiang chi* 酹江集, compiled by Meng Ch'eng-shun 孟稱舜 (vols. (101-20).

Ku-pen Yüan Ming tsa-chü 孤本元明雜劇. Ch'ang-sha: Commercial Press, 1941. A typeset edition with an introduction by Wang Chi-lieh 王季烈.

The 144 plays of this collection are all from *Mo-wang kuan ch'ao-chiao pen ku chin tsa-chü*. 36 of these plays have been placed in the Yüan dynasty, and 17 others are possibly of the same period.

Yüan ch'ü hsüan wai-pien 元曲選外編 (*Selected Yüan Plays: A Supplement*). Compiled by Sui Shu-sen 隋樹森. Peking: Chung-hua Book Co., 1959. Reprint, 1961. 3 vols.

A collection of 71 plays (62 titles), these volumes include the best available texts of all the extant Yüan plays not found in *Yüan ch'ü hsüan*. The plays are grouped by authors, who are listed chronologically as well as can be determined. The source of each text is noted in the table of contents. As many of these plays were discovered in this century and are scattered in various collections, this compact edition, as a supplement to *Yüan ch'ü hsüan,* is a great convenience for students in the field.

Yüan jen tsa-chü hsüan 元人雜劇選 *(Selected Plays by Yüan Authors).* Edited by Ku Chao-ts'ang 顧肇倉. Peking: Jen-min wen-hsüeh ch'u-pan-she, 1956.

Contains fifteen Yüan plays with copious and excellent annotations.

2. INDIVIDUAL AUTHORS OR WORKS

Kuan Han-ch'ing hsi-ch'ü chi 關漢卿戲曲集 *(A Collection of Kuan Han-ch'ing's Plays).* Edited and collated by Wu Hsiao-ling 吳曉鈴 *et al.* 2 vols. Peking: Chung-kuo hsi-chü ch'u-pan-she, 1958.

This collection of eighteen plays attributed to Kuan Han-ch'ing has copious annotation and commentary. Kuan Han-ch'ing's non-dramatic *ch'ü* are included in the appendix.

Kuan Han-ch'ing hsi-ch'ü hsüan 關漢卿戲曲選 *(Selected Plays of Kuan Han-ch'ing).* Peking: Jen-min wen-hsüeh ch'u-pan-she, 1958.

A collection of eight plays by Kuan. Good annotations.

Ta hsi-chü-chia Kuan Han-ch'ing chieh-tso chi 大戲劇家關漢卿傑作集 *(Masterpieces of the Great Dramatist Kuan Han-ch'ing).* Edited by Wu Hsiao-ling 吳曉鈴 *et al.* Peking: Chung-kuo hsi-chü ch'u-pan-she, 1958.

A collection of six plays by Kuan. A glossary is appended, with the entries transcribed in the *P'in-yin* system, and arranged in alphabetical order. The vocabulary list (pp. 133-260) is long and the explanations are detailed and helpful. An index of Chinese characters, arranged by the number of strokes, is also appended (pp. 261-71).

Wang Shih-fu 王實甫. *Hsi hsiang chi* 西廂記 *(The Romance of the Western Chamber).* Edited and annotated by Wang Chi-ssu 王季思. Shanghai: Hsin-wen-i ch'u-pan-she, 1954.

Contains extensive annotation.

————. *Hsi hsiang chi* 西廂記 (*The Romance of the Western Chamber*). Edited and annotated by Wu Hsiao-ling 吳曉鈴. Peking: Tso-chia ch'u-pan-she, 1954.

————. *Hsi hsiang chi chu* 西廂記注 (*The Romance of the Western Chamber with Annotation*). Edited by Wang Yü-chün 王毓駿. Peiping: Wen-hua hsüeh-she, 1938.
Extensive annotation dealing with linguistic and lexical matters.

B. SECONDARY SOURCES

A Ying 阿英 (pseud. of Ch'ien Hsing-ts'un 錢杏村). "Yüan-jen tsa-chü shih" 元人雜劇史 ("History of Yüan Drama"), *Chü-pen* 劇本 (*Drama*), no. 4 (1954), 12-128; no. 6 (1954), 123-33; no. 7 (1954), 156-65; no. 8 (1954), 140-52; no. 9 (1954), 146-61; no. 10 (1954), 119-28.

Aoki, Masaru 青木正兒 *Shina kinsei gikyoku shi* 支那近世戲曲史 (*History of Chinese Drama in the Recent Centuries*). Tokyo, 1929. Translated into Chinese by Wang Ku-lu 王古魯, *Chung-kuo chin-shih hsi-ch'ü shih* 中國近世戲曲史, 1931. Reprinted by Peking: Tso-chia ch'u-pan-she, 1958. Reference here is to the Chinese version.

————. "Hokkyoku no ikyo" 北曲の遺響 ("Traces of Music of Northern Songs"), *Tōhōgakuhō* 東方學報 (Kyoto), VIII (Oct., 1937), 1-10.

————. *Yüan jen tsa-chü hsü-shuo* 元人雜劇序說 (*An Introductory Study in Yüan Drama*). Translated into Chinese by Sui Shu-sen 隋樹森 and edited by Hsü T'iao-fu 徐調孚. Shanghai: Kai-ming, 1941. Reprint, Hong Kong: Chien-wen Book Co., 1959. References are to the 1959 Chinese version.

Bazin, M. *Introduction au théâtre chinois des Youén*. Paris, 1938.

Berman, Laurence, editor. *Words and Music: The Scholar's View*. Cambridge: Harvard University Press, 1972.

Birch, Cyril. *Anthology of Chinese Literature*. New York: Grove Press, 1965.

————. *Stories from a Ming Collection.* Bloomington: Indiana University Press, 1959.

Bishop, John L. *The Colloquial Short Story in China: A Study of the San-Yen Collections.* Cambridge: Harvard University Press, 1956.

Brooks, E. Bruce. "Chinese Aria Studies." Seattle: University of Washington, 1968. A Ph.D. dissertation.

Brower, Robert and Earl Miner. *Japanese Court Poetry.* Stanford: Stanford University Press, 1961.

Chang, Hai-p'eng 張海鵬. *Kung tz'u hsiao-tsuan* 宮詞小纂. In *Chieh-yüeh-shan-fang hui-ch'ao ts'ung-shu* 借月山房彙鈔叢書, 1812. Shanghai: Po-ku-chai 博古齋 reprint, 1920.

Chang, Hsiang 張相. *Shih tz'u ch'ü yü tz'u-hui shih* 詩詞曲語辭滙釋 (*A Glossary of Words and Terms from Shih, Tz'u and Ch'ü Forms of Poetry*). Shanghai: Chung-hua Book Co., 1953. 2 vols. Revised and printed as *Shih tz'u ch'ü yü tz'u-tien* 詩詞曲語辭典 Taipei: I-wen Book Co., 1957.

Chang, Hua 張華 (232-300). *Po wu chih* 博物志 (*A Miscellany of Marvels*). *Ssu-pu pei-yao* edition listed below.

Chang, Yen 張炎 (1248-ca. 1315). *Tz'u yüan* 詞源 (*Sources of the Tz'u*). In *Tz'u hsüeh ts'ung-shu* 詞學叢書 (*A Collection of Studies on Tz'u*). Edited by Ch'in En-fu 秦恩復, 1810.

Chao, Ching-shen 趙景深. *Hsi-ch'ü pi t'an* 戲曲筆談 (*Discourses on Drama*). Peking: Chung-hua Book Co., 1962.

————. *Yüan-jen tsa-chü kou-ch'en* 元人雜劇鉤沈 (*Excerpts of Lost Yüan Plays*). Shanghai: Ku-tien wen-hsüeh ch'u-pan-she, 1956.

————. *Tu ch'ü hsiao chi* 讀曲小記 (*Notes on Traditional Drama*). Peking: Chung-hua Book Co., 1959.

Chao, Yin-t'ang 趙蔭棠. *Chung-yüan yin yün yen-chiu* (*A Study of Chung-yüan yin yün*) 中原音韻研究. Shanghai: Commercial Press, 1936.

Ch'en, Li-li. "Outer and Inner Forms of *Chu-kung-tiao,* with Reference to *Pien-wen, Tz'u* and Vernacular Fiction," *Harvard Journal of Asiatic Studies,* XXXII (1972), 124-48.

Ch'en, Shou-yi [陳受頤]. "The Chinese Orphan: A Yüan Play. Its Influences on European Drama of the Eighteenth Century," *T'ien Hsia Monthly,* III, no. 2 (Sept. 1936), 89-115.

Ch'en, Wan-nai 陳萬鼐. *Yüan Ming ch'ing chü-ch'ü shih* 元明清劇曲史 (*History of the Yüan, Ming, and Ch'ing Drama*). Taipei: Commercial Press, 1966.

Cheng, Chen-to 鄭振鐸. *Ch'a-t'u pen Chung-kuo wen-hsüeh shih* 插圖本中國文學史 (*An Illustrated History of Chinese Literature*). Peking: Wen-hsüeh ku-chi k'an-hsing-she, 1959.

————. *Chung-kuo su wen-hsüeh shih.* 中國俗文學史 (*History of Chinese Vernacular Literature*). 1938. Reprint, Peking: Wen-hsüeh ku-chi k'an-hsing-she, 1959.

————. *Chung-kuo wen-hsüeh yen-chiu* 中國文學研究 (*Studies in Chinese Literature*). Peking: Tso-chia ch'u-pan-she, 1957.
Contains several essays on Yüan drama.

Cheng, Ch'ien 鄭騫. *Ching-wu ts'ung pien* 景午叢編 (*Collected Works of Cheng Ch'ien*). Taipei: Chung-hua Book Co., 1972. 2 vols.
Contains 24 articles on the subject of Yüan drama, including a few listed here.

————. *Pei ch'ü hsin p'u* 北曲新譜 (*Metrical Patterns of Northern Songs*). Taipei: I-wen ch'u-pan-she, 1973.

————. "Pei ch'ü ke-shih te pien-hua" 北曲格式的變化 ("Changes of Form of Northern Songs"), *Ta-lu tsa-chih* 大陸雜誌 I, no. 7 (July, 1950), 12-16.

————. *Pei ch'ü t'ao-shih hui-lu hsiang chieh* 北曲套式彙錄詳解 (*An Analysis of the Northern Song-suites*), Taipei: I-wen ch'u-pan-she, 1973.

————. "Tsang Mao-hsün kai-ting Yüan tsa-chü p'ing-i" 臧懋循改訂元雜劇評議 ("A Critique on Tsang Mao-hsün's Editing of the Yüan Plays"), *Wen shih che hsüeh-pao* 文史哲學報 (Taipei), no. 10 (August 1961), 1-13.

————. *Ts'ung shih tao ch'ü* 從詩到曲 (*From Shih Poetry to Ch'ü Songs*). Taipei: K'o-hsüeh ch'u-pan-she, 1961.

————. "Yüan-jen tsa-chü te chieh-kou" 元人雜劇的結構 ("The Structure of Yüan Drama"), *Ta-lu tsa-chih* 大陸雜誌, II, no. 12 (June 1951).

Ch'i Kung 啓功. "Lun Yüan-tai tsa-chü te pan-yen wen-t'i" 論元代雜劇的扮演問題 ("On Staging Yüan Drama"), *Wen-hsüeh i-ch'an tseng-k'an* 文學遺產增刊, I (1955), 286-96.

Ch'ien, Chung-shu 錢鍾書. "Tragedy in Old Chinese Drama," *T'ien Hsia Monthly,* I (1935), 37-46.

Ch'ien, Nan-yang 錢南揚. "Sung Chin Yüan hsi-chü pan-yen k'ao" 宋金元戲劇搬演考 ("The Staging of Dramas in the Sung, Chin, and Yüan Periods"), *Yen-ching hsüeh-pao,* 燕京學報, XX (Dec. 1936), 177-94.

————. *Sung Yüan hsi-wen chi i* 宋元戲文輯佚 (*A Collection of Sung and Yüan Hsi-wen Excerpts*). Shanghai: Ku-tien wen-hsüeh ch'u-pan-she, 1956.

Chih An 芝菴 (also referred to as Yen-nan Chih An). *Ch'ang lun* 唱論 (*Discourse on Singing*). Yüan period (this work was included in *Yang ch'un pai hsüeh* compiled by Yang Chao-ying). In *CKKT*, Vol. I, pp. 153-66.
A compilation of 31 brief statements on the art of singing; some of these are now incomprehensible.

Chin shih 金史. (*History of the Chin Dynasty*). In *Erh-shih-ssu shih* listed below.

Ch'ing-p'ing-shan-t'ang hua-pen 清平山堂話本 (*Ch'ing-p'ing-shan-t'ang Collection of Stories*). Reprint, Peking: Wen-hsüeh ku-chi k'an-hsing-she, 1955.
The title is a modern one given to the extant fragmentary collection containing 27 stories. Originally in six sets of ten

stories each, they were printed by Hung P'ien 洪鞭 of the Chia-ch'ing period (1522-66).

Chiu T'ang shu 舊唐書 (*The Old History of T'ang*). In *Erh-shih-ssu shih* listed below.

Chou, Hsiang-yü 周祥鈺 *et al.,* compilers. *Chiu kung ta-ch'eng nan pei tz'u kung-p'u* 九宮大成南北詞宮譜 (*Scores of Northern and Southern Songs in the Nine Musical Modes*). 1746. Reprint, Shanghai, 1923.

Chou, I-pai 周貽白· *Chung-kuo chü-ch'ang shih* 中國劇場史 (*A History of the Chinese Theatre*). Shanghai: Commercial Press, 1936.

————. *Chung-kuo hsi-ch'ü lun chi* 中國戲曲論集 (*A Collection Of Essays on Traditional Chinese Drama*). Peking: Chung-kuo hsi-chü ch'u-pan-she, 1960.

————. *Chung-kuo hsi-chü shih* 中國戲劇史 (*History of Chinese Drama*). Shanghai: Chung-hua Book Co., 1954. 2nd ed. 3 vols.

————. *Chung-kuo hsi-chü-shih chiang-tso* 中國戲劇史講座 (*Lectures on the History of Chinese Drama*). Peking: Chung-kuo hsi-chü ch'u-pan-she, 1958.

————. *Hsi-ch'ü yen-ch'ang lun-chu chi-shih* 戲曲演唱論著輯釋 (*A Collection of Writings on the Performance of Drama*). Peking: Chung-kuo hsi-chü ch'u-pan-she, 1962.

Chou, Mi 周密 (1232-1298). *Wu-lin chiu shih* 武林舊事 (*Memoirs from Wu-lin*). Completed 1280-1290. Reprint in *Tung ching meng hua lu; wai ssu chung,* listed below.

Chou, Te-ch'ing 周德清· *Chung-yüan yin yün* 中原音韻 (*Sound and Rhymes of the Central Plains*). With a preface dated 1324. In *CKKT,* Vol. I., pp. 167-285.

————. *Yüan pen Chung-yüan yin yün* 元本中原音韻 (*A Yüan Edition of the Sound and Rhymes of the Central Plains*). Modern reprint: T'ieh-ch'in-t'ung-chien-lou 鐵琴銅劍樓 edition, 1922.

A photo-reprint of a Yüan dynasty block-print edition, formerly in the collection of Ch'ü Shao-chi 瞿紹基 of the

Ch'ing dynasty. T'ieh-ch'in-t'ung-chien-lou was the name of Ch'ü's library.

Chu, Chü-i 朱居易. *Yüan-chü su-yü fang-yen li-shih* 元劇俗語方言例釋 (*A Glossary of Colloquial Expressions and Dialect Terms in Yüan Drama*). Shanghai: Commercial Press, 1956.

Chu, Ch'üan 朱權. *T'ai-ho cheng-yin p'u* 太和正音譜 (*The Sounds of Universal Harmony*). Preface dated 1398. References are made to the *CKKT* edition, Vol. III, pp. 1-231.

Ch'üan-hsiang p'ing-hua wu chung 全相平話五種 (*Five Fully Illustrated P'ing-hua*). 1321-24. Photo-reprint, Peking: Wen-hsüeh ku-chi k'an-hsing-she, 1956.

    The five historical romances are *Ch'üan-hsiang Wu wang fa Chou p'ing-hua* 全相武王伐紂平話, *Yüeh-yi t'u Ch'i ch'i kuo ch'un-ch'iu* 樂毅圖齊七國春秋, *Ch'üan-hsiang hsü Ch'ien Han shu p'ing-hua* 全相續前漢書平話, *Ch'üan-hsiang Ch'in ping liu kuo p'ing-hua* 全相秦併六國平話, *Hsin ch'üan-hsiang san kuo chih p'ing-hua* 新全相三國志平話. Given on the title-page of this last work is the time of publication: (Yüan) Chih-chih 至治 (1321-24); given also in four of the five works are the place of publication and the name of the publisher: Chien-an Yü-shih 建安虞氏 (Fukien province). An original copy is in the Imperial Cabinet Library, Japan.

Ch'üan T'ang shih 全唐詩 (*The Complete Collection of T'ang Poetry*). Compiled by Ts'ao Yin, 曹寅 *et al.,* under imperial auspices. 1707. Peking: Chung-hua Book Co., 1960. References here are to the 1960 edition.

Chuang-tzu 莊子. *Nan-hua chen ching* 南華眞經. In *SPTK so-pen* listed below.

Chūgoku bungakuhō 中國文學報 (*Journal of Chinese Literature*), (Kyoto University), I (1954)-XXIV (1974). Each issue contains substantial bibliographical information on Yüan drama.

Chūgoku koten gikyoku goshaku sakuin 中國古典戲曲語釋索引. Prepared by Ōsaka shiritsu daigaku bungakubu, Chūgoku gogaku, Chūgoku bungaku kenkyūshitsu 大阪市立大學文學部中國語學中國文學研究室. 1970.

Chung-kuo ku-tien hsi-ch'ü lun-chu chi-ch'eng 中國古典戲曲論著集成 (*A Collection of Writings on Traditional Chinese Drama*). Prepared by Chung-kuo hsi-chü yen-chiu yüan. Peking: Chung-kuo hsi-chü ch'u-pan-she, 1959. 10 vols.

Chung-kuo shih-hsüeh lun-wen so-yin 中國史學論文索引. Peking: K'o-hsüeh ch'u-pan-she, 1957.
    Contains bibliographical information on Chinese traditional drama (pp. 476-90).

Chung-kuo shih-hsüeh lun-wen yin-te 中國史學論文引得 (*Chinese History: Index to Learned Articles*). Compiled by Yü Ping-kuen 余秉權. Hong Kong: East Asian Institute, 1963, Vol. I; Cambridge: Harvard-Yenching Library, 1970, Vol. II. Vol. I contains articles of 1902-1962; Vol. II contains articles of 1905-1965.

Chung-kuo ts'ung-shu tsung-lu 中國叢書綜錄. Shanghai: Chung-hua Book Co., 1959-1962.
    Contains bibliographical information on traditional Chinese drama. (I, pp. 923-45; II, pp. 1647-68.)

Chung-kuo wen-hsüeh shih 中國文學史 (*A History of Chinese Literature*). Prepared by Chung-kuo k'o-hsüeh yüan wen-hsüeh yen-chiu so. Peking: Jen-min wen-hsüeh ch'u-pan-she, 1963. 3 vols.

Chung, Ssu-ch'eng 鍾嗣成. *Lu kuei pu* 錄鬼簿 (*A Register of Ghosts*). Preface dated 1330. In *CKKT*, Vol. II, pp. 85-274.

Crump, James I. "The Conventions and Craft of Yüan Drama," *Journal of the American Oriental Society,* Vol. 91, no. 1 (Jan.-Mar. 1971), 14-29.

———. "The Elements of Yüan Opera," *Journal of Asian Studies, XVII,* no. 3 (May 1958), 417-34.

———. "Yüan-pen, Yüan Drama's Rowdy Ancestor," *Literature East and West,* XIV, no. 4 (1970), 473-90.

————. Review of *Genkyokusen shaku* 元曲選釋, *Far Eastern Quarterly,* XII (1953), 329-32.

Demiéville, P. "Archaismes de prononciation en chinois vulgaire," *T'oung Pao,* XL (1951), 1-59.

Denlinger, Paul B. "Studies in Middle Chinese." Seattle: University of Washington, 1962. Unpublished Ph.D. dissertation.
Discusses mainly the pronounciation of Old Mandarin.

Dew, James Erwin. "The Verb Phrase Construction in the Dialogue of Yuan *Tzarjiuh:* A Description of the Arrangements of Verbal Elements in an Early Modern Form of Colloquial Chinese." Ann Arbor: Univ. of Michigan, 1965. Unpublished Ph.D. dissertation.

Dolby, A.W.E., "Kuan Han-ch'ing," *Asia Major,* XVI, parts 1-2 (1971), 1-60.

Dolezelová-Velingerová, M. and J. I. Crump. *Ballad of the Hidden Dragon, Liu Chih-yüan chu-kung-tiao.* Oxford: Clarendon Press, 1971.

Erh-shih-ssu shih 二十四史. (*Twenty-four Histories*). Edited by Chang Yüan-chi 張元濟. Shanghai: Commercial Press, 1930-37. *SPTK Pa-na* 百衲 edition.

Feng, Meng-lung 馮夢龍, compiler. *Ku-chin hsiao-shuo* 古今小說 (also known as *Yü-shih ming-yen* 喻世明言). 1620-1621. 40 *chüan.* Reprint, Shanghai: Commercial Press, 1947.

Feng, Yüan-chün 馮沅君. *Ku-chü shuo-hui* 古劇說彙 (*Studies in Traditional Drama*). 1947. Peking: Tso-chia ch'u-pan-she, 1956, revised edition.
Detailed discussions of terminology in Yüan drama.

————. "Tsen-yang k'an-tai *Tou O yüan* chi ch'i kai-pien pen" 怎樣看待竇娥冤及其改編本 ("How to View *Tou O yüan* and its Revised Version"), *Wen-hsüeh p'ing-lun* 文學評論, IV (August 1965), 42-50.

Forke, A. "Die Chinesische Umgangssprache im XIII Jahrhundert," *Actes du Douzième Congrès International des Orienta-*

listes. Rome, 1899, II, 49-67.

Based upon three Yüan plays: *K'an-ch'ien-nu* 看錢奴, *Wu-t'ung yü* 梧桐雨, and *Huo-lang tan* 貨郎旦, this is an early Western study of grammar and vocabulary of Chinese colloquial language

Fu, Hsi-hua 傅惜華. *Ku-tien hsi-ch'ü sheng yüeh lun-chu ts'ung-pien* 古典戲曲聲樂論著叢編 (*A Collection of Essays on Music in Traditional Drama*). Peking: Yin-yüeh ch'u-pan-she, 1957.

—————— *et al., eds. Shui-hu hsi-ch'ü chi* 水滸戲曲集 (*A Collection of Plays on Liang-shan Heroes of The Water Margin*). Shanghai: Ku-tien wen-hsüeh ch'u-pan-she, 1957.

——————. *Yüan-tai tsa-chü ch'üan mu* 元代雜劇全目 (*A Complete List of Yüan Plays*). Peking: Tso-chia ch'u-pan-she, 1957.

Fu, Ta-hsing 傅大與. *Yüan tsa-chü k'ao* 元雜劇考 (*A Study of Yüan Drama*). Taipei: Shih-chieh Book Co., 1960.

Gernet, Jacques. *La vie quotidienne en Chine à la veille de l'invasion Mongole (1250-1276)*. Paris: Hachette, 1959. English translation by H. M. Wright, *Daily Life in China*. New York: The Macmillan Company, 1962.

Haenisch, E. "Beiträge zur Geschichte der Chinesischen Umgangssprache," *Mitteilungen des Seminars für Orientalische Sprachen (Ostasiatische Studien)*, Jahrgang XXXV. Berlin, 1932, pp. 106-35.

This study on the early Chinese colloquial language is based on the *Yüan-ch'ao pi-shih* (*Secret History of the Yüan Dynasty*).

Han shu 漢書 (*History of the Han Dynasty*). In *Erh-shih-ssu shih* listed above.

Han, Yü 韓愈. *Chu Wen-kung chiao Ch'ang-li hsien-sheng chi* 朱文公校昌黎先生集 (*A Collection of Chang-li's Writings Edited by Chu Wen-kung*). In *SPTK so-pen* listed below.

Hanan, Patrick D. *The Chinese Short Story: Studies in Dating,*

Authorship, and Composition. Cambridge: Harvard University Press, 1973.

————. "The Development of Fiction and Drama," in Raymond Dawson, ed., *The Legacy of China.* Oxford: Oxford University Press, 1964.

Hawkes, David. "Reflections on Some Yuan *Tsa-chü,*" *Asia Major,* XVI, parts 1-2 (1971), 69-81.

Hayashi, Kenzō 林謙三 (pseud. Nagaya Kenzō). *Sui T'ang yen yüeh tiao yen-chiu* 隋唐燕樂調研究 (*A Study on the Modes of Courtly Entertainment Music in the Sui and T'ang Periods*). Translated into Chinese by Kuo Mo-jo 郭沫若. Shanghai, 1936. Reference is to the Chinese version.

Hayashi, Yukimitsu 林雪光. "*Genkyokusen*-chū no shikusa-kuin" 「元曲選」中の詩句索引 ("Index to the Poetry in *Selected Yüan Plays*"). *Kōbe gaidai ronsō* 神戶外大論叢, X (March 1960), 143-74.

Hayden, George A. "The Judge Pao Plays of the Yüan Dynasty". Stanford: Stanford University, 1971. Unpublished Ph.D. dissertation.

Hightower, James R. "Review of *Genkyokusen shaku* [a mimeographed edition]," *Far Eastern Quarterly,* IX (Feb. 1950), 208-14.

————. "Yüan Chen and the Story of Ying-ying," *Harvard Journal of Asiatic Studies,* 33 (1973), 90-123.

Hsi-hu lao-jen 西湖老人. *Hsi-hu lao-jen fan-sheng lu* 西湖老人繁盛錄 (*The West-lake Old Man's Account of the Splendors [of Lin-an]*). Ca. 1253. In *Tung ching meng hua lu; wai ssu chung,* listed below.

Ho, Ch'ang-ch'ün 賀昌羣. *Yüan-ch'ü kai-lun.* 元曲概論 (*A General Study on Yüan Drama*). Shanghai: Commercial Press, 1930.

Ho, Liang-chün 何良俊 (fl. 1560). *Ch'ü lun* 曲論 (*Notes on Ch'ü*). In *CKKT,* Vol. IV, pp. 1-14.

Hou Han shu 後漢書 (*History of the Later Han Dynasty*). In *Erh-shih-ssu shih* listed above.

Hsia, C. T. 夏志清. *The Classic Chinese Novel*. New York: Columbia University Press, 1968.

Hsia, Po-ho 夏伯和 (T'ing-chih 庭芝, born ca. 1316). *Ch'ing lou chi* 青樓集 (*The Green Mansions*). 1355. In *CKKT*, Vol. II, pp. 1-84.

Hsiao, T'ung 蕭統、ed. *Liu ch'en chu Wen-hsüan* 六臣註文選 (*An Anthology of Literature*). In *SPTK so-pen*. 2 vols.

Hsieh, Wan-ying 謝婉瑩. "Yüan-tai te hsi-ch'ü" 元代的戲曲 ("Drama in the Yüan Dynasty"), *Yen-ching hsüeh-pao* 燕京學報, I (June 1927), 15-52.

Hsü, Chia-jui 徐嘉瑞. *Chin Yüan hsi-ch'ü fang-yen k'ao* 金元戲曲方言考 (*A Glossary of the Dialect Terms in Chin and Yüan Dramas*). Shanghai: Commercial Press, 1948. Revised edition, 1956.
   Entries are arranged by number of strokes. Brief meanings are given and often followed by citations from Yüan plays as well as from other vernacular literature of the Yüan-Ming period. A slim volume.

Hsü, Fu-tso 徐復祚 (1560-1630). *Ch'ü lun* 曲論 (*A Discourse on Ch'ü*). In *CKKT*, Vol. IV, pp. 229-48.

Hsü, Mu-yün 徐慕雲. *Chung-kuo hsi-chü shih* 中國戲劇史 (*History of the Chinese Theatre*). Shanghai: Shih-chieh Book Co., 1938.

Hsü, Shuo-fang 徐朔方. *Hsi ch'ü tsa-chi* 戲曲雜記 (*Miscellaneous Notes on Drama*). Shanghai: Ku-tien wen-hsüeh ch'u-pan-she, 1956.

———. "Yüan ch'ü chung te Pao-kung hsi" 元曲中的包公戲, ("The Judge Pao Plays in Yüan Drama"), *Wen shih che* 文史哲 (Tsing-tao), no. 9 (1955), 14-16.

Hsü, Ta-ch'un 徐大椿 (Ch'ing dynasty). *Yüeh-fu ch'uan sheng* 樂府傳聲 (*The Sounds of Music*). In *CKKT*, Vol. VII, pp. 145-88.

Hsü, Ti-shan 許地山. "Fan chü t'i-li chi ch'i tsai Han chü shang ti tien-tien ti-ti" 梵劇體例及其在漢劇上底點點滴滴 ("The Structure of Sanskrit Drama and a Few Notes on Its

Trivial Influence on Chinese Drama"), *Hsiao-shuo yüeh pao* 小說月報, extra edition, no. 17 (June 1927), 1-36.

Hsü, Tiao-fu 徐調孚, ed. *Hsien ts'un Yüan jen tsa-chü shu-lu* 現存元人雜劇書錄 (*Bibliography of Extant Plays by Yüan Authors*). Shanghai: Shanghai wen-i lien-ho ch'u-pan-she, 1955.

Hsü, Wei 徐渭 (1521-1593). *Nan tz'u hsü-lu* 南詞敍錄 (*Notes on Southern Songs*). In *CKKT,* Vol. III, pp. 233-56.
　　Although it is mainly on Southern drama, it contains much information on earlier Northern *ch'ü.*

Hsüeh, Feng-sheng. "Phonology of Old Mandarin: A Structural Approach." Bloomington: Indiana University, 1968. Unpublished Ph.D. dissertation.

Hu, Chi 胡忌. *Sung Chin tsa-chü k'ao* 宋金雜劇考 (*A Study on the "Variety Play" of the Sung and Chin Periods*). Shanghai: Ku-tien wen-hsüeh ch'u-pan-she, 1957.

Hu, Chu-an 胡竹安. "Sung Yüan pai-hua tso-p'in chung te yü-ch'i chu-tz'u" 宋元白話作品中的語氣助詞 ("Intonational Particles in the Colloquial Writings of the Sung and Yüan Dynasties"), *Chung-kuo yü-wen* 中國語文, no. 72 (June 1958), 270-74.

Hu, Tzu-shan 胡紫山 (1227-1293). *Tzu-shan ta-ch'üan chi* 紫山大全集. (*The Complete Works of Tzu-shan*). In *San-i-t'ang ts'ung-shu* 三怡堂叢書, Honan, 1924.

Hu, William C. C. "A Bibliography for Yüan Opera (*tsa-chü*)," *Occasional Papers* (Ann Arbor: Center for Chinese Studies, The University of Michigan), no. 1 (1962), 1-37.

Huang, Li-chen 黃麗貞. *Chin Yüan pei-ch'ü yü-hui chih yen-chiu* 金元北曲語彙之研究 (*A Study of the Vocabulary of the Northern Drama in the Chin and Yüan Periods*). Taipei: Commercials Press, 1968.

Huang, P'i-lieh 黃丕烈 (Ch'ing dynasty). *Yeh-shih-yüan ts'ang shu ku chin tsa-chü mu-lu* 也是園藏書古今雜劇目錄 (*A Catalogue of the Old and New Plays in the Yeh-shih-yüan Library*). In *CKKT,* Vol. VII, pp. 373-406.

Huang, Wen-yang 黃文暘. *Ch'ü hai* 曲海 (*A Bibliography of Plays* [from the 13th to the 18th century]). Compiled in 1777-1781. A revised edition in *CKKT,* Vol. VII, pp. 313-72.

Hung, Mai (1123-1202) 洪邁. *I-chien chih* 夷堅志 (*I-chien's Jottings*). Shanghai: Commercial Press, 1927.

Huo, Sung-lin 霍松林. *Hsi hsiang chi chien shuo* 西廂記簡說 (*A Brief Discourse on The Romance of the Western Chamber*). Peking: Tso-chia ch'u-pan-she, 1957.

Idema, W. L. "Storytelling and Short Story in China," *T'oung Pao,* LIX (1973), 1-67.

Iida, Yoshirō.飯田吉郎. "Genkyoku joji nōto — shu toshite *a* ni tsuite" 元曲助字ノート—主として「阿」について ("Notes on Auxiliary Words in Yüan Drama — Chiefly on *a*"). *Chūgoku bunka kenkyūkai kaihō* 中國文化研究會會報, I, no. 1 (Dec. 1950), 7-8.

―――. "Tō *Seishō* no kōsei" 董西廂の構成 ("The Structure of Tung's *Western Chamber*"), *Chūgoku bunka kenkyūkai kaihō* 中國文化研究會會報, II, no. 4 (July 1952), 77-82.

Ikeda, Takeo 池田武雄. "Gen jidai kōgo no kaishi ni tsuite" 元時代口語の介詞について ("On Prepositions in the Vernacular Language of the Yüan Period"), *Ritsumeikan bungaku* 立命館文學, CLXXX (1960), 170-79.

Iriya, Yoshitaka 入矢義高. "Genkyoku joji zakkō" 元曲助字雜考 ("A Study of Auxiliary Particles in Yüan Drama"), *Tōhōgakuhō* 東方學報 (Kyoto), XIV, no. 1 (1943), 70-97. Revised and translated into Chinese by Chi Po-yung 紀伯庸, in *Kuo-wen yüeh-k'an* 國文月刊, no. 70 (August 1948), 5-11.

Iwaki, Hideo 岩城秀夫. *"Genkan kokon zatsugeki sanjūshu no ryūden."* 元刊古今雜劇三十種の流傳 (*"History of the Transmission of the Yüan Edition of Thirty Plays"*), *Chūgoku bungakuhō* 中國文學報 (Kyoto), XIV (1961), 67-89.

————. "Sōdai engeki kikan" 宋代演劇窺管. ("A Limited View of the Sung Dynasty Theatrical Performance"), *Chūgoku bungakuhō,* XIX (Oct. 1963), 102-27.

Jao, Tsong-yi, ed., and Paul Demiéville, translator. *Airs de Touen-houang (Touen-houang k'iu), Textes à chanter des VIIIe-Xe siècles.* Paris: Centre National de la Recherche Scientifique, 1971.
    With an introduction in Chinese by Jao Tsong-yi, and a French translation of the introduction and the songs by Paul Demiéville.

Jen, Pan-t'ang 任半塘. *T'ang hsi-nung* 唐戲弄. (*Theatricals in the T'ang Period*). Peking: Tso-chia ch'u-pan-she, 1958.

Johnson, Dale R. "One Aspect of Form in the Arias of Yüan Opera," *Michigan Papers in Chinese Studies,* (Ann Arbor: Center for Chinese Studies, The University of Michigan), no. 2 (1968), 47-98.

————. "The Prosody of Yüan-*ch'ü*". Ann Arbor: University of Michigan, 1968. Unpublished Ph.D. dissertation. 2 vols.

————. "The Prosody of Yüan Drama," *T'oung Pao,* LVI, nos. 1-3 (1970), 96-146.

Kano, Naoki 狩野直喜. "Genkyoku no yurai to Haku Jinho no *Gotōu*" 元曲の由來と白仁甫の梧桐雨 ("The Origin of Yüan Drama and Po Jen-fu's *Rain on the Wu-t'ung Trees*"), *Geibun* 藝文, II, no. 3 (March 1911), 1-12.

Kishibe, Shigeo [岸邊成雄]. "The Origin of the *P'i-p'a,* with Particular Reference to the Five-stringed *p'i-p'a* preserved in the Shô-sô-in," *Transactions of the Asiatic Society of Japan,* ser. 2, XIX (Dec. 1940), 259-304.

————. "Tō no zokugaku nijū-hachi-chō no seiritsu nendai ni tsuite" 唐の俗樂二十八調の成立年代について ("On the Date of the Emergence of the Twenty-eight Modes of Popular Music in the T'ang Dynasty"), *Tōyōgakuhō* 東洋學報, XXVI (1939), 437-68 and 578-631; XXVII (1939), 121-33.

Kuan Han-ch'ing chi ch'i hsi-ch'ü lun-wen so-yin 關漢卿及其戲曲論文索引 (*Index to Works on Kuan Han-ch'ing and His Plays*). Prepared by Peking: Chung-kuo k'o-hsüeh-yüan wen-hsüeh yen-chiu-so, 1959.

Kuan Han-ch'ing hsi-chü yüeh-p'u 關漢卿戲劇樂譜 (*Musical Scores of Excerpts from Plays by Kuan Han-ch'ing*). Compiled by Yang Yin-liu 楊蔭瀏 *et al.* Peking: Yin-yüeh ch'u-pan-she, 1959.

Kuan Han-ch'ing yen-chiu 關漢卿研究 (*Studies on Kuan Han-ch'ing*). Peking: Chung-kuo hsi-chü ch'u-pan-she, n.d.

Kuan Han-ch'ing yen-chiu lun-wen chi 關漢卿研究論文集 (*A Collection of Articles on Kuan Han-ch'ing*). Shanghai: Ku-tien wen-hsüeh ch'u-pan-she, 1958.

Kuan-p'u-nai-te-weng 灌圃耐得翁 (pseud.). *Tu ch'eng chi sheng* 都城紀勝 (*The Wonders of the Capital* [Lin-an]). Preface d. 1235. Reprint in *Tung ching meng hua lu; wai ssu chung,* listed below.

Legge, James. *The Chinese Classics.* Hong Kong, 1861-1872. 5 vols.

Leung, Pui Kam. *Kuan Han-ch'ing yen-chiu lun-wen chi-ch'eng* 關漢卿研究論文集成 (*Research Theses on Kuan Han-ch'ing*). Hong Kong: Arts' Study, 1969.

Li, Chia-jui 李家瑞. "Yu shuo-shu pien-ch'eng hsi-chü te hen-chi" 由說書變成戲劇的痕迹 ("Traces of Change from Oral Narratives to Drama"), *Bulletin of the Institute of History and Philology* (*Academia Sinica*), VII, no. 3 (1937), 405-18.

Li, Hsiao-ts'ang 李嘯蒼. *Sung Yüan chi-i tsa-k'ao* 宋元伎藝雜考 (*A Study on the Performing Arts of the Sung and Yüan Periods*). Shanghai: Shang-tsa ch'u-pan-she, 1953.

Li, Tche-houa [李治華]. "Le théâtre des Yuan, et présentation d'une pièce du théâtre des Yuan," in *Aspects de la Chine,* II, Paris, 1959.

———. "Le dramaturge chinois Kouan Han-k'ing," in *Les théâtres d'Asie.* Paris, 1961.

Li, Yü 李玉 *et al.* (fl. 1644). *Pei tz'u kuang cheng p'u* 北詞廣正譜 (*The Standard Metrical Patterns of the Northern Songs*). Ch'ing-lien shu-wu. Reprint, Peking: Peking University Press, 1918.

Liao, Hsün-ying 廖珣英. "Kuan Han-ch'ing hsi-ch'ü te yung yün" 關漢卿戲曲的用韻 ("The Use of Rhyme in Kuan Han-ch'ing's Plays"), *Chung-kuo yü-wen* 中國語文, no. 125 (April 1963), 267-74.

Liu Chih-yüan chu-kung-tiao 劉知遠諸宮調 (*Liu Chih-yüan Medley*). Chin dynasty, 1115-1234. A woodblock edition. Photolithographic reprint, Peking: Wen-wu ch'u-pan-she, 1959. (For translation, see M. Dolezelová-Velingerová and J. I. Crump.)

Liu, Chün-jo 劉君若. "A Study of the *Tsa-chü* 雜劇 of the 13th Century in China." Madison: The University of Wisconsin, 1952. Unpublished Ph.D. dissertation.
Contains an English translation of three plays (*Tou O yüan, Wu-t'ung yü, Li K'uei fu ching*) in the appendix.

Liu, Hsiang 劉向 (77-6 B.C.). *Lieh nü chuan* 列女傳 (*Biographies of Illustrious Women*). 1825: A facsimile edition by Yü Ching-an 余靜庵 of the 1214 Sung edition.

Liu, Hsiu-yeh 劉修業. *Ku-tien hsiao-shuo hsi-ch'ü ts'ung-k'ao* 古典小說戲曲叢考 (*Classic Chinese Fiction and Drama: Biographical and Bibliographical Studies*). Peking: Tso-chia ch'u-pan-she, 1958.

Liu, James J. Y. [劉若愚]. *The Art of Chinese Poetry*. Chicago: University of Chicago Press, 1962.
Contains a perceptive analysis of many passages from Yüan plays.

———. *The Chinese Knight-Errant*. Chicago: University of Chicago Press, 1967.

———. "Elizabethan and Yüan: A Brief Comparison of Some Conventions in Poetic Drama," *Occasional Papers* (London: The China Society), no. 8 (1955), 1-12.

—————. "The *Feng-yüeh chin-nang*" 風月錦囊 ("Brocade Pouch of Romances"), *Journal of Oriental Studies* (Hong Kong), IV, nos. 1-2 (1957-1958), 79-107.

Liu, Nien-tzu 劉念茲. "Chung-kuo hsi-ch'ü wu-t'ai i-shu tsai shih-san shih-chi ch'u-yeh i-ching hsing-ch'eng" 中國戲曲 舞台藝術在十三世紀初葉已經形成 ("The Establishment of Chinese Dramatic Performing Art in the Early Thirteenth Century"), *Hsi-chü yen-chiu* 戲劇研究 (Peking), no. 2 (1959), 60-65.

—————. "Yüan tsa-chü yen-ch'u hsing-shih te chi tien ch'u-pu k'an-fa" 元雜劇演出形式的幾點初步看法 ("A Few Preliminary Observations on the Staging of Yüan Drama"), *Hsi-ch'ü yen-chiu* 戲曲研究, no. 2 (1957), 66-85.

Liu, Te-chih 劉德智. *Yin chu Chung-yüan yin yün* 音注中原 音韻 (*The Pronunciation of Graphs in Sound and Rhymes of the Central Plains*). Taipei: Kuang-wen Book Co., 1962.

Liu, Wu-chi 柳無忌. *An Introduction to Chinese Literature*. Bloomington: Indiana University Press, 1966.

—————. "Notes on the Sex of a Yüan Dramatist," *Tsing Hua Journal of Chinese Studies*, New Series, I, no. 2 (April 1957), 246-52.

—————. "The Original Orphan of China," *Comparative Literature*, V, no. 3 (1953), 193-212.

Liu, Yung-chi 劉永濟. *Sung tai ko wu chü ch'ü lu-yao* 宋代 歌舞劇曲錄要 (*Selections of Sung Dynasty Songs, Dances and Dramatic Lyrics*). Shanghai: Ku-tien wen-hsüeh ch'u-pan-she, 1957.

Lo, Ch'ang-p'ei 羅常培. "Chiu chü chung te chi-ko yin-yün wen-t'i" 舊劇中的幾個音韻問題 ("Some Phonological Problems in Traditional Drama"), *Tung-fang tsa-chih* 東方 雜誌, XXXIII, no. 1 (1936), 393-410.

Lo, Chin-t'ang 羅錦堂. *Hsien ts'un Yüan-jen tsa-chü pen-shih k'ao* 現存元人雜劇本事考 (*A Study on the Stories of Extant Yüan Plays*). Taipei: Chung-kuo wen-hua shih-yeh Co., 1960.

————. *Pei ch'ü hsiao-ling p'u* 北曲小令譜 (*Metrical Patterns of Northern Non-dramatic Songs*). Hong Kong: Huan-ch'iu wen-hua fu-wu-she, 1964.

Lo, K'ang-lieh 羅慷烈. *Pei hsiao-ling wen-tzu p'u* 北小令文字譜 (*Northern Non-dramatic Songs and Their Metrical Patterns*). Hong Kong: Lung-men Book Co., 1962.

Lo, Yeh 羅燁. *Tsui weng t'an lu* 醉翁談錄 (*A Drunken Old Man's Notebook*). Reprint, Shanghai: Ku-tien wen-hsüeh ch'u-pan-she, 1957.

Lu, Chih-wei 陸志韋. "Shih *Chung-yüan yin-yün*" 釋中原音韻 ("A Study of the Phonology of the *Chung-yüan yin yün*"), *Yen-ching hsüeh-pao* 燕京學報, XXXI (1946), 35-70.

Lu kuei pu hsü-pien 錄鬼簿續編 (*A Supplement to A Register of Ghosts*). Anonymous Ming author, probably Chia Chung-ming (1343-1422). In *CKKT*, Vol. II, pp. 275-300.

Lü shih ch'un-ch'iu 呂氏春秋 (*The Spring and Autumn Annals of Lü*). Compiled under the patronage of Lü Pu-wei 呂不韋. 3rd century B.C. In *SPTK so-pen*.

Lu, Tan-an 陸澹安, ed. *Hsiao-shuo tz'u yü hui-shih* 小說詞語匯釋 (*A Dictionary of Phrases and Idioms from Chinese Vernacular Fiction*). Peking: Chung-hua Book Co., 1964.

Lu, Yüan-chün 盧元駿. *Kuan Han-ch'ing k'ao-shu* 關漢卿考述 (*A Study on Kuan Han-ch'ing*). Taipei: n.p., 1961.

Meng, Ssu-ming 蒙思明. *Yüan tai she-hui chieh-chi chih-tu* 元代社會階級制度 (*The Social Class System in the Yüan Dynasty*). Peking: Harvard-Yenching Institute, ca. 1938. Reprint, 1967.

Meng, Yüan-lao 孟元老. *Tung ching meng hua lu* 東京夢華錄 (*Reminiscences of the Splendor of the Eastern Capital [Pien-liang]*). Preface d. 1147. Reprint in *Tung ching meng hua lu; wai ssu chung*, listed below.

Miller, Robert P. "The Particles in the Dialogues of Yüan Drama: A Descriptive Analysis". New Haven: Yale University, 1952. Unpublished Ph.D. dissertation.

Mote, Frederick W. "China Under Mongol Domination," in *Cambridge History of China.* Cambridge University Press, forthcoming.

————. "Confucian Eremitism in the Yüan Period," in *Confucianism and Chinese Civilization.* Edited by Arthur F. Wright. New York: Atheneum, 1964.

Nemoto, Makoto 根本誠. *Sensei shakai ni okeru teikō seishin* 專制社會における抵抗精神 (*The Spirit of Resistance in Authoritarian Society*). Tokyo: Sōgensha, 1952.

Nozaki, Shunpei 野崎駿平. "Gen no zatsugeki ni arawareta 'riji' ni tsuite" 元の雑劇にあらわれた「詈詞」について ("About the 'Abusive Terms' in Yüan Drama"), *Chūgokugogaku* 中國語學, 58 (Jan. 1957), 3-12.

Osada, Natsuki 長田夏樹. "Tō Seishō bumpō hikki (jō)" 董西廂文法筆記(上). ("Notes on the Grammar of the Language in Tung's *Western Chamber* (Part I).") *Kōbe gaidai ronsō* 神戶外大論叢, XI (1960), 113-31.

Pian, Rulan. *Sonq Dynasty Musical Sources and Their Interpretation.* Cambridge: Harvard University Press, 1967.

Picken, Laurence. "The Music of Far Eastern Asia," *The New Oxford History of Music.* London: Oxford University Press, 1957, vol. I.

Po, Chü-i 白居易. "P'i-p'a hsing" 琵琶行 ("The Lute Song"), in *Po shih Ch'ang-ch'ing chi* 白氏長慶集 (*Collected Works of Po Chü-i*). In *SPTK so-pen.*

Polo, Marco. *The Travels of Marco Polo, the Venetian.* London and New York: Dutton Co., 1908.

Průšek, Jaroslav. "La Fonction de la Particuli *ti* dans le Chinois Médiéval," *Archiv Orientální,* XV, nos. 3-4 (June 1946), 303-40.

————. "The Realistic and Lyric Elements in the Chinese Medieval Story," *Archiv Orientální,* XXXII (1964).

Reischauer, Edwin O., translator. *Ennin's Diary, The Record of a Pilgrimage to China in Search of the Law.* New York: The Ronald Press, 1955.

Ruhlmann, Robert. "Les jeux et le théâtre au temps des Song", in *L'Art de la Chine des Song,* catalogue pub. by the Musée Cernuschi, Paris, 1956.

————. "Traditional Heroes in Chinese Popular Fiction," in *Confucianism and Chinese Civilization.* Edited by Arthur F. Wright. New York: Atheneum, 1964.

San kuo chih 三國志 (*History of the Three Kingdoms*). In *Erh-shih-ssu shih* listed above.

San kuo chih p'ing-hua 三國志平話. In *Ch'üan-hsiang p'ing-hua wu chung* listed above.

Schlepp, Wayne. *San-ch'ü Its Technique and Imagery.* Madison: The University of Wisconsin Press, 1970.

Scott, A. C. *The Classical Theatre of China.* London: George Allen & Unwin, 1957.

Seaton, Jerome P. "A Critical Study of Kuan Han-ch'ing: The Man and His Works." Bloomington: Indiana University, 1969. Unpublished Ph.D. dissertation.

Shakespeare, William. *The Complete Works,* ed. by G.B. Harrison. New York: Harcourt, Brace and Company, 1948. Revised edition, 1952.

Shen, Ch'ung-sui 沈寵綏. *Tu ch'ü hsü chih* 度曲須知 (*On the Composition of Ch'ü*). c. 1644. In *CKKT,* Vol. V, pp. 183-319.

Shen, Te-fu 沈德符 (1578-1642). *Ku ch'ü tsa-yen* 顧曲雜言 (*Miscellaneous Notes on Ch'ü*). 1618. In *CKKT,* Vol. IV, pp. 192-228.

Shih chi 史記 (*Records of the Historian*). In *Erh-shih-ssu shih,* listed above.

Shih, Chung-wen [時鍾雯]. *Injustice to Tou O* (*Tou O Yüan*) *A Study and Translation.* Cambridge: Cambridge University Press, 1972. In the Princeton-Cambridge Studies in Chinese Linguistics series.

Shih, Nai-an 施耐菴 and Lo, Kuan-chung 羅貫中. *Shui-hu ch'üan chuan* 水滸全傳. (*The Water Margin*). Modern edition, Peking: Jen-min wen-hsüeh ch'u-pan-she, 1954. 3 vols.

Shionoya, On 鹽谷温. *Genkyoku gaisetsu* 元曲概說 (*A General Study on Yüan Drama*). Translated into Chinese by Sui Shu-sen 隋樹森. Shanghai: Commercial Press, 1947.

Shu chih 蜀志. (*History of the Kingdom of Shu*). Part II of *San kuo chih.* In *Erh-shih-ssu shih,* listed above.

Sickman, L. "Wall-Paintings of the Yüan Period in Kuang-Sheng-Ssu, Shansi," *Revue des Arts Asiatiques* (Paris), XI, no. 2 (June 1937), 53-67.

Spuler, Bertold. *History of the Mongols.* Berkeley: University of California Press, 1972.

Ssu pu pei yao 四部備要. Shanghai: Chung-hua Book Co., 1927-1935.

Ssu pu ts'ung-k'an so-pen 四部叢刊縮本. Taipei: Commercial Press, 1965.

Size reduced facsimile edition of *Ssu pu ts'ung-k'an,* edited by Chang Yüan-chi 張元濟. Shanghai: Commercial Press, 1920-1922; second and third series, 1934-35.

"Staging Yüan Drama: A Colloquium," *Literature East and West,* XIV, no. 4 (1970), 547-67.

Stimson, Hugh. *The Jongyuan In Yunn.* New Haven: Yale University Press, 1966.

————. "Phonology of the *Chung-yüan yin yün,*" *Tsing Hua Journal of Chinese Studies,* New Series, III, no. 1 (May 1962), 114-59.

————. "Song Arrangements in Shianleu Acts of Yuan Tzarjiuh," *Tsing Hua Journal of Chinese Studies,* New Series V, no. 1 (July 1965), 86-106.

Su, Ch'e 蘇轍. *Luan ch'eng chi* 欒城集 (*Luan City Collection*). In *SPTK so-pen* listed above.

Sui, Shu-sen 隋樹森, ed. *Ch'üan Yüan san-ch'ü* 全元散曲 (*A Comprehensive Collection of Yüan Non-dramatic Songs*). Peking: Chung-hua Book Co., 1964. 2 vols.

Sun, K'ai-ti 孫楷第. *K'uei-lei-hsi k'ao-yüan* 傀儡戲考原 (*A Study of the Origin of the Puppet Shows*). Shanghai: Shang-tsa ch'u-pan-she, 1952.

————. *Su-chiang shuo-hua yü pai-hua hsiao-shuo* 俗講說話 與白話小說 (*Popular Lectures and Vernacular Fiction*). Peking: Tso-chia ch'u-pan-she, 1956.

————. *Ts'ang-chou chi* 滄州集 (*Ts'ang-chou Collection*). Peking: Chung-hua Book Co., 1965. 2 vols.

————. *Yeh-shih-yüan ku chin tsa-chü k'ao* 也是園古今雜 劇考 (*A Study of the Yüan Plays in the Yeh-shih-yüan Library Collection*). Shanghai: *Shang-tsa ch'u-pan-she*, 1953.

————. *Yüan ch'ü-chia k'ao-lüeh* 元曲家考略 (*A Short Study on Yüan Dramatists*). Shanghai: Shang-tsa ch'u-pan-she, 1953.

Sung shih 宋史 (*History of the Sung Dynasty*). In *Erh-shih-ssu shih*, listed above.

Ta T'ang San-tsang ch'ü ching shih-hua 大唐三藏取經詩話 (*Tripitaka of the Great T'ang in Search of Scriptures in Prose and Verse*). Sung-Yüan period. Photolithographic ed., 1916. Colophon by Lo Chen-yü. Reprint, Peking: Wen-hsüeh ku-chi ch'u-pan-she, 1955.

Ta Yüan sheng cheng kuo-ch'ao tien-chang 大元聖政國朝 典章 (generally referred to as *Yüan tien-chang* 元典章 [*Yüan Code*]). Compiler unknown. *Chien-yang shu-fang* 建陽書坊, 1322. Photolithographic reprint, Taipei: Palace Museum, 1972.

T'ai-p'ing yü-lan 太平御覽 (*An Imperial Collection Compiled in the T'ai-p'ing Era*). Compiled by Li Fang 李昉 (925-996) and others. Completed in 983. Reproduction of a collated Sung edition by Commercial Press, 1935.

Tai, Wang-shu 戴望舒. *Hsiao-shuo hsi-ch'ü lun-chi* 小說戲曲 論集 (*A Collection of Essays on Fiction and Drama*). Edited by Wu Hsiao-ling 吳曉鈴. Peking: Tso-chia ch'u-pan-she, 1958.

Takahashi, Moritaka 高橋盛孝. "Genkyoku ni arawareta kogo to shinji" 元曲に現われた胡語と襯字 ("Foreign Words and Non-metric words in Yüan Drama"), *Chūgokugogaku* 中國語學, 112 (August 1961), 1-2.

T'an, Cheng-pi 譚正璧. *Hua-pen yü ku-chü* 話本與古劇 (*Hua-pen and Old Drama*). Shanghai: Shanghai Ku-tien wen-hsüeh ch'u-pan-she, 1956.

————. *Yüan ch'ü liu ta-chia lüeh-chuan* 元曲六大家略傳 (*Brief Biographies of Six Master Yüan Playwrights*). Shanghai: Ku-tien wen-hsüeh ch'u-pan-she, 1957.

————. *Yüan-tai hsi-chü-chia Kuan Han-ch'ing* 元代戲劇家關漢卿 (*The Yüan Dynasty Playwright Kuan Han-ch'ing*). Shanghai: Shanghai Wen-hua ch'u-pan-she, 1957.

Tanaka, Kenji 田中謙二. "Gen zatsugeki no daizai" 元雜劇の題材 ("The Subject Matter of Yüan Drama"), *Tōhōgakuhō* 東方學報 (Kyoto), XIII, no. 4 (Sept. 1943), 128-58. Revised and translated into Chinese by Chi Yung 紀庸 in *Kuo-wen yüeh k'an,* no. 71 (1948), 14-22.

————. "Genjin no ren'aigeki ni okeru futatsu no nagare" 元人の戀愛劇における二つの流れ ("Two Schools of Thought in Yüan Love Plays"), *Tōkō* 東光, 3 (Jan. 1948), 34-42.

————. "Gengeki ni okeru fuchi no ichirei" 元劇における布置の一例 ("An Example of the Structure in the Yüan Drama"), *Shinagaku* 支那學, XII, no. 5 (Aug. 1947), 147-51.

————. *Genkyoku tekisuto no kenkyū* 元曲テキストの研究 (*Studies on the Texts of Yüan Drama*). *Monbushō kagakukenkyūhi Kenkyū-hōkoku-shūroku* 文都省科學研究費研究報告集錄. Nov. 1951.

————. "*Seishōki* banbon no kenkyū" 西廂記板本の研究 ("A Study of the Editions of *The Romance of the Western Chamber*"), *Biburia* ビブリア, I (Jan. 1949), 107-48.

————. "*Seishōki* shohon no shinpyōsei" 西廂記諸本の信憑性 ("The Authenticity of the Various Versions of *The*

Romance of the Western Chamber), *Nihon Chūgokugakkai kaihō* 日本中國學會會報, II (1950), 89-104.

―――. "*Tō Seishō* ni mieru zokugo no jo-ji" 董西廂に見える俗語の助字 ("Auxiliary Words in the Colloquial Language Found in Tung's *Western Chamber*"), *Tōhōgakuhō* 東方學報 (Kyoto), XVIII (1950), 55-77.

―――. "Yüan ch'ü chung chih hsien-yün" 元曲中之險韻 ("Difficult Rhymes in Yüan Drama"). Translated into Chinese by Chi Yung 紀庸 in *Kuo-wen yüeh k'an* 國文月刊, no. 63 (Jan. 1948), 17-22.

―――. "Zatsugeki *Seishōki* ni okeru jinbutsu seikaku no kyōchō" 雜劇「西廂記」における人物性格の強調 ("Emphasis on Characterization in the Play *The Romance of the Western Chamber*), *Tōhōgaku* 東方學, XXII (1961), 67-83.

T'ao, Tsung-i 陶宗儀 (fl. 1360). *Ch'o keng ku* 輟耕錄 (*Jottings During Intervals of Farming*). In *SPTK so-pen* listed above.

T'ien-i-ko lan-ke hsieh-pen cheng hsü Lu kuei pu 天一閣藍格寫本正續錄鬼簿 (*T'ien-i-ko Handwritten Edition of A Register of Ghosts: Original and Supplement.*) An enlarged version by Chia Chung-ming 賈仲明 of Chung Ssu-ch'eng's *Lu kuei pu*. Chia's preface is dated 1422. It is given the present title in the photolithographic reprint by Shanghai: Chung-hua Book Co., 1960.

Tōdō, Akiyasu 藤堂明保. "Development of Mandarin from 14c. to 19c.," *Acta Asiatica*, VI (1964), 31-40.

Tōyōgaku bunken ruimoku 東洋學文獻類目 (*Annual Bibliography of Oriental Studies*. Formerly 東洋史研究文獻類目 and 東洋學研究文獻類目). Kyoto daigaku jimbun kagaku kenkyūjo 京都大學人文科學研究所. The first volume appeared in 1934.

Gives bibliographical information on Yüan drama in section X. 7 in each issue.

Ts'ai, Mei-piao 蔡美彪. "Yüan-tai tsa-chü chung te jo-kan i-yü" 元代雜劇中的若干譯語 ("Some Foreign Expressions

Found in Yüan Drama"), *Chung-kuo yü-wen* 中國語文, no. 55 (Jan. 1957), 34-36.

Ts'ai, Ying 蔡瑩. *Yüan chü lien-t'ao shu-li* 元劇聯套述例 (*Song-Sequences in Yüan Drama*). Shanghai: Commercial Press, 1933.

Ts'ao, Ch'ou-sheng 曹惆生, compiler. *Chung-kuo yin-yüeh, wu-tao, hsi-ch'ü jen-ming tz'u-tien* 中國音樂，舞蹈，戲曲人名詞典 (*A Dictionary of Names of People in the Field of Chinese Music, Dance, and Drama*). Peking: Commercial Press, 1959.

Ts'ui, Ling-ch'in 崔令欽 (T'ang dynasty). *Chiao-fang chi* 教坊記 (*An Account of the Music Academy*). In *CKKT*, Vol. I, pp. 1-30.

Tu, Shan-fu 杜善夫. "Chuang-chia pu shih kou-lan" 莊家不識构闌. In *Ch'ao-yeh hsin sheng t'ai-p'ing yüeh-fu*. Edited by Yang Chao-ying (ca. 1324). In *SPTK so-pen* listed above.

"Tu *Yüan ch'ü hsüan* chi" 讀元曲選記 ("Selected Notes on the *Yüan ch'ü hsüan*"), *Tōhōgakuhō* 東方學報 (Kyoto). Prepared by Tōhō bunka kenkyūjo 東方文化研究所 renamed Jimbun kagaku kenkyūjo, Kyoto University.

Notes on *Ch'en T'uan kao wo* 陳搏高臥, XI, no. 1 (1940), 111-22; *Jen feng-tzu* 任風子, XI, no. 3 (1940), 408-17; *Yü hu ch'un* 玉壺春, XI, no. 3 (1940), 417-27; *Yü ch'iao chi* 漁樵記, XI, no. 3 (1940), 427-39; *Mo-ho-lo* 魔合羅, XII, no. 1 (1941), 140-56; *Yen Ch'ing po yü* 燕青博漁, XII, no. 1 (1941), 156-68; *Chiu feng-ch'en* 救風塵, XII, no. 2 (1941), 297-308; *T'ao-hua nü* 桃花女, XII, no. 3 (1941), 437-49; *Hsieh T'ien-hsiang* 謝天香, XII, no. 4 (1941), 581-92.

Tuan, An-chieh 段安節 (late ninth century). *Yüeh-fu tsa-lu* 樂府雜錄 (*Miscellaneous Notes on Songs*). In *CKKT*, Vol. I, pp. 31-89.

Tung *chieh-yüan* 董解元 (Scholar Tung, fl. 1190-1208). *Hsi hsiang chi chu-kung-tiao* 西廂記諸宮調 (*The Western Chamber Medley*). Peking: Wen-hsüeh ku-chi k'an-hsing-she, 1955.

Tung ching meng hua lu; wai ssu chung 東京夢華錄（外四種）(*Reminiscences of the Splendor of the Eastern Capital [Pien-liang]; and Four Additional Accounts [of Lin-an]*). Shanghai: Chung-hua Book Co., 1958; reprint, 1962.

See the listing of these accounts under the individual authors: Chou Mi, Hsi-hu lao-jen, Kuan-p'u-nai-te-weng, Meng Yüan-lao and Wu Tzu-mu.

Tung, T'ung-ho 董同龢. *Chung-kuo yü-yin shih* 中國語音史 (*A History of Chinese Phonology*). Taipei: Chung-hua wen-hua ch'u-pan shih-yeh-she, 1954.

A concise text on Chinese historical phonology, it contains comments on Northern *ch'ü* and on tone, initials, and finals as described in *CYYY*.

————. *Han-yü yin-yün hsüeh* 漢語音韻學. Taipei, 1968.

A revised and much enlarged version of *Chung-kuo yü-yin shih;* published posthumously.

Voltaire, Jean Francois Marie Arouet de. *Oeuvres complètes de Voltaire*. Paris: Antoine-Augustin Renouard, 1819. Tome IV, pp. 377-454: *L'orphelin de la Chine*.

Waley, Arthur. *Ballads and Stories from Tun-huang*. New York: The Macmillan Co., 1960.

Wang, Chi-lieh 王季烈 and Liu Fu-liang 劉富樑. *Chi-ch'eng ch'ü p'u* 集成曲譜 (*Chi-ch'eng [A Comprehensive] Collection of Musical Scores*). Shanghai: Commercial Press, 1925.

Wang, Chi-ssu 王季思. "Kuan Han-ch'ing tsa-chü te jen-wu su-tsao" 关汉卿杂剧的人物塑造 ("Character Portrayal in Kuan Han-ch'ing's Plays"), *Wen-hsüeh yen-chiu* 文學研究, 2 (1958), 39-50.

————. *Ts'ung Ying-ying chuan tao Hsi hsiang chi* 從鶯鶯傳到西廂記 (*From "The Story of Ying-ying" to The Romance of the Western Chamber*). Shanghai: Shanghai ku-tien wen-hsüeh ch'u-pan-she, 1955.

————. "Yüan-chü chung hsieh-yin shuang-kuan-yü" 元劇中諧音雙關語 ("Puns in Yüan Drama"), *Kuo-wen yüeh-k'an* 國文月刊, no. 67 (May 1948), 15-19.

Wang, Chi-te 王驥德. *Ch'ü lü* 曲律 (*Music of the Ch'ü Songs*). 1624. In *CKKT,* Vol. IV, pp. 43-191.

Wang, Ching-ch'ang 汪經昌. *Ch'ü hsüeh li shih* 曲學例釋 (*A Study on Ch'ü with Illustrating Passages*). Taipei: Chung-hua Book Co., 1962.

Wang, Cho 王灼 (d. 1160). *Pi-chi man chih* 碧鷄漫志 (*Random Notes Written at Pi-chi*). In *CKKT,* Vol. I, pp. 93-149.

Wang, Chung-min 王重民 *et al.,* eds. *Tun-huang pien-wen chi* 敦煌變文集 (*A Collection of pien-wen from Tun-huang*). Peking: Jen-min wen-hsüeh ch'u-pan-she, 1957. 2 vols.

Wang Hsiao-ch'uan 王曉傳, compiler. *Yüan Ming Ch'ing san tai chin hui hsiao-shuo hsi-ch'ü shih liao* 元明淸三代禁毀小說戲曲史料 (*Historical Materials on Banning and Destroying Fiction and Drama in the Yüan, Ming, and Ch'ing Dynasties*). Peking: Tso-chia ch'u-pan-she, 1958.

Wang, I 王易. *Tz'u ch'ü shih* 詞曲史 (*History of Tz'u and Ch'ü*). Reprint, Taipei: Kuang-wen Book Co., 1960.

Wang, I-ch'ing 王奕淸 *et al.,* compilers. *Ch'in ting ch'ü p'u* 欽定曲譜 (*Formularies of the Ch'ü-songs Compiled under Imperial Auspices*). 1715. Photo-reprint, Shanghai: Sao-yeh shan-fang 掃葉山房, 1924.
    Includes Northern and Southern songs.

Wang, Kuang-ch'i 王光祈. *Chung-kuo yin-yüeh shih* 中國音樂史 (*History of Chinese Music*). Shanghai: Chung-hua Book Co., 1934. Reprint, Hong Kong, 1962.

Wang, Kuo-wei 王國維. *Sung Yüan hsi-ch'ü shih* 宋元戲曲史 (*History of Sung and Yüan Drama*). Shanghai: Commercial Press, 1915.

————. *Wang Kuo-wei hsi-ch'ü lun-wen chi* 王國維戲曲論文集 (*A Collection of Wang Kuo-wei's Writings on Traditional Drama*). Peking: Chung-kuo hsi-chü ch'u-pan-she, 1957.

Wang, Li 王力. *Han yü shih kao* 漢語史稿 (*Draft History of the Chinese Language*). Peking: K'o-hsüeh ch'u-pan-she, 1958. 3 vols.

————. *Han-yü shih-lü hsüeh* 漢語詩律學 (*Chinese Poetics*). Shanghai: Chiao-yü ch'u-pan-she, 1958. Revised edition, 1962.
A study of the prosodic rules of Chinese poetry, containing an extensive section on the tones and rhymes of Yüan ch'ü.

————. *Han-yü yin-yün hsüeh* 漢語音韻學 (*Chinese Phonology*). Peking: Chung-hua Book Co., 1956. (Originally *Chung-kuo yin-yün hsüeh* 中國音韻學. Ch'ang-sha: Commercial Press, 1937.)

Wang P'ei-lun 王沛綸. *Hsi-ch'ü tz'u-tien* 戲曲辭典 (*A Dictionary of Theatre*). Taipei: Chung-hua Book Co., 1969.

Wang, Po-ch'eng 王伯成 (fl. 13th century). *T'ien-pao i shih chu-kung-tiao* 天寶遺事諸宮調 (*A Medley on Events in the T'ien-pao Era*). Reference is to selections found in *Yung-hsi yüeh-fu* (listed on p. 239 above).

Wang, Shih-chen 王世貞 (1526-1590). *Ch'ü-tsao* 曲藻 (*On Ch'ü*). In *CKKT,* Vol. IV, pp. 15-42.

Wang, Yü-chang 王玉章. *Yüan tz'u chiao lü* 元詞斠律. Shanghai: Commercial Press, 1936.

Wang, Yün 王惲 (1227-1304). *Ch'iu-chien hsien-sheng ta-ch'üan wen-chi* 秋澗先生大全文集 (*The Complete Works of Ch'iu-chien*). In *SPTK so-pen.*

Wu, Hsiao-ling 吳曉鈴. " 'Hsi yu chi' yü 'Lo-mo-yen shu' " "西遊記" 與 "羅摩延書" (*"Travels to the West* and *The Rāmāyana"*), *Wen-hsüeh yen-chiu* 文學研究, no. 1 (1958), 163-69.

————. "Shih-lun Kuan Han-ch'ing te yü-yen" 試論關漢卿的語言 (*"A Tentative Discourse on Kuan Han-ch'ing's Language"*), *Chung-kuo yü-wen,* VI (1958), 264-67.

Wu, Mei 吳梅. *Ku ch'ü chu t'an* 顧曲塵談 (*Talks on Chinese Dramatic Poetry*). Shanghai: Commercial Press, 1916. 2 vols.

————. *Yüan chü yen-chiu* 元劇研究 (*A Study on Yüan Drama*). Shanghai: Ch'i-ming Book Co., 1929.

Wu, Tzu-mu 吳自牧 (fl. 1270). *Meng liang lu* 夢梁錄 (*Records of a Dream Life [in Lin-an]*). Ca. 1275. Reprint in *Tung ching meng hua lu; wai ssu chung* listed above.

Yang, Daniel S. P. *An Annotated Bibliography of Materials for the Study of the Peking Theatre.* Wisconsin China Series, no. 2. Wisconsin: The University of Wisconsin, 1967.
　　Several entries pertain to early traditional Chinese drama.

Yang, Lien-sheng 楊聯陞. "*Lao Ch'i-ta, P'u T'ung-shih* li te yü-fa yü-hui" 「老乞大」「朴通事」裏的語法語彙 ("Vocabulary and Syntax in *Lao Ch'i-ta* and *P'u T'ung-shih*"), *Bulletin of the Institute of History and Philology* (*Academia Sinica*), XXIX (1957), 197-208.

Yang, Paul Fu-mien 楊福綿. *Chinese Linguistics: A Selected and Classified Bibliography* 中國語言學分類參考書目. Hong Kong: The Chinese University of Hong Kong, 1975.
　　Contains bibliography on Medieval Chinese 中世漢語 (nos. 1534-1601) and Old Mandarin 古代官話 (nos. 1602-1960).

Yang, Richard Fu-sen 楊福森. *Chung-kuo hsi-chü ku-shih hsüan-chi* 中國戲劇古事選集 (*A Collection of Tales from Yüan Plays*). Taipei: Tung-fang ch'u-pan-she, vol. I-IV, 1966-1969.

————. "Lü Tung-pin in the Yüan Drama." Seattle: University of Washington, 1955. Unpublished Ph.D. dissertation.

————. "The Function of Poetry in the Yüan Drama," *Monumenta Serica,* XXIX (1970-1971), 163-92.

————. "The Social Background of Yüan Drama," *Monumenta Serica,* XVII (1958), 331-52.

Yang, Wei-chen 楊維禎 (T'ieh-ya 鐵崖, 1296-1370). *T'ieh-ya san chung* 鐵崖三種 (*Three Works by T'ieh-ya*). Shanghai: Sao-yeh shan-fang, 1921.

Yang, Yin-liu 楊蔭瀏. *Chung-kuo yin-yüeh shih kang* 中國音樂史綱 (*An Outline History of Chinese Music*). Peking: Yin-yüeh ch'u-pan-she, 1955.

———— and Ts'ao An-ho 曹安和. *Hsi hsiang ch'i ssu chung yüeh-p'u hsüan ch'ü* 西廂記四種樂譜選曲 (*Selections from the Music Scores of Four Versions of The Romance of the Western Chamber*). Peking: Yin-yüeh ch'u-pan-she, 1962.

Yao, Hsin-nung [姚莘農]. "The Theme and Structure of the Yüan Drama," *T'ien Hsia Monthly*, 1 (1935), 388-403.

Yeh, T'ang 葉堂. *Na-shu-ying ch'ü p'u* 納書楹曲譜 (*Na-shu-ying Collection of Musical Scores*). 1784-1792.

Yeh, Te-chün 葉德鈞. *Sung Yüan Ming chiang-ch'ang wen-hsüeh* 宋元明講唱文學 (*Oral Literature in the Sung, Yüan, and Ming Periods*). Shanghai: Ku-tien wen-hsüeh ch'u-pan-she, 1957.

Yen-nan Chih An 燕南芝菴. See Chih An.

Yen, Tun-i 嚴敦易. *Yüan chü chen i* 元劇斟疑 (*Deliberations on Problems Pertaining to Some Yüan Plays*). Peking: Chung-hua Book Co., 1960.

Yoshida, Tamako 吉田多滿子. "Gen zatsugeki no kenkōsa no ichimen" 元雜劇の健康さの一面 ("One Aspect of the Soundness of Yüan Drama"), *Tōhōgaku* 東方學, XIX (1959), 87-97.

Yoshikawa, Kōjirō 吉川幸次郎. *Gen zatsugeki kenkyū* 元雜劇研究 (*Studies in Yüan Drama*). Tokyo: Iwanami Book Co., 1948. Translated into Chinese (*Yüan tsa-chü yen-chiu*) by Cheng Ch'ing-mao 鄭清茂. Taipei: I-wen Book Co., 1960. References here are to the Chinese version.
　　Much of the material had appeared as articles: "Gen zatsugeki no sakusha" 元雜劇之作者, *Tōhōgakuhō* 東方學報 (Kyoto), XIII, nos. 3-4 (1942), 1-72, 530-80; "Gen zatsugeki no kōsei" 構成, *Tōhōgakuhō*, XIV, nos. 2-4 (1944), 191-229, 412-40, 514-33; "Gen zatsugeki no bunshō" 文章, *Tōhōgakuhō* XV, no. 1 (1945), 35-82; "Gen zatsugeki no yōgo" 用語, *Tōhōgakuhō*, XV, no. 3

(1946), 283-313; "Gen zatsugeki no chōshū"聽衆, *Tōyōshi kenkyū* 東洋史研究, VII, no. 5 (1942); "Gen zatsugeki no shiryō"資料, *Shinagaku*支那學, XII, no. 1 (Sept. 1946).

―――. "*Kangū shū* zatsugeki no bungakusei" 漢宮秋雜劇 の文學性 ("Literary Characteristics of the Play *Autumn in the Han Palace*"), *Nihon Chūgokugakkai kaihō* 日本中國 學會會報, XVII (Oct. 1965), 108-28.

Yüan Ming Ch'ing hsi-ch'ü yen-chiu lun-wen chi 元明清戲曲 研究論文集 (*A Collection of Essays on Drama in the Yüan, Ming, and Ch'ing Periods*). Prepared by Peking: Tso-chia ch'u-pan-she, 1957.
　　Contains 28 articles on Yüan drama (pp. 1-244; 303-16).

Yüan Ming Ch'ing hsi-ch'ü yen-chiu lun-wen chi erh-chi 元明 清戲曲研究論文集二集 (*A Collection of Essays on Drama in the Yüan, Ming, and Ch'ing Periods: Second Collection*). Prepared by Peking: Jen-min wen-hsüeh ch'u-pan-she pien-chi-pu, 1959.
　　Contains 18 articles on Yüan drama (pp. 1-252).

Yüan shih 元史 (*History of the Yüan Dynasty*). In *Erh-shih-ssu shih* listed above.

Yüan-tai hsi-ch'ü lun-wen so-yin 元代戲曲論文索引. Peking: Chung-kuo k'o-hsüeh-yüan wen-hsüeh yen-chiu-so, 1957.

Yüan tien-chang 元典章 (*Yüan Code*). See *Ta Yüan sheng cheng kuo-ch'ao tien-chang* above.

Zucker, A. E. *The Chinese Theatre*. Boston: Little, Brown & Co., 1925.

C. TRANSLATIONS

1. JAPANESE LANGUAGE

Genjin zatsugeki 元人雜劇. Translated and annotated by Aoki Masaru 青木正兒. Tokyo: Shunjūsha, 1957.

Translations of three plays: *Wu-t'ung yü* (*YCH* 21), *Huo-lang tan* (*YCH* 94), and *Mo-ho-lo* (YCH, 79). The volume includes a glossary (pp. 229-94) with words listed in the order in which they appear.

Genkyoku Kinsenki 元曲金錢記. Translated by Yoshikawa Kōjirō 吉川幸次郎. Tokyo: Chikuma shobō, 1943.
This work includes notes and a commentary dealing with many lexical and grammatical problems of the language of the play.

Genkyoku Kokukan tei 元曲酷寒亭. Translated by Yoshikawa Kōjirō. Tokyo: Chikuma shobō, 1948.
This work includes notes and commentaries.

Genkyoku sen 元曲選. Translated by Shiyonoya On 鹽谷温. Tokyo: Meguro shoten, 1910.

Gikyoku shū 戲曲集. Compiled by Aoki Masaru. *In Chūgoku koten bungaku zenshū* 中國古典文學全集. Vol. 33. Tokyo: Heibon sha, 1959.
Contains translations of six Yüan and Ming plays, the four Yüan plays being *Chiu feng-ch'en* (*YCH* 12), *T'ieh-kuai Li* (*YCH* 29), *Mo-ho-lo,* (*YCH* 79) and *Ho han-shan* (*YCH* 8).

Gikyoku shū 戲曲集. Edited by Tanaka Kenji 田中謙二. In *Chūgoku koten bungaku taikei* 中國古典文學大系 Vol. 52. Heibonsha, 1970.
Contains translations of the following: *Hsi hsiang chi* (*WP* 117), *Chiu feng-ch'en* (*YCH* 12), *Tou O yüan* (*YCH* 86), *T'ieh-kuai Li* (*YCH* 29), *Ho han-shan* (*YCH* 8), *K'u-han t'ing* (*YCH* 58), *Chin-ch'ien chi* (*YCH* 2) and *Pai-yüeh t'ing* (*WP* 102).

2. WESTERN LANGUAGES

(i) Collections

(Individual plays in the following works are listed by title in Section ii below.)

Bazin, Antoine Pierre Louise. *Théâtre chinois, ou Choix de pièces de théâtre composées sous les empereurs mongols.* Paris, 1838. Contains translations of four Yüan plays.

————. *Le Siècle des Youên.* Paris, 1850. Contains summaries of a number of plays.

Li, Tche-houa [李治華]. *Le signe de patience, et autres pièces du théâtre des Yuan.* Gallimard, 1963.
Contains translations of three plays.

Liu, Chün-jo. "A Study of the *Tsa-chü* of the 13th century in China." Madison: The University of Wisconsin, 1952. Unpublished Ph.D. dissertation.
Contains translations of three Yüan plays.

Liu, Jung-en. *Six Yüan Plays.* Middlesex, England: Penguin Books, 1972.

Rudelsberger, Hans. *Altchinesische Liebes-Komödien,* 1923. Free renderings of five Yüan plays.

Yang, Hsien-yi and Gladys Yang. *Selected Plays of Kuan Han-ch'ing.* Peking: Foreign Languages Press, 1958.
Contains translations of eight plays.

Yang, Richard Fu-sen. *Four Plays of the Yüan Drama.* Taipei: The China Post, 1972.

(ii) Individual Works

(The number after the title refers to the play's order in *YCH* and *WP*; see pp. 225-234 above.)

Chang sheng chu hai (98)
Liu, Jung-en "Chang Boils the Sea," pp. 159-87.

Chao shih ku-erh (85)
Julien, Stanislas. *Tchao-chi-kou-eul, L'Orphelin de la Chine.* Paris, 1834. 131 p.
Le Père Prémare. *L'Orphelin de Tchao,* in *Description de la Chine,* par le Père du Halde. Paris, 1735, III: 339-78. Two English translations of du Halde's work

(London, 1736; 1741) contain translations of Father Prémare's version.

This abridged translation by a French Jesuit provided the basis for Voltaire's *L'Orphelin de la Chine,* 1755. It also inspired an English play by William Hatchett: *The Chinese Orphan: an Historical Tragedy, Alter'd from a Specimen of the Chinese Tragedy in du Halde's History of China. Interspers'd with Songs, after the Chinese Manner.* (London: Charles Corbett, 1741. 75 p.) For details, see Ch'en Shou-yi, "The Chinese Orphan: A Yüan Play. Its Influences on European Drama of the Eighteenth Century," *T'ien Hsia Monthly, III* (1936), 89-115.

Liu, Jung-en "The Orphan of Chao," pp. 41-81.

Ch'ien nü li hun (41)
Bazin. *Siècle,* pp. 215-320 (summary).
Liu, Jung-en "The Soul of Ch'ien-nü Leaves Her Body," pp. 83-113.
Yang, Richard. "Ch'ien-nü's Soul Left Her Body," pp. 143-80.

Chin ch'ien chi (2)
Bazin. *Siècle,* pp. 213-29 (summary).

Chiu feng-ch'en (12)
Yang and Yang. "Rescued by a Coquette," pp. 106-29.

Ch'iu Hu hsi ch'i (32)
Bazin. *Siècle,* pp. 201-09 (summary).

Chuan K'uai T'ung (5)
Bazin. *Siècle,* pp. 237-39 (summary).

Han kung ch'iu (1)
Davis, J. F. *Han Koong Tsew, or the Sorrows of Han, a Chinese Tragedy.* London, 1829, 18 p. Songs are omitted in the translation.
Keene, Donald. "Autumn in the Palace of Han." In *Anthology of Chinese Literature,* ed. by C. Birch. New York: Grove Press, 1965, pp. 422-48.
Laloy, Louis. *Le Chagrin au palais des Han.* Paris, 1912.
Liu, Jung-en "Autumn in the Han Palace," pp. 189-224.

Ho han-shan (8)
Bazin. "Ho-Han-Chan, ou la Tunique confrontée," *Théâtre,* pp. 135-256.

Williams, S. W. "The Compared Tunic, a Drama in Four Acts," *Chinese Repository,* XVIII (1849), 116-55. Translated from Bazin's French version.

Hao t'ien t'a (48)
Bazin. *Siècle,* pp. 336-48 (summary).

Hsi hsiang chi (117)
Chen, Pao-ki. *Si syang ki.* Lyon, 1934.

Hart, Henry H. *The West Chamber.* Stanford: Stanford University Press, 1936.

Hsiung, S. I. *The Romance of the Western Chamber.* London: Methuen, 1935. Reprinted with a critical introduction by C. T. Hsia. New York: Columbia University Press, 1968.

Hundhausen, Vincenz. *Das West-zimmer.* Peking, 1926.

Julien, S. *Si-siang-ki, Histoire du Pavillon d'Occident.* Genève, 1872-1880.

Soulié de Morant. *L'amoureuse Oriole, jeune fille.* Paris, ca. 1928.

Hsiao Hsiang yü (15)
Crump, James. *Hsiao Hsiang yü* (Act IV), in "Colloquium and Translation," in *Asian Drama, a Collection of Festival Papers.* Edited by Henry W. Wells. The College of Fine Arts, University of South Dakota, 1966, pp. 68-86. Mimeographed version.

Hsieh T'ien-hsiang (9)
Rudelsberger. "Die Ehen des Fräuleins Schmetterling," pp. 55-76. (Free rendering.)

Hsüeh Jen-kuei (19)
Bazin. *Siècle,* pp. 261-68 (summary).

Hu-tieh meng (37)
Yang and Yang. "The Butterfly Dream," pp. 79-105.

Huang-liang meng (45)
Bazin. *Siècle,* pp. 322-34 (summary).

Laloy, Louis. *Le Rêve du millet jaune, drame taoiste du* xiiie siècle. Paris: Desclée de Brouwer, 1935.

Rudelsberger. "Das Leben ist ein Traum," pp. 97-111. (Free rendering.)

Hui-lan chi (64)

Forke, Alfred. *Der Kreidekreis*. Leipzig: Philipp Reclam, 1927.

Hume, Frances. *The Story of the Circle of Chalk*. From the French of Stanislas Julien. With illus. by John Buckland-Wright. London: The Rodale Press, 1954.

Julien, S. *"Hoei-lan-ki" ou l'histoire du cercle de craie*. Londres, 1832.

Klabund (pseud.). *Der Kreidekreis*. Berlin: I. M. Spaeth, 1925. Adapted from the Chinese.

Laver, James. *The Circle of Chalk*. Translated from Klabund's German version. London: W. Heinemann, 1929.

Van Der Veer, Ethel. "The Chalk Circle," in *World Drama*. Edited by Barrett H. Clark. New York, London: D. Appleton and Co., 1933, pp. 227-58.

Huo-lang tan (94)

Bazin. "La Chanteuse," *Théâtre,* pp. 257-320.

Jen tzu chi (61)

Bazin. *Siècle,* pp. 367-76 (summary).
Li, Tche-Houa. "Le signe de la patience," pp. 29-134.

K'an ch'ien nu (91)

Li, Tche-Houa. "L'Avare," pp. 135-253.

Yang and Yang. "A Slave to Money," in *Chinese Literature* (Peking), (Sept. 1962), 53-92.

K'u Ts'un-hsiao (104)

Yang and Yang. "Death of the Winged-Tiger General," pp. 205-37.

Lai sheng chai (18)

Bazin. "La Dette (payable dans) la vie a venir," *Siècle,* pp. 249-61 (summary).

Lao sheng erh (22)

Bruguiere de Sorsum, A. *Lao-seng-eul, comèdie chinoise, suivie de San-iu-leau, ou les trois étages consacrés, conte moral.* Paris: Rey et Gravier, 1819, 227 p.

Davis, J. F. *Laou-seng-urh, or An Heir in His Old Age.* London: J. Murray, 1817, 115 p.

Li K'uei fu ching (87)

Crump, J. I. "Li K'uei Carries Thorns," in *Occasional Papers* (Ann Arbor: Center for Chinese Studies, The University of Michigan), no. 1 (1962), pp. 38-61. With annotation. (The annotation was later deleted in the version in *Anthology of Chinese Literature,* edited by C. Birch, New York: Grove Press, 1965.)

Liu, Chün-jo. pp. 1b-38b.

Lien-huan chi (89)

Liu, Jung-en "A Stratagem of Interlocking Rings," pp. 225-79.

Lu Chai-lang (49)

Yang and Yang. "The Wife Snatcher," pp. 48-78.

Pao chuang ho (84)

Bazin. *Siècle* pp. 402-19 (summary).

Tan tao hui (105)

Yang and Yang. "Lord Kuan Goes to the Feast," pp. 178-204.

T'ieh-kuai Li (29)

Bazin. *Siècle,* pp. 276-98 (summary).

Rudelsberger. "Die Seelenwanderung des Mandarinen Lu," pp. 77-96. (Free rendering.)

Tou O yüan (86)

Bazin. "Le Ressentiment de Teou-Ngo," *Théâtre,* pp. 321-409.

Liu, Chün-jo, pp. 1a-54a.

Liu, Jung-en "The Injustice Done to Tou O," pp. 115-58.

Shih, C. W. *Injustice to Tou O (Tou O Yüan),* pp. 36-325.

Yang and Yang. "Snow in Midsummer," pp. 21-47.

Yang, Richard. "Tou O Was Wronged," pp. 1-46.

Tsou Mei-hsiang (66)
Bazin. "Thao-mei-hiang, ou les intrigues d'une soubrette," *Théâtre,* pp. 3-134. Reprinted as a single book by Paris: L'Imprimerie royale, 1935, 115 p.

Tung-t'ang lao (13)
Li, Tche-Houa. "Le Fils Prodigue," pp. 255-371.

Wang chiang t'ing (153)
Yang and Yang. "The Riverside Pavilion," pp. 130-52.

Wu ju t'ao yüan (78)
Bazin. *Siècle,* pp. 394-98 (summary).

Wu-t'ung yü (21)
Liu, Chün-jo, pp. 1c-44c.
Yang, Richard. "Rain on the Wu-t'ung Tree," pp. 97-141.

Yü ching t'ai (6)
Rudelsberger. "Doktor Ching und seine Base oder der Yadis-spiegel," pp. 37-53. (Free rendering.)
Yang and Yang. "The Jade Mirror-stand," pp. 153-77.

Yüan-yang pei (4)
Bazin. "Le Couverture du lit nuptial," *Siècle,* pp. 230-37 (summary).
Rudelsberger. "Die Liebesdecke," pp. 9-36. (Free rendering.)

Yüeh-yang lou (36)
Yang, Richard. "The Yellow Crane Tower." Appendix to "Lü Tung-pin in the Yüan Drama." Seattle: University of Washington, 1956. Unpublished Ph.D. dissertation.

————. "The Yüeh-yang Tower," pp. 47-95.

Glossary

THE glossary excludes authors and titles already in the Bibliography and in the list of extant plays in the Appendix; for page reference to the Chinese characters of these authors and titles, see the Index.

An Lu-shan 安祿山

An-shih 安石
    (Wang An-shih 王安石)

ch'a-tan 搽旦

ch'an-ta 纏達

ch'ang 倡

Ch'ang-an 長安

Chang Ch'ien 張千

Chang Ch'ien-nü 張倩女

Chang Chün-jui 張君瑞

Chang Fei 張飛

Chang Hai-t'ang 張海棠

"Ch'ang hen ke" 長恨歌

Chang Heng 張衡

Chang Hsieh 張協

Chang Hsieh chuang-yüan
    張協狀元

Ch'ang Hung 萇弘

Chang I 張儀

Chang K'o-chiu 張可久

Chang Kuei 張珪

Chang Kuo-pao 張國寶

Chang Lin 張林

Chang Shan-yu 張善友

Chang Shao 張劭

Chang Shou-ch'ing 張壽卿

Chang Ting 張鼎

Chang-tsung 章宗

Chang Yeh-t'ang 張野塘

ch'ang yen tao 常言道

ch'ang-yu 倡優

Chao 趙

Chao-chün 昭君
    (See Wang Chao-chün)

Chao Hsüan-lang 趙玄朗

Chao Kung-fu 趙公輔

Chao Ling-chih 趙令時

Chao P'an-erh 趙盼兒

Chao P'ien-hsi 趙偏惜

Chao shu 趙書

Chao Shuo 趙朔

Chao T'ien-hsi 趙天錫

"Ch'ao t'ien-tzu" 朝天子

Chao T'ing-yü 趙廷玉

Chao Tun 趙盾

Chao Wen-yin 趙文殷

Chao-yang 朝陽

Chao Yung 趙用

ch'e (ch'ih) 尺

Che-hsi 浙西

"Che-ku" 鷓鴣

"Che kuei ling" 折桂令

Ch'en Chi-ch'ing 陳季卿

"Chen chung chi" 枕中記

"Ch'en-tsui tung feng" 沉醉
東風

ch'en-tzu 襯字

Cheng-chou 鄭州

Cheng Kuang-tsu 鄭光祖

Cheng-kung 正宮

cheng-ming 正名

cheng-mo 正末

Ch'eng Po 程勃

cheng shih 正是

cheng-tan 正旦

Ch'eng-tu 成都

Cheng Tzu-ch'an 鄭子產

Cheng-yang *men* 正陽門

Ch'eng Ying 程嬰

Ch'i 齊

Chi-chai sou 己齋叟

"Chi hsien pin" 集賢賓

Ch'i-seng 乞僧

"Chi-sheng ts'ao" 寄生草

Chi Shih-lao 吉師老

Chia-chung 夾鐘

Chia Chung-ming 賈仲明

chia-ma 家麻

chia-t'ou tsa-chü 駕頭雜劇

Chiang-che 江浙

Chiang-nan 江南

Ch'iao Chi 喬吉

chiao-fang 教坊

Ch'iao Kung 喬公

"Ch'iao-mu-cha" 喬木查

"Ch'iao p'ai-erh" 喬牌兒

Chiao-tso 焦作

chieh 節

chieh-yüan 解元

Ch'ien chin chi 千金記

ch'ien-chuang 錢庄

Ch'ien Chung-shu 錢鍾書

ch'ien-hu 千戶

Ch'ien K'o 錢可

chih 徵

Chih An 芝菴
(Yen-nan Chih An)

Chih-cheng 至正 (1341-68)

ch'ih chien ma ch'an 叱奸罵
讒

Chih-i 支乙

Chih Tu 郅都

Chin (a state in the Spring and
Autumn period) 晉

Chin [dynasty] 金

Ch'in 秦

ch'in 琴

"Chin chan-erh" 金盞兒

Ch'in Kuan 秦觀

Chin Sheng-t'an 金聖嘆

chin-shih 進士

chin-t'i 近體

chin-t'ung 金童

ching 驚

Ch'ing 清

ching [role] 淨

Ching-chou 荊州

"Ch'ing-ko-erh" 青哥兒

Ch'ing-ming 清明

"Ch'ing tung yüan" 慶東源

Ch'iu Hu 秋胡

"Ch'iu Hu pien-wen" 秋胡變
文

Chiu-shan shu-hui 九山書會

"Ch'iu ssu" 秋思

chiu-wei tui 救尾對

Cho Wen-chün 卓文君

Chou 周

ch'ou 丑

Chou Fang 周昉

Chou Pang-yen 周邦彥

Chou She 周舍

Chou Yen 周延

Chou Yü 周瑜

Ch'u 楚

ch'ü 曲

ch'ü [tone] 去

chu ch'en ku tzu 逐臣孤子

"Ch'u ch'iang hua to-to" 出
牆花朵朵

Chu Chin-hsiu 朱錦繡

Chu Ching 朱經

Ch'u-chou 楚州

Chu Ch'üan 朱權

Chu Hsi 朱熹

chu-ju 侏儒

Chu-ko K'ung-ming 諸葛孔明
(Chu-ko Liang 諸葛亮)

chu-kung-tiao 諸宮調

Chu Lien-hsiu 朱簾綉

Chu lin ssu 竹林寺

"Chu ma t'ing" 駐馬聽

Chu Su 朱橚(Yu-tun 有燉)

chüan 卷

ch'uan-ch'i 傳奇

"Chuan-sha" 賺煞

"Chuan-sha wei" 賺煞尾

chuang-ku 裝孤

chuang-shang 莊上

Chuang-tzu 莊子

chuang-yüan 狀元

chüeh 角

"Ch'üeh t'a chih" 鵲踏枝

chün ch'en tsa-chü 君臣雜劇

chün-tzu 君子

chung 忠

chung ch'en lieh shih 忠臣烈
士

Ch'ung-Kuan 崇觀

chung-lang 中郎

Chung-li Ch'üan 鍾離權

Chung-lü 中呂

ch'ung-mo 冲末

Chung-nan 終南

Ch'ung-ning 崇寧

ch'ung-tieh tui 重疊對

Chung Tu-hsiu 忠都秀

Ennin 圓仁

erh pai wen 二百文

"Erh-sha" 二煞

fa 髮

fan 凡

Fan K'ang 范康

Fan Shih 范式

Fen (ho) 汾 (河)

feng hua hsüeh yüeh 風花雪
月

Feng-su t'ung 風俗通

fu 拂

fu (rhyme-prose) 賦

fu-ch'a 浮槎

Fu-ch'ai 夫差

fu-ching 副淨

fu-mo 副末

Fu-seng 福僧

ha-la 哈喇

ha-sa-erh 哈嗽兒

Hai-t'ang 海棠

Hai-yen 海鹽

Han 漢

Han Chüeh 韓厥

Han-lin 翰林

Han-tan 邯鄲

Han Wei Hsien 漢韋賢

Hangchow 杭州
  (See Lin-an 臨安)

ho 合

"Ho hsi hou t'ing hua" 河西後庭花

Ho-chung 河中

"Ho hsin-lang" 賀新郎

ho-pi tui 合璧對

Hou-ma 候馬

"Hou t'ing hua" 後庭花

hsi 覡

Hsi Ch'ien-chin 喜千金

"Hsi ching fu" 西京賦

Hsi-hu wu yeh-erh 西湖梧葉兒

Hsi Shih 西施

hsi-t'ai 戲台

hsi-wen 戲文

hsia 下

Hsia-hou Tun 夏候惇

Hsiang 襄

"Hsiang mo pien-wen" 降魔變文

hsiao 孝

hsiao i lien chieh 孝義廉節

hsiao-mo 小末

Hsiao-shih tiao 小石調

hsiao-shuo 小說

Hsiao Sun t'u 小孫屠

hsiao-tan 小旦

"Hsiao t'ao hung" 小桃紅

Hsiao Te-hsiang 蕭德祥

"Hsiao-yao le" 消遙樂

hsieh-tzu 楔子

hsien 仙

Hsien-lü (kung) 仙呂（宮）

"Hsin shui ling" 新水令

Hsin-yeh 新野

Hsü Chien 許堅

Hsü-chou 許州

Hsüan-so Hsi-hsiang 弦索西廂

hsüan-so tiao 弦索調

Hsüan Tsang 玄奘

Hsüan-tsung 玄宗

Hsüeh Pa 薛霸

Hsün-yang 潯陽

Hu-han-yeh 呼韓耶

hu-la-hai 忽剌孩

Hu t'ing i sheng meng ching 忽聽一聲猛驚

Hu Tzu-shan 胡紫山

hua 花

Hua (shan) 華（山）

hua chao-erh 花招兒

Hua Li-lang 花李郎

"Hua-mei hsü" 畫眉序

"Hua shan nü" 華山女

hua-tan 花旦

hua-tan tsa-chü 花旦雜劇

Huan-men tzu-ti ts'o li-shen 宦門子弟錯立身

Huan sha chi 浣沙記

Huang (surname) 黃

huang (yellow) 黃

huang (deserted) 荒

Huang-chung (kung) 黃鐘（宮）

"Huang-chung sha" 黃鐘煞

Huang-chung shang 黃鐘商

"Huang-ying-erh" 黃鶯兒

hun 昏

"Hun-chiang lung" 混江龍

hun-tan 魂旦

"Hung hsiu hsieh" 紅繡鞋

Hung-niang 紅娘

"Hung shao-yao" 紅芍藥

Hung-tung 洪洞

Hung-tzu Li-erh 紅字李二

Hung-ya 洪涯

i [musical note] 乙

i 義

I-chai sou 已齋叟

"I chih hua" 一枝花

I Ching 義淨

i kuan hsia shih 倚官挾勢

"I pan-erh" 一半兒

"I-sha" 一煞

I-tse 夷則

I-yang 弋陽

I Ying fu T'ang 伊尹扶湯

Jen-ch'en 壬辰

Jen Feng-tzu 任風子

jen shen 人身

ju [tone] 入

ju tzu 辱子

ju-tzu (a mattress) 褥子

Juan Chao 阮肇

juan mo-ni 軟末尼

Jui-pin 蕤賓

K'ai-feng 開封 (See Pien)

k'an ch'ien-mien (look ahead) 看前面

k'an ch'ien mien 看錢面

kan-pang 桿棒

K'ang Chin-chih 康進之

k'ao-pei 靠背

k'ao ting kuan han 靠定棺梜

Kao-tsu 高祖

Kao-tsung 高宗

Kao Wen-hsiu 高文秀

ko-chü tui 隔句對

k'o pu tao 可不道

"Ko-wei" 隔尾

kou 勾

Kou-chien 勾踐

kou-lan 構（勾）闌

Ku Chung-ch'ing 顧仲清

Ku-hsien (Ku-hsi) 姑洗

"K'u huang-t'ien" 哭皇天

ku-tzu-tz'u 鼓子詞

"K'uai-huo-san" 快活三

k'uai-pan 快板

kuan (coffin) 棺

kuan 官

Kuan Ch'ing 關卿

Kuan Han-ch'ing 關漢卿

kuan-mu 關目

Kuan-t'ao 館陶

Kuan-yin 觀音

Kuan Yü 關羽

Kuang-sheng 廣勝

Kuang-wu 光武

k'uei-lei-tzu 窟礧子（傀儡子）

"Kuei san t'ai" 鬼三臺

kuei-yüan tsa-chü 閨怨雜劇

K'un-ch'ü 崑曲

"Kun hsiu ch'iu" 滾繡球

K'un-shan 崑山

kung [musical note] 工

kung [musical mode] 宮

kung-an 公案

Kung-sun Ch'u-chiu 公孫杵臼

kung-tiao 宮調

Kung T'ien-t'ing 宮天挺

"Kung tz'u" 宮詞

K'ung Wen-ch'ing 孔文卿

Kuo Ma-erh 郭馬兒

Kuo Piao 葛彪

kuo yen tao 果言道

Kuo Yü-ti 國玉弟

Lan Ling 蘭陵

"Lan Ling wang ju chen ch'ü" 蘭陵王入陣曲

Lan Shan-ching 藍山景

Lan Ts'ai-ho 藍采和

lao-tan 老旦

Li Chiao-erh 李嬌兒

Li Hsing-tao 李行道

Li K'o-yung 李克用

Li K'uan-fu 李寬甫

Li K'uei 李逵

Li Po 李白

Li Po-t'ou 李薄頭

Li sao 離騷

Li Shang-yin 李商隱

"Li-t'ing-yen-sha" 離亭燕煞

Li Ts'un-hsin 李存信

Li Tzu-chung 李子中

Li Wa 李娃

"Li Wa chuan" 李娃傳

Li Wen-wei 李文蔚

li-yüan ling-hsiu . . . tsa-chü pan-t'ou 梨園領袖...雜劇班頭

Li Yung-tsu 李榮祖

Liang Ch'en-yü 梁辰魚

Liang Chin-chih 梁進之

"Liang-chou" 梁州

"Liang-chou ti-ch'i" 梁州第七

Liang-shan 梁山

Liang-shan-po 梁山泊

Liang wu kung 兩無功

Liao-yang 遼陽

lien-chu tui 聯珠對

lien-pi tui 聯璧對

lien-t'ao 聯套

Lin-an 臨安 (Hangchow 杭州)

lin ch'üan ch'iu-ho 林泉丘壑

Lin-chung 林鐘

Lin Hsiang-ju 藺相如

ling 伶

ling-kuai 靈怪

liu 六

Liu 劉

Liu Ch'en 劉晨

Liu Ch'ing-fu 劉慶甫

"Liu chuan" 六轉

Liu Hsiu 劉秀

Liu Pei 劉備

Liu Piao 劉表

Liu Shua-ho 劉耍和

liu-shui 流水

Liu T'ang-ch'ing 劉唐卿

liu tzu san yün 六字三韻

"Liu-yao hsü" 六么序

"Liu-yao ling" 六么令

"Liu yeh-erh" 柳葉兒

Liu Yung 柳永

Lo-chia (shan) 落伽（山）

"Lo-ssu-niang" 絡絲娘

Lo-yang 洛陽

Lu 魯

Lu Chai-lang 魯齋郎

Lu Chih-shen 魯智深

"Lu Ch'iu chieh fu" 魯秋潔婦

lü-lin tsa-chü 綠林雜劇

lü-lü 呂律

Lu Su 魯肅

Lü Tung-pin 呂洞賓

luan-feng-ho-ming tui 鸞鳳和鳴對

Ma Chih-yüan 馬致遠

Ma Chün-ch'ing 馬均卿

"Ma lang-erh" 麻郎兒

Ma Tan-yang 馬丹陽

Ma-wei (shan) 馬嵬（山）

man-pan 慢板

"Man t'ing fang" 滿庭芳

Mao Yen-shou 毛延壽

"Mei hua chiu" 梅花酒

"Meng Chiang nü pien-wen" 孟姜女變文

Meng Chüeh-ch'iu 孟角毬

mi-han 米罕

Mi-li-ha 米里哈

Ming 明

Ming fei 明妃

Ming-huang 明皇

Ming-ying-wang 明應王

mo 末

Mo-ho-lo 魔合羅（磨喝樂）

mo-lin 抹鄰

mo-ni 末泥

Mu-lien 目蓮

Mu-lien chiu mu 目蓮救母

Mu-lien chiu mu ch'üan shan hsi-wen 目蓮救母勸善戲文

"Mu yang kuan" 牧羊關

"Na-cha ling" 哪吒令

Nan hsi 南戲

Nan-lü 南呂

Nei-jen shuang-lu 內人雙陸

Ning Ch'eng 甯成

Nü-e (wa) 女娥（媧）

nu-men 弩門

pa 罷

pa-se 把色

"Pa sheng Kan-chou" 八聲甘州

Pai-hsi 百戲

pai-ling 白翎

pai-ling-ch'üeh 白翎雀

"Pai tzu chih ch'iu ling" 百字知秋令

p'ai-yu 俳優

Pan-she (tiao) 般涉（調）

Pao Cheng 包拯
　（Pao-kung 包公）

Pei-ch'ü 北曲

P'ei Hsing-nu 裴興奴

pei huan li ho 悲歡離合

p'i-p'a 琵琶

"P'i-p'a hsing" 琵琶行

p'i p'ao ping hu 披袍秉笏

Pien 汴（Pien-ching 汴京，Pien-liang 汴梁，K'ai-feng 開封）

pien-chih 變徵

pien-kung 變宮

pien-wen 變文

p'ing [tone] 平

P'ing-yang 平陽

P'ing-yang nu 平揚奴

Po Chü-i 白居易

Po Hua 白華

po-lao 孛老

Po P'u 白樸

"Po pu tuan" 撥不斷

p'o tao 朴刀

p'o tao kan pang 鏺刀趕棒

P'u-chiu ssu 普救寺

pu-erh 卜兒

"Pu fu lao" 不伏老

pu-hsiao 不孝

pu-kuan ch'uan-mu 佈關串目

sa-t'a-pa 莎塔八

sa-yin 撒因

Sai Lu-yi 賽魯醫

san-ch'ang 散場

San ch'i Chou Yü 三氣周瑜

san-ch'iang 三槍

san-ch'ü 散曲

san-pan 散板

"San-sha" 三煞

san-yüeh 散樂

Sang 桑

se-tan 色旦

"Sha-wei" 煞尾

shan-mien tui 扇面對

Shan-yang 山陽

Shang [musical mode] 商

shang [musical note] 上

shang [tone] 上

Shang-chüeh tiao 商角調

Shang Chung-hsien 尚仲賢

"Shang-hua shih" 賞花時

"Shang ma chiao" 上馬嬌

Shansi 山西

shen-cheng 神崢

Shen Chi-ch'i 沈濟齊

shen fo tsa-chü 神佛雜劇

shen-hsien tao hua 神仙道化

shen t'ou kuei mien 神頭鬼面

Shen Ts'ai 沈采

sheng 聲

"Sheng hu-lu" 勝葫蘆

"Sheng yao wang" 勝藥王

shih 詩

Shih-ching 詩經

Shih-chiu San-jen 史九散人

Shih Chün-pao 石君寶

Shih Hui 施惠

Shih Le 石勒

"Shih mei jen shang yüeh" 十美人賞月

Shih-tsu 世祖

"Shou chiang nan" 收江南

Shou-lang 壽郎

"Shou-wei" 收尾

Shu-Han 蜀漢

shu-hui 書會

"Shua hai-erh" 耍孩兒

shuang-kuan yü 雙關語

shuang-lu 雙陸

shuang sheng 雙聲

Shuang tiao 雙調

"Shun-tzu pien-wen" 舜子變文

Shuo-chi 說集

shuo kung-an 說公案

ssu [musical note] 四

Ssu-ma Ch'ien 司馬遷

Ssu-ma Hsiang-ju 司馬相如

Ssu-ma Hui 司馬徽

Ssu-ma Kuang 司馬光

"Ssu pien ching" 四邊靜

Su Ch'e 蘇轍

su-chiang 俗講

Su Ch'in 蘇秦

Su Chung-lang 蘇中郎

su-men 速門

Su Shih 蘇軾 (Tung-p'o 東坡)

Su *shih* 蘇石

Su Shun 蘇順

"Sui-sha" 隨煞

Sun Ch'üan 孫權

Sun Shu-ao 孫叔敖

Sun Yung 孫榮

Sung 宋

Sung Chiang 宋江
   (Kung-ming 公明)

Sung Yin-chang 宋引章

Szechwan 四川

ta-ch'ü 大曲

Ta-kuan 大觀

ta-la-sun 答剌孫

Ta-lü (Tai-lü) 大呂

Ta mien 大面

Ta p'o sha kuo, wen tao ti 打
   破沙鍋璺到底

Ta-shih tiao 大石調

Ta-tu 大都

T'a-yao niang 踏搖娘

"T'ai ch'ing ko" 太清歌

T'ai-hang 大行

T'ai-hang *san-yüeh* Chung
   Tu-hsiu *tsai-tz'u tso-ch'ang*
   大行散樂忠都秀在此作場

T'ai-i 太乙

t'ai-i-yüan-yin 太醫院尹

"Tai ku to" 呆骨朵

Tai-mien 帶面

Tai Shan-fu 戴善甫

T'ai-ting yüan nien ssu yüeh
   太定元年四月

T'ai-ts'ou (T'ai-ts'u) 太簇

T'ai-tsung 太宗

T'ai-yüan 太原

tan [role] 旦

tan 狚

T'ang 唐

"T'ang hsiu-ts'ai" 倘秀才

t'ao-shu 套數

"Tao-tao ling" 叨叨令

"Te-sheng ling" 得勝令

Ti Chün-hou 狄君厚

"Ti-liu-tzu" 滴溜子

t'i-mu 題目

t'i t'ien hsing tao 替天行道

ti-tzu 笛子

"T'i yin teng" 剔銀燈

"T'iao-hsiao ling" 調笑令

"T'iao-hsiao ling chuan-t'a"
   調笑令轉踏

"Tieh lien hua" 蝶戀花

t'ieh-tan 貼旦

tieh tzu 疊字

tieh yün 疊韻

"Tien chiang ch'un" 點降唇

"Tien ch'ien huan" 殿前歡

"T'ien ching sha" 天淨沙

T'ien ho hui 天河會

"T'ien-hsia le" 天下樂

T'ien-jan hsiu 天然秀

T'ien-lai chi 天籟集

T'ien-t'ai 天台

ting 錠

t'ing 聽

ting-tsu tui 鼎足對

t'o-po 脫膊

t'o-po tsa-chü 脫膊雜劇

"Tou ha-ma (hsia-ma)" 鬪蝦蟆

Tou O 竇娥

Tou T'ien-chang 竇天章

tsa 雜

tsa-chü 雜劇

"Ts'ai ch'a ko" 採茶歌

ts'ai-jen 才人

tsai shang 在上

Ts'ai Shun 蔡順

ts'ai-tzu chia-jen 才子佳人

Ts'an-chün 參軍

Ts'ao Chin-hsiu 曹錦秀

Ts'ao Ts'ao 曹操

tse [tone] 仄

"Tseng ling-jen Chao Wen-i" 贈伶人趙文益

"Tseng Sung shih hsü" 贈宋氏序

tso-ch'ang 作場

Tso chuan 左傳

Tsou Yen 鄒衍

"Ts'u hu-lu" 醋葫蘆

"Ts'u yü lin" 簇御林

"Tsui ch'un feng" 醉春風

"Tsui chung t'ien" 醉中天

"Tsui fu kuei" 醉扶歸

Ts'ui Tzu-yü 崔子玉

Ts'ui Ying-ying 崔鶯鶯

ts'un 寸

"Ts'un-li ya-ku" 村裏迓鼓

T'u-an Ku 屠岸賈

Tu Fu 杜甫

Tu Shan-fu 杜善夫 (San-jen 散人)

"T'u ssu-erh" 禿厮兒

"Tuan-cheng hao" 端正好

Tuan-yün 端雲

Tun-huang 敦煌

Tung Ch'ao 董超

Tung-hai 東海

Tung-lin 東林

Tung-p'ing 東平

Tung-t'ang lao 東堂老

tz'u 詞

"Tzu hua-erh hsü" 紫花兒序

Tzu-kuei 秭歸

wa 娃

wa-she 瓦舍

wa-ssu 瓦肆

wai 外

wai-tan 外旦

wan-hu 萬戶

Wang An-shih 王安石

Wang Chao-chün 王昭君
  (Ch'iang 嬙)

Wang Ch'iang 王嬙
  (See Wang Chao-chün)

Wang Chin-pang 王金榜

Wang Ho-ch'ing 王和卿

Wang Hsiu-jan 王脩然

Wang Lin 王林

Wang Liu 王留

"Wang Lu shan p'u-pu" 望
  廬山瀑布

Wang Mang 王莽

Wang Pa-se 王把色

Wang Po-wen 王博文

Wang-ti 望帝

Wang T'ing-hsiu 王廷秀

Wang Wen-chü 王文舉

Wei 魏

Wei Liang-fu 魏良輔

"Wei-sheng" 尾聲

Wei Tao-tao 魏道道

wen (crack) 璺

wen (ask) 問

wen tao ti 璺到底; 問到底

Wen T'ing-yün 溫庭筠

wu [musical note] 五

wu (shaman) 巫

Wu [state] 吳

Wu Han-ch'en 武漢臣

Wu Hsüeh-chiu 吳學究

Wu-i (Wu-she) 無射

wu-lun 五倫

wu-t'ung 梧桐

Wu Tzu-hsü 伍子胥

"Wu Tzu-hsü pien-wen" 伍
  子胥變文

yang 陽

Yang-chou nu 揚州奴

Yang Kuei-fei 楊貴妃

"Yao" 么

"Yao p'ien" 么篇

Yao Shou-chung 姚守中

yao-shu 妖術

yen (feast) 宴

yen-chu-fei-hua tui 燕逐飛花對

yen-fen 煙粉

yen-hua fen-tai 煙花粉黛

Yen Shan-hsiu 燕山秀

yen-tso 嘸作

Yen Tzu-ling 嚴子陵

yin 陰

yin-chü le tao 隱居樂道

Yin-ho 銀河

yin-hsi 引戲

Yin-sun 引孫

yin-tai 引帶

yin-yang 陰陽

Ying-chung 應鐘

Ying Shao 應劭

Ying-ying (See Ts'ui Ying-ying)

"Ying-ying chuan" 鶯鶯傳

yu 優

yü 羽

Yü Ch'i-chi 魚齊即

Yü Chi-fu 庾吉甫

Yü Chin 于禁

yu-hsia 遊俠

"Yu hu-lu" 油葫蘆

Yü-lan-p'en 盂蘭盆

yü-nü 玉女

Yü Po-yüan 于伯淵

"Yu ssu men" 遊四門

Yu "T'o-tzu" 尤駝子

Yü-yao 餘姚

Yüan 元

Yüan Chen 元稹

Yüan *ch'ü* 元曲

Yüan Hao-wen 元好問 (I-shan 遺山)

Yüan-ho 元和

"Yüan-ho ling" 元和令

Yüan "Hu-tzu" 袁鬍子

yüan huo 原活

Yüan I-shan (See Yüan Hao-wen)

"Yüan kung tz'u" 元宮詞

yüan-pan 原板

yüan-pen 院本

"Yüeh-chi Ts'ao shih shih yin" 樂藉曹氏詩引

yüeh-ch'uang 樂床

yüeh-fu 樂府

Yüeh Shou 岳壽

Yüeh tiao 越調

Yung-chi 永濟

Yung-lo ta-tien 永樂大典

Index

Italic numerals refer to the pages on which the Chinese characters can be found. Authors and titles appearing solely as references in the footnotes are not included in the index.

Library of Congress Cataloging in Publication Data

Shih, Chung-wen
  The golden age of Chinese drama, Yüan tsa-chü.

  1. Chinese drama—Yüan dynasty, 1260-1368—History
and criticism. 2. Theater—China—History. I. Title.
II. Title: Yüan tsa-chü.
PL2384.S5   895.1'2'409   74-2979
ISBN 0-609-06270-6